BLAMED

DANA GRIFFIN

Also By

Dana Griffin

The Cover-Up

Coerced

Calamity

For Pat Jarvis,

Whose friendship I value

And Hunter and Charlie,

Faithful companions lost, but never forgotten

Chapter One

The crushing pain radiating up from my legs yanked me out of unconsciousness. My arms dangled above my head and my hands rested on the overhead panel of the aircraft. Comprehending I was upside down was difficult to grasp with the fear of blacking out again threatening to overtake me.

I yelled and squirmed in an attempt to stop the slide into nothingness and to relieve the agony in my legs. Neither relaxed the all-consuming pain. If anything, my thrashing sharpened it.

We were on approach to Dallas-Fort Worth when... what? Nothing came forth that explained why I'd be upside down and in such misery. A black hole occupied my memory of what happened between everything being normal as we approached the runway and... now.

Wind whistled through the smashed cockpit windows, ruffling my hair. Shards of glass littered the overhead panel. Smoke that stank of burned jet fuel and something else I couldn't place drifted in.

Where there's smoke, there's... Fire! I had to get the flight attendants and passengers to safety! Then a realization hit me. We had been ferrying the empty aircraft from a maintenance facility in San Salvador.

Ned! Why hadn't the first officer, who had been the pilot flying, made a sound?

When I looked across the cockpit, I shrieked.

The overhead panel had bowed in and crushed the forty-something husband and father's head backward at an extreme angle against his headrest. A lifeless eye bulged from his distorted, bloody face. It stared straight ahead.

The laid-back pilot with a dry sense of humor looked like a ghoul from a Hollywood movie.

How could he be dead? He'd been joking with me just moments ago.

To distance myself from the sight, I squeezed my eyes shut while fumbling for the seatbelt buckle of my five-strap harness, then hesitated. If I released it, I would plant my head into the overhead panel, which was filled with numerous toggle switches. Even if I didn't impale on a switch or break my neck, the agony in my legs made me question if I could work them enough to crawl from the aircraft.

I risked a glance. Whatever had happened to us had bent the instrument panel down, trapping my lower extremities under it. The femur in my right leg poked out through a tear in my pants. A constant stream of blood ran from the tip of the broken bone.

I recoiled, and the bone moved.

An intense spike of nausea erupted, emptying my stomach. Vomit burned my throat, ran into my eyes, and up my nose.

I swiped my face with my arm to clear my vision. This movement sent a wave of blackness rolling through me. A part of me welcomed it to end my misery. Another part worried I wouldn't ever wake from it. I couldn't leave my wife, son, and daughter.

The sounds of large diesel engines approached. Air brakes hissed. Were they from the crash and rescue trucks?

"Help." My cry was a gurgle from the vomit in my mouth. I spit.

The smoke outside was now so thick, I couldn't see the ground. Would they find me before I was consumed by fire? "Help!"

I didn't detect any movement or hear any voices. I *would not* become a victim. I had to get out.

A stabbing pain in my side had grown in intensity, making it harder to breathe. When the yoke was rammed into me, had it broken a rib or my sternum? Punctured a lung?

A shove on the yoke to move it forward proved futile.

With a heave, I pushed against the edge of the glareshield, normally at shoulder height but now waist level, hoping to ease the pressure against my chest. The crushing force didn't slacken.

It also intensified the torture in my legs. I doubted a chainsaw cutting into them would hurt worse. The bellow I unleashed didn't summon the strength needed to distance me from the yoke.

I sat as still as I could, panting.

The gulps of air I took didn't relieve my shortness of breath.

If I could slide the seat back, I might breathe easier and free my legs.

Why hadn't I thought of the seat adjustment lever?

Twisting to yank that lever at the base of my seat felt like a knife stabbing my chest. With my free hand, I shoved on the crushed instrument panel. The intensity of the torment was so great, I almost blacked out.

If I did, I might either bleed or burn to death.

Through gritted teeth, I pushed on the glareshield, yanking on the seat adjustment lever. When I didn't move, I unleashed a howl.

I stayed rammed against the yoke.

When I attempted to shove with my feet, unimaginable agony consumed me, bringing on the darkness I'd been fighting.

Chapter Two

Senior Director of Flight Standards and Training for Sphere Airlines, Neal Reeves, stared out his west-facing office windows with a view of the Denver skyline and the Front Range without seeing it. The image being broadcast on all the news stations filled his head with the horror of one of their aircraft resting upside down atop a regional jet where it had come to rest in Dallas.

At this time, the number of deaths and injuries on the regional jet was unknown.

Sphere's six year run of being accident-free had just ended.

Being responsible for the procedures and training administered to Sphere's pilots, he didn't doubt he'd take a hit about the accident's cause.

Since the majority of accidents were caused by human factors, the adequacy of the safety programs he had worked hard to develop the last five years would be questioned. His career advancement had probably come to a halt.

One of the six fleet managers, Bryce Marling, entered his office, pulling Reeves' attention back from contemplating the unknown.

Marling was responsible for the Edwards Aerospace EA-220, an aircraft comparable to Boeing's 737, which had been in the accident. He developed the procedures for how the aircraft was flown and supervised the thirty instructors who trained the pilots who flew this model.

Marling's mid-fifties face wasn't creased with the accident's burden the way Reeves thought his decade-older visage must have been.

"What have you learned?" Reeves dropped into his desk chair.

"The captain," Marling consulted his notepad, "William Kurz, has been with us for twenty-one years and an EA-220 captain for eleven of those years."

"In that time, he should've learned how to land in a crosswind. What else do we know about him? Has he had any trouble with training? Is he one of our antagonistic pilots?"

"No record of failed check-rides, or the necessity for additional training. The instructors I questioned couldn't remember him until they looked up his photo."

Reeves knew from his time as instructor that Kurz must've done a good job during training. Instructors usually only remembered the ones who had difficulty.

"He was an unknown to the Denver Chief Pilot. They have no reports of him pissing off first officers or flight attendants. Nor are there any complaints from dispatchers or gate agents."

"Just great." Reeves shook his head. "If one of our model pilots can't land during a thunderstorm and prevent the aircraft from cartwheeling off the runway, what will the public think of the remainder of our pilots?" Reeves held up his hand to tell Marling he wasn't expecting an answer to his question.

"If anything, that's a blessing," Marling said. "The media and lawyers for those who died or were injured would question why we kept an inept pilot employed."

Reeves blew out a sigh. "Yeah, you're right. What about the first officer? Any issues with him?"

"He, too, is another unknown." The pages of his notepad crinkled when he flipped them. "He's been with us for seven years and had no issues with training. He was scheduled to go through captain upgrade curriculum next month."

"Why did two of our competent pilots go off the runway?" Hearing it was two capable pilots made the accident even harder to comprehend.

"From the initial reports, the wind gusts from the approaching thunderstorm were forty knots at times. They might've exceeded the crosswind limits of the aircraft."

Since only a few hours had passed since the accident, there were more unknowns than answers.

"Who will be our liaison to work with the National Transportation Safety Board?" Reeves asked.

"Josh Pringer. He's an EA-220 instructor."

"I want to hear what he finds out when they listen to the CVR."

Marling screwed up his face as if he'd tasted something repulsive. "The NTSB will make him sign a confidential agreement preventing him from discussing what was heard on the cockpit voice recorder. Only the members on the NTSB's CVR committee will be able to discuss the recording until the surviving crew members have listened to it. In this case, that's Kurz."

"The NTSB doesn't need to know Pringer talked to us." Reeves pointed a penetrating look at Marling to convince him it wasn't a request.

"If the NTSB discovers he leaked confidential information, they'll kick him off the investigation. Because of that transgression, whoever replaces him will be kept on the fringes."

The stubble on Reeves' cheeks bristled when he scrubbed his face, hoping to rub the long day's fatigue away. "Bureaucrats seem to go out of their way to make running an airline as difficult as possible. It's bad enough during normal operations. But when there's a crisis, as we face now, they entrench themselves in their rules and procedures, taking even longer to make a decision or pass along information that could be helpful. Their constant worry that something might be mentioned negatively in the media makes the already turtle-paced organizations practically shut down."

Being a good subordinate, Marling didn't say anything.

Reeves expelled a loud breath. "Maintenance is claiming the aircraft came out of its inspection with no defects. They're adamant nothing was overlooked that contributed to the accident. We need to know if that's true before they convince the FAA and NTSB, as well as the VPs, that the accident was flight training's fault. Until Kurz can tell us what happened, let's hope the CVR and DFDR exonerate our department."

Marling gave a nod.

"How long before the NTSB gets the data from the DFDR?" Reeves asked.

"The digital flight data recorder will be flown to their lab in D.C. tomorrow. Maybe the day after that."

"As soon as Pringer hears what happened, I want to know. I don't want to be getting second-hand information from another department."

"When Pringer calls me, I'll conference call you," Marling said.

"Good. The NTSB will be talking to the pilots who have recently flown with Kurz and Partin. I want you to do that before they do. Find out what the other pilots will say about these two unknowns."

Marling scribbled a note.

"Put together a list of any information the NTSB or FAA might discover. Phone calls, faxes, emails, messages sent from the aircraft, anything dealing with these two pilots and this flight. I want to know what we'll be confronted with so we can prepare our defense."

Marling nodded. "The big unknown is what Kurz will say when he's interviewed."

"What's his condition?"

"Still unconscious in intensive care."

"How soon after he wakes up will the NTSB interview him?" Reeves asked.

The palms of both of Marling's hands turned up. "I doubt a doctor will let them while he's still in the ICU."

"I want you at the hospital ready to interview him as soon his doctor will allow. I want to know what he remembers."

Marling made another note.

"Assist Kurz, or his family, in whatever needs they may have. If it seems we're trying to help him through this ordeal, he might be more willing to open up to us."

"Good idea," Marling said.

"What about the union? Will they have someone there to look out for Kurz's rights?"

"I'm guessing until they hear he's healthy enough to be interviewed, they won't waste the resource to station someone at the hospital."

"Good," Reeves said. "We don't want them urging Kurz to not talk to you."

The phone on Reeves' desk rang. He glanced at the caller ID. "I have to take this. Find someone we can blame for this accident."

Chapter Three

The hiss and sigh of the air compressor in our hangar disrupted my sleep. It should have stopped once the tank was full. If the effort to open my eyes wasn't so great, I might've investigated why it continued malfunctioning. I would deal with the annoying machine after another nap.

A honking tone disrupted my hibernation. Just when I'd begin to drift off, the alarm went off again.

I'd never heard that warning from the air compressor. The pull back into nothingness was too great to worry about it now.

But the annoying alarm continued.

Something was stuck in my mouth and ran down my throat. I chewed on it, but it stayed in place. The alarm on the air compressor went off again. Had I stuck the dirty, stiff air hose in my throat?

That didn't make any sense. I'd never do that.

I woke enough to wonder why I was sleeping in the hangar instead of working on the airplane I was building. And why had I chosen such an uncomfortable place to nap? Pain consumed me. My legs screamed. Each time I breathed, a stab of agony raced through my chest. The torment wasn't as bad as what I had experienced in the nightmare of being trapped in an aircraft wreck.

Voices murmured around me. Someone with cold hands took one of mine in theirs. I pried my eyes open and quickly closed them. It was bright, even though the hangar had few lights on.

"Bill, wake up, honey. Come on, Bill."

My wife's voice was insistent, demanding. Had my nap in the hangar made me late for something? With effort, I pried my eyes open a slit.

Natalie stood at my side and lifted the corners of her mouth. Her usually vibrant blue eyes were filled with worry. Dark bags circled under them. Instead of looking forty as she usually did, she appeared a decade older than her fifty-two years of age.

"Hi." She caressed my forehead.

I tried to speak, but that thing in my mouth and throat prevented it. A band was wrapped around my head holding it there. I tried to reach for it, my arms moving slowly as if through water, but they were grasped and held.

The struggle to free myself brought on a wave of pain as intense as I had experienced in the nightmare.

"Mr. Kurz, it's alright," a male voice beside me said. "Mr. Kurz, you can't touch the tube."

I became aware of the suspended ceiling, an IV pole with several containers of liquid hanging from it, a bed, and glass walls.

The man across from Natalie who held one arm wore gray scrubs. The woman beside my wife holding the other arm was dressed in blue ones.

"It's okay, Bill." Natalie held each side of my face. Her eyes locked on mine. "You're in a hospital. You've been intubated and a ventilator is assisting your breathing."

A puff of air filled my lungs without any effort from me. Although her hands had a calming effect on me, disorientation, confusion, and fear ruled me. Why was I in a hospital? Why was a machine assisting my breathing? The tube in my throat prevented me from asking these questions.

The throbbing that radiated up from my lower extremities and chest took away my desire to break free from the clutches on my wrists. I couldn't shove the pain down and fight to get the object out of my mouth.

Natalie continued to caress my face with her gaze locked on mine.

I relaxed, but my anxiety over why I was in a hospital lay dormant, ready to control my emotions if I allowed.

Was this a nightmare or reality? Had the airplane I'd been flying crashed? My thoughts were slow and fuzzy.

"Mr. Kurz, I'm Steve. I'm a respiratory therapist," the guy to my side said. "You've begun to breathe over the ventilator. Your O2 sats are good, so we can remove the tube."

Natalie smiled, which suggested this was a good thing. She stepped to the foot of the bed where I could continue to see her.

Steve unfastened the strap around my head. "On the count of three, I want you to cough. Once the tube is out of your mouth, don't swallow. Let me suck out your mouth first."

The desire to get the thing out of my throat took away any thought of why my mouth would need to be vacuumed.

On three, I let out a cough that would expel the worst phlegm from my lungs. A stabbing pain darkened the edges of my vision. The tube sliding up my throat felt like barbs were attached to it. As excruciating as the procedure was, a sense of relief swept through me when the end had cleared my lips. But with it came gunk I fought to not swallow. Being a good pilot required following procedure. I complied with Steve's instruction.

He sucked out my mouth, removing my need to rid my mouth of that stuff.

The nurse placed a cannula under my nose and wrapped the hose around my ears.

"I bet that feels better." Natalie smiled.

"Why am I here?" My throat was so raw, my words came out a whisper.

"Would you like a drink of water?" the blue scrub woman asked.

I nodded.

The cool water soothed my throat.

"How's our patient doing?" A dark-haired guy wearing a lab coat stepped into the room and scanned the monitor above my head that showed my vital signs. "I'm Dr. Gummelt, a hospitalist. It's good to have you back with us."

Gummelt dropped his gaze to me. "It's probably difficult to take a deep breath because you fractured a rib that punctured your lung. Your liver was lacerated. You'll be sore for a while. On a scale of one to ten, ten being the worst, how's your pain?"

I wanted to say three thousand, but when I said ten afterward, they might not believe me. "Eight or nine." My voice was a raspy whisper I didn't recognize as mine. "What happened to me?"

"You were in an accident," Gummelt said.

That I knew, but I didn't know how.

"You broke your right leg above and below your knee." Gummelt used a voice that hinted he sympathized. "We operated on it and put a pin in your femur and stabilized your tibia with an external fixator. There was extensive damage to the muscle and tendons where the bones protruded through the skin. Your big toe and two bones in your left foot were also fractured."

His words seemed to come through a filter that prevented me from processing them as fast as they were delivered.

"The bones will heal adequately, but recovering the use of your leg from the damage to the muscle, ligaments, and tissue surrounding your knee will take some time," Gummelt continued as if I was following everything he said.

Thankfully, Natalie was a nurse practitioner. Her gaze flicked from Gummelt to me. I had seen her pursed lips enough times to know she was concerned.

Her apprehension heightened my anxiety, but it was a minor thing compared to the pain, from what I assumed was my fractured ribs and crippled leg and foot. I squirmed and regretted that action. "Ahh! Ahh!" Even the groan caused agony.

Gummelt placed in my hand a cord with a push button. "You're attached to a morphine drip. Whenever you need a shot of the pain reliever, push the button."

I gave the button an enthusiastic push, holding it for several seconds. Should I keep it depressed? Knowing it would hurt to ask that, I withheld my question. Moments later, the level of anguish ebbed, never completely going away.

Gummelt pulled the sheet back at my feet and pressed his fingers to my ankles. "The color and pulses in your feet are good." He poked my toes and foot in several places with a pen, asking if I could feel that, which I could. "You don't seem to have lost any circulation or feeling. Barring any further complications, we've managed to save your leg. Unfortunately, it will probably never be one hundred percent again. You'll always have a limp and will experience arthritis later in your life."

I ran his last words over in my head. *Managed to save your leg. Never be one hundred percent. Always have a limp.*

How could I be in this situation? Ned and I were on approach to Dallas-Fort Worth and had just lowered the landing gear. We planned to make a normal landing before the approaching thunderstorm closed the airport. The landing was... what? I couldn't remember the landing.

When I shook my head, the room swirled. I pressed my head into the pillow and concentrated on Natalie while holding myself as still as possible.

"Are you okay?" she asked.

"Dizzy."

"Try not to move your head rapidly," Gummelt said.

Yeah, no shit.

"With rehabilitation, you should be able to resume your life with some limitations." Gummelt pasted on a smile as if I would find that reassuring.

How could I? I hadn't wrapped my head around the *barring no further complications*, and *never be one hundred percent,* and *always have a limp*. Would I be able to fly again? Natalie and I skied twenty times a season. Would I not be able to tear up a black diamond trail again? Being close to the numerous ski areas was one of the reasons we lived in Denver.

Wait. I resisted the urge to shake my head again. If I'd been flying into Dallas, how could Natalie be here? "Where am I?"

"Baylor Hospital," Gummelt said.

Where was that?

My confusion must've shown, as Natalie said, "In Dallas."

How'd she get here so soon? We would have landed around five in the afternoon. By the time she had been notified of the accident and gone to the airport, could she have made the last flight to Dallas?

"What day is this?" It amazed me they could hear my murmur.

"After we repaired the laceration to your liver, re-inflated your lung, and operated on your leg, we kept you sedated," Gummelt said.

Did he answer my question?

"Three days," Natalie said. "The accident was three and a half days ago."

I settled into the bed, limp with the cold realization that while on approach or during the landing, something significant had happened. I should be able to remember something that would haunt me until I died.

"What happened?"

Chapter Four

Instead of answering me, Gummelt exchanged a glance with Natalie. "The best thing for your recovery is lots of rest."

"We'll check on you in a while." The nurse patted my arm. She and the doctor left the room.

Natalie came to my side. She lifted a leg as if to sit on the edge of the bed but seemed to reconsider and took my hand in hers.

With her other hand, she straightened the sheet, pulled the IV tube out from under the pillow, and stared at the drip of the liquid from the IV bag into the line. "Are you warm enough? Can I get another blanket?"

Although a medical professional and in tune with the environment of my room, I knew her busy work was to avoid talking about why I was in the hospital.

The dose of morphine I'd given myself was enveloping me in the desire to close my eyes and drift away. It'd be so easy to slip into the blanket of darkness again, but I knew that when I woke, I'd still be in a hospital and wouldn't know what happened to put me here.

I gave the hand of the amazing woman I married twenty-nine years ago a squeeze. "What happened?"

For a long moment, I didn't think she was going to answer me. Then she sighed. "It seems something happened when you landed."

Why was she being vague? Natalie gave me a hard time when I used the words *seemed, kind of,* or *maybe* when making a point that I knew could be taken negatively. I frowned, trying to remember the landing.

A gust of wind rocked the airplane and lifted us, making the aircraft go high on the glideslope. Ned already had the power at idle to slow to our approach speed. If he lowered the nose to increase our rate of descent to put us back on the glideslope, it would increase our airspeed. Something we were trying to decrease.

"Gear down. Flaps fifteen," Ned said.

I moved the landing gear and flap lever. The aerodynamic drag from both would assist in slowing us. Three green lights lit up indicating the landing gear legs had lowered to the landing position. Then...

My mind was a blank after that until I woke hanging upside down. My leaving the present to conjure up the past made my rebellious eyelids increase their desire to close. I blinked several times and concentrated on holding them open.

My wide-eyed expression must've suggested to Natalie that I remembered what happened because she bent closer and caressed my face. "It's okay. It'll all work out."

"What'll work out?" I cleared my throat, grimacing at the burn that effort created. "What happened on the landing?" The standby rudder ON light had been illuminated. It indicated the two main actuators were not powering the rudder and that only the single standby rudder actuator was. Had it affected our ability to control the aircraft?

She studied me. "You don't remember?"

I almost shook my head but managed to stop myself. I didn't need the room spinning again. "No."

She glanced at the door.

Was she stalling, or checking to be sure the doctor or nurse weren't coming back?

"Your aircraft went off the runway and cartwheeled, crashing into—" Her lips pursed before she turned her attention to the IV bags.

Before I could form the question of what happened on the landing roll, Ned's head, bent at an extreme angle, and his bulging, lifeless eye flashed into my conscience. "Ned. Is he..." She wouldn't know who Ned was. I flew with a different first officer on every trip. "The first officer, is he..."

Tears pooled in Natalie's eyes. Her grasp on my hand tightened. "I'm sorry."

Although her apology confirmed what I suspected, I didn't want to believe what had happened to him. "Did he... did he... die?"

Her nod was subtle, but it unleashed a cascade of emotion.

A sob that began in my gut and traveled through my chest flared the stabbing burn beneath my ribs. The pain didn't deter the moan that erupted from me.

Although I'd only flown with Ned three times, twice in the last six months, I'd connected with him. His dry sense of humor and easygoing manner mirrored mine. How could someone so carefree be gone?

Natalie rested her forehead against mine, holding both sides of my face. Her tears wet my cheeks, or were they mine?

I needed her in my arms.

When I lifted my arms, the agony overwhelmed me. I slipped over the edge into darkness.

Chapter Five

I lapsed in and out of consciousness, never knowing how long I'd slept. Each time I came to, the realization of why I was in a hospital came crashing down on me. Then, I'd wish I could slip back into unconsciousness, hoping that when I woke next, I would realize it'd all been a dream. But as quickly as I wished that, I knew there was no escaping the predicament I was in.

What the hell had happened?

As bad as it seemed for me, Ned would never get to see his children grow. My concern about limping the rest of my life and an inability to do the things I loved seemed so trivial in comparison. These thoughts overwhelmed me, pushing me into a black void where any choice was a bad one. I would wallow there until I gave myself a dose of morphine and lost any conscious thought.

Most of those times, Natalie was there, trying to be upbeat by telling me about family or friends who had called and expressed their desire to help.

As comforting as these assurances were, I could not conjure any enthusiasm.

The only time Natalie had mentioned the accident, she said we cartwheeled, which would've made our landing headline news. How often had the aircraft I'd been trapped in been shown to millions? How many times had pictures of me and Ned been broadcast so that the public could put a face to the two who would have been labeled incompetent pilots?

How could we have cartwheeled?

If we had penetrated a microburst while on approach, the downdraft could have exceeded the aircraft's climb capabilities, slamming us to the ground. The downward and forward motion, especially if one wing hit before the other, could have sent the aircraft tumbling.

But Natalie had said it *seemed* we went off the runway on landing. I tried to picture what might've sent the aircraft rolling across the ground like a child's toy that had been kicked. If we had landed and one or all the landing gear legs collapsed, we should've slid along on the aircraft's belly and been able to walk from the accident.

One time when I returned to consciousness, I found my son Lucas in a chair, reading from a tablet computer. As reassuring as it was to see Natalie each time I woke, a different kind of tenderness came over me, that of shared jokes and interests that only father and son shared. "Hi." The rawness of my throat still made my voice a whisper.

He came to the bed. "How are you feeling?"

My leg and foot screamed as if they were being cut off with a dull knife until I gave myself a dose of morphine. The slightest movement of my upper body sent a stabbing pain across my chest. Yet the nurses, doctor, Natalie, and now Lucas asked this question with maddening regularity.

I shrugged and grimaced from the pain.

"Rib fractures are painful." My son, a third-year med student, scrunched up his face. "It's hard to do anything without moving your chest some."

I flashed appreciation for my son's attempt to educate me. "Yeah, no shit, Dr. Kurz."

The worry on Lucas' face was replaced with a smile.

"When did you get here?" I asked.

"Lindsey and I got here the day after the..." He squeezed his eyes closed. "Ah... you were admitted."

I wished everyone wouldn't avoid talking about the accident. Did they think by skirting around it, I wouldn't think about it? "Lindsey's here too? The swimmers on Martha's Vineyard won't be safe without her watchful eye."

Lucas smiled. "She and Mom went to get something to eat other than hospital food."

I couldn't blame them. What little I'd managed to eat had been pretty bland. "How bad is it?"

When Lucas began reciting my medical condition, I realized I should've specified the accident. Natalie had avoided this question by changing the subject, acting cheerful.

I lifted a hand, pausing my son's narration. "How bad was the accident?"

Lucas sighed. "It's not good."

Hence one of the reasons I was glad he was here alone. I knew he'd tell me what was going on. Through Lucas's rebellious teenage years, we had learned to respect one another if we didn't lie to each other. There were times for both of us when it would have been easier to dance around the truth. Me, for not being able to provide for him the way his friends' parents could. Him, for being a teenager and wanting to test his independence.

I lifted my eyebrows.

"Mom says you don't remember the landing?"

I nodded.

"That's common with traumatic injuries."

I tried to find comfort in the fact that I hadn't suppressed the experience so I wouldn't have to confront it. Prior to this moment, I had worried my lack of memory was from knowing I hadn't prevented Ned's death. "Will I regain those memories?"

He shrugged. "Some people do. Some never do."

Remorse consumed me at the prospect of never remembering. I'd forever rack my mind for why I hadn't prevented it.

"They're saying you landed just as a thunderstorm moved over the airport."

I remembered the storm. It was centered south of the airport with the torrential downpour dropping visibility to zero at the southern end of the runways. We had approached from the north. The winds and visibility were adequate for landing.

"Just after you touched down, you encountered a wind gust from the side."

I frowned, trying to remember that, but couldn't.

Lucas watched me as if worried what he said might be traumatic. "Your aircraft swerved and went off the runway. The left wing hit an excavator that was digging up a taxiway, which spun you further and sent you tumbling."

I tried to visualize what he was telling me, hoping a memory would pop into my head, but something akin to sensory deprivation resided where memories of the landing should be. I widened my eyes when the memory of fear popped to the surface. The yell and need-to-be-anywhere-else kind-of horror like I'd never experienced before.

What Lucas said explained why we ended up upside down. But it didn't make sense why we would've gone off the runway. Had the brakes locked up and blown the two main gear tires? Still, we should've been able to keep the aircraft on the runway. Unless having only the standby rudder actuator prevented full use of the rudder.

"How strong a gust was it?"

"I don't know. They aren't saying. Maybe they don't know yet."

"They" would be the NTSB, the National Transportation Safety Board.

I had previously landed the EA-220 in gusting crosswinds that I suspected were at the aircraft limits of thirty-eight knots and had never come close to going off the runway. One of those times had been flying with Ned several months ago. Even though Ned had been flying the day of the accident, he had demonstrated earlier that he was capable of landing in the conditions Lucas described.

"Is the accident all over the news?"

The nod Lucas gave was subtle. He fidgeted, glanced out at the nurse's station, then poked at his tablet. "Mom will kill me for showing you this." Holding the tablet in front of me, he began playing a video. The screen was blurry.

"I need my reading glasses." I hated I lay there as an invalid, depending on my son to do something as simple as retrieve my own damn glasses.

Lucas glanced around the room, then opened and closed several drawers in the cabinet at the side of the room. "I don't know where they are."

Were they lying in the wreckage? Where was the suitcase that I had dragged behind me on every trip for the last ten years? Would I get it or my laptop and wallet back? Were the NTSB and FAA examining my dirty underwear and contents of my computer like every other part of the airplane? Years from now, when I'd managed to put most of the trauma of the accident behind me, would my things finally be returned to reopen that wound?

"Let me see if a nurse will lend me some." Lucas left the room, returning a moment later with a pair of glasses he intentionally placed crookedly on my face.

My apprehension of watching what Natalie didn't want me to see prevented me from commenting on his attempt to lighten my mood.

After working to suppress a smile, he straightened the readers.

The glasses' prescription was stronger than mine, but I wasn't going to complain if I got answers to my many questions.

Lucas held the tablet in front of me again and selected the video. "This has been played over and over on the news."

The recording was of low quality and shaky. There were water droplets in the foreground. Occasionally, the corner of a window came into view that made me suspect the video was taken by a passenger on an airliner.

A Sphere Airlines EA-220 with its aqua-green stripe down the side approached a runway with its landing gear and flaps extended. I recognized the background as the north side of DFW airport.

"Here comes another one," a voice said that must have been the photographer's. His drawl suggested he was from Texas.

The wings on the approaching aircraft rocked. The nose rose to flare for landing. When the main landing gear was a few feet above the concrete, the aircraft's nose swung to align it with the runway. The wings continued to rock and the nose swerved back and forth a few degrees, but the pilot did a good job of compensating for the gusting winds.

"Pretty windy," the photographer said.

I watched in the same detached way I might consider another crew's arrival. The video didn't trigger any memories.

The mains touched down in a smooth landing. A moment before the nose gear made contact with the runway, the aircraft slewed to the left as if yanked.

Instinctively, I pushed with my right leg as if pushing on the rudder pedal. The spike of agony stole my concentration. I worked to push through it, needing to see what happened.

"Hang onto it," the photographer said.

The nose gear slammed to the ground as the aircraft increased its curve toward the side of the runway. When it left the concrete, the aircraft was angled forty-five degrees from the centerline.

"Holy shit!" the photographer said.

Although no flashes of memory came to me, my heart had begun to thump hard. I clenched my fists.

On the video, voices shouted. "Oh, my God!"

"Look!"

"Fuck!"

The cabin sidewall of the aircraft came into view as the photographer attempted to track the airplane's path, leaving a quarter of the screen still showing the 220's tail as it traveled across the grass.

The video jerked around as if the photographer struggled to move to a position that allowed him to continue filming. Flashes of legs clad in jeans, then the back of the seats, the cabin sidewall, a click like a seatbelt being released, and the aircraft's window filled the screen. The image continued to jerk as the video zoomed in, then out.

After a second or two of this commotion, the aircraft came into view. In the lower corner of the screen, the boom of an excavator and the left wing collided.

The tail of the aircraft rose and twisted as if the hand of God had lifted it.

Even though no memories of being a part of the wild ride came to me, I shook as if cold.

The aircraft continued to roll, slamming onto its top and not pausing in its momentum. Wingtips and parts of the rudder and vertical stabilizer were flung from the aircraft as it continued to roll another couple of revolutions.

The video recorded more shrieks, yells, and swearing.

Was my memory loss caused by blacking out from the centrifugal forces rolling the aircraft so violently? How had I lived?

During the aircraft's tumble, a flash of memory popped into my head: I was looking through the windshield. One hand white-knuckled the yoke, the other braced on the glare shield. The view out the windshield was grass before it was quickly replaced with the horizon viewed upside down, then nothing but sky.

The aircraft continued to tumble, flinging debris and dirt. On the right side of the screen, the tail of an Embraer 145, a fifty-seat regional jet, slid into view.

I lifted my hands to cover my eyes, knowing what I would witness. But I needed to see this, to know what I had caused.

"No! Not that plane! Not that plane," someone on the video yelled.

The 220 slammed diagonally across the top of the smaller jet.

Chapter Six

Two days after watching the devastating video, I was moved from the intensive care unit to a single room on the medical/surgical floor. This room that would be my home for at least a week had a window with sunlight streaming through, something I didn't want. Natural light brightened the dark pit I'd mentally crawled into.

Many on the regional jet must've perished. How did I move on when I'd been responsible for ending so many lives?

I wished I had died, too.

"This should be more pleasant." Natalie smiled, but there was no enthusiasm in her eyes.

"Yeah, this is much cheerier." Lindsey's voice, like her mother's, rose at the end of her sentence.

My glum mood generated this false cheerfulness. I had no enthusiasm for anything.

The twenty-something blonde nurse, who'd introduced herself as Megan, set a pitcher of ice water on the table over my bed. "Let me know if you need anything." She smiled at Lucas before leaving.

His gaze followed the nurse out the door. "Yeah, this is much better."

For the first time since awakening in the hospital, I peeked over the edge of my pit, appreciating that my family might move past what I'd done to them.

When I reached for the TV remote, Natalie snatched it up and set it on the windowsill out of my reach.

"You feel like reading?" Her smile had been replaced with a furrowed brow I'd seen numerous times in twenty-nine years. "The gift shop has a pretty good selection of books and magazines."

I noted she didn't mention newspapers. "Sure. You know what'll interest me."

At some point, I'd have to confront her determination to avoid discussing the accident. But hadn't killing so many on that regional jet caused her enough grief? Shouldn't I allow her some control of our situation for what I was putting her through?

But any day now, the NTSB and FAA would question me. Afterward, the FAA would determine if I kept my pilot license. Depending on what the NTSB ruled as the accident's cause, Sphere Airlines might fire me. If the families of those on the regional jet sued Sphere, there'd be depositions and trials I would have to sit through. We couldn't avoid reality by not facing it.

The TV in the ICU unit had always been tuned to something that sheltered me from what was going on outside the hospital. The fog generated by the morphine made me apathetic.

Since the morphine pump had been removed and my mind was clearer, I needed to know what happened and figure out how to survive this nightmare—physically, mentally, and financially.

Six days had passed since the accident. A part of me hoped the media found more newsworthy content in something one of the presidential candidates had said than the incompetent pilot who killed many. At the same time, I also needed to learn what the NTSB concluded had caused the accident. They must have analyzed the cockpit voice recorder and digital flight data recorder by now.

"Why don't you all get away for a bit?" I pasted on an expression of encouragement. "I'll be fine."

Lucas and Lindsey brightened.

"You mean it?" our daughter asked.

I nodded. "Yes. I've got some guys coming over to drink beer and play cards."

Our children showed a trace of a smile. I didn't fool my wife. She studied me with her lips pursed.

"I'll probably take a nap. PT wiped me out." Physical therapy, or what I secretly called torture, and the Percocet I took afterward made a nap something I could easily do.

Although I had ulterior motives for urging my family to take a break, the strain of hanging around the hospital was showing on them.

Yesterday Lindsey and Lucas had a disagreement over something trivial. Sibling bickering was something they did often, something Natalie and I detested, but yesterday, their tone and words were sharper than normal.

The usual warm expression that Natalie wore had been replaced by bags under her eyes and a downturned mouth. She stared off into space, picking at her fingernails, something she never did before.

"Go on. Get out of here." I made a shooing motion with my hand. "Go eat someplace that isn't fast food. Have a couple of drinks. I appreciate you being here, but you need to live. I'll be all right."

"You guys go ahead." My wife nodded at the door.

"No." I beckoned her over. "Please get away for a while. I need you strong." I gestured to the monitor over my head that displayed my vitals. "Big Brother is watching. If anything happens, they'll be here in a flash. You don't need to be constantly at my side."

"What you're going through is traumatic," Natalie said. "You don't have to go through it alone."

"I'm not." I gave her hand a squeeze. "I know all of you are here for me. But I need you mentally, emotionally, and physically strong. Please, get away for a while." I pasted on what would be my usual expression of nonchalance. "If it were you in this bed, since you wouldn't be able to stop me, I'd be out shopping." I didn't shop.

Some of the life that normally filled her eyes returned before she glanced at her watch. Her chest rose and fell. "Maybe for a little bit."

After they'd been gone long enough that I knew they weren't coming back, I pressed the call button for the nurse. When Megan came, I pointed to the windowsill. "Will you toss me the remote please?"

I channel surfed until I found an all-news station. For several minutes, all that was mentioned was the coverage of this year's presidential election.

The next showed a variation of the first. Next channel.

A reporter stood with an airport in the background and several aircraft taxiing behind the chain-link fence. "...Safety Board member Burton Meckes informed us that the data from the flight recorder revealed the pilot did not maintain control of the aircraft."

Pain burned through my chest when I sat up straighter. Prior to now, it had annoyed me that the media never got aviation details correct—and overly dramatized them. They always made it seem there was only one pilot, not two, in the cockpit. Today, I had another reason to hate the media's reporting of aviation. I, *we*, would've maintained control if we could have.

The scene changed to show a podium with the crest of the breast of an eagle surrounded by the words *National Transportation Safety Board* on the front of it. A middle-aged man with a round face stood behind the bank of microphones. "Analysis of the flight data recorder revealed that four-point-three seconds after touchdown, the crew experienced a gust of wind from their left of fifty-six knots, forty-eight degrees from the runway heading."

I lifted my brow. Without a crosswind chart to verify it, I suspected that gust exceeded the 220's crosswind capability. Had the crosswind been greater than the aircraft's designed limit, making it impossible for us to stay on the runway?

"The crew compensated for the crosswind by only applying forty percent of the available rudder. That was not an adequate displacement to counter the effects of a gust this strong."

I narrowed my eyes. Forty percent? We would've pushed the rudder pedal to the stop to use all the available rudder.

The scene changed back to the reporter standing at the airport. "Later, Board Member Meckes would not speculate why the crew would use less than half the available rudder. Until they question the captain of the flight, who still has not issued a statement, the National Transportation Safety Board will not know why the crew did not prevent their aircraft from crashing into another one."

I clenched my fists, hating that they made me look like I was hiding from the media and had allowed the accident that killed so many. Why didn't they mention the main rudder actuators were not working and we only had the standby rudder control? Had that fact become old news at this point?

The reporter's next statement sent me spiraling deeper into the dark pit I'd been occupying.

"We also just learned that two of the twelve who survived the accident have died. That now brings the death toll to thirty-eight, including the first officer of the doomed flight, and ten in critical condition."

Thirty-eight!

I laid my head back, engulfed in an emptiness that replaced the constant throbbing of pain. Thirty-eight had died from my actions or, it now seemed, lack of them.

"Thanks, Victor." The screen changed to show the anchor accompanied by a man dressed in a blue suit, coiffured dark hair with streaks of gray, and a lowered brow. "We're now joined by Captain Louis Culbertson, who is a former accident investigator and airline captain."

I groaned. This would be one of the many self-proclaimed aviation experts the media always dragged out whenever there was an accident or incident.

"Captain Culbertson, do you glean any information from what the NTSB reported today?"

"Well, Jenny, the use of less than half the available rudder is eye-opening. I'm sure the NTSB will be looking into the pilots' training and question pilots they have flown with to see if either one had trouble landing in a crosswind."

They wouldn't find a problem with either Ned or me.

"What I find troubling is this crew continued to Dallas and attempted to land during a thunderstorm," the so-called expert said. "They overflew Houston, where they could've landed until the storms moved out of the Dallas area. One of the things the NTSB will be looking into is this captain's judgement, which at this time seems inadequate."

I considered throwing the remote at the TV.

"Are we now finding out this accident might've been prevented if a more qualified pilot had been flying the aircraft?" Jenny plastered on an expression of bewilderment.

Culbertson considered this question before answering. "I can't say. It does look troubling that this captain didn't land at an airport with good weather and didn't use all the available rudder to keep the aircraft on the runway. These are all things the NTSB will be considering."

This so-called expert was proving to be a Monday morning quarterback speculating on information to boost his image. People not knowing any better would feel what he said was accurate when in reality it was a fabrication.

When we overflew Houston, the weather in Dallas was adequate for a safe landing.

No wonder Natalie kept me from watching the news since my decisions and actions were crucified.

I clicked to another channel.

"... captain was one to not follow standard procedures," a guy with close-cropped hair and a gruff expression said. "Any aircraft coming out of maintenance is to be flown by the captain. Since he allowed the less experienced first officer to fly, he obviously wasn't one to follow procedures. Or he was concerned about his ability to land in the crosswind they encountered."

Even though I shook my head, I couldn't dismiss the guy's logic. Since waking in the wreckage, I had questioned if I had flown the flight instead of Ned, would I have prevented the accident?

On the video Lucas had shown me, Ned aligned the nose of the aircraft with the runway just before touchdown. To have done that, he would have had to input some right rudder. It would have taken minimal effort to put in all the available rudder to keep us on the runway when the gust hit us.

While I was questioning why he hadn't prevented the accident, I had to ask why hadn't I? My feet would have been just off the pedals, ready to take over if needed. It would have taken me less than a second to stomp on the rudder pedal when I saw he was losing control.

That would be a question I knew the NTSB would ask. My missing memory prevented me from coming up with an answer, making me want to smack myself until a memory was dislodged.

Knowing I felt so strongly about Ned's ability, some might argue I had let my earlier experience with him allow me to be complacent. Possibly, since during the part of our arrival I remembered, he'd done an excellent job flying the aircraft. But if he was sharp and competent earlier, why would he have suddenly become inept in the critical seconds before we went off the runway?

When nothing of substance was being broadcast on other channels, I turned the TV off and questioned why the media wasn't making a bigger deal of the aircraft coming out of maintenance and that the rudder was powered only by the standby actuator. On the flight from San Salvador, Ned and I had relayed to Sphere's maintenance department that the main rudder controls had failed.

Something in the aircraft's inspection must have been overlooked or put together incorrectly. Had something in the rudder mechanism prevented us from pushing the pedal to the stop? Wouldn't the NTSB realize that was why the aircraft had crashed?

I was able to quiet the turmoil in my mind and fall asleep. When I woke, it was dark outside.

Natalie stood at the window, talking on her cell phone in a hushed tone. "They surrounded us as we left the hospital, shouting questions, like, 'Why hasn't Bill issued a statement?' And 'Is he exaggerating his injuries to avoid facing up to what he's done?'"

Wasn't it bad enough I ruined so many lives? Why did the media have to needle my family when they too were victims of my actions?

Being trapped in a hospital bed, unable to come to their aid overwhelmed me, blurring my vision with tears.

"I thought Lucas was going to run them over when they surrounded our car."

My shuddering and sob turned Natalie's attention to me.

"Bill's awake now. I'll call you later." She lowered her phone, looking concerned. "You okay?"

"The media is hounding you?"

"Oh, it's nothing." She worked to brighten her face.

"It didn't sound like it to me."

She busied herself with straightening the bedding, paused, then moved the TV remote to the windowsill and studied her phone's screen.

"Swish," I said, "how bad is it outside this room?"

Her gaze remained locked on her phone. "I'm sorry you heard my conversation with Janice. It's nothing you need to worry about."

She downplayed this to shelter me. Maybe I should make a statement. "Has someone from the union been by?" There were experts at the pilot's union who could help me prepare a statement that wouldn't incriminate me.

She shook her head. "A fleet manager has been around and has been very helpful."

That put me on edge, while at the same time it comforted me. "Who?"

"Bryce Marling."

I'd had no interactions with him, so I didn't know if he would be looking out for me or for the airline.

Chapter Seven

The next day, while Natalie and the kids went to lunch, I had Megan retrieve the TV remote off the windowsill again, then flipped through the news channels, stopping when the accident was mentioned. All that was reported was headline news in length, without going into much detail.

I was about to turn the TV off when an anchor announced, "After a break, we have an exclusive interview with Sphere Airlines First Officer Adam Obermiller."

What did this pompous twerp have to say?

When Obermiller was introduced, the anchor asked, "First Officer Obermiller, you previously flew with Captain Kurz?"

I smiled briefly at the use of my rank and name. When I had become a captain years ago, I would spiel out to family and friends with a puffed-up chest, "Captain Kurz, captain on the Sphere Airlines 220. Whose mission is to boldly go where no 220 has gone before." After the first time, they didn't find it funny.

"Yes. Recently." Obermiller sat upright in his pressed uniform and had spent some time in front of the mirror gelling his hair so that it stuck up in the fashionable way young men his age wore it.

Looking the part of a pilot was the only thing the asshole did right.

"I understand you had a landing incident with Captain Kurz. Tell us about it."

Obermiller cleared his throat. "He was landing in a similar situation to the one in Dallas-Fort Worth last week. Because of the strong crosswind, he had to fly at a crab to the runway." Obermiller moved one flattened hand above the other at an angle to signify an aircraft moving over a runway with the nose pointed to the side into the wind.

"Just before touchdown, the procedure is to apply upwind rudder to align the nose with the runway."

"I understand that's not what Captain Kurz did," the anchor said.

Obermiller nodded. "You're right. He didn't."

I straightened, my narrowed eyes glued to the TV.

"What did Captain Kurz do?"

"It's not what he did, but didn't do. He was going to allow the aircraft to land in the cocked angle."

Fucking. Lying. Bastard.

"And why would that be bad?" the anchor asked.

"Well, at the angle we would've touched down, he possibly could have collapsed the landing gear."

The anchor's eyebrows rose. "Obviously, that wouldn't be good. So what did you do?"

"I ordered a go-around," Obermiller said with confidence.

"A go-around? Isn't that where the aircraft climbs away from the airport? How did Captain Kurz take a first officer telling him what to do?"

"He must not have liked it, as he initially did nothing."

"Nothing?"

Obermiller nodded. "Nothing. Just as I was reaching to take the controls and perform the go-around, Kurz realized he had no choice and complied with the procedure."

"What happened then?"

"After we got to altitude and were being vectored for another approach, I told him he had been about to land crooked. He agreed and said he would do better this time."

"And did he?"

Obermiller squirmed in his seat. "No."

"What did he do?"

"Again, he flew in a crab to line up with the runway, but just before touchdown, he didn't make any corrections to align with the runway."

"What happened then?"

Obermiller's turned his gaze down. "We were low on fuel and couldn't do another go-around, so I took the controls and landed the aircraft."

I gritted my teeth and breathed deeply.

"So you had to take the controls from the captain and land the aircraft?" the anchor asked, as if what he was hearing was preposterous. "Why would Captain Kurz have considered landing crooked?"

"I don't know. I can only assume he was nervous. Or incompetent."

I clenched and unclenched my fists.

"Could it have been he'd never landed in conditions like that before?"

Obermiller squirmed again. "Possibly. It seems hard to believe this hadn't happened with another pilot on another flight. I'm just glad I was there that day instead of a first officer who might not have spoken up."

"We are too. What did Captain Kurz say afterwards?"

"What are you watching?" Natalie asked, suspicion filling her tone as she, Lindsey, and Lucas walked into the room.

"An outrageous lie." I pointed to the TV. "He's claiming he took the airplane away from me when it was the other way around."

She looked at the TV, then reached for the remote. "You don't need to watch that."

My face warmed. "Yes, I do. Someday soon I will have to explain what happened. Everyone who questions me will know everything that has been reported. To defend myself, I need to know too."

Behind her, Lindsey and Lucas stared at us wide-eyed.

"Look at your heart rate and blood pressure." Natalie pointed to the monitor. "Both are abnormally high. This stress is hampering your ability to heal."

As we argued, Obermiller told the TV anchor, "I wish I had told the chief pilots about Captain Kurz's landing. Maybe the accident wouldn't have happened."

I pointed the remote at the screen. "He's lying and making me out to be incompetent."

Lucas and Lindsey moved into the room so they could see the TV.

Natalie reached for the remote, but I swung my hand away and was punished with a stab of pain in my chest.

My grimace must have shown.

"That's why you need to remain calm." Natalie held her open hand out in front of her like she had done to the kids when they were younger.

I considered doing what Lucas had done when he was fifteen and thrown the remote across the room and yelled, "This is not fair!"

Natalie's blue eyes nailed mine with defiance.

I glared back at her. "We can't pretend the accident will go away by ignoring it."

Her expression was one I'd seen numerous times when I'd erroneously accused her of not understanding my point. "I'm not ignoring it."

A very small voice in my head told me I wasn't considering what she was experiencing, or her medical knowledge. My anger stifled it. "You can't shelter me from what is being said. I need to know."

She lifted her face to the ceiling and exhaled a deep breath, splaying her fingers at her sides.

Lucas eased out of the room. Lindsey watched his retreat and turned back with her mouth agape.

I wanted to massage my chest where it burned, but would not give Natalie the satisfaction of knowing she was right about the physical effects of anger.

I clicked the TV off and shoved the remote at her.

Again, she placed it on the windowsill and stayed facing the window.

Lindsey's expression showed a conflict of emotion.

In a calmer voice, I said, "I'm sorry you're going through this. All of you. I wish I could spare you this pain. I wish your lives could go on as they were. But your husband, your father, will now always be considered the incompetent pilot who killed thirty-eight."

"You're. Not. Incompetent," Natalie said through clenched teeth before turning to me.

I laid my head back against the pillow. "Tell that to the families of those who died."

"I'm sure once everyone hears you didn't cause the accident, they won't think that of you," Lindsey said.

My daughter's positive outlook filled my chest with a good kind of pain. At the same time, I thought her judgement was clouded. "We don't know that I didn't."

"I do." Natalie's voice was confident. She came to my side and clasped my hand. "I don't care what the so-called experts say. I know you would have prevented that accident if you could have."

Her faith in me made emotion travel up my throat and bring tears to my eyes. I wish I had the same faith in my actions. "I wish I could remember."

She pulled my hand to her chest and held it there.

I blinked to hold back my tears. Why had I become such a crybaby? It must be the narcotics. "I watch the news, hoping something will jog my memory. I could be fired. Or lose my pilot license. We could be sued. I need to know what we face."

I tried to see if the impact of my words hit my wife. But instead of seeming troubled by them, she said, "I can't imagine what it is like to not remember something that others feel was your fault. I'm sure it's awful." Her eyes pleaded. "But being in a constant state of anger and worry will prolong your healing process. Stress lowers your immune system. The more you dwell on the accident's cause and wallow in guilt, the longer it'll take you to recover."

I hated not knowing what happened. I certainly didn't want to prolong my recuperation.

"Please, *for me*, work at getting healthy so I can have you back." Natalie squeezed my hand. "I hate seeing you so broken and morose."

"Me too, Dad. I want the father that makes me laugh."

It hadn't been their intention, but I slid further down into the gloom of guilt for not being the person they needed.

"I can't tell you," Natalie swallowed, "how devastated I was when I heard about the crash and that you were in critical condition. Or could be an amputee." Her eyes had pooled.

I hadn't considered the fall-to-her-knees-numbness she must have experienced when word reached her.

"When I saw that video," she nodded when my eyes widened, "yeah, I watched it too. I couldn't see how you survived. Since then... I can't leave. What if you have a setback?"

My daughter turned her face away and wiped a finger under each eye. That sight brought on a flood of my own tears.

I craved to do something about my reputation being stomped on. But I knew I should care more about easing my family's burden. If sitting idly by could help them get through this, shouldn't I grant them that? Wasn't this similar to what Natalie and I preached to Lindsey and Lucas: that it didn't matter what others thought of them as long as they were true to themselves?

"I would like to promise you I'll ignore the news and not think about the accident, but I don't have that luxury."

My devoted wife worked her mouth back and forth, a gesture I normally loved when she considered a request.

"I already think about the accident constantly. Won't a little education ease the stress I'm experiencing by not being informed?"

I hated that I was adding conflict. Prior to the accident, our marriage had been tested numerous times. Besides the normal stress any couple experienced, we had to deal with the incredible amount of time I was away from home and the uncountable birthdays, holidays, and special events I had missed. Add in the temporary pay cuts we suffered when I moved up from a regional airline to Sphere, and two airline bankruptcies, it was a wonder we had survived.

I had a profound gratitude that we had made our marriage work. So I didn't want to reject her opinion of what she thought best.

She shook her head. "Promise me you'll limit the amount you watch and avoid the reports that are the most upsetting to you."

I pulled her hand to my lips and kissed it. "I promise."

I didn't realize that compromise would be tested so very soon.

Chapter Eight

The next day while my family was away, a tall, thin man with hair graying at the temples knocked on my door and stepped into the room. He seemed at ease wearing a sport coat over a tieless dress shirt and pressed khaki pants as if he dressed that way often.

My pulse began to pound as we eyed each other. He seemed familiar, making me suspect he was the fleet manager Natalie mentioned, but I worried he was a family member of one of the ten severely injured in the accident. They were recovering somewhere in this hospital. How did I convey how sorry I was without it seeming trite?

"Captain Kurz?" my visitor asked.

I swallowed. "Yes."

"Bryce Marling." He moved to the bedside with an extended hand. "I'm the EA-220 fleet manager."

"Bill Kurz." Although the name was familiar from training bulletins, my unease didn't go away as I shook his hand. "Did I miss a check-ride and you're here to see why?"

Marling smiled until his gaze traveled over me. Physical therapy had just left and I hadn't pulled the blanket over my legs until I cooled down.

The Fleet Manager grimaced as he took in the bandage that ran the length of my leg, and the external fixator with its rods that pierced my skin. "No, I think it's evident why you're lounging around." He averted his gaze from my leg. "I came to be of assistance in any way I can."

"Thank you, and for all you've done for my family."

"Hey, no problem." He waved a hand. "Whatever you need, let me know and I'll do everything I can to see you get it. I can't imagine what you and your family are going through."

He had no idea. "Thank you."

As helpful and congenial as he appeared, I knew I had to be careful what I said to someone from management. I had been responsible for putting the airline under scrutiny from the NTSB and FAA, tarnished its reputation to the traveling public, and opened it up to numerous lawsuits. I didn't know if management would try to pin the blame on me or support me. Before I said anything to them, the NTSB, or FAA, I had to talk to a union rep or hire an attorney.

"Outside of my family, you're the first person who has come to visit."

Marling's hand waved again. "No problem. Glad I could be here." He glanced at the chair beside my bed.

After a tip of my head in its direction, he sat.

"I'm surprised someone from the union hasn't stopped by." By referring to the pilot's union's lack of support, I hoped to deter him from questioning me without a representative looking out for my interests.

"They haven't been here? Hmmm. Doesn't surprise me."

I frowned. "Why?"

"Oh, well, they've been at the accident scene and the various meetings the NTSB has conducted. And they're formalizing the agreement they've reached with us on the pilots' contract." He smiled. "You're getting a pay raise. It's about time, isn't it?"

"Yeah." Even though his justification seemed legitimate, it still bothered me no one had made an appearance.

"Besides, until a few days ago, they weren't letting you have visitors. What with the Memorial Day holiday and all, I'm sure they didn't feel a pressing need."

Even though I had never been a pin-wearing, fist-pumping supporter of the union, I had paid my monthly dues all through my career. Shouldn't they have given me a little support?

"Your wife tells me you might be moved to a rehabilitation facility in a week."

"Yeah. I hope the food's better there." I gave a wry smile.

He chuckled. "Yeah, I'm sure. I'm working on getting you into a place in Denver. I'm sure that'll be easier for your wife."

"Thanks. I appreciate it." The thought of being closer to home lifted my spirits. I would get to see Natalie more than if I stayed in Dallas. But, being close, she would feel the need to visit often, adding burden to her already busy life.

Regardless, it piqued my interest that someone from the training department was working on my behalf, and not someone from the chief pilot's office. Usually, the latter took care of pilots' needs.

"Have you been watching the news?" he asked.

I nodded.

"Then you must know the data from the DFDR says you guys didn't adequately compensate for the gust which caused the aircraft to go off the runway. Regardless of what the data says, we don't believe you guys would've sat there and gone on that wild ride intentionally. That was one nasty storm at the end of the runway."

Some of the edginess tightening my shoulders relaxed.

The home remodeling show on TV caught his attention. "My wife watches this. Gives her ideas to add to the honey-do list."

"Yeah, mine does too."

We watched for several minutes as the clients argued with the contractor about the unplanned costs. Marling seemed content to sit and enjoy the show.

I had no illusions of why he was here, yet found myself in a debate of asking why the news didn't mention the main rudder actuators weren't working. That would open a question and answer session. But there was something I could inquire about to deflect attention away from my actions.

"What will happen to First Officer Adam Obermiller for allowing himself to be interviewed?"

Marling's forehead wrinkled. "What do you mean?"

With a gesture at the TV, I said, "Yesterday, he was interviewed and claimed he had to take the airplane away from me during a landing in a crosswind."

Marling pursed his lips before speaking. "This is the first I'm hearing of this. When, exactly, what station and who interviewed him?"

"I was channel surfing yesterday afternoon and don't remember which station I stopped on. CNN maybe."

"I'll look into it." He appeared deep in thought.

I assumed the airline's PR department would've have been watching and reading everything that had been said about the accident so they would know how to respond during press conferences. Word of a pilot being interviewed, in uniform, should have come to their attention.

"What he said was an outright lie."

"Why? What'd he say?" Marling's eyes narrowed.

"He claimed a couple of months ago I attempted to land without correcting for a crosswind and he ordered me to go around. On the second approach I was going to do so again, but he took the aircraft away from me and landed safely."

"Why is that a lie?"

"He was the one flying and I ordered the go-around. While being vectored for the second approach, I suggested I land the aircraft. But he said he was sorry and would do better the next time."

"And did he?"

"No. We didn't have the fuel to go around again, so I took control and landed."

Marling scratched his head. "So, you claim he said it was you who had the problem landing?"

My heart thumped in my chest. "I'm not claiming that. That's what he said."

"Did you report this to the chief pilot's office?"

I smoothed out the sheet. "No."

"Why not? If he needed additional training, you should've brought that to their attention."

"Yeah, I know." I sighed, wishing I hadn't fallen for Obermiller's justification that he had a lot on his mind. "Regardless, he's telling the traveling public you have a captain who was incompetent."

"I can see why that would upset you." His tone suggested he was attempting compassion.

"It doesn't matter whether it upsets me. He's lying. Add that to the fact the NTSB is saying Ned and I didn't adequately compensate for the crosswind, the public will think Sphere is unsafe. I'm sure the FAA will question why we allowed a pilot with a history of poor skill to continue flying without being trained properly."

I didn't need to look at the monitor to know my vitals were elevated.

"So you're upset he's claiming it was you who had the problem landing when it really was him?"

Prior to this exchange, I always smiled at the belief line pilots held that the ones in management were clueless suck-ups trying to get into a position of power. Now I wondered if there wasn't some truth to this myth. "Wouldn't you be?"

Marling clasped then unclasped his hands. "This will be a delicate situation."

"Why?"

"Well, since you didn't report this, you are in fact as guilty as you claim the company should be for allowing an unsafe pilot to continue flying without additional training."

I lowered my head. *Shit!*

"If he's already gone on the news once, and we approach him now for additional training, what's to stop him from going on camera again claiming that because he spoke up, we're punishing him?" Marling held out his hands, palms up.

"Unless he gets permission to be interviewed, knowing he could be facing suspension should shut him up."

A deep breath escaped Marling. "Yeah I suppose. But you have to look at it from the company's perspective. We have an accident with a captain who appears to not adequately compensate for a crosswind. Now we hear of an earlier landing in which he might've had difficulty with this same procedure. But you claim it was the first officer who had the problem, yet didn't report that. Can you see how we might think you're trying to cover up your negligence?"

My sigh was louder than I intended, but I hated that my giving another pilot a break was coming back to make me look like the incompetent one.

Marling studied my downturned face. "I'll investigate this and get back to you."

✈ ✈ ✈

The airplane rocked from the turbulence. The runway rushed up to greet us. We flared and the nose of the aircraft aligned with the runway as we touched down on the left main landing gear, followed by the right.

Just before the nose gear touched the concrete, the airplane began to swing to the left.

"Rudder! Rudder," I yelled.

When the corrective application of right rudder wasn't applied, I glanced at Ned to see why he wasn't stopping the aircraft from going off the runway. Ned wasn't occupying the first officer position. Adam Obermiller was. He gave me a devious grin.

The aircraft tumbled over and over with parts being flung from it.

I woke with my heart racing. The sheets of my hospital bed were soaked in sweat.

If pain made a noise, my leg would be screaming from my quivering.

After my heart rate slowed and the pain subsided some, I longed for the ability to roll over and try to return to sleep, hoping that when I woke, I didn't remember the nightmare.

I closed my eyes and the horror replayed in my head. During the accident, had I yelled for Ned to apply more rudder? Or had my mind fabricated that, like it had put Obermiller in the first officer's seat?

Eventually I would get to hear the cockpit voice recorder. Even if I heard I had ordered Ned to apply more rudder, it didn't absolve me of not stomping on it myself.

✈ ✈ ✈

The next morning after my sponge bath—how I looked forward to when I could take a long, hot, shower—Marling knocked on my door before entering. He carried two Starbucks venti-sized plastic cups of a tan frozen drink.

"You look like a mocha Frappuccino type of guy."

I fought the urge to lick my lips. "Yes. Thank you. Room service hasn't delivered the one I ordered hours ago."

While sucking on his straw, Marling smiled.

How many times in the past had I swung into a café without appreciating that freedom?

We drank in silence until Marling stirred his drink. "We've talked to Adam Obermiller."

"Yeah? What did he say?"

"He's claiming what he said during his interview is correct."

"Really?" My face warmed. "What are you going to do about him being interviewed without getting approval by the company?"

"Well... we're going to let this issue fade away."

"What? In recurrent training every year, we're warned that giving statements to the media is grounds for termination. How can this *fade away*?"

"The accident has been in the news enough. We're anxious for the media to tire of it and move on to something else. If we were to fire Obermiller, no doubt he'd arrange another interview explaining he was wrongfully terminated for blowing the whistle on an unsafe captain."

As much as I didn't want to believe what I was hearing, logically I understood Sphere's thinking and knew what Marling would say next, dreading it.

"Since the captain in question was just involved in an accident similar to the time Obermiller described, and we have no record of Obermiller's lack of skill, he'll be given a warning and told to keep his mouth shut."

I set my half-finished drink down. Either I was getting a brain freeze or this discussion was giving me a headache. Why did I give the pompous ass a break several months ago?

"Put him in a simulator with a strong crosswind, or talk to other captains who have flown with him in windy conditions and you'll learn he's lying."

"Since no other captain has come forward agreeing with you, we'd just as soon let this go away."

I shook my head.

Marling offered me an appeasement. "What we will do is note that his crosswind landing techniques need to be evaluated when he goes for recurrent training."

"When will that be?"

Every Sphere Airlines pilot would be experiencing crosswind landings during recurrent training. It would be something the NTSB would recommend.

"Five months."

I lifted my brow. "A check-airman should give a line check on one of his flights."

Marling bore his gaze into me. "Don't you think we thought of that? If it's a calm day and he does fine, he could claim we're harassing him."

"If he's involved in an incident and the company hasn't done anything, how will you explain that?"

Marling shook a finger at me. "You better hope that doesn't happen for your sake, since you didn't report him."

Several seconds elapsed while Marling drank his drink. In a calmer tone he said, "Since you claim he's lying, prove to me you're not the one who has difficulties landing in a crosswind. Walk me through the approach and landing that put you in that bed."

I turned TV remote over and over, weighing how much to tell him. Or, more accurately, letting him know how little I could tell him.

"Who was flying? You or Partin."

"Ned was."

"How was his approach?" He paused, waiting for my answer. "Was it stable?"

Most landing accidents resulted from the crew being too high, too fast, or both of these high-energy states. Every airline had stabilized approach criteria to which crews had to adhere. If they fell outside those parameters, they were supposed to go around.

He had to know I was reluctant to talk by my diverted attention. But I felt compelled to take blame off Ned's performance. "Yes. He did a great job of keeping us on glideslope and approach speed considering the turbulence."

"So, he touched down. Then what happened?"

When I took a deep breath, I realized the stab of pain I got when I did that was lessening every day. "I'm not sure how much I should say until I talk to a union rep."

"Really? You want to play that game? Your buddies at the union haven't been to see you and reassure you they're looking out for your interests. Meanwhile, the airline has flown your family to be at your side, put them up in a hotel, and arranged for you to have a private room."

I didn't realize the single room was a result of Sphere actions. "Thank you. I appreciate all you've done for us."

"Knowing that, instead of helping us figure out what happened, you want to stall the investigation while you wait for the union to get off its ass?"

No, I didn't. But if I could regain the use of my leg, I wanted a job to come back to.

"I see your point." I pointed my face to my lap.

Although I heard him sucking on his straw, I felt his gaze resting on me.

It would be so easy to spill my guts since he gave the appearance of doing what was best for me and my family, while the union's presence had been non-existent. If it was determined I hadn't done enough to prevent the accident, would I keep my job if I opened up and helped the airline with the investigation? If the FAA pulled my license, would the airline give me a non-flying job? Or kick me to the curb even though I'd tried to do the right thing?

If the union advised me to remain silent, what assurances did I have that I wouldn't still be fired?

"You see... the problem is... I don't remember the landing."

Marling stared at me, then blinked. "What do you mean?"

Revealing I had no memory of the accident didn't lift a weight off my shoulders. It had the opposite effect. Had I made a grave mistake and should've remained mute until I spoke to a union rep?

But I'd opened this door and might as well step through it. "After we put the gear down on the approach," I licked my lips, "I don't remember anything until I woke trapped in the wreckage."

"Really?" He studied me. "You're not shitting me?"

"No." I swallowed. I put my hands under the sheet, hoping to hide their quivering.

"You remember putting the gear down but nothing else until you woke up in the wreckage?"

"That's correct."

I knew during the investigation I'd be asked the same question numerous times to gauge if I gave a different answer. It still annoyed me that Marling repeated what I had said like he didn't believe it.

"Nothing? Not a thing?"

"I have one brief memory of a glimpse out the windshield when we were tumbling across the airport."

"So you don't know if either you or Partin applied full rudder but found the crosswind was greater than the rudder's authority?"

I shook my head. "I wish I could."

A long second passed while he stared at me. "Jesus. That must be awful. To be lying here in bed, not knowing if you did all you could to have prevented that."

Although his comment suggested he felt sorry for me, would he now use this revelation against me?

"Wow." He sucked the last of his drink and set it aside. "Does anyone else know this?"

"Just my family."

"Do you know if you'll ever get the memory back?"

Lucas had looked it up and told me it was inconclusive. Some who had suffered traumatic events and lost their memories never regained them. Others got back fragments. Over time, a few eventually remembered everything. I explained this to Marling.

"Well, that certainly puts a different light on things."

I hoped it wasn't a laser beam of a light that sliced away my career.

"Maybe it's a good thing you don't remember that wild ride you went on. Have you seen the video that has played on every news station endlessly?"

It flashed through my mind. I gave a nod.

"If that didn't bring back any memories, I don't know what will." He lifted his phone from his belt and glanced at the screen.

I hadn't heard a chime or vibration.

"I'm going to have to cut my visit short today. I've got a crisis to deal with."

Like letting his bosses know I couldn't remember the landing? "Thanks for the drink."

"Hey, no problem. I'll talk to you soon." He left the room.

I didn't see him again for several weeks.

Chapter Nine

The sun was setting behind the Front Range out Neal Reeves' office windows when he met with Marling.

"Is Kurz using memory loss as a ploy to cover up his incompetence?" Reeves asked. "Or is it a side effect of the heavy drugs he's on? He must be looking for a way to absolve himself of blame."

"Hmmm... I hadn't thought of the drugs." Marling rubbed his chin.

"Isn't Kurz's wife in the medical profession? She might've fed him the information on memory loss after traumatic accidents."

"Possibly. Especially with Obermiller coming out and claiming he had to take the airplane away from Kurz."

"How did Kurz react to that?" Reeves lifted his brow.

"Not well. He claims Obermiller is lying."

"Of course he does." Reeves shook his head. "Doesn't surprise me."

"If Kurz is telling the truth, we have to question his judgment in not reporting the first officer's need for additional training. That doesn't show a captain prioritizing the safe operation of the airline."

"Yeah, you're right." Reeves rubbed his face. "That'll add to the training department's failures. The NTSB will claim we have inadequate crosswind training and don't catch pilots with poor judgement. Do we have a problem, or was Kurz a fluke that slipped through the cracks?"

"Well, that's the problem with training. We can't train every situation crews will experience on the line."

Although true, Reeves knew the NTSB and public wouldn't accept that explanation.

"From the NTSB's initial analysis, the gust Kurz experienced right after touchdown was at the aircraft's crosswind limit. It doesn't seem likely, but Kurz might've been lucky and never experienced such conditions. Or, it happened to be the other pilot's turn to fly the flights that did."

What were the odds of that happening?

"Other than Obermiller, none of the other pilots I've questioned remember Kurz or Partin having a problem landing in a crosswind."

"Why did Kurz let Partin fly that flight?" Reeves asked. "If I were flying an aircraft that just came out of heavy maintenance, you can be damn sure I would've been at the controls."

"Well, since we don't a have policy stating the captain will be the flying pilot," Marling shrugged, "for me it would depend on the first officer. Since Kurz and Partin had previously flown together, Kurz must've felt confident in Partin's skills. Especially if Kurz worried about his ability to land in a crosswind."

"So how do we deal with our problem pilot?"

"Most likely, we won't have to," Marling said. "Kurz lost consciousness in the accident. The FAA will pull his medical and not reinstate it until he can prove he has no symptoms caused from traumatic injury. Memory loss might be a reason to not re-issue it. Then there is the problem of regaining the use of his leg to work the rudders. If he had difficulty landing in a crosswind before, it'll probably be impossible with a bum leg."

"Good point," Reeves said. "Then Kurz will be blamed for the accident."

Chapter Ten

The aircraft's wings rocked as it approached the runway. Just as it would touch down, a wing dropped, rolling the aircraft into a ninety-degree bank. The wingtip contacted the runway and the aircraft began cartwheeling.

I sat up in bed, clutching the bed rails as pain burned in my chest. With the realization that I was still in my hospital room and not onboard a tumbling aircraft, I eased back against the pillow and willed my pounding heart to slow. Images of items being flung around the rotating cabin were still vivid in my mind.

It didn't take a degree in psychology to figure out why I had this nightmare. In the morning, I'd be flown on an air ambulance to a rehab facility in Denver.

The horrendous dream conjured up a new concern. Even if my leg recovered enough that I could resume flying, would the fear of another accident prevent me from returning to the sky?

I lay awake thinking about that and the upcoming move.

It had come as a shock to Natalie and me that I would be transferred to Denver. Sphere's health insurance provider had declined the air ambulance flight from Dallas. After my conversations with Marling, I suspected Sphere covered the costs.

Maybe they weren't going to use the partial amnesia to blame me for the accident.

✈✈✈

While being wheeled to the ambulance that would transport me to the airport, Natalie, who'd gone home a week ago but had returned to assist in my transfer, walked alongside the stretcher, holding my hand. "I wish I could fly with you. But you'll be just fine. My flight lands after yours. I'll come by on my way home. Maybe I could stop and get... "

The rest of her words were lost on me as I concentrated on calming my tremors. I tried to convince myself that I was a pilot with twenty thousand hours and only one accident. The odds against having another in my lifetime were huge. To get my mind off the nightmare planted in my head, I speculated on what aircraft I would be flown in. Some air ambulances used Learjets, which were on my bucket list of airplanes I wanted to pilot. I hated that the first time I might fly in one, I would be horizontal in the back and not in the captain's seat.

"Bill?" Her eyes crinkled. "You didn't hear me, did you?"

I pasted on an apologetic expression.

The caring mien she conveyed had calmed me numerous other times, but not now.

"Don't worry." She patted my hand. "They'll give you Ativan before they load you onto the airplane. You probably won't care that you're flying."

I balled the sheet in my fists as the exit door came into view. I needed to man up and prove I didn't need medication to fly.

Outside, a light breeze ruffled my hair. I inhaled deeply, smelling freshly cut grass. The hiss of a sprinkler was mixed in with traffic on the street. I savored the smells and sounds that I didn't realize I had longed for in my two-week exile in the hospital with its antiseptic smells and routine din.

Before I was lifted into the ambulance, the paramedic gave me a shot.

When he pulled away, Natalie bent and kissed me.

When we separated, I knew my peck had lacked the get-lost-in-the-moment hers attempted to convey. I regretted that my anxiety prevented me from showing her how much she meant to me.

She caressed both sides of my face with hers, hovering inches above me. "It'll be alright. In no time at all, you'll be in Denver. I'll come by every day and we'll get you walking on your own. Then life will return to normal."

She made it sound so simple. My wishing I had died seemed so short-sighted. To think I would bring that pain to this incredible woman was such a selfish idea.

"Asking you out on our first date was the best decision I've ever made."

She beamed and wiped away the tears that had leaked out of my eyes. Damn, I was turning into such a crybaby. After another kiss, she straightened. "I'll see you soon."

"I love you."

"You'd better." She smiled at what was our joke to each other.

At the airport, before the back doors opened, I steeled myself. *You can do this, Bill.*

The aircraft was a Cessna Citation, not a Learjet. I ran my gaze over it the way passengers apprehensive of flying must. The polished aluminum leading edges had no dents. There were no oil streaks running aft on the engine nacelles.

One of the pilots was doing the walk-around, and, unlike myself, he had no gray hair. The captain's head, visible behind the windshield, was a blonde. As quickly as I wished for a more mature crew, I remembered when I flew for a regional airline in my twenties, hating the comments from passengers about the *teenagers* flying the aircraft.

Still, I watched the first officer preflighting the aircraft to make sure he bent under the wing to inspect it and the landing gear for worn tires, fluid leaks, or damage to the airframe.

As he worked his way around the tail of the aircraft, I started not caring. My rigidity eased and I marveled at the cumulus clouds floating high above.

I was vaguely aware of taxiing to the runway and taking off. After we had climbed for a few minutes, the air smoothed out from the mild low-level turbulence created by the uneven heating of the ground.

I woke to the sound of the engines shutting down and fresh air enveloping me.

"There, that wasn't so bad now, was it?" the flight nurse asked.

I rolled my head on the pillow to look out the aircraft's oval windows. "Are we there?"

"Yep. Ambulance is pulling up. They'll have you at your rehab facility in no time."

Cool.

When my stretcher was out of the aircraft, the lack of humidity in the air made the visibility limitless. I picked out to the west the soaring peaks of Lookout and Bear Mountains, and Mt. Morrison, places Natalie and I had hiked and mountain biked with Lucas and Lindsey. I breathed in the air and smelled pavement and jet fuel, and smiled. Not the breath of fresh mountain air I had been hoping for, but still a familiar scent. Rejuvenation lifted my soul that I was in my home town.

I had left behind the fear of being interviewed by the media, or bumping into the victims on the regional jet. A sense of distancing myself from it all took some of the tension from my shoulders.

I didn't realize the accident's investigation would follow me to Denver so soon.

Chapter Eleven

The next day, two physical therapists were helping me out of bed when a guy in his forties and soft all over waltzed into my room.

"Captain Kurz?" the guy asked.

"Yes."

"Don Loring from the union. I'm here to prep you for the NTSB hearing."

The two physical therapists helped me ease into a wheelchair. Each day, this process became less painful, but it still made me grimace. Unfortunately, it masked my annoyance toward my visitor.

"Thank you," I said to the therapists. I made a show of studying my watch. "Well, you'll have to wait an hour and a half. I have to get to physical therapy."

"Can you postpone it? I was hoping to catch a flight home in a few hours."

The two therapists stood by my side, looking from Loring to me. I guessed they sensed my irritation.

"So... Now you're getting around to supporting me."

Wrinkles spread across Loring's brow. "Excuse me?"

"The accident was over two weeks ago and you're the first from the union to show up."

"Look," Loring stuffed his hands in his pants pockets, "I help pilots who have been involved in an incident or accident to prepare their testimony to the NTSB and FAA. If you don't want my help, I got plenty I can do."

"Would it have been too much for someone to take an hour to swing by and let me know they were looking out for me?"

Loring held out his hands, palms up. "That's why I'm here now."

"I'm wondering if the NTSB's hearing wasn't in a few days if you would be here now."

The union rep turned his head down. His shoulders rose and fell. "Look, I'm sorry if someone hasn't come by before now. When I heard about the hearing, I came as soon as I could."

I had never had any dealings with the union, something of which I was proud. My job performance had not required they represent me in a meeting with a chief pilot or the FAA. Most representatives were pilot volunteers who held various duties they fulfilled when not flying. Taking my frustration out on someone who wasn't responsible for the organization's lack of support was not warranted.

His attitude could use some work though.

"If you had called, I could've told you when I was available." I gestured to the two therapists. "I don't set my schedule." As anxious as I was to discuss the hearing, I couldn't postpone physical therapy.

Loring sighed. "All right. If I have to spend the night, so be it."

"When I return, I'm going to be craving a Percocet and not be very coherent after that."

He sighed. "When is a good time?"

"First thing tomorrow morning."

He handed me his business card. "See you then."

Chapter Twelve

After Loring left the next day, I was mulling over his advice on how to respond to questions at the NTSB hearing when my friend Russell strolled in. He carried a white paper bag with grease stains.

"Beware of pilots bearing gifts," he beamed.

The scent of fried food accompanied him. "Ahh. Is that Touch and Go's cheeseburgers and fries?"

His gaze ran over me, lingering on my legs. His Adam's apple bobbed before he worked his smile back into place. "Do you think I'd bring anything else?"

My mouth watered as I opened the bag and retrieved several fries. "Mmmm." I chewed with my eyes closed. "You don't know how much I've missed Sheila's cooking. The only way this could taste better is if we had flown there in your airplane to get it."

Russell had built an RV-7, a two-seat kit-built aircraft constructed of aluminum, identical to the one I was creating. With a cruise speed of one-hundred-eighty knots and capable of aerobatics, I'd been dying for the day when I would finish mine. Would I have the courage to take it aloft now?

Russell often assisted me with the construction. He was a great resource for describing how to accomplish the thousands of tasks needed to complete it.

"Well, if you'd get off your ass, we could go now."

"Well, you know me." I lifted my left leg with its hard-sole cast. "I'll probably hang out here and watch TV."

A moment of silence passed while I stuffed my face. Prior to that day that changed my life, we could converse about any subject with ease. Now, I was at a loss as to how to ease into the conversation I knew he would want to discuss.

Russell shook his head. "The lengths to which some people will go to draw attention to themselves."

"Yeah, that's so me, wanting the media to hound my family and say negative things about me." I paused, mid-bite, and slumped my shoulders. "How've you been?"

"Compared to you, I can't complain. Wouldn't help if I did anyway."

Normally, his familiar line would've drawn a smile out of me. "Oh, I have it pretty good. Not everyone gets to take a dump in a bedpan."

The warmth on his face fell away. "Natalie warned me you're taking the accident hard. Can't say as I blame you. I would too."

I stared at the half-eaten burger before wrapping it up and putting it in the bag. "I don't have much of an appetite these days." I wanted my friend to know it wasn't his choice of subjects or that I wasn't grateful for the food he'd brought me.

"You going to eat those fries?"

The familiarity of his stealing my fries lifted some of my gloom. I passed the container to him. "How's the plane running?"

He chewed on a fry while watching me. "Great. Hey... I'm sorry I didn't come by as soon as you were flown back to Denver."

"I would have understood if you didn't want to."

"That would've made me a pretty lousy friend."

I didn't realize how much I had missed him until that moment. My worries over how he and others would act seemed absurd now.

He used a fry as a pointer. "Even though your wife has threatened me with bodily harm if I discuss the accident, talk to me."

Natalie's idle threat lit up my face.

"Tell me what you went through. We both know it'll be the only way to move past that time."

I paused. Did I want to vocalize my memories? I would expose the numerous things I had two weeks to wish I had done differently. Being a retired airline pilot, Russell could ask questions that might lower my already low self-esteem.

Then I realized how ridiculous that thought was. While building my aircraft, he would point out something stupid I did in a gentle way, then question if that was as good as I could do. Sometimes all it took was a shake of his head to let me know I could have driven a rivet better. I didn't doubt his questions would help consider the flight in another light and prepare me better for the NTSB hearing.

After a moment's reflection, I spilled my guts. As I relived the flight in details that only another airline pilot would understand, tranquility worked its way through me in a way I hadn't experienced since waking in the wreckage. If Russell judged me, it was not apparent by his questions.

No matter what the NTSB ruled as the accident's cause, I knew Russell would still be my friend. He'd be there to help me work my way through the deaths of the victims.

When I had finished with the narration, I felt lighter. The constant ache in my shoulders from tension had eased. I knew I had climbed a couple of steps out of the dark place I had occupied.

"You only remember the one glimpse out the windshield while you tumbled?" he asked.

I nodded. "In two days, I'll have to talk to the NTSB."

"Better you than me." Russell worked to hide his smile before he grew serious. "As difficult as that will be, it'll probably be good to get that behind you."

I hoped so. "Since I've told you everything I know, why don't you sit in for me?" I batted my eyes.

"I would if I could."

If the situation were reversed, I would for him too.

"What if the NTSB and FAA don't believe me? What if they continue to blame Ned and me?"

Russell's reply was immediate. "You can't worry about that. We pilots are proud individuals whose reputations as skilled aviators are important to us. But what should matter more are our morals. If you go through this investigation telling the truth and admitting when you made errors, as hard as it may be that you aren't exonerated, in the end you'll know you've been true to yourself."

Chapter Thirteen

Two days later, Natalie wheeled me from my room to the conference room of the rehab facility. From home, she had brought me a shirt, tie, sport coat and a pair of khakis. She had cut a slit up both legs so we could pull them up over the external fixator on one leg and the cast on the other. After wiggling and squirming to get dressed, I craved a Percocet. Since I wanted to be clear-headed, I took eight hundred milligrams of ibuprofen and tried to sit as still as possible to not aggravate my injuries.

On the trip from my room, I swallowed often even though my mouth was dry.

I was more nervous than when I took my check ride to be an EA-220 captain. Then, the instructor administering the check-ride was being observed by the FAA to become an Aircrew Program Designee so that he could give this examination in the future without the FAA observing. Not only was I worried about not screwing up, I had additional pressure to do well so that the instructor, who was also nervous, would have an easy ride to grade.

Like that time, the FAA would be in attendance today, to determine if I had violated any FAA regulations or did not fly to the standards of my Airline Transport Pilot certificate, the highest level of pilot licenses. What I stated today could determine if I retained my pilot certificate.

"When you're done, I can go out and get you a steak and a milkshake. Would you like that?" Natalie asked.

Although I had heard her, and a small part of me appreciated her wanting to give me something to look forward to, my mind was on the group of people we approached. I nodded. If I spoke, she wouldn't understand my quivering voice.

"There's a place just down the street I'm sure will do takeout."

In a few moments, I'd have to talk. I might as well exercise my voice. "Thank you. That'd be nice."

She gave my shoulder a squeeze. "You'll do great. I know you will."

I wish I had the same confidence.

The twelve in the conference room stood in small groups conversing. A few talked on their phones. All turned their gazes to me as we approached.

My already thumping heart picked up its pace.

A petite woman with bright, brown eyes wearing a suit approached with her hand held out. "You must be Captain Kurz. I'm Lori Masters with the NTSB. I'm sorry we have to meet under these circumstances."

"Bill Kurz." I shook her hand, hoping she didn't notice the tremor in mine. "This is my wife, Natalie."

"It's a pleasure to meet you." As Natalie pushed me into the room, Ms. Masters pursed her lips before speaking. "I'm sorry. I'm going to have to ask you to remain outside. It's NTSB policy only the crewmembers and those pertinent to the investigation hear the testimony."

"It's okay." I patted Natalie's hand. "I'll be all right." I hoped.

She kissed me on the cheek. "I'll be sitting right there." She indicated some chairs located down the hall.

I wheeled myself into the room with Ms. Masters following.

"Why don't you put yourself on the end." She pointed to the oblong table that would seat a dozen. A chair was missing from the end she indicated.

Microphones sat evenly spaced around the table. Each word, quiver of my voice, stutter, umm, could be replayed later to determine if my statements were true.

I glanced around the room as everyone took a seat, hoping for a familiar face. Other than Loring, the union rep, there wasn't one.

Before he sat, he stepped over and shook my hand. "You ready for this?"

No, I wasn't. Unless I was willing to fake a physical reason that prevented me from giving my testimony, I had to go through with it. Although it wouldn't take much to become nauseous. "Yeah, I guess."

"Remember what I said," Loring whispered. "Try to be factual and to the point. Don't ad lib. If you don't know something, state that."

I nodded.

Sitting to my right, Ms. Masters said, "Why don't we get started? I'm sure Captain Kurz would like to return to his room so he can continue his recuperation."

The conversations died off. Chairs scraped, papers rustled, pens clicked.

Twelve sets of eyes stared at me.

Chapter Fourteen

Ms. Masters stated into the microphone in front of her the date, time, my presence, and the purpose of the hearing. She then had everyone in the room introduce themselves and with whom they were affiliated.

I remembered none of the names except Loring's and one other individual's, a Sphere EA-220 instructor named Pringer. I had heard of him but had never experienced his training.

There was a maintenance investigator from Sphere, as well as representatives from Edwards Aerospace, the engine manufacturer, Pratt and Whitney, another from the NTSB besides Ms. Masters, and two from the FAA.

Once introductions were complete, Ms. Masters got right to the point. "Captain Kurz—"

"You can call me Bill, if you'd like." I hoped the quiver in my voice wasn't obvious.

She smiled. "Bill it is then. On May twenty-first of this year, were you the captain on flight 9100 from San Salvador to Dallas-Fort Worth?"

I leaned forward to get close to the mic. "Yes."

Ms. Master slid the microphone toward me. "You shouldn't have to lean over."

I nodded.

She asked preliminary questions. In my answers, I explained we were picking up the airplane after it had come out of a maintenance inspection. Ned and I were to ferry it to Dallas-Fort Worth so it could fly a revenue flight.

"Did you fly another aircraft to San Salvador that you exchanged for the one you picked up?" Ms. Masters asked.

"No." I thought of saying no more, as Loring had suggested, but decided I would help move the process along. "First Officer

Partin and I dead-headed there late in the afternoon the day before." The more I talked, the less nervous I felt. But I kept my quivering hands in my lap. "We were to fly the aircraft to Dallas-Fort Worth the next morning at eight."

The papers in front of Ms. Masters rustled as she thumbed through them. "But you didn't leave San Salvador until two twenty-three. Why the delay?"

"When we got to the hangar, the aircraft wasn't ready." I remembered the disappointment Ned's and I had felt. We had hoped to be in Dallas in time to catch noon flights to Denver and be home for dinner.

"Why wasn't the aircraft ready?"

"Unknown. It was sitting outside the hangar with portable scaffolding at the tail. None of the guys at the base of the scaffolding spoke English. When I tried to go into the hangar to find someone who could explain the delay, I was prevented by a couple of guys."

Ms. Masters scribbled notes on the pad beside her. "What did you and First Officer Partin do while you waited for the aircraft to become ready?"

"We sat in first class, killing time."

"I'm curious as to what you did during that time." Her face expressed curiosity, not judgment.

I wondered what that had to do with anything but thought she might want to know if we were fatigued or frustrated, or if she was attempting to relax me. "Ned," I squeezed my eyes shut a moment, "First Officer Partin watched a movie on his iPad, then napped. I sent a couple of messages to our dispatcher asking for an update on when the aircraft would be ready, read a novel I had brought with me, and napped."

Around the room, the others stared at me or made notes. A few typed into tablet computers or their phones.

"How did you send these messages?" Ms. Masters asked.

"Through Arinc with the aircraft's message function."

"How did you learn the aircraft was ready for flight?"

"One of the guys who seemed like a supervisor and spoke English brought us our dispatch paperwork and said the aircraft was ready."

"Did you confirm this with your company?"

"Yes. I sent a message asking for verification that the aircraft was ready for flight."

"And the response was?"

"They confirmed the aircraft was airworthy by sending an airworthiness release over the aircraft's printer and telling us to fly to DFW ASAP."

"Since it seemed they wanted the aircraft in DFW as soon as possible, did you jump in the cockpit, fire up, and go?"

"No. Ned... uh, First Officer Partin did an exterior inspection while I reviewed the dispatch paperwork."

"Did First Officer Partin find any discrepancies during his walk-around?"

"No." Now, I wished he had. He might still be alive.

"Do you know if he did a cursory preflight, or a detailed one?"

It was important to me to establish how good a pilot Ned was. I didn't want the cause of the accident blamed on him. "While waiting, we discussed our mistrust with the guys working on the aircraft who couldn't tell us what they were doing. Because of that, and judging by the length of time First Officer Partin was outside the aircraft, I know he would've looked the aircraft over carefully."

"Do you know that for a fact, or are you covering for the fact that First Officer Partin might've missed something?" This was asked by one of the FAA guys across the table from Ms. Masters. "I should remind you we've heard the cockpit voice recorder and know both of you didn't adhere to FAA regulations during the flight."

Until that point, answering Ms. Masters' questions had empowered me that I was getting to tell my side of the story. This reminder that everything we had said while sitting in the cockpit had been recorded caused my body to shudder each time my heart beat. I racked my mind for any deviation from standard operating procedures we might've made.

"I want to remind everyone," Ms. Masters glared across the table at the FAA guy, "the NTSB will conduct the first portion of this hearing. You'll all get a chance to ask your questions later."

"I think it's important to remind Captain Kurz that we know for a fact that while at their cruise altitude, he violated the FARs" the FAA guy said. "Both pilots left their position without the other donning their oxygen mask. If he would not follow this common procedure, what others might he have transgressed?"

Inwardly, I berated myself. At the time, I thought we could have donned our masks in the fifteen seconds of useful consciousness we would have had if the aircraft lost pressurization while the other was in the bathroom. But to the FAA, a rule didn't matter if there were no passengers or eight hundred.

"You'll get your chance to ask your questions later." Ms. Masters annunciated each word. "I'll also remind you that you are not to discuss with others what was recorded on the CVR until Captain Kurz has heard it and agreed to release it to the public."

The FAA guy sat back, wearing a scowl.

"Even with that warning," Ms. Masters faced me with her head cocked, "was that a Duran Duran song you were singing during the flight?"

I frowned.

"Something about being hungry."

The tension I felt a moment ago eased as I remembered what she was referring to. "Yes. 'Hungry Like a Wolf.',," As we had preflighted the aircraft, Ned had remarked how hungry he was. The lyrics to that song popped into my head and I now remembered mouthing them during the flight. I thought I'd been singing to myself.

"I like that song." Ms. Masters consulted her notepad. "You stated First Officer Partin did not discover any discrepancies during the walk-around."

"That's correct."

They wouldn't have heard my conversation with Ned about that, as the cockpit voice recording was one hundred and twenty minutes long. The flight had been over three hours. The recording would've begun when we had been at our cruise altitude awhile.

"You stated a moment ago you were looking over the dispatch paperwork. What was the weather at your destination?"

I was sure she already knew the answer to this question and it was an attempt to verify if I had done as I claimed. "I remembered it as being good, at that time. I think it had high broken clouds with winds, I think, out of the southwest at ten knots, gusting to twenty. But the forecast predicted a chance of thunderstorms at the time of our arrival."

"Did you need an alternate?"

"According to the forecast, no." I knew my next actions would be judged. "But based on the forecast, I asked for more fuel anyway."

"Why?"

"I worried that the thunderstorms might slow down arrivals and I wanted a cushion in case we had to hold or divert."

"How much fuel did you have?"

"I don't remember the specific number, but we would arrive at DFW with just over an hour's worth of fuel."

"Did you get the additional fuel?"

Regret tightened my stomach. "No." For once, I took Loring's advice and didn't add any further comment even though the need to justify that decision was strong. If we had waited, I might not be sitting at this hearing in a wheelchair with a leg that throbbed. Ned and thirty-seven others would be alive.

"Why not?"

With my head turned down, I rubbed my hands on the wheelchair's armrest. "We waited half an hour for the fuel truck. When the non-English speaking ground crew couldn't tell us how much longer it would be, and knowing the company needed the aircraft to fly a flight, First Officer Partin and I decided to go without it." I hated how I appeared to change my mind on decisions I previously thought important.

I didn't add we both had been away from home for five days. If we delayed much longer, we would miss the last flight from DFW to Denver and would spend another day away.

"Do you feel this accident might've been prevented if you had waited for the additional fuel?"

I caught myself before nodding, and took Loring's advice. "I don't know."

Ms. Masters walked me through the steps we had taken to start and taxi to the runway. "So, you're cleared for takeoff. Who would be the pilot flying?"

"First Officer Partin."

"With the aircraft having come out of a maintenance inspection, why did you have the first officer fly the flight?"

I too had questioned countless times if I should have flown. I didn't think I was a better pilot than Ned, but the what ifs constantly tore at me. And, remembering how the media had played up Asshole Obermiller's accusations and berated this decision, I knew my answer had to prove I wasn't the incompetent pilot I'd been made out to be.

I took a drink of water to give me a second to form my answer. "Since we weren't informed this was a test flight, nothing prevented First Officer Partin from flying the flight."

Ms. Masters lifted an eyebrow. "When is a test flight required?"

"When a flight control has been removed from the aircraft."

"And you weren't told that had happened during this inspection?" Her lifted brow remained in place. She acted like I should know that had happened during the inspection.

Had the rudder been removed and not put back on properly? "That's correct."

"Regardless, since the aircraft had major maintenance procedures performed on it, shouldn't you, the pilot in-command, have flown the flight?" Since Ms. Master's expression still conveyed curiosity, I didn't feel she was being judgmental.

"There are only four times in the Sphere Airlines Operations Manual that state the captain is required to make the takeoff." I lifted a finger. "When the visibility will be less than half a mile."

I raised another finger. "When the captain has less than one hundred hours as captain of that model aircraft and the visibility is less than a mile." I lifted another. "When the first officer has less than one hundred hours in that model of aircraft and taking off from an airport in mountainous terrain."

All four of my fingers now stuck in the air. "When the aircraft is required to have a test flight. Since this flight didn't satisfy any of these conditions, and First Officer Partin was as competent as any other Sphere Airlines pilot—" I disliked that I was putting Obermiller into this group—"I saw no reason why he couldn't fly the flight."

Ms. Masters gave a small nod. "How did you decide First Officer Partin would be the pilot flying?"

I suspected she was digging to see if Obermiller's allegations had any bearing. Even though they did not, I knew my answer might make us seem unprofessional. But as Russell had suggested, I had to be truthful. "We played paper, scissor, rock."

For a moment, Ms. Masters pulled in the corners of her mouth, trying to hide a smile. "Did the decision to have First Officer

Partin fly have anything to do with the thunderstorms forecast to be at DFW at the time of your arrival?"

And there it was. I met Ms. Masters' eyes before turning my gaze to the others around the table. "No," I stated firmly. I stifled the urge to say more.

"We'll return to this decision shortly." Ms. Masters flipped the page of her document.

"I look forward to it." I hoped my bravado didn't come back to bite me later.

Ms. Masters snapped her attention to me, searching my face, before the corners of her mouth lifted momentarily.

She worked through the taxi portion of the flight and the clearance for takeoff. "Was the takeoff roll normal?"

"No."

The gazes of the others in the room sharpened on me.

"Why not?" Ms. Masters asked.

"The standby rudder ON light illuminated." I stifled the urge to detail the steps when it came on, feeling it would be better for Ms. Masters to pull them out of me.

She exchanged frowns with the NTSB guy sitting beside her. Tippen, I think his name was. Their shared look suggested this was the first time they were made aware of this malfunction. "When on the takeoff roll did it illuminate?" she asked.

Why hadn't Sphere shared this revelation with the NTSB? "After one hundred knots, but before V1. It's been several weeks, but I think it happened about one hundred and twenty-five knots."

The FAA guy who'd given me grief earlier watched me with his eyebrows pulled down.

"What was your V1 airspeed?" Her frown was still present.

"I don't remember for sure, but I think around one hundred thirty-eight." Loring's subtle shake of his head reminded me I should've answered I didn't remember.

"Did you consider rejecting the takeoff?" Ms. Masters asked.

"No. That is not one of the criteria Sphere Airlines recommends rejecting a takeoff for." I now wish we had.

The FAA guy scribbled a note.

"What did you do then?"

"Once airborne and after we had retracted the landing gear and flaps, I complied with the abnormal procedure listed in the quick reference handbook."

Ms. Masters now questioned me without consulting the document in front of her. "What did it require you to do?"

"Other than stating the crew was to avoid large rudder pedal inputs, nothing."

Around the table, everyone alternated their attention from me to making notes. A few huddled and whispered.

"After you completed the abnormal procedure, what did you do?" Ms. Masters asked.

"Once we climbed through ten thousand feet, I sent a message to our dispatcher, telling him of the malfunction and asking if we should return to San Salvador."

Again, she glanced at Tippen, who shook his head.

"Just for clarification… you sent a message to your dispatcher stating the standby rudder ON light illuminated on the takeoff roll. Is that correct?"

A suspicion crept up from my stomach that I now knew why the media hadn't made a big deal out of us not having the main rudder control. Sphere must've withheld this information.

"That's correct," I said to Ms. Masters.

"Did your dispatcher respond to that message?"

"Yes." Since it seemed this was information the NTSB did not know, I took Loring's advice and didn't add anything further. I didn't know why Sphere would withhold this detail, so I didn't want to implicate myself by ad libbing.

"What did he say?" I noted she knew the dispatcher was not a woman.

"To continue to DFW."

The FAA guy furiously scribbled a note, wearing a scowl.

"Did you question that decision?" Ms. Masters asked.

"The first officer and I were discussing that when the dispatcher sent us an MEL for the standby rudder ON light."

Ms. Masters again glanced at Tippen, who shrugged.

"So, your dispatcher sent you relief to fly with an inoperative piece of equipment through the communications function on your flight management computer." Ms. Masters' speech halted as if she were forming the sentence as she went. "Is that correct?"

"Yes."

Every item installed on the aircraft was supposed to work. Some didn't have to if it was listed in an FAA-approved manual called a Minimum Equipment List.

"Do you remember the number of the MEL?" She turned to the maintenance investigator for Sphere.

With his attention on his notepad, he missed her glare.

"No, I do not. But I do remember the first officer and I thinking the MEL issued was incorrect."

"Why was that?" Her surprise was evident in her tone.

"The MEL procedure gave relief to operate the aircraft if the standby rudder ON light was illuminated when it should be off. But there was a maintenance procedure that needed to be accomplished before the aircraft could fly, to verify the main rudder actuators were still powering the rudder."

"So," Ms. Masters had her face lifted as if thinking, "the standby rudder light was on and your maintenance department sent a message that listed it inoperative, or, MELed. Is that correct?"

"Yes."

She whispered to Tippen. He whispered a reply back. Others around the table were doing the same. Some of the burden I carried lifted with the knowledge that I was revealing a defect that might've caused the accident.

"Captain Kurz," she blinked, "Bill, normally what does the illumination of the standby rudder light indicate?"

"That both of the two main hydraulic systems, or their actuators, are not powering the rudder, and the standby hydraulic system is powering the standby rudder actuator."

Another exchanged glance went between Ms. Masters and Tippen. "What do you understand the intent of the MEL for this component is to be used for?"

"It's to be used when the standby rudder light is illuminated, but shouldn't be."

"So, for clarification, you do not feel the MEL was used correctly?"

The Sphere aircraft maintenance investigator kept his gaze on his notepad.

Had Sphere withheld from the NTSB that the main rudder control was not working to hide they had incorrectly issued an MEL?

"That's correct," I said.

After another pause, she asked, "And the aircraft was handling normally."

"I was unaware of it having any handling abnormalities."

"Was it turbulent?"

I lifted my head while remembering the climb. "Other than some low-level light turbulence, no, I would not say it was turbulent."

"Did you have any more conversation with your dispatcher or maintenance department about the issuance of the MEL?"

"No."

After staring off into space a moment, she consulted the document from which she was asking her questions. "Do you remember any issues during the climb or after you leveled off?"

"No."

"During the cruise portion of the flight, did you check the weather in DFW?"

Under the table, I counted on my fingers the number of times we had checked the weather at our destination. "Yes. Twice. Once before we flew out over the Gulf of Mexico, when we would lose communication with Arinc. Then as soon as we neared the coast of the U.S."

"Did the weather at DFW give you concern during either of those times?"

And here came the questions about my decision to fly past Houston and continue to Dallas.

"No before we flew over the Gulf, but yes when we hit landfall." Now that I'd revealed the reason why there was an accident, the burden weighing me down was lifted and I felt freed to answer without any apprehension. I thought they would not find our decision to continue to Dallas faulty.

"Why were you concerned?"

"At that point, we were about an hour from landing and the thunderstorms that were forecast were now listed as being visible to the west," I said. "But they were not over the airport."

"What did you do?"

"I sent a message asking our dispatcher if anyone was having difficulty landing in DFW."

"And their reply was what?"

"We didn't get one until we were half an hour from landing. But I remember the message stated arrival rates had slowed, but there were no reported difficulties."

"At that point, did you foresee any issues making a normal landing?"

I took a moment to question if she meant the looming thunderstorms, or the issue of having only standby rudder power. It didn't matter. The answer was the same. "No."

"Did you experience any delays or holding on the arrival?"

"Sort of. We were slowed to two hundred and fifty knots earlier than normal, then two-ten. We were vectored significantly to the north before being put on final to land to the south."

"You stated earlier you desired more fuel than was required, but you left before you received that fuel. Did being slowed early and sent further to the north than you expected cause any concerns about what your arrival fuel would be?"

"Yes." I clamped my mouth shut to not elaborate.

"Did that factor into your decision to continue with the approach instead of waiting until the thunderstorms had passed?"

Obviously, she was trying to determine if I felt pressured to land because we were low on fuel. "Since the thunderstorms were moving across the southern edge of the airport and we were arriving from the north, and flights were still landing at the airport, I thought we would land with adequate fuel."

Since this portion of the flight would have been recorded on the cockpit voice recorder, they would've heard Ned and me deciding that if we had to divert, we would go to Fort Worth Alliance, located fifteen miles to the northwest of DFW. The thunderstorms had passed by there.

"Did the first officer have any difficulty handling the aircraft while on final?"

That, too, we had discussed and would be on the recording. "No, considering the turbulence we began to encounter as we neared the airport."

As we approached the portion of the flight I could not remember, I feared some might feel I claimed this in an attempt cover up my incompetence. I had begun to tremble, especially since the digital flight data recorder revealed Ned or I hadn't used all the available rudder, something that baffled me.

"Did you experience any windshear?"

I pointed my face at the table. "Up until we put the landing gear down, no."

"What about after you put the gear down?"

"Ah... I ah... I don't remember."

"Was it still turbulent?" Ms. Masters' tone suggested she found my response peculiar.

I squirmed, sending a jolt up my right leg. "Ah... I... I... don't remember."

My last responses, I realized, made it seem that I was avoiding the inevitable question of why we did not use all the available rudder.

"You don't remember any turbulence at all?"

I squeezed my eyes closed, willing the missing time in my life to return. When it didn't, I took Russell's advice and stated the truth. "You see... I, ah... I don't remember anything after the landing gear was lowered.

Chapter Fifteen

Silence that lasted several seconds filled the room.

Ms. Masters broke it by asking, "Please explain what you mean."

"I… I don't remember the approach, landing, or the accident." I rested my head in my hands and rubbed my temples. "After we put the gear down, my next memory is waking in the wreckage, trapped in my seat."

Out of the corner of my eye, I saw the FAA inspector shake his head.

A second passed while the only noise was the flow of air and a cough.

"So… you remember putting the landing gear down, but nothing else until you woke in the wreckage?" Ms. Masters asked.

"That's correct." I faced her. "I wish I could."

Why did this seem a surprise? Hadn't Marling forwarded this information to the NTSB? If not, why?

Her face scrunched up in either an apologetic expression or one of frustration. If she were Natalie, I would have known she expressed sympathy.

"You have no memory or fragments of memory of the touchdown or the accident?" She sighed.

"No."

"Then you can't explain the crucial moments after you touched down and… departed the runway?"

"The closed head trauma from the accident gave me partial amnesia. You don't know the frustration I feel trying to recall that time. I would love to explain our actions, or lack of them, so I would know if I had done all I could to prevent thirty-eight people from dying. Or, if I screwed up."

Around the table, no one would meet my eyes—except the FAA inspector. His gaze bore into me. He had a smirk on his face.

Paper rustled as she flipped through several pages of her document. "If you'll bear with me, we'll back up a bit. We questioned several pilots both you and First Officer Partin have recently flown with."

My frustration dissolved, replaced with eagerness to address Asshole Obermiller's lies.

"Almost all spoke positively of both you and First Officer Partin. How would *you* categorize First Officer Partin?"

"Ned Partin was as good a pilot as any other Sphere Airlines pilot." I wished I'd thought of a different way to explain that than the one I had already used. "The cause of this accident wasn't from anything he did, or should have done."

"How do you know that?" Ms. Masters asked.

I told her about flying with him months ago and his landing in a strong gusty crosswind.

"I realize you don't remember the landing of the accident flight, but do you feel you might've prevented the accident if you had been flying?"

I shook my head. "If Ned couldn't have prevented it, I doubt I could have." As soon as the words left my mouth, I realized I had set up her next question.

"One of the pilots we spoke to has questioned your ability to land in a crosswind."

I gritted my teeth.

"He claims several months ago, he had to take the aircraft from you during a crosswind landing. Is that true?"

I met her eyes, then the others sitting around the table. "No. First Officer Obermiller's comments are lies. I had to take the aircraft from him."

"But your airline has no record of you recommending him for additional training?"

I lowered my head. "Something I now regret."

The smirk on the FAA guy widened as he scribbled a note.

Ms. Masters thumbed through her document, then said, "I have nothing further at this time. I'll turn the hearing over to Bob Cramp, from the FAA's office of investigation and prevention."

Cramp, the guy who'd spoken up earlier during the hearing, straightened in his chair and pointed his narrowed eyes my way after he consulted his notepad. "Now, Captain Kurz, you claim the standby rudder light came on during the takeoff roll, but you didn't return to San Salvador. Why not?"

"First off, I don't *claim* it illuminated. It did. To answer your question, yes. Now, I wish I had rejected the takeoff."

His eyebrows shot up. "So you wish you had aborted the takeoff for something you claim is not a malfunction your airline recommends you abort for?"

"Looking back on what happened, in hindsight, yes, I do."

"How would you have explained you aborted a takeoff for something that shouldn't trigger an abort?"

I frowned, questioning the logic of his question. Did he think I would have a hard time explaining why we rejected the takeoff? "When we taxied to the maintenance hangar, the mechanics would have seen the standby rudder ON light was illuminated. That would be explanation enough."

"What if they couldn't find the cause of the alleged issue? How would you have justified delaying the flight?"

I didn't know all the parameters the flight data recorder captured, but I thought the main rudder actuators not powering the rudder would be one of them. "The light was illuminated on the overhead panel. That would be justification enough." I hated that my defensiveness prevented me from thinking of a different explanation.

"So you say," Cramp said. "Let's think about this differently. If what you say is true, you have an annunciator telling you the primary control mechanisms powering the rudder have malfunctioned and you continue on a three-hour flight on the sole standby system. Does that sound like a good decision to you?"

I swallowed. "Nowhere in the *FAA approved* Quick Reference Handbook for this procedure does it state a landing should be performed as soon as possible."

He seemed unfazed. "You stated earlier you didn't agree with the issuance of the MEL by your maintenance people, but didn't discuss this further with them. You were on a backup flight control system and you disagreed with the procedure your company has issued. Don't you think it would have been wise to land and sort this out on the ground?"

"That was something I intended to do when we landed in DFW." My trembling had elevated the throbbing in my leg.

"So, instead of landing immediately, you thought it safe to fly over the Gulf of Mexico with what you thought was a malfunctioning flight control?"

The others around the table watched my grilling with rapt attention. Ms. Masters wore a frown.

One of the *what ifs* I'd berated myself with the last two weeks had been this very topic.

"As I've stated, since the QRH didn't lend any suggestion to the severity of this malfunction, and our maintenance people, who should know the aircraft's systems better than I since they work on them, thought it okay to continue, yes, I thought it safe to fly to DFW."

Cramp shook his head. "You have me confused. A second ago, you said you wished you had aborted the takeoff. Now you're saying it was okay to continue. Which is it?"

I craved a Percocet to relieve the agony in my leg. If I requested the hearing be recessed, I knew it would seem I was trying to avoid these questions.

"What I said earlier was looking back on it in hindsight, meaning, now, knowing it might have been the cause of the accident, I wished I had *rejected* the takeoff. But since I didn't know that, at that time, I based my decision on the information I had *at that time*." I hated how my ramblings made me sound defensive.

"Did First Officer Partin have a chance to voice his disagreement with your decision?"

That question came out of nowhere. I tried to remember if Ned had disagreed with anything I had suggested, but couldn't. Had the cockpit voice recorder captured an instance that I didn't remember?

"I encouraged every first officer I flew with to voice their opinion even if it disagreed with mine."

"You didn't answer my question. I'll rephrase it so you might understand."

My face burned.

"Did First Officer Partin, on flight 9100, flown on May 21st of this year have a chance to say he thought continuing to Dallas-Fort Worth with a flight control operating on its sole backup was a wrong decision?"

Ms. Masters glared at Cramp now.

"Yes, he did."

"But you ignored his advice."

"I didn't say that." My heart pounded. "Ned and I discussed why the standby rudder ON light illuminated and how we thought the issuance of the MEL was incorrect. But he never thought we should do anything differently than continue to DFW."

"So you say."

I hoped Loring, my union rep, might step in and defend me. He sat slouched in his chair, his face pointed at the table.

The questioning continued, picking apart the decisions I had made, or skewing them as wrong. Cramp shredded my decision to not wait for the additional fuel, making it seem I couldn't make a wise decision.

Prior to this hearing, I too had questioned if we had waited for the fuel, would the thunderstorm have passed by Dallas when we arrived. Or, we could have held, waiting for them to pass, which we probably wouldn't have done. We hadn't felt the need a month ago. I still felt if there hadn't been a problem with the rudder, we would have landed successfully.

"You've been vague about the weather in Dallas. You couldn't recall exactly what your takeoff speed was, how much fuel you would have when you landed in DFW," Cramp said. "Yet you could recite, I'm assuming, verbatim, the procedure for when the standby rudder light comes on. Don't you think that comes across as someone who has had weeks to think of an excuse he can claim caused the accident?"

Every nerve in me hummed. "I can see why you'd think that. But those items you mentioned are things that change on every flight, so there is no point in memorizing them. We need to recall the aircraft systems and company procedures at any time. Regardless, I assume the digital flight data recorder will back up what I've said."

"What if I told you the DFDR did not record this alleged malfunction? Would you like to change your testimony?"

My jaw dropped. Having only a vague awareness of what is captured on the flight data recorder, I questioned why it didn't. I spilled water onto my tie when I attempted a drink.

Cramp didn't hide his smile.

"No. The standby rudder ON light illuminated during the takeoff roll and remained on through the rest of the flight." My voice quivered so much, the audacity I tried to convey was lost. "Otherwise, why would I have sent the messages to our dispatcher about it?"

"There are no messages to your dispatcher mentioning not only this alleged malfunction, but any malfunctions." Cramp enunciated each word, while staring at me as if he'd caught me in a lie.

I frowned, not believing what he'd said. "Yes, there… there were. I… I sent some."

The Sphere representatives, Loring, Pringle, and the maintenance investigator avoided looking my way.

"Put yourself in our position. First, you requested additional fuel but left before you got it. Flew over an airport with clear weather, continuing to one with a thunderstorm. Then continued an approach with the thunderstorm over the airport. Now you claim there was a malfunction that there is no proof of. And also claim to not remember the landing and your failed attempt to keep the aircraft on the runway. Aren't these elaborate attempts to cover up your incompetence?"

I inhaled a deep breath that I held even though it stabbed. My face must've been crimson. Erupting with vulgarities would deflate the miniscule esteem I had left. I bore my gaze into the FAA investigator's eyes. "I can understand your skepticism. As traumatic as it might be, I'd love nothing more than to remember the missing period of time."

Cramp smirked. "So you say."

For the first time in my life, I wished I had never become a pilot. If I hadn't, I would not be sitting through this interrogation. I wouldn't limp the rest of my life, nor carry the weight of thirty-eight deaths.

The pain in my leg had gone from throbbing to consuming most of my conscious thought. I had been rubbing it continuously for the last half hour.

"I have nothing further at this time," Cramp said. "I'm sure I'll have plenty later."

During the last several minutes, Ms. Masters had watched me with pursed lips. "Why don't we conclude this hearing and reconvene at another time."

I mouthed *thank you* to her.

She handed me a business card. "I'll let you know if and when we wish to set up another hearing. Call if you think of anything you feel would be pertinent to the investigation."

I nodded as I wheeled myself from the table. If Cramp had handed me a card, I would have torn it up.

Chapter Sixteen

After the hearing, Lori Masters stopped in the ladies' room before leaving for her flight back to D.C. When she exited, she found Bob Cramp leaning against the wall across the hall. "What's with the attitude, Bob?"

"Me? Tell me you aren't buying that guy's story?"

"How do you know he's not telling the truth?"

His eyebrows lifted. "Seriously?"

She began to walk down the hall, causing Cramp to hurry and catch her.

"There is no evidence the *two* main rudder control systems had failed," he said.

"Do you remember United Airlines flight 585 in Colorado Springs, or USAir flight 427 in Aliquippa, Pennsylvania?"

"The Boeing 737 accidents? Vaguely."

"For some time, we couldn't figure out why the aircraft would suddenly roll out of control. No one could believe a crew would allow such a wild deviation from normal flight, yet that's what the data concluded. After extensive investigation, we realized the rudder control value under certain conditions could command the rudder to go to its limit. If the crew tried to counteract that action by applying opposite rudder, it would only aggravate the problem."

"That was back when the FDR recorded eight parameters. The accident airplane's is digital and records eighty-eight. With those kinds of details, there's no way what Kurz is claiming could have happened without us having already known about it."

"Possibly." Kurz said he'd sent messages that they had no record of, and that bothered her. "Yet your belief is the same one many had years ago before we discovered the rudder control value issue."

"The accidents you quoted were on the older model 737s before the FAA required additional backups of the rudder control on newer types. The EA-220 was manufactured after that rule change."

Lori stopped and stared at him, hoping he would realize the obvious.

"What? You can't possibly believe we could allow an aircraft to be certified under the new regulations that would have rudder issues?"

"It's something we need to consider."

"Really?" Disbelief filled Cramp's expression. "In the fifteen years the EA-220 has been manufactured, and probably a thousand or more having flown over a million hours, there has never been an incident or accident that *might* be linked to a rudder problem."

"Except the one we're now investigating."

Cramp gave his head a vigorous shake. "The one flown by a captain with a known problem landing in a crosswind. *Who*, I might add, did not use all the available rudder. So, his claim," he made air quotes, "'he can't remember the accident' proves he screwed up and doesn't want to admit it. He hopes to distract us from the real cause of the accident."

"Memory loss from traumatic head injuries is a common occurrence."

"Exactly." Cramp pointed a finger at her. "In the time this guy has had to think about it, he learned of this condition. You heard how he stated the condition. Closed head trauma. No one other than a medical profession uses words like that. His wife is a medical professional. She fed him this information."

Lori resumed her walk down the hall with Cramp hurrying to catch up. "Or, he remembered the language his doctor used to explain his missing memory," she said

"What is it about this guy that makes you want to believe his fabrications?"

"He seemed sincere and full of remorse." She had to back up her gut feeling with data that could be proven. Feeling sorry for a crippled pilot with haunted eyes wouldn't prove anything.

"Were we at the same hearing? And what was with that, 'What was that song you were singing' bullshit?"

"I was trying to get the guy to relax. Do you think we would have learned there might be a larger problem if we relied on your intimidating interrogation techniques? What was next? Waterboarding?"

"I was making sure he knew how serious the consequences of his sub-standard piloting skills were. Something you didn't seem to want to do."

Lori faced Cramp with narrowed eyes. "He knows. If you hadn't been so intent on blaming him, you would have heard and seen his remorse. I believed him when he said he wished he could remember so he would know he had done everything possible to prevent loss of life."

Cramp smirked.

Lori tamped down her rising infuriation. Then it dawned on her why the FAA investigator seemed so obtuse. "You're worried we'll look into the certification of the 220s. To prevent that, you have to pin this on the crew."

It was brief, but Cramp' gaze flicked away before returning to hers. "Your *desire* to believe the captain doesn't justify stalling an investigation and wasting resources running down a fictitious problem."

It was her turn to shake a finger at him. "You're wrong. I don't want to discover an issue with the aircraft's certification. If there was, that would mean the agency I and millions of others trust to oversee safety was delinquent in their job."

Red blossomed on Cramp's cheeks. "What's next, Masters? Reviewing the maintenance on the aircraft that we've already dismissed as the cause?"

"That too needs to be re-evaluated." Her footsteps echoed as she continued down the hall.

"You'll find the FAA's support lacking in your pursuit of innuendos."

This made her wonder why.

Chapter Seventeen

Two weeks after the hearing, the cast on my left foot was removed. The external fixator would remain on my right leg another couple of weeks. Since I had gotten adept at getting around on crutches and caring for my daily needs, I was released from rehab.

On the ride home, I left the window in Natalie's Toyota Venza down, savoring the fresh, clean, smell of outside air. The satisfaction of driving past familiar places must've shown.

She beamed. "Feels good to be free?"

"Oh, yeah."

"Want to do anything on the way home?"

Home. For the last month, I'd longed to be there. But seeing the hangar would remind me of the airplane I was building that I might never fly.

"Let's go for a hike up in the mountains."

"If I had known, I would've brought our hiking boots." She tried and failed to look disappointed she'd let me down.

This was one of the many reasons I loved her so much. "No. Home, James. I have matters of importance there."

Ten years ago, we had found a motivated seller with a house and hangar that had taxiway access on the Erie municipal airport. It was located on the northwest side of Denver, which required me to drive an hour to the international airport. The drive didn't bother me, as I thrived on living here.

Often when I approached the stone and lap-sided two-story home, I found it surreal we got to live in such a gorgeous place with unobstructed views of the Front Range.

Today, when Natalie pulled into the driveway, the same awe I had felt the day the realtor showed it to us had me leaning forward to take in the place.

Natalie's sigh pulled me back to reality. "I'm going to miss living here."

"Yeah, me too."

"How much sick leave do you have left?" She hit the garage door button on her mirror.

"Four months. Then I'll be on long term disability."

"Which is fifty percent of your salary?" She parked in the middle of the garage since my car sat in the employee lot at the airport.

"Fifty-five percent."

"It still won't meet our expenses."

She stated that as a fact, but it reminded me of how I had failed us, and threatened to send me into the pit in which I often dwelled. A mental shake shoved those thoughts aside so that they wouldn't ruin my homecoming.

Thinking about how our living arrangements would have to change, I wondered how Ned's wife, Alicia, faced these same decisions over the family farm they had inherited. I would have Natalie by my side during that emotional process of modifying how we lived. Alicia and her young children would go through it without Ned.

Natalie opened her door. "I'll help you out in a sec. There's someone who wants to see you."

When she opened the door to the house, Casey came bounding out and circled around her, whining the entire time. Then our golden retriever must have smelled me, as she lifted her head and sniffed the air.

A smile shattered my glumness as I threw open my door. "Hey, girl. How's my dog?"

Casey hurried around the car, her whining higher in pitch, and threw her front legs up onto my lap. One of her paws landed atop my mending femur.

"Ahh!" I shoved her out of the car and rocked. Although the pain was tear evoking, I regretted my rough handling of our faithful friend.

Unfazed, Casey jumped up again. Natalie caught her collar and held her back. "You okay?"

I nodded.

"I'm sorry. I didn't realize she'd get so excited."

When sliding my lower leg back and forth didn't cause me to black out, I reached out and petted Casey. "It's okay. She didn't know."

With her front legs resting on the door sill, Casey leaned in and lapped at me. I lowered my face so she could kiss me, savoring the warmth our dog showed me. Even though a throb traveled the length of my leg, I didn't realize how much I had missed Casey as I ran my hand along her silky fur before pulling her into a hug.

She sprang from the car and ran into the house.

With a grunt, I swung my legs out.

Natalie handed me my crutches, which I tucked under my armpits. A tennis ball dropped in front of me and rolled up against my sneaker.

Casey sat as we had taught her and stared at me.

"He can't do that now, Case." Natalie moved to kick the ball away, I assumed, so that I wouldn't stumble on it.

"Give it to me, please." I held out a hand.

With the ball in my hand, Casey's gaze tracked my movement as I wound up and threw it out of the garage. She took off after it. The ball bounced a couple of times across the driveway before rebounding against the overhead door of the hangar. Casey caught it in mid-air and trotted back to the garage.

For a moment, I considered hobbling over and entering my hideaway to look at the airplane. I visualized the tools lying where I had left them, ready for when I returned from San Salvador. How much dust had accumulated on the wings?

"Let's get you inside."

Natalie must have sensed what was going through my mind and didn't want me wandering over to where she had jokingly accused me of having an affair.

In the past month, she had probably wandered through our home with her own anxiety about our future. Alone, she had paid the bills and kept the place up while working and taking time to visit me. It would be selfish of me to ignore her excitement of having me home.

"Yeah, let's see if you've kept the house spotless in my absence, woman." I mocked being gruff.

"Oh, shit!" She hurried around the car before turning back to me with her blue eyes gleaming.

Inside, the familiar scent of freshly bathed dog and baked cookies greeted me. My mouth watered. The familiar sight of a pile of mail sat on the end of a countertop. A couple of plastic grocery bags sat near the fridge. The corner of a box of K-Cup pods for my coffee maker poked out. She must've stocked up before coming to get me.

Now, as when I returned from a trip, the satisfying sense of being home dropped the facades I erected. Here, I could be myself and the real healing would begin.

Natalie began putting away the groceries.

I moved close to her. "Come here." I leaned the crutches against the counter and opened my arms.

I held my slender wife and our bodies melded into each other. I'd forgotten how well her ass fit in my hand and her head rested just under my chin, so natural and comforting. Other than the clumsy hugs and brief kisses we gave each other while I lay in bed or sat in a wheelchair, we hadn't shown each other the affection that lingered in my mind afterward.

"It's great to be home."

She rested a hand on my cheek. "Coffee, or..." her eyebrows danced, "me?"

Her alluring expression had me grinning like a schoolboy. "You."

Sex in my condition would be difficult. I knew we'd make it work.

On the way to the bedroom with Natalie trailing me, her hands resting on my hips, the phone rang.

"It might be one of the kids calling." She left to answer.

They could wait. But our children calling to welcome me home warmed me in a different way than our lovemaking would.

The doorbell rang, followed by a knock.

Chapter Eighteen

Natalie tossed me my phone on her way to the door.

The caller ID said Sphere Airlines. "Bill, it's Bryce Marling. I thought you should know the NTSB has released—"

From the front door came, "Jessie Purnell, Denver 7 news. With the NTSB's release of the—"

"—the preliminary report," Marling said.

"—blaming your husband, what does he have to say?"

My heart hammered. I was having trouble following both conversations, and each one troubled me. "What?" I said to Marling.

"The NTSB has released the preliminary report of the accident."

"We have no comment." Natalie's voice was shrill. "Get off our property." The door slammed.

Casey barked continuously.

"The media is here. I'll have to call you back," I said to Marling.

"Don't talk to them." His tone was urgent. "I've emailed you a copy of the report. Call me after you've read it."

I hung up. Like I would discuss the report with the guy I thought was looking to blame me for the accident.

Natalie's mouth was pursed as she moved into the dining room. Her face had lost color.

Peering out the frosted glass of the side-lite I watched someone descend the steps.

Natalie yanked the blinds closed.

A cameraman appeared in the other one, his camera aimed at me. "He's over here."

Before Natalie got the other window blocked, the reporter tapped on it. "Captain Kurz, what do you have to say about being blamed for the accident?"

Natalie got the slats twisted, blocking the media's view of us.

"What the hell?" Every nerve in me hummed. How could these assholes invade our privacy with flippant disregard?

At my side, Casey continued to bark.

My petting silenced her, but she kept her face pointed at the window. A tap on it started her up again. I gave thought to letting her out the door. But she'd look for a ball to take with her, hoping to play catch with them.

As if the house was on fire, Natalie hurried into the great room and pulled the curtains closed.

"They won't come around to the back of the house." Would they? Was the local media as bad as paparazzi outside celebrities' homes? Or was this just a precaution on Natalie's part?

In the breakfast room, she closed the plantation shutters. "Where's the phone?" I had seen the scowl she wore more times than I cared to remember.

This time, I was glad it wasn't from something I had done. Then my relief shattered as I realized I had caused the disruption of our solitude.

Also troubling was how our hiding played into the media portraying me as the cause of the accident.

When Natalie found my phone on the couch where I'd tossed it, she dialed three numbers, then put the handset to her ear. "This is Natalie Kurz." She gave our address. "We have trespassers on our property."

"Yes, again."

Again?

The doorbell rang numerous times. Casey scampered to the front door, barking.

After Natalie disconnected, I asked, "Has the media been here before?"

Without a glance my way, she stepped into the kitchen, her eyes burning.

I followed her. "Have they bugged you before?"

With her butt resting against the countertop edge, she examined a fingernail.

"Swish?"

She sighed. "Yes. The police will come and run them out into the street, making it difficult for the neighbors to pass."

A month ago, I would have mirrored her position beside her, so that together we could face our problem. Unable to do that now, I stayed in front of her, attempting to catch her eye while leaning on my crutches. "For how long?"

With a quick glance at me, she moved to the pile of mail and thumbed through it. "The last time... a day."

A day? Even though I hadn't planned to leave the house, the thought of us being trapped here added to the hopelessness dragging me down.

I ran my hand through my hair. "Why didn't you tell me?"

She flipped over another envelope. "What could you have done?"

Anger and understanding fought to be the dominant emotion.

Other than listen to her, and wallow in guilt for the disquiet I brought into her life, there was nothing I could've done. But the curt way she stated that fact suggested she held resentment toward me.

"You could've shared with me what you were going through. So we could talk about it. Isn't that what married couples do?"

I hobbled to the couch and eased onto it, fighting the urge to throw my crutches to the floor. If it wouldn't have been difficult to retrieve them later, I might have.

The doorbell finally stopped ringing and with it, Casey's barking.

Natalie sat beside me and took my hand. She didn't say anything for a moment. "You were already feeling so down. I didn't want to add to it."

I squeezed her hand knowing I would've done the same thing. "I don't know if it's the caveman in me who feels the need to stand in the yard and beat my chest to scare off the reporters." That elicited a lift of the corners of her mouth. "Or the need to know how badly I've screwed up our lives. But we can't go through this not talking about what we're going through. It'll tear us apart."

She sighed. "I know."

"Have the kids been pestered too?"

"No."

Thank God for that.

Deep down, I knew I should get her to talk about what she was feeling. If I was a good husband who allowed my wife the freedom to express whatever thoughts she had, even if they were negative toward me, I would have. Right then, I couldn't handle being brought further down.

I stared straight into space, wondering how much more I'd screw things up.

That morning, as I anticipated leaving rehab, I vowed to get off the pity pot. Time to live up to that promise. I gave myself a mental shake.

"That was Marling on the phone. He said the NTSB has released the preliminary accident report. Obviously, it's not good. He emailed me a copy. Can you—"

She stood and went to the basement, where we had an office.

When she returned, she carried several sheets of paper. She split them in half and handed me a copy of the NTSB's report.

Before I could ask, she went to the kitchen and returned with my glasses.

We sat beside each other, reading.

I skimmed the first third of the report that gave the details of the airline, the aircraft's age, the fact that the aircraft had come out of a maintenance inspection, Ned's and my experience and that we had flown together, and the weather at the time of the accident.

When the report described the approach, landing, and subsequent accident, I took in each word, trying to remember the approach after we lowered the gear. The video Lucas had showed me helped visualize what was being described, but no forgotten memories surfaced.

Natalie read, without a word, even though I suspected she had questions about things someone outside the industry would not understand.

The final few pages summarized my interview, saying that I stated the two primary rudder actuators had become inoperative and the single standby actuator powered it. To this, the report said:

Since the aircraft had come out of maintenance after an inspection, a mechanical issue affecting the rudder was a possibility that investigators evaluated. The digital flight data recorder (DFDR) showed no evidence of a hydraulic or flight control malfunction that could support the captain's claim. Due to the extensive damage to

the vertical stabilizer and rudder, the rudder control mechanism could not verify a problem had existed that was not captured by the DFDR.

Shit! I'd hoped after the hearing that an examination of the wreckage would reveal a problem they hadn't noticed before.

All indications reveal the rudder functioned properly. 3 seconds prior to touchdown it was deflected 18 percent to the right. That aligned the aircraft track with the runway magnetic heading. During the flare and initial roll out, the rudder traveled from 12 to 28 percent as the pilot corrected for the gusting wind of 12 to 28 knots.

4.3 seconds after the main landing gear touched down, the aircraft experienced a gust of 56 knots, 48 degrees from the runway heading, changing the aircraft track 30 degrees to the left. During this time, the rudder was not deflected more than 45 percent to the right. This was an insufficient amount of deflection to counteract the gust and realign the aircraft with the runway.

Since the surviving pilot cannot remember if he or the deceased pilot applied corrective rudder to counteract the change in aircraft track, the NTSB concludes neither pilot applied more than recorded by the DFDR.

An examination of the wreckage did not reveal a restriction that prevented the crew from applying 100 percent of the rudder.

Double fucking shit! That had been a thought I'd considered after learning we only applied forty percent of the rudder.

I dropped the pages, wishing for a cocktail. Or two. Then resumed reading.

Natalie finished before I did and waited until I caught up. I could tell from her frown that she had questions.

When I threw the pages onto the coffee table, she asked, "Were you pressured to continue the approach?"

That wasn't the question I thought she'd ask. *Why wouldn't you use all the rudder* was the one on my mind. Obviously, she thought of the accident's cause differently.

"No."

"But this statement here," she flipped several pages and read, "The captain thought it was okay to continue the approach with thunderstorms over the southern edge of the airport. The NTSB concludes he had been mission-oriented in his focus to deliver the aircraft to Dallas-Fort Worth so it could fly a revenue flight. Adding to his decision was the fact the only airport in the Dallas area airlines had service to, Dallas-Love Field, was closed due to thunderstorms."

"They must've misunderstood what I said at the hearing." I shook my head. "They asked if I felt pressured to continue the approach to deliver the aircraft. But I said I saw no reason to delay it since the aircraft in front of us were not having trouble landing. They must've interpreted that to mean I didn't want to bail out since no one in front of us had. It's known as herd mentality. If the aircraft before us landed, and the one behind us continues, we might as well too."

"Did you fall into this *herd* mentality?"

"No."

Her mouth worked back and forth. I wondered if she was comparing how in traffic I would stay in one lane and follow along at whatever speed the traffic traveled while she continuously changed lanes.

"What about being low on fuel?" she asked. "Did that pressure you to land?"

"No more so than any other time."

She frowned.

"Ask any pilot when an aircraft has too much fuel and they will say only when it is on fire."

Her frown deepened. She had never liked my crass comments concerning serious matters.

"Since an aircraft burns more fuel the heavier it is, no airline wants their pilots to carry more than is required to safely fly the flight. The FAA requires us to land with at least forty-five minutes plus the fuel required to fly to an alternate airport if one is needed. Sphere's policy is to land with an hour plus alternate fuel."

"How much would you have landed with?"

I shoved down the frustration that surfaced from her questions. It was easy to assume she doubted my decisions, when in fact she was trying to understand what had put us in this predicament.

"A little over an hour."

"That doesn't seem like much. What would you have done if the thunderstorm had prevented you from landing?"

"We would not have hesitated to fly to Fort Worth Alliance, an airport to the west of DFW."

"So you weren't feeling pressured to land because of low fuel?"

"Pressured, no. But in the back of my mind, I knew how frustrating a diversion to Fort Worth Alliance would be. Without station representatives to assist us, we'd have had to arrange for fuel and how we were going to pay for it. It would also have made us miss our flights home."

She glanced at my legs before throwing the report onto the coffee table.

She probably thought the same thing I had a thousand times in the last month. If we had diverted, thirty-eight wouldn't have died, ten wouldn't have been severely injured, and I wouldn't be crippled.

"What will happen now?" she asked.

"The NTSB will continue to investigate stuff like the structural integrity of the aircraft, maintenance procedures, crew training, and the airline operations to conclude if any of them need to be modified to prevent another accident."

She leaned against me, easing the turmoil running rampant through me. "Will they find something that'll alleviate you of being responsible for the accident?"

"I don't know." I stared into space, thinking. "One thing about this report that bugs me is there is no mention of the messages I sent concerning the standby rudder ON light being illuminated. They have to wonder why I'd send them if there wasn't a problem. I sent those hours before we approached DFW."

"Is Sphere hiding them from the NTSB so that you'll take the blame instead of them?"

"If so, I don't understand why. Yes, we have the media parked out in front of our house, but they're getting trashed too. Why would Sphere deliberately keep evidence from the NTSB about a rudder problem?"

"Could they be fined or... sued if it was their fault?"

"Maybe."

She took in our home. "Will we be sued? Will we lose the equity we have in this house and our retirement?"

Those thoughts had kept me from sleeping well. "I don't know."

Chapter Nineteen

Several days later, my friend Russell drove me home from physical therapy after the therapist had worked me hard. I'd forgotten to take a Percocet with me to make the ride more tolerable, something I certainly wouldn't forget again.

I let Casey out the back door and followed her out onto the deck. This early July day was cloudless and warm, but not so hot, yet, that sitting in the sun would be uncomfortable. The doorbell rang before I lowered into a chaise lounge. Had I forgotten something in Russell's car?

Casey beat me to the front door and stood waiting with her tail wagging.

The painkiller hadn't dulled the biting pain in my leg yet. If Russell had returned, thinking my silence in the car was an indication of loneliness, I'd have to persuade him I was not receptive to visitors.

The intruder could be the media since we had received several calls requesting an interview. But I hoped the NTSB's preliminary report of their shitty investigation had been replaced with something more newsworthy.

Peering out the frosted sidelight, a lone figure stood on the steps. It didn't resemble Russell's slender figure. Was it a neighbor coming to see how I was?

When I opened the door, a stocky guy stood on the steps. He wore jeans, a shirt with the waist untucked, a tie loose around his neck, and wrap-around sunglasses. In his hand was a sheaf of paper wrapped in a light blue paper. "William Kurz?"

The sudden dryness of my mouth made it difficult to speak. I swallowed. "Who's asking?"

"Are you William Kurz?"

If I didn't acknowledge my identity, could I stall the process that was beginning? "I don't give my name to strangers who come to my door."

Casey stood in the door's threshold, preventing me from closing it. Before I could call her back, she stepped out onto the steps, sniffing at the stranger. Knowing her, she hoped to make a new friend.

Sunglasses gave her a pet before wrapping an arm around her neck and squeezing.

Casey let out a yelp and scrambled to break free of the headlock.

"Hey!" Stunned, it took me a second to react. Anyone manhandling a dog that way did not have pure intentions. I swung a crutch at Sunglasses.

He backed up out of my reach, dragging Casey with him. "Are you William Kurz?"

"Let go of my dog!" I thought about throwing a crutch at him. But he might use it to beat her. When his grasp on her didn't slacken, I yelled, "Yes."

The papers were thrown at my feet. "You've been served." Sunglasses flung Casey off the front steps and ran to his car.

She scrambled to her feet and barked in a deep, guttural growl I'd never heard from her. As she ran after the asshole, I yelled for her to stop.

My heart was in my throat. I feared he'd pull a gun and shoot her.

Sunglasses got his car door closed before Casey threw her front paws on it, her growl menacing.

I hobbled down the steps, hating how slow I was. I had to restrain her before Sunglasses hurt her.

He threw open the door.

I cringed when a thud knocked Casey backward.

A smirk filled the asshole's face as he backed out of the driveway with Casey running after him.

"Casey," I continued to yell, to no avail.

She chased the car down the street until it rounded the corner and went out of sight, then came trotting back.

I looked for a limp and breathed a sigh when there wasn't one.

She stopped in front of me, panting, staring at me with an expression that questioned if I thought she had done well. If I could have knelt, I would have hugged her.

Bending as much as the crutches allowed, I petted her. "You're a brave dog. Let's go inside."

When inside with the door locked, I used a crutch to kick the sheaf of papers next to a chair. Lowering into it, I picked them up, read, then flung them across the room.

The next morning, Natalie and I were shown into the office of attorney Tori Killinger. The thirty-something woman with long blonde hair came around her desk and shook our hands.

On her desk were stacks of haphazardly piled paper. On the credenza were pictures of two girls younger than ten. I questioned if Ms. Killinger was the lawyer we wanted to defend us in the lawsuit brought against us by the estates of two of the people in the regional jet who had been killed. Someone grizzled in appearance who had practiced civil litigation for several decades with no distractions at home might be more appropriate.

But she had come recommended by a doctor in Natalie's medical practice. Unless we wanted to take our chance on someone we found online, she was our best bet.

After we exchanged pleasantries, Ms. Killinger got to the point. "First off, Denver police talked to the guy who served papers to you yesterday. He's a courier some attorneys hire to notify parties that they are named in a lawsuit. He claims while in the process of serving you, your dog attacked him."

I shook my head.

"Oh, that's ridiculous." Natalie huffed.

"He's got scratches on his driver's door that he showed the police," Ms. Killinger said. "But he's not interested in pressing charges."

"Which really means he knows that's not the truth and hopes we don't take the matter further." There was no denying the anger in Natalie's voice.

"I can pursue this, if you want. But since you don't have any evidence that he assaulted your dog, other than your word, Mr. Kurz, it'll end up being his word against yours."

"So he gets to continue doing his job in whatever manner he wants." I wished the guy would come to the door again. He'd find a crutch planted in the side of his head. Maybe I'd be successful this time.

Ms. Killinger lifted her hands, palms up. "I don't like it either, but unless you have a video of him to back up your claim, all you'll do is run up a legal bill in a case that may go nowhere."

Natalie and I exchanged a subtle shake of our heads. We did not have the financial luxury to legally chase after assholes. Besides worrying about meeting our house payment after my sick leave ran out, another huge uncertainty was the medical expenses Sphere's crappy health insurance didn't cover.

"Now, you need to understand this lawsuit brought against you. This is a class action case in which the attorneys are representing the estates of two residents of Colorado who died in your accident. They are suing everybody they feel they can get money from. Also named in the suit are Edwards Aerospace, Pratt and Whitney, Sphere Airlines, the Federal Aviation Administration, Dallas Fort Worth Airport, the estate of a Ned Partin..." She lifted her gaze from the document, seeking an explanation.

Ned's wry grin flashed in my mind. Guilt consumed me that I hadn't expressed my condolences to his wife, who was also being sued. "He was the first officer on the flight."

Ms. Killinger made a note. "The attorneys for the plaintiffs will try to get as much money from everyone as they can. They'll plan on Edwards Aerospace and Sphere Airlines being the big paychecks, but they'll go after anyone involved who has assets."

The knot in my stomach tightened. We would lose the equity in the house, our retirement fund, and whatever I could get for the partially completed airplane.

"How can we win this lawsuit?" Natalie's face had paled.

"Since the NTSB has ruled you, Mr. Kurz, as a cause in the accident, you're liable. The only way you could not be held accountable is if your involvement in the cause of the accident was coincidental."

Chapter Twenty

Natalie and I said nothing to each other after leaving Ms. Killinger's office until in the car.

"Ten thousand for a retainer." Natalie backed out and drove off. "And she estimates that the lawsuit will cost *at least* an additional one hundred thousand. I should have become a lawyer."

Those dollar amounts had been ping-ponging in my head too. "You wouldn't have liked being one. You don't like to argue."

A heavy sigh escaped her. "The retainer took a chunk out of our savings. We'll have to list the house as soon as possible."

The thought of having to move so soon overwhelmed me. I wanted to wake from this nightmare to find it wasn't real.

"I'll need to paint Lindsey's room. No one will buy the place with that hideous bright green. Why did we let her choose that color?"

I knew I should be participating in this diatribe, but the self-pity that now seemed a part of my personality pulled me further into the dark place I now dwelled within.

"I'll have to stain the deck that *we* were going to do last summer. I guess it'll get done now." A scowl got shot my way.

Last summer, I had been focused on finishing the fuselage of the airplane so I could mate the wings to it. What I estimated would be a two-month task turned into four. Natalie had waited for me to help with the staining until fall had set in, hoping I'd get out of the hangar and spend time with her, even if it was to do a chore.

"I'll help."

A snort. "How are you going to help?"

I didn't like her thinking of me as an invalid. "I'll slide around on my butt."

"Forget it. I know you don't want to stain it."

"That's not true."

"Isn't it?"

Our voices were escalating and I willed myself to be calm. "I'm sorry I decided to build the damn airplane." I faced her. "Truly, I am. If I hadn't, I wouldn't have picked up the flight from San Salvador that put us in this fucking position."

From the time I ordered the kit two years ago, I had been flying as much extra time as I could to pay for it. When home, if I wasn't skiing, I spent all my time in the hangar.

Prior to the crate arriving with the airplane parts that I would assemble, we spent our days off together. Since then, we had had numerous arguments about the time I spent alone across the driveway.

Building an airplane was something I had wanted to do since I had become a pilot thirty-five years ago. When Lucas and Lindsey were out of college, I thought we were in a financial position that we could afford to fulfill my dream. When it was finished, I hoped Natalie and I could travel in it.

Natalie pulled to a stop at a light and stared straight ahead, her face a mask of neutrality. After a expelling a sigh, she gave my arm a little shake, then rested her hand there. Her warmth went straight to my heart.

"You don't deserve this." I put my hand atop hers.

"You don't either." She gave me a glance that lifted me. "I'm sure I've done stuff you grudgingly went along with."

"None that made us move out of our home to a one-room dump."

When she removed her hand so she could hug herself, the place on my arm cooled. I worried our relationship over the next several months would, too.

The light changed and we remained silent for several minutes while she drove.

The guilt of all I was causing her consumed me. "If you want out of this, I don't blame you." I held my breath.

She turned to me with narrowed eyes. "What? A divorce?"

I met her stare expressing understanding until she turned back to watch the road.

"If we divorce before this lawsuit gets rolling, with the equity in the house, whatever I can get for the airplane, and your salary, you should be able to live comfortably. You can get a place the kids aren't embarrassed to come visit."

She yanked the steering wheel, whipping the car into a parking lot. The stop was so sudden, the shoulder strap of my seatbelt locked.

"What the hell is wrong with you?" A vein in her forehead protruded. I had only seen this a few times. "Do you think so little of me that I would bail out on *us* because we have to make a few changes? Jesus!"

Although a part of me was relieved, I was shocked by the venom of her words and sank in my seat. "It's not just a few changes."

A deep breath expelled through her nose before she turned away. "I know you feel guilty for what happened, and the narcotics you're taking can cause depression." She faced me. "But damn it, Bill, I don't deserve this. And I'm not talking about worrying where and how we'll live."

I hung my head.

"You've done some things that I didn't agree with and a couple that made me angry. But I never, *including now*, ever considered leaving you."

This showed me how I misjudged her. After I began spending all my time in the hangar, I thought she might've considered a divorce.

In a calmer tone, she said, "I realize you're trying to be chivalrous. But it pisses me off you'd think I'd consider walking out on you."

A horn honked behind us.

"Oh go fuck yourself." She yelled at the mirror before pulling into a parking spot.

I smiled, lifting some of my remorse. Natalie never, ever, used that word.

Her face was warm on my palm when I placed it there. I rubbed my thumb along her skin under her eye. "I had to offer."

"Well don't ever offer again." She shook a finger at me.

"Okay."

We stared at each other a moment before leaning close and kissing, then held each other as best we could. The console dug into my ribs, sending a stab of pain that originated at the site of my fracture. I accepted the pain so that I didn't end this moment.

When we were back on the road, I stared at this incredible woman.

"What?"

"You're pretty hot when you're pissed off. And scary, too."

"Pfff." Her eyes were filled with mirth before it faded. "What are we going to do?"

It was a rhetorical question, but I shared what had been on my mind. "I need to talk to the NTSB."

"About those messages?"

"Yeah. How can they dismiss there was a problem with the rudder if I sent messages hours before we landed? There has to be a record of them somewhere."

"Let's hope so."

Chapter Twenty-One

When we got home, Natalie handed me the plastic bag filled with the stuff that had accumulated in my room at the rehabilitation center. After I dumped it onto the kitchen table, we sorted through the discharge paperwork, flying magazines, and books. In amongst this mess was Ms. Masters' card.

I took a moment to compose myself. I didn't want to come across as an angry lunatic so that Ms. Masters would not consider what I had to say. Nor might she be willing to share how the NTSB had determined the preliminary cause of the accident.

While I punched in her number and put the phone to my ear, Natalie sat across from me, her hands wrapped around a mug of tea.

"Masters."

"Ms. Masters, this is Bill Kurz."

"Hello, Captain… Bill. It's *Mrs*. Masters. How are you getting along?"

I appreciated that she didn't ask the question everyone else asked. "Better, now that I'm home."

"That's good to hear."

I took a breath. "I've read the preliminary accident report. I was wondering why the rudder being powered solely by the standby actuator wasn't mentioned."

"It was." Her tone suggested a bit of hesitancy. Computer keys clicked. "I'm pulling up the report now."

I covered the phone and said to Natalie, "Can you get the accident report, please?" I should have gotten it before I made this call.

There were a few moments of silence, then Mrs. Masters said, "On page twenty-four." Her voice became flatter as she read. "The captain stated the standby rudder ON light illuminated during the takeoff roll in San Salvador and remained on the remainder of the flight. Investigators considered the possibility—"

Natalie handed me the report which I thumbed through to the page she read from.

"—but no evidence could be found that proved this had occurred, or was a contributing factor."

I remembered reading this now and thought the pain medication must be making my memory not what it was prior to the accident. "How can that be? Didn't the flight data recorder show that the A and B main actuators were not powering the rudder?"

"The DFDR does not tell us what system is powering any flight control," she stated as a matter of fact. "It only tells us how much the flight control moved."

Satisfaction spread through me that they had missed a crucial point. "So you don't know that the A and B actuators were not powering the rudder."

"That's not an accurate statement."

I frowned.

"You're right," she said. "We don't know that they were disabled. But we also don't know that they were still active."

In my head, I pictured the rudder system schematic. "Does the DFDR record hydraulic valve position, or which warning lights illuminated?"

"No. We wish it did, as it would make our jobs easier. But the regulations, at this time, require the aircraft manufacturers to capture eighty-eight parameters. I can email you a link to the regulation that lists what those parameters are."

"Okay." I gave her my email address. "I'm like most pilots and thought the flight data recorder captured every switch position, gauge reading, and what the pilots ate."

She chuckled.

I hadn't found talking to her as confrontational as I thought it might be. If the subject weren't so critical to the future of Natalie's and myself, this conversation would be as engaging as talking to another pilot who had built an RV-7.

My next comment might change this mood. "So, the fact that you can't prove that the standby system was powering the rudder makes me think you discounted what I said."

"It's not that we doubt you, it's that we can't prove what you said."

"Then how can you say we didn't *try* to correct for the strong crosswind when there is the possibility the rudder didn't respond as it should have?" My tone was sharper than I intended.

"The data that is available to us does not support that claim."

"The aircraft had just come out of maintenance. Don't you think something might've been done to the rudder controls that prevented us from staying on the runway?" *Calm down*, I mentally told myself.

"We went over the maintenance records from the inspection the aircraft underwent in San Salvador. We also talked to the technicians who worked on it." Mrs. Masters' voice remained conversational in tone. "The rudder and its systems were inspected, but no repairs were required."

"Didn't they have to take components apart during this inspection that might not have been put back together correctly?"

"According to the maintenance records and statements from the technicians, no. And unfortunately, the rudder and vertical stabilizers were too damaged in the accident to verify those facts."

"Do you see how frustrating that may be for me? You're willing to believe the technicians, but not the person who is a victim in the accident."

From Natalie's pursed mouth, I knew I needed to calm down.

"As I've said, it's not that we don't believe you." Her tone wasn't as casual. "We can't prove what you said."

"You can't prove what the technicians said either."

"I know how frustrating this might be."

"I doubt that. We're being sued. We'll be financially ruined. The doctors question if I'll ever fly again."

"Actually, Bill, I do know. I was in an accident in a Cessna Citation that injured my back. That was a couple of years ago and I've recovered fully. My accident didn't kill anyone and I wasn't sued. But as far as being questioned about my part in the accident and second-guessing my actions, I *do* know what you're going through."

My anger deflated. "I'm sorry. I didn't know."

"There were some issues with your statement that made the NTSB consider some of what you said might not be entirely truthful."

I straightened. "Like what?"

"Your memory was vague on some things, but you could recite verbatim the procedure for the standby rudder ON light illuminating. You also claimed an MEL had been issued that there is no record of."

The FAA inspector at my questioning had grilled me on these facts. Did he, or his agency, force the NTSB to dismiss what I had said?

"I explained why I couldn't recall certain items exactly at the hearing." I said that with my teeth clamped together.

"Yes, you did. There are those who feel that since you can state verbatim a procedure that could be used to absolve you of blame, you might've had a month to come up with it."

"That's not what I did."

Natalie shook her head.

In a calmer tone, I said, "For most of that month, I was on such powerful drugs I couldn't remember what day it was. Studying a manual to figure a way out of this mess was out of the question."

"I believe you when you say you can't remember the accident. But if you did and could state that you or the first officer used all the available rudder to keep the airplane on the runway, but it was ineffective, we'd be more inclined to believe your statement that there was something wrong with it."

I massaged my forehead as if it would conjure up a memory suppressed since the accident. Then something I had dwelled on surfaced.

"In the time I've had to lie around and think, I've questioned why my *right* leg was injured so severely and not both. If I had straightened out my right leg to push the rudder to the stop, it would have been under the instrument panel when it was bent down in the accident. But my left leg would have been pushed back by the left rudder pedal and consequently out from under the panel."

Mrs. Masters said nothing for several seconds.

"If I hadn't stepped on the rudder, like the data claims, why don't I have compound fractures on both legs?"

"I'm pulling up the pictures of the cockpit," she said.

"Can you send them to me?"

"No, I cannot. We don't release data in an active investigation."

I sighed. "I thought I might see something that'll trigger a memory."

Several seconds went by without a sound from her.

"You still there?" I asked.

"Yes. I'm here. Can I call you back in a few hours?" There was hesitancy in her voice.

"I'll have to cancel a tennis match. But, yeah, I'll be here. I want to discuss why there's no mention of the messages I sent stating we had a problem with the rudder. I promise not to yell at you this time."

"Okay. I'll call you back."

Chapter Twenty-Two

After Lori studied the wreckage photos of Sphere Airlines EA-220 and reviewed the data from the flight data recorder, she paced within her cubicle, tapping a finger on her lips. After some deliberation, she decided there was no point in putting off sharing what she had discovered with the investigator in charge, Jeff Hume.

How receptive he would be to her findings kept her thinking of how to present it while she weaved through the other cubicles to Hume's office.

He was typing on his computer. Lori could see his email screen. "Hey, what's up?"

"We should re-evaluate the preliminary cause of the Sphere Airlines accident."

Hume rested his head in his hand. "Why?"

"The captain from the flight called—"

"And wasn't happy with the preliminary cause."

Lori tamped down her frustration. "Obviously. But he brought up a good point. If he didn't step on the right rudder, why was his right leg injured more than his left?"

Hume's eyes moved left and right. "If I remember correctly, the right side of the cockpit was damaged more than the left. Hence the reason the FO died. So, the instrument panel must've been bent down more over his right leg, crushing it."

"That's a good assumption until you look at the pictures."

Hume lifted his brow.

"Pull up the pictures." Lori gestured to his computer as she scooted a chair up and sat.

Hume clicked through several layers of file branches until the thumbnails of the accident photos were displayed.

"Start with this one." She pointed to a photo.

Hume clicked on it, enlarging the photo to the size of his monitor.

It was taken from the cockpit door, looking forward at the instrument panel. Jagged pieces of the windshield and side windows were visible at the picture's edges. The overhead panel was caved in, with the right side significantly lower than the left.

Blood smeared the switches and gauges.

Both pilots had been removed from the wreckage hours before the NTSB arrived. But Lori estimated if this picture had been taken before Kurz was removed, the overhead panel would have been close to impacting his head, too.

"I'm not sure what I'm supposed to see," Hume said.

"See how the instrument panel is bent down." Lori ran her finger horizontally along the edge of it. "On the first officer's side, it cants down to the right. But on the captain's side, it is parallel with the aircraft's lateral axis."

"Mmmmm... maybe. It's hard to tell from this photo. Everything is so out of position."

"Move ahead four pictures." Lori swiped her finger as she might on a touch screen.

The photo Hume pulled up was taken from approximately where Kurz's seat would have been, if it hadn't been cut out to remove him.

"See how the top of the instrument panel on the captain's side is bent down evenly in comparison to the FO's?" She ran her finger on the screen. On the right side of the photo in front of the first officer, the glareshield dipped down significantly.

Hume studied the photo a moment before clicking back to the previous one and examining it. "Maybe. It's hard to tell from these photos without some frame of reference."

Lori had to admit that it was. It was easier for her to visualize the damage since she had spent more time at the wreckage and had taken these photos. And had spent several body-trembling moments crouched in the cockpit, visualizing what the crew had gone through while the aircraft tumbled over and over.

"We should go back to Dallas and re-examine the wreckage."

A smirk filled Hume's face. "Because the pilot who caused the accident isn't happy?"

"When you see the wreckage again, you'll see he has a valid point. If his right leg was extended to push on the rudder, his left would have been out from under the instrument panel."

Hume turned back to his monitor and studied the photos. "Maayybbee. But if he pushed the right rudder partially, that might have put his left leg in a position to not be injured."

It was a good point, considering the data from the digital flight data recorder revealed the pilots had not used all the rudder.

"No. We've overlooked something else."

"What?" Hume was more annoyed then curious.

"Pull up the data from the DFDR."

A sigh escaped him before he did as she suggested.

"Now move to just before the aircraft touched down."

Hume moved the slider bar until near the end of the file.

Lori pointed to a spot on one of the graphs representing the readings from one of the eighty-eight parameters that the digital flight data recorder captured. "Notice here right before touchdown, the rudder moves left and right a degree or two, obviously correcting a gusting crosswind. Then there is this deflection to the right of eighteen percent. That would have been when the first officer pushed on the rudder pedal to align the aircraft's track with the runway, then backed off that input here, and increased it here."

A nod. "Okay. So?"

"That corresponds to what the rudder pedal displacement also shows. The right pedal moved eighteen percent, then backed off to twelve, then increased to twenty-eight." She pointed to the graph representing the rudder pedal movement.

Hume turned from the monitor to her. "You're not pointing out anything we haven't already looked at."

"I'm getting to it. Notice for several seconds, the rudder continues to move. It goes from twelve to twenty-eight percent. That corresponds to what the rudder pedal indicators show." She slid her finger up and down to both graphs.

"Yeah." Impatience laced Hume's tone.

"Now here, when the aircraft experienced the gust of fifty-six knots, the rudder moves to forty-five percent. But the right rudder pedal moves forty percent. Both remain in that position for the next twenty-three seconds. In that time, the aircraft departs the runway, collides with the excavator, and begins tumbling."

Hume stared at his monitor as if the longer he looked at it an answer to this dilemma would be revealed. "The rudder moved more than the pedal." He said nothing for another second. "Why?"

Lori sat back in her chair, working at containing her excitement. "I have a theory. Before we leave this subject, look at the rudder graph from when the aircraft experienced the gust until it begins tumbling in relation to the rudder pedal displacement. Never does the rudder go more than forty-five percent to the right. Nor does it back off even one percent. The rudder pedals also remain displaced forty percent, never changing."

"What are you getting at?"

"In those twenty-three seconds, why didn't the rudder ever move? Even one percent?"

Hume studied the graphs. "The pilots must've frozen up and kept the pedal partially depressed."

"The aircraft collided with an excavator and somersaulted. That jolt would have shifted the pilot's feet some. But the graph doesn't reveal that."

Hume was silent while he studied his monitor.

"What if the pilots shoved the rudder pedal to its limit, but it didn't respond like it should have? While they rolled nose to tail several times, their right legs remained locked, holding the pedal at its stop?"

"They didn't." Hume tapped the rudder pedal graph. "The rudder pedals never moved more than forty percent."

"Do you agree, though, that it'd be more logical for the pilots to not move the pedals even a degree if they had one rammed against its stop, than pushed in partially?"

Recognition registered on Hume's face before he turned back to his monitor.

"What if the rudder pedal potentiometer was defective and didn't measure displacement more than forty percent?" Lori asked.

"Whoa, that's a stretch. If your *theory* is correct, why didn't the rudder move a corresponding amount?"

"First off, we've seen through the initial part of the touchdown, the pilots move the rudder pedals and the rudder moves a corresponding amount. Except when they experience the gust."

"Okay."

"The captain stated that the standby rudder ON light illuminated during the takeoff in San Salvador. In that scenario, the two main rudder actuators are not powered by the two powerful main hydraulic pumps. The sole standby actuator controls the rudder from the weaker standby hydraulic pump. The abnormal procedure for this malfunction is to avoid large rudder displacements. The standby actuator must not have had the power to move the rudder more than forty-five percent."

She let him absorb that a moment. "Wouldn't the gust they experienced require a large pedal displacement?"

A long sigh escaped Hume as he slouched in his chair. "So, you *theorize* that one or both pilots tried to move the rudder to the right more than the data reveals, but an alleged malfunction of the rudder actuators prevented it from following that command?"

Lori bristled at his use of *theorize*, but it was a legitimate point. Until she proved it, it was just a theory. "Yes."

Hume rubbed his jaw. "And this is based on the fact the captain thinks both legs should be injured equally?"

"No. That got me to considering why his right one was injured more than the left. The data," she pointed to his monitor, "reveals we haven't considered all possibilities. Like why didn't the rudder pedals move after they were shoved to forty percent?"

Hume drummed his fingers on the desk. "Is this because I was selected as the IIC for this accident instead of you?"

Lori recoiled. "What? No."

"I know you were pulled some time ago, unfairly I might add, from the investigation you were in charge of for inappropriate remarks to the press. I have to consider if you're bitter over that decision."

She resisted the urge to stand and pace while she formed an appropriate response to his outrageous thought. Then the words her husband had stated to her on occasion came to her: *You need to remove emotion from this subject.*

Hume had a valid point. But he was potentially overlooking something that might have caused Sphere's accident if he didn't consider her hypothesis. That could have drastic consequences if another Edwards Aerospace 220 had a similar problem.

She flexed her hands, willing the irritation out through her fingertips. "During the accident you speak of, I learned I'm probably not cut out to be the investigator in charge. I often felt pulled in too many directions to effectively run the investigation as it should have been. I'm happy to be running the operations portion of this one under your leadership."

Hume studied her before giving a subtle nod. "How do you propose we figure out if your assumption is correct?"

She hid the smile that wanted to spring forth. "We need to take measurements of the accident aircraft's cockpit to see if both of the captain's legs would have been injured equally if he *hadn't* stepped on the rudder. Or stepped on it partially. We'll have to compare those measurements to an undamaged aircraft."

Hume swayed his head back and forth. "Just so we can satisfy the captain that his theory is correct?"

"No." She swallowed, knowing her next suggestions would be met with resistance now that they had decided on a preliminary cause. "We'll also have to test the rudder pedal potentiometers to see if they'll measure movement more than forty percent."

"Seriously?" Hume asked.

"Then we'll have to measure the output pressure of the standby hydraulic pump to see if it was sufficient to move the rudder more than forty-five percent. Next, we'll need to inspect the hydraulic lines to see if there were restrictions, or leaks, that prevent delivered pressure from reaching the actuator. If the actuator had not been destroyed, we would also verify it would move the rudder to its limit. Obviously, we can't do that now."

Hume blew out his lips. "If we discover the rudder pedal potentiometer is defective, we're going to open up a pit of snakes. The captain and his pilot's union will claim that he and the first officer must have shoved the rudder pedal to the floor to keep the aircraft on the runway, but the aircraft didn't respond. They'll claim there is either a design or a maintenance problem."

Either one of those problems had Lori worried.

"If it's a design problem, the FAA will have to determine if the entire fleet of 220s need to be grounded."

Which Lori knew they'd be reluctant to do. The airlines flying that aircraft would lose millions while their aircraft sat. They would lobby Congress about the FAA's unreasonable demands. The FAA would be diligent in proving they had not overlooked something when they certified the aircraft, a process that might take months. The Administrator and others would be appearing before Congressional hearings and would possibly lose their jobs if something had been overlooked.

"Edwards Aerospace is going to claim their aircraft's design met certification standards and had flown millions of hours since then," Hume said. "They'll try to prove it hadn't been maintained correctly. Sphere Airlines will claim they maintained it in accordance with the manufacturer's procedures, which were approved by the FAA. So they'll claim either Edward's maintenance procedures are incorrect or there must be a defect in the rudder control mechanism."

Which reminded Lori of the conversation she had with FAA Inspector Cramp.

Hume shook his head. "Everyone is going to claim we're trying to find a problem that isn't there, since we've already determined a preliminary cause that everyone agreed with."

"Then we need to do these tests to either confirm the preliminary cause is correct or that there is a bigger issue than suspected." Lori folded her hands in her lap.

Hume scrubbed his face with both hands. "Oh brother. Are you trying to make my life miserable?"

Lori was about to respond when the corners of his mouth lifted.

"I'll have to run this by Ratliff." Their superior, the Director of Aerospace Safety. "He'll probably need to consult with the chairman."

"Do you want me to be present when you do?" Lori wasn't convinced Hume grasped the details she had pointed out.

"No, that's not necessary."

"Should I take a team to Dallas to take measurements and test the rudder pedal potentiometer and pump pressure?"

"No. Don't do anything until I talk to Ratliff," Hume said.

Chapter Twenty-Three

While waiting for Mrs. Masters to call me back, I sat on a kitchen chair doing long arc quads. I would lift my lower leg horizontally and hold it there until I couldn't take the ripping-my-leg-off agony in my quads.

Most of the time, I did this and other exercises with the determination to walk normally again, to get back in the air, and resume skiing. But there were days when the prospect of months of agony from therapy overwhelmed me. In a month and a half, I had only progressed from a walker to crutches, and it would be months before I'd walk without the devices. I'd wallow in self-pity that I would always limp and never be able to ski or fly.

But Natalie and the physical therapists had been adamant: If I wanted any semblance of a normal life, I *must* do the therapy.

I hated that my life consisted of constant pain, popping narcotics, going to PT, and doing these damn exercises that I grunted and cursed through. But if I wanted this lifestyle to change, I had to put in the effort.

It had been more than a couple of hours since I had talked to Mrs. Masters and I figured she was blowing me off. I wasn't sure how I'd prove they had overlooked the rudder issue if they kept me on the fringes of the investigation.

I had just lifted my foot for another rep when the phone rang. The cordless handset was across the kitchen and Natalie had taken Casey for a walk.

The answering machine picked up before I could get my crutches and hobble across the room. "Bill, this is Lori Masters from the NTSB."

Although I attempted to hurry, I moved deliberately so I didn't risk a fall that would put me back in the hospital.

"When you get this would you call me back, please? There's something I'd like—"

"Hello. I'm here."

"Oh. I thought you might've gone to your tennis match," she said.

Her remark lifted the corners of my mouth and I would have continued with the charade, but my anxiety she might have discovered something occupied my thoughts. "You said there was something you wanted to discuss?"

There was hesitation before Mrs. Masters spoke. "Are you able to travel?"

"Like... on an airline?"

"Yes."

Good question. The fear of having the external fixator bumped while out in public kept me close to home. I was scheduled to have it removed in several days. Aside from that, I went to physical therapy three times a week. Until I was released from it months from now, I couldn't go too far. Was I ready to board a flight without a shot of Ativan?

"Possibly." That was false bravado talking.

"Could you come to D.C.? We'll need you to listen to the recording from the cockpit voice recorder. Only those on the CVR panel can discuss the recording among themselves until you listen to it and agree to release it."

With the phone cradled between ear and shoulder, I attempted to hobble over to the chair I'd vacated. The phone slipped and clattered onto the floor. "Shit."

"Are you okay?" I heard faintly.

I sat and picked up the phone. "Sorry. I dropped the phone."

"You had me worried you might've fallen."

Did I want to hear the recording? Would I hear some crucial mistake I had made that I couldn't remember and have to live with the guilt of knowing I'd screwed up? I already second-guessed my actions. Reliving the two hours that were captured might make me regret even more the many things I wish I had done differently.

Could I stand to hear Ned's last breath or the anguish he'd experienced before dying? "Ummm... how soon after other accidents have other pilots listened to the CVR?"

"There is no set time we suggest pilots wait. It's dependent on when the pilots are ready."

Was I ready? Would I ever be?

"I realize replaying… that time may be traumatic for you. If it's too soon… that's okay."

Should I? Or shouldn't I?

"You said you hoped looking at the photos might trigger a memory. Listening to the CVR might also unlock something your brain suppressed."

The thought of wishing I had died after watching the video floated to my consciousness. Would hearing what I couldn't remember make me wish again that my life had ended too? "I'll have to think about it. When do you need to know?"

"Ah, well… the sooner the better."

"Why?" What did it matter to the NTSB, or was she checking off a task that needed to be completed?

"It's… best to review ah… review these details while they're still fresh in the pilot's mind."

She was usually very articulate and spoke without hesitation. Why not now? Did she feel she was forcing me into something I wasn't ready for? Or…

"I'm curious. You're asking me to do this after I mentioned the difference in my leg injuries. Have you discovered something you feel listening to the CVR might clarify?"

Another pause. "Possibly."

What the hell did that mean? "Do you want my help for your benefit or mine? If my coming there would be to place more blame on me, you can forget it."

"You're going to have to trust me, Bill. I can't go into why I'd like you to review the data, but it would help the investigation." A moment passed. "It'll help you."

Help me what? Not blame myself so much? Or help the NTSB realize Ned and I couldn't have prevented the accident?

If it were the FAA guy, Cramp asking, I'd tell him to go to hell. But she had been sincere and cordial to me since I met her. I doubted she wanted to bury me further.

I glanced around the kitchen. For a month, I had craved coming home to languish in the comfort Natalie and I had made here. Now I was considering leaving it after only a week and a half.

"Okay." I explained about getting the apparatus removed from my leg. "How long will I need to be there?"

"A morning or afternoon should be plenty of time."

I did the logistics in my head. With flights both ways, it would be a long day I wasn't capable of yet. That meant spending a night. "Okay. I'll call you after I get the metal brace taken off."

"Good. I'll make arrangements here."

I should've consulted Natalie. She was going to be pissed.

Chapter Twenty-Four

While in the hospital and the rehab facility, I had vowed to be a better husband to make up for all I was putting Natalie through. Our discussion about building the airplane reminded me how quickly I made decisions that affected our lives without discussing them with her.

Yet here I was, repeating that same behavior.

The front door opened and Casey's claws clacked across the hardwood floor. She stopped in front of me, receiving a pet before going to her bowl and slurping up water.

"You're done with your exercises already?" Natalie frowned. "What's wrong?"

I sighed, worried I'd made it overly dramatic. "Mrs. Masters called back."

"And?"

"She wants me to come to D.C. and listen to the cockpit voice recorder."

Her forehead lifted. "You can't travel yet."

I thought she'd say that.

Casey sat between my legs, giving me the chance to look away from Natalie while I petted our best friend.

"You told her you'd come?"

Guilt twisted my stomach. I ran my hands along both sides of Casey's face, something she seemed to love, so I didn't have to face my wife.

"You can't travel."

Again, she made me feel like an invalid. Instead of laying out why I needed to go, I allowed my hurt pride to make me defensive.

"Why not?" I regretted that my voice was sharper than I had intended. "I told her it would have to wait until I got this off." I lifted my leg.

"Why not? Seriously?" In hurried movements, she gathered up the newspaper that we'd left strewn on the table. "Oh, gee, let me see. You can't dress yourself. You need help getting in and out of the shower. You can't walk more than a few house lengths without being tired. So how are you going to make it through a terminal? Do I need to go on?" She threw the last remark over her shoulder as she went into the garage to drop the paper in the recycle bin.

None of those reasons were entirely true, which she knew. Alone, twisting to get into a shirt, or pulling up a pair of shorts required contortions that sent spikes of pain through me, but I could do it. I also could have gotten myself onto the stool in the shower this morning but didn't mind her getting naked and assisting me.

She hadn't thrown out my need to be drugged the last time I flew. I hoped she hadn't knowing how much that would hurt.

Although her reasoning was justified, I knew underlying these excuses was her worry for me. And since she knew me so well, she knew how unsettled I'd be after hearing the cockpit voice recorder. If I had explained why I needed to go, we wouldn't be having this argument.

When she returned to the kitchen, I waited for her to voice whatever thoughts she'd formed before I justified the trip.

She filled a glass with water from the dispenser on the refrigerator door. "I can't take any more time off."

"I know."

She faced me. "You agreed to go when you knew I couldn't go with you?"

I screwed up my face in an apology.

She sat at the table but didn't look at me. "Traveling this soon will be exhausting for you. You won't be clearheaded and able to process what you'll hear as well as you would if you wait."

"I'm sorry." I lowered my head. "I shouldn't have agreed to go without discussing it with you first." She would still be worried, but I would not have made another decision that affected our lives without her.

"Why did you?"

"There was something in the way she asked that made me think she suspects the accident wasn't my fault."

"Did she tell you what that was?"

"No," I said. "I told her I wouldn't come so she could place more blame on me."

"What'd she say to that?"

"That I'd have to trust her."

Natalie frowned. "Really? And you fell for that?"

I wondered if that was protectiveness or a woman's mistrust of another. "She's been honest and upfront with me so far. From what she was trying *not* to say, I think she's discovered something... or suspects something... but needs me to hear the cockpit voice recorder to confirm it."

Natalie glanced around the kitchen. "Probably nothing I'll say will convince you it's too soon for you to be traveling on your own."

"If I don't now, we'll—" Her glare told me she hadn't finished.

"I do understand how important it is for you to clear your name. Not just so we don't lose everything, but so you'll know you weren't the cause of that accident."

It warmed my heart that she understood me so well.

"Promise me you'll be careful and not push yourself."

I gave thought to holding up three fingers like a Boy Scout but knew my typical smart-aleck gesture wasn't appropriate at the moment. "I promise."

Chapter Twenty-Five

Neal Reeves read over the tentative agreement the airline had reached with the pilots' union focusing exclusively on the sections that affected pilot training. The negotiations for the pilots' contract had dragged on for almost two years. Then, within days after the accident, they'd come to an agreement. Reeves looked over the portion dealing with training in the hopes the management who had negotiated the contract hadn't compromised it to make the pilots come to an agreement.

Marling knocked on his open office door. "You got a sec?"

Reeves gestured to the chair across from his desk.

"Kurz called. He wants a positive space pass to D.C. and back, as well as a hotel room. The NTSB wants him to listen to the recording from the cockpit voice recorder."

Reeves frowned. "I know it's standard procedure for the surviving crew members to listen to the recording. But to request that so soon after he's been released from a medical facility is curious. Did he give any idea why now and not in a couple of months?"

"No. I tried to press him, but he was kinda vague about it."

"Do you suppose he initiated it? The preliminary report put the majority of the blame on him and the FO. Is he hoping to hear something that'll absolve him?"

"Possibly."

Reeves rubbed his chin. "I'm curious what he thinks he'll hear that the CVR committee hasn't already uncovered? Is he going alone?"

"He asked for only one pass."

"Really? Can he get around that well now?"

Marling shrugged. "I would've guessed no, but I haven't seen him in over a month. Pringer said he went to his hearing in a wheelchair."

A glint shone in Reeve's eyes. "He'd probably appreciate some assistance. Why don't you go with him?"

Marling smiled. "So I can learn what he does."

Chapter Twenty-Six

Russell picked me up after my physical therapy session to drive me to the Denver airport. Knowing I was traveling, the physical therapist had taken it easy on me.

"How's it feel to have that hardware off your leg?"

I smiled, remembering how he had averted his gaze from my leg. "Better today. Yesterday, I don't know if it was unscrewing the rods from the bone, or…"

His grimace suggested this wasn't a topic he was comfortable with.

"I'll spare you the details."

"Thanks." He glanced at the sky. "Should be a good day to fly. You ready?"

A few white, fluffy cumulus clouds floated in the sky. Combined with the unlimited visibility, it was the kind of day pilots lived for. I took a deep breath. "I hope so. I didn't sleep well last night. I had another nightmare. I hope getting this flight behind me might end those."

"Time will tell."

I didn't want to dwell on the upcoming flight. The anticipation would only elevate my anxiety. "When I get home, I'm going to put the airplane up for sale."

His shoulders rose and fell. "That sucks. When I was building mine, I know how upset I would've been if I had to sell it before I'd finished it."

"I think upset is too mild an adjective. Fucking pisses me off might be better."

He smiled, then it dissolved. Only another aircraft pilot/builder would understand the love put into building an airplane they'd never fly.

"When I find a buyer, can I hire you to help dismantle it so it can be trucked to its new home?"

With his forehead lowered, he glanced at me. "I'm offended. Hire me? You couldn't afford me."

"I realize someone of your incredible expertise is in high demand, but how about for a couple bottles of bourbon?"

"Now you're getting close to meeting my price. But only if you'll help me drink it."

"As soon as I'm off these damn narcotics, you've got it."

When we neared the airport and paralleled runway 25/7, a Sphere Airlines EA-220 began its takeoff roll to the west.

"That is a nice-looking aircraft." Russell alternated his gaze between the road and the runway.

It was built into a pilot's DNA to stare at an airplane as it took off or landed. Pride had always filled me that I was one of thirty-five hundred of Sphere's ten thousand pilots who flew the EA-220. Deepening that pride was the knowledge I was fortunate to be one of one hundred thousand in the U.S. who made my living by being a pilot.

Playing in my head what the captain of that flight was experiencing and thinking, a lump formed in my throat. It threatened to choke me.

When they reached 100 knots, they'd be committed to continuing the takeoff unless they had an engine failure or fire.

For the next several seconds, the captain would be spring-loaded to yank the thrust levers to idle and reject the takeoff, if needed, or continue accelerating down the runway. Once they reached rotation speed, he—or she—would ease the yoke back, raising the nose of the aircraft, causing the wing to generate lift. The captain would be eager to get the 180,000-pound machine into the air before they ran out of runway.

The nose gear left the concrete and the aircraft rolled on its main landing gear for several seconds before lifting off.

How I loved that intense concentration followed by the sheer joy so many millions fantasized about.

My vision blurred from the tears that filled my eyes. A blink sent them rolling down my cheeks. I turned away and wiped my face, hoping Russell didn't notice.

As embarrassing as it might be, I glanced back to watch the landing gear retract and the airplane bank into a turn to the northwest.

Before I got caught being emotional, I averted my gaze and took a shaky breath.

Russell gave my shoulder a squeeze.

"Damn narcotics," I choked out and swiped my cheeks.

A moment of silence passed, then he said, "I sure don't miss those o'dark ugly flights." The reminiscent tone Russell used was one I had heard often. "The ones so early that regardless of what time you went to bed, you never got a good night's sleep. Maybe the all-night flights were worse. Don't miss those either."

My grief over the career I might have to give up slackened. It was easy to remember the flying and status of the job and forget the frustrating aspects that I, too, griped about.

"I also don't miss holding for an hour while the airport was being plowed, then having to divert and run out of duty time. Then the passengers would throw dagger-stares at us as we made our way to the hotel van."

A final swipe dried my face. "Or those dried out, mystery-meat crew meals they'd feed us."

"You got meat in your meals? I wish we had."

I chuckled and risked a glance at him.

His expression was flat, his gaze on the road.

"Thanks. For everything."

"You know," he said and glanced at the runway as a Boeing 787 lined up for takeoff, "what I'd give to get back in a 757 and fly another flight." He sighed. "If I were in your situation, I'd feel the same way."

His understanding threatened to bring more tears. Several blinks and a deep breath held them back.

At the terminal, I got out of his car and put my crutches under my arms. When I turned to let Russell put my backpack on me, I spotted Marling hurrying over, accompanied by an attendant pushing a wheelchair.

"Here, let me get that." He took the pack from Russell.

Marling had told me he'd meet me at the airport, but I expected it would be at the gate. Although I anticipated getting through security and to the gate on my own, as Natalie had pointed out, it would be the longest I'd walked. My stupid pride had prevented me from requesting a wheelchair.

I eased into the wheelchair. "Thanks. I appreciate this."

"Oh, sure. Whatever I can do to help."

Inside, people scampered about to get in the security line. Some stared at the monitors and then their boarding passes as if trying to decipher them. People got annoyed at the TSA agents who ordered them to put their phones down and pass through the x-ray machine.

I registered all this and might've savored the chaos that had been a normal part of my life. But my thoughts dwelled on the upcoming flight.

The closer we got to the gate, the more I trembled and the drier my mouth became.

Marling was going on about a crew that refused to fly together during a check-ride that he had to deal with before picking me up. I nodded occasionally but had trouble following the conversation.

The gate agents boarded me before the other passengers. When I glanced in the cockpit, I didn't recognize either pilot. I'd hoped I had flown with the first officer, or had passing acquaintance with the captain. Knowing one of them might've eased my anxiety.

None of the flight attendants were familiar, which eased my trepidation. I wouldn't have to explain why I was on crutches. It would also be embarrassing if I rocked in my seat with my eyes closed.

A seat in first class with its ample legroom would have been a dream. Instead, I had a window seat in the middle of coach. My crutches were put in a closet at the front of the airplane. The fact that the nearest emergency exit was several rows behind me added to my fear. Could I evacuate from the airplane without my crutches?

A glance at my watch revealed I had to wait another hour before I could take a Percocet to dull the throb in my leg and calm myself. If I took one now, would I begin the slide toward becoming addicted to them?

The passengers boarded, the cabin door was closed, and the aircraft pushed back from the gate. I was grateful the seat beside me was empty so I didn't have to be social. Marling sat across the airplane and a row ahead of me.

I white-knuckled the armrests during the takeoff roll. At every bump on the runway, I imagined a tire disintegrating, or an engine failing and the crew not compensating for the asymmetric loss of thrust while we shot off into the grass.

Once the wheels thunked into the wheel wells, I flexed my fingers and mopped my brow. Maybe agreeing to fly to Washington so soon was a bad idea.

When it was time, I swallowed the narcotic and relaxed enough to rest my head against the sidewall and doze. I sat up with a start when the engines went to idle and the aircraft began descending.

My fingers made new impressions in the armrest during the descent. The pilots touched down on the short runway at Ronald Reagan Airport with the gentlest of thumps. That didn't ease my death grip. I suspected Ned and I had touched down anticipating an uneventful rollout.

While the engines roared in reverse thrust and the airplane decelerated, I imagined the brakes failing, colliding with an aircraft on a crossing runway, or running off the end and into the Potomac. If it had been windy, causing the aircraft to rock from the turbulence, it would have been a depiction of one of my nightmares. I'd probably be crying out.

Only after the aircraft turned off the runway did I realize I had been holding my breath. I let out a long gush and tried to relax my tense limbs.

I was glad we weren't going to the NTSB today. I needed a shower.

If riding on a smooth flight caused me to be this big a wreck, how would I be tomorrow listening to the cockpit voice recorder?

Chapter Twenty-Seven

Marling and I arrived at the NTSB offices at L'Enfant Plaza in D.C. promptly at eight. This was a miserable time to be up for me. For the last two months, I had been on Central or Mountain Time. I also hadn't slept much, too stressed over what I would hear on the recording. The nightmare I had during the brief period I slept didn't help.

To give myself adequate time to shower, shave, and dress on my own, I got up at five. If Natalie could've come, I might have gotten another hour of sleep. I also could've used her smile to bolster my confidence.

The receptionist called Mrs. Masters to announce Marling and I were there. She exited an elevator a few minutes later and smiled at me before frowning when she noticed Marling. "Bill, thank you for coming."

"I'm glad I can help. Do you know Bryce Marling, our EA-220 fleet manager?"

"Hello again." She extended her hand to him. "I hope you understand, Captain Marling, that since you aren't on the panel the NTSB convened to listen to the CVR, you won't be able to join us today."

Thank God!

Marling pursed his lips. "Oh, but I'm sure Bill won't mind. I'm here to help him in whatever way I can."

Hell, yes I minded.

Before I could form an objection, Mrs. Masters said, "Regardless of whether Bill gives his consent, until he's heard the entire recording, we cannot allow you to."

Yes! I hoped I hid my gratitude.

"I'll have to ask you to wait here in the lobby. Or, you could go see the sights in D.C. The receptionist can give you a map of the area and direct you to the places you might want to visit."

"I suppose… I can get some work done." An overly dramatic sigh came from him, then he held up his phone. "If you need me for anything, Bill, I'll be here."

Not likely. "Okay." I followed Mrs. Masters to the elevator.

Once the doors had closed, she glanced at my sneakers. They were the only thing comfortable enough to wear on my tender left foot. "Did you know your shoes are untied?"

"Yes. I'm starting a new style that I'm sure will be trending."

She grinned.

"It hurts too much to bend down and tie them and I didn't want to ask Marling."

"I'm guessing you didn't ask him to accompany you here."

Her acumen surprised me. "No, I didn't."

"Why is he here?"

"When I called him to get flight and hotel reservations, he volunteered to accompany me. I thought I could manage on my own, but he's been helpful."

Most likely his motivation for accompanying me had nothing to do with support. Since I wasn't sure of the hidden agendas, I kept that to myself.

Before we went to the Cockpit Voice Recorder Lab, Mrs. Masters took me to two different offices to meet the occupants. Both Aaron Ratliff, the director of aerospace safety, and Jeff Hume, the investigator in charge of my accident, seemed surprised by my presence. The frowns they shot at Mrs. Masters suggested her inviting me there was not run by them first.

Was she attempting to go around them to prove what she suspected?

Inside the Cockpit Voice Recorder Lab was a long conference table with a dozen headphones in front of each seat. Two men sat at the table. One, who was in his twenties with a soul-patch under his lower lip, sat at a computer at the head of the table. The other I remembered as sitting beside Mrs. Masters at my hearing.

"Do you remember Aaron Tippen?" Mrs. Masters asked.

"Yes." We shook hands.

"And this is Brandon Bosimen. Brandon is the CVR analyst assigned to your accident."

"Bill Kurtz."

Brandon leaned over his computer and shook my hand.

"We'll start at the beginning of the recording and play it until the recording stops." Mrs. Masters took a seat. "If at any point you want the recording stopped to ask a question or to point out something pertinent, just raise your hand."

"Okay." I lowered myself into a chair across the table from her and Tippen. What did I do if I heard something I didn't want to live with? I donned the headphones while taking a deep breath.

She nodded and Bosimen clicked his mouse.

Chapter Twenty-Eight

A roaring noise was the first thing I heard through my headphones. It took a couple seconds before I realized the recording would have begun after we had reached our cruise altitude of 41,000 feet. What I heard was air rushing by the cockpit at four hundred and fifty knots.

The air traffic controllers and pilots of the other flights on the radio frequency spoke in Spanish. Occasionally the controller would speak English to a non-Hispanic flight.

Since Ned and I had spent the morning waiting for the aircraft, we had caught each other up since we had flown together months ago, and were silent. Several minutes into the recording, I smiled as I heard myself faintly sing the words to Duran Duran's "Hungry Like A Wolf."

Since we didn't have the intercom microphone activated, Ned wouldn't have heard me.

Today I buried my face in my hands, embarrassed that my inability to carry a tune had been recorded.

Mrs. Masters' face was turned down, engrossed by the document in front of her so I couldn't tell if she was trying not to smile. Tippen stared off into space.

My singing was interrupted by Ned's drawling voice. My spirits lifted—until I remembered he was dead.

I have to use the little boy's room, he said.

There were several clicks and rattles of his seatbelt being unbuckled, the seat sliding to the side, a grunt, then a faint thud of the first-class lavatory door closing.

This was the instance FAA Inspector Cramp had referred to at the hearing. I should have put on my oxygen mask before Ned left his seat. Was a letter from the FAA on the way stating I'd be fined or my pilot's license suspended for a month or so? Other than the fine, did it matter at this point?

After Ned returned, for the next hour and a half, we talked occasionally. He hoped to make it home that night as he had a well driller scheduled to put in another well from which Ned could irrigate his fields. We discussed how this year's crop was growing and Ned's wish to buy another five-hundred-acre farm and work both full-time. Like many pilots, he loved the flying but hated being away from home so much. He thought the two farms could support him comfortably without his pilot salary.

I explained Natalie would be working the next day and I hoped to finish plumbing the brake lines on my airplane. Since Ned loved to tinker on his farm equipment, he was full of questions about building the airplane.

During this conversation, I answered radio calls from the controller and switched frequencies several times.

Our discussion turned to the rumor that Sphere Airlines' quarterly profit was so good, we might get a good pay raise in the pilot contract presently being negotiated.

I heard the mechanics got a healthy raise in their contract, Ned said.

They just voted that in, didn't they? I asked.

Yeah, I think a couple of days ago.

Listening to the casual nature of our conversation, tears pricked my eyes. I cherished hearing it, knowing it would be the last time I'd hear his voice. He didn't feel the need to fill silence with conversation, unlike a few pilots I had flown with. His interest in what I had to say was genuine. Beside the fact he was an excellent pilot, our mutual respect of each other made me appreciate the times I had flown with him. We never called each other, or got together with our wives, but I would miss him and think of him often.

This time when I rested my head in my hands, it was to cover the tears I tried to suppress.

The airplane flew normally then, not requiring us to talk about the standby rudder ON light being illuminated. During the climb to altitude, we had discussed it and maintenance's error in applying the MEL. That portion of the recording would have been overwritten with what I was now listening to. If the recording was longer, or our flight less than two hours, my proof we had a rudder problem would've been captured.

My tearing a piece of paper off the printer was captured on the recording. *Weather in Dallas is still good,* I said. *The thunderstorms forecasted haven't hit there yet.*

I had handed Ned the printout of the weather in Dallas I had just downloaded.

Yeah, should be no problem. Ned's tone showed the same lack of concern mine had.

During the monotonous time while we cruised across the Gulf of Mexico, Mrs. Masters alternated between reading from the bundle of paper she brought with her or seeming to stare off into space.

Tippen doodled or sat with a vacant stare.

Bosimen, for the most part, stared at his monitor, often stifling a yawn.

How many times had each of them heard this recording? Knowing that most of the recordings they listened to ended with the pilots dying, did they ever burn out from listening to this mundane time that ended with the terror that ruined lives?

After Ned and I neared the coast of the U.S., The air traffic controller in Houston called us. *Sphere 9100, radar contact. Cleared direct, Humble.*

Sphere 9100, direct Humble. I responded, acknowledging the clearance to fly directly to the initial point just north of Houston that began the arrival route into Dallas-Fort Worth.

Another tearing sound, then I said: *It looks like those thunderstorms have moved closer to the airport.*

But they're moving to the southeast, Ned said. *Hopefully they'll miss the airport.*

Yeah.

Our tones agreed with my memory. We were unfazed by the weather. We both had flown to airports with much nastier weather than what was being reported.

Any time now, dispatch, I said on the recording. *I hope arrivals haven't slowed down, causing us to hold.*

The Houston controllers passed us off to the Dallas-Fort Worth controllers. The pace of the transmissions increased.

I sat up a little straighter and held my quivering hands in my lap. In less than half an hour, I'd hear the events that had changed my life forever. I strained to hear something that the NTSB had missed that would prove we had done all we could to prevent the accident.

We'll plan on the Cedar Creek Eight arrival, Ned said as he began the descent and approach briefing. He gave the pertinent information required to be discussed. ... *touchdown elevation is five-sixty-two. If we miss... well, this has us going straight ahead right into those storms. What'll you want to do? Request an immediate left from tower?*

Yeah. That'll work. I said.

When he finished the briefing, I did the descent checklist.

Shortly afterward, the controller said to us, *Sphere 9100 maintain two hundred and fifty knots in the descent.*

After I replied, Ned said, *I suppose getting slowed down now is better than having to hold later.*

When he deployed the speed brakes, the rumbling from the disrupted air atop the wing was captured on the recording.

Yeah, I guess. If that weather keeps moving, we shouldn't have a problem.

I took a swig from the bottle of water beside me to relieve the dryness of my mouth. I hoped the tremble of the bottle didn't give away my terror.

Dispatch says arrivals have slowed down, but no one is holding or diverting, I said.

Maybe we can still catch the flight to Denver. Ned had smiled and lifted his eyebrows several times.

The roar of the air rushing past the cockpit decreased in volume as Ned slowed us to the assigned speed.

While in the descent, we were handed off to the approach controller. *Dallas, Sphere 9100 fourteen three descending on the Cedar Creek eight with xray.*

Sphere 9100 after Dietz fly heading three five five, the controller responded. *Descend and maintain ten thousand.*

We had just passed the airport flying north on a parallel course to final. We would continue in that direction for another forty miles before turning back to the airport.

Several minutes later, we were slowed to one hundred and eighty knots.

Flaps 5, Ned said. The ambient noise diminished as our speed slowed.

There were two clunks as I moved the flap lever to the commanded position.

The controller was heard stating to everyone on the frequency, *Tower reports arriving aircraft experienced a windshear with a gain and loss of ten knots.*

If we experience windshear, I said on the recording, *the callouts are max power stow the speed brake.*

Got it.

Mrs. Masters stopped the recording. "Were you feeling any pressure to continue the approach even with the reported windshear?"

I was so engrossed in the recording, it took me a second to respond. "What? Oh. Ah… No. I just wanted to remind both of us what the callouts were in case we experienced it."

Was she questioning if I had fallen into the herd mentality that I had discussed with Natalie? Now, I wished instead of continuing the approach, I had told Ned we were diverting. I suspect that decision would have been met with a frown. The pilots at Sphere often landed with reports of windshear of ten knots.

"Okay." Mrs. Masters made a note as Bosimen resumed the recording.

Sphere 9100, turn left one four zero intercept the one seven center localizer. Descend and maintain five thousand feet.

Several minutes later, the controller said, *Sphere 9100, you're cleared the ILS one seven center.*

I acknowledged the clearance, then said, *It looks like that storm is just sitting off the end of the runway.*

Now that we faced the airport, I remembered we could see the storm out the windshield and its depiction on the weather radar.

Ned had nodded.

I stared at a spot on the table right in front of me so the NTSB investigators didn't see the terror I must be expressing.

Sphere 9100, contact the tower.

After I had changed frequencies, we heard: *American 562, turn right taxiway mike seven and contact ground control on point six five. Did you experience any windshear?*

Negative, the voice of one of the pilots on the American flight responded.

Tower, Sphere 9100 twenty out one seven center, I radioed to the tower.

Sphere 9100 cleared to land runway one seven center. Wind one four zero at twelve gusting to twenty-five. Previous aircraft have reported windshear with a loss and gain of fifteen knots.

Now, as then, I didn't hear any urgency in the controller's voice. The controller didn't seem concerned with the wind or the ominous black storm sitting on the southern boundary of the airport.

Cleared to land, I replied to the controller. To Ned I said, *Somewhere, the winds are going to shift.*

The recording was stopped and Mrs. Masters asked, "Why did you feel the wind would shift?"

"The wind readout on the map display showed the wind from the south, but the tower just reported it from the southeast." Did the three NTSB investigators detect the quiver of my voice?

At the time, I hadn't been concerned by this aspect, as I had landed numerous times with the wind several thousand feet above the ground and twenty miles from the runway different than what the tower reported.

"Can we... um... listen to the recording to the end and discuss... uh... discuss it later?" I lifted my face to meet Mrs. Masters' eye.

Initially, she conveyed a look of concentration on what she was hearing on the recording so she could peel back the subtle layers. That expression fell away as she took in my face. She nodded, portraying an expression that sympathized with what I was going through.

When the recording resumed, Ned said, *If American can handle it, it'll be a piece of cake for us.* Bravado filled his voice.

Later, when we discussed the recording in more detail, I withheld from the NTSB that he had mocked chewing his nails. I didn't want them considering that even though he appeared to have been joking, it was an attempt to mask his concern. Also, knowing he would never utter another word in a few minutes, I wanted everyone's memory of him portrayed in a favorable light.

Aware that he was about to die, I wished I could key a microphone and warn him to go around.

Over the next few minutes, the tower told two more arriving flights that landed before us to contact ground control. The aircraft that was two in front of us reported a gain and loss of fifteen knots of airspeed one hundred feet off the ground. That was typical with a gusty wind.

Let's see how this will handle. The double chime of Ned disconnecting the autopilot sounded.

Several moments later, I said, *Any problems?* He had made several shallow turns using more rudder than needed.

Doesn't seem to be. Gear down. Flaps fifteen. Landing check.

Up to this point, I had remembered everything I had heard, so I tried to stuff my anxiety down so I could concentrate, hoping I'd hear something that would open the door to my suppressed memories.

There was a clunk followed by a roar of the air being disturbed by nose gear lowering, a familiar noise I had heard thousands of times before.

At the same time, the flight landing before us reported to the tower, *The winds on the landing roll are squirrelly.*

Massaging my forehead didn't help me remember that comment. The previous crew had hinted that the winds made it difficult to track the runway centerline. Although they didn't claim it was dangerous, it must have concerned them enough that they thought it needed to be passed along.

Yet Ned and I didn't discuss that. Had we been so preoccupied with configuring the aircraft for landing that we missed it? Or were we confident we could handle it if the previous crew had managed to?

Had my mind blocked this warning, knowing it was crucial information I should have acted on?

I squirmed to fight the urge to rock. "Don't land," I wanted to scream.

Speed brake is armed. Gear down three green, I said while completing the landing checklist.

Down three green, Ned confirmed. *Flaps thirty.*

A couple of clunks sounded as I moved the flap lever, then said, *Flaps are thirty, green light. Landing checklist complete.*

I blinked, but no memory of accomplishing the checklist returned from the black void of this time. Hearing myself say something of which I had no memory was eerie.

Several seconds later, the whine of the engines increased. Ned would have had them at idle to slow to our approach speed, then increased power to maintain that speed while tracking the electronic glideslope.

I blocked out the steady radio calls while listening to every squeak and vibration. A trickle of sweat ran down my back.

Go around. Go around, I chanted to myself as if willing a different outcome could change what mine and thirty-eight other families had experienced the last couple of months.

The whine of the engines remained steady, then dropped as Ned must've reduced power to stay on the electronic glideslope without gaining airspeed. A moment or two later, it increased.

One thousand, I called out indicating we were one thousand feet above the runway.

Set missed approach altitude, Ned said.

The whine of the engines increased, then increased significantly for a second or two before reducing to the tone that suggested the normal approach power setting. Ned must have encountered a significant downdraft that made the airplane begin to go below the glideslope.

Missed approach altitude set, I said.

Knowing the transformation our lives would take in just a few moments, it amazed me how calm we sounded.

My present breaths came in quick pants.

Five hundred, I said like I had a thousand times before.

Mrs. Masters seemed to be staring at something just above and to the side of me. Bosimen appeared engaged by something on his computer monitor. Tippen's face pointed at the table. No one seemed to notice my trembling or continuous squirming. How could they seem so calm?

One hundred. The airplane's automated voice called out our height above the runway.

Then, *Fifty.*

Thirty.

Twenty.

I squeezed my eyes closed and gave thought to ripping off my headphones. Did I want to hear the accident? If I continued breathing this way, would I hyperventilate?

The power decreased. *Ten.*

A couple of seconds later, there was a muffled thud. Followed by me saying, *Nice.* Ned's touchdown must've been smooth and I had complimented it.

My heart threatened to pound out of my chest.

The whine of the engines increased when Ned selected reverse thrust.

There was a gasp from one or both of us. Then a bang, accompanied by a chirp that must have been when the nose gear slammed onto the runway.

The video Lucas had shown me helped visualize what was going on. I wrapped my arms tight around my chest, knowing we were in the process of leaving the runway.

Whatthefuck? No! No! No! I yelled each *no* shouted louder.

Fuck. I can't make it, Ned cried.

Why won't it?

Fuck!

Rumbling that must have been the aircraft rolling across grass filled my headphones. The inevitable was moments away.

No! Fuckno!

Shit!

Our shouts were mixed in with each other's.

I sat huddled as tight as I could, cringing and braced for the collision with the excavator.

Come on. Come on. Come on, I said real fast. This was mixed in with Ned's yell of, *No. No. No!*

A bang—as loud as a gunshot—startled me even though I was anticipating it.

Grunts came from both of us.

The groan of metal being bent sliced through my headset.

I caught a glimpse of Mrs. Masters staring at me, wide-eyed and pale. She glanced at Tippen before turning back to me.

A crash louder than the bang startled me. It must've come when the aircraft slammed onto its back. Glass shattered. It made me duck as if to avoid the flying pieces.

Banging, thuds, and tearing metal screwed through my head. It lasted an eternity but might have been a less than a minute. Mixed in amongst these sounds were shrieks that were Ned's and mine.

Then those screams were solitary.

I grasped my headset to yank it off, but stopped. I had to hear this.

Then silence filled my headphones. It went on for several seconds.

Feeling the recording was about to end, I almost pulled off the headset until I heard a groan.

Then I did again.

Then I gasped. Followed by, *Ah. Ah. Ah!* Each of my exclamations louder than the previous one. The last one was a shriek.

I flashed back to waking in the wreckage. Excruciating pain from my mangled leg and foot, broken ribs, and lacerated liver consumed me.

Now, those areas of my body throbbed. Though not as torturous as they had two months ago.

On the recording, I vomited and spit. The image of my femur protruding through my pants and the constant stream of blood dripping from it came back to me, as gruesome as it had been that day.

A muffled roar, the source of which was impossible to distinguish on the recording, reminded me of the emergency vehicles approaching.

Help, came out a gurgle, followed by me spitting again. *Help!*

I would have to leave this room if the recording did not stop.

Mrs. Masters sliced her hand across her throat. "We've heard enough."

I clawed my headset off and stumbled to my feet, almost falling.

Mrs. Masters hurried around the table and helped me with my crutches. "Are you okay?"

"Men's room?" I spoke so rapidly, it amazed me she understood.

"Down the hall to the left."

She held the door to the CVR lab open for me.

I hobbled down the hall as fast as I could.

Tippen hurried ahead of me.

This was going to be close.

He held open the door to the men's room, then followed me in. I wished for privacy but my constant swallowing prevented me from forming words.

Kneeling in a stall would be impossible. I bent at a sink and emptied my stomach.

Chapter Twenty-Nine

When my retching stopped, I continued to brace myself at the sink, allowing my heart rate to slow. The sweat on my face cooled.

"You okay?" Tippen ran water at the sink next to mine and handed me wet paper towels.

I spit—remembering that I did that on the recording—trying to get the awful taste out of my mouth, then accepted the towels. "Thanks." *Okay?* I had just heard the aircraft I was in command of crush thirty-eight lives. How would I ever be okay?

The sounds from the recording continued to play in my head, refreshing my memory of my feeble cry for help, bellows of pain, and the horror of seeing Ned's lifeless eye. My leg, foot, and ribs throbbed as if to reinforce what I'd experienced.

Besides my injuries, I now had the menacing sounds of the aircraft being destroyed. And Ned's and my cursing when we couldn't keep the aircraft on the runway.

None of that helped me remember anything after I put the landing gear down.

The paper towels I placed on my face with trembling hands were cool and refreshing. Although physically feeling better, I wished I could crawl into bed and not talk to anyone.

I ran the water and tried to wash my vomit down the drain.

"Don't worry about that. I'll get the janitorial service to come clean it up. You've got some…" Tippen pointed to the sleeves of my shirt.

I wiped at the vomit stains with a fresh batch of towels. "You wouldn't have any gum or mints, would you?"

"After I escort you back to the CVR lab, I'll get some."

I felt like a convict who couldn't be left alone. In my debilitated state, he probably worried I would fall and sue the NTSB.

When we returned to the lab, Mrs. Masters was gone. Tippen left me with Bosimen, who occupied himself at his computer. I smelled vomit and hoped it wasn't noticeable to the others.

Mrs. Masters returned with a bottle of Pepsi that she set down in front of me. "It helps me."

I swallowed a mouthful, dulling the bile taste in my mouth.

Tippen returned and slid a pack of gum across the table to me. He and Mrs. Masters left the room and stood just outside the door, conversing in hushed tones.

After popping a piece in my mouth, I drank more soda, wishing it were Scotch. It would dull the sounds ricocheting around in my head. A glance at my watch revealed I wasn't due to take a Percocet for another two hours.

Fishing a tablet from my pocket, I swallowed it, justifying that if ever there was a time for its sedating effect, it was now. Wasn't that what addicts told themselves?

Why won't it? No! No! No! I tried to make sense of the words I had shouted. Had I stepped on the rudder but the airplane wouldn't respond? Or had I sat still and questioned why Ned wasn't correcting the swerve? If so, I deserved to limp the rest of my life.

Rubbing my temples didn't bring back any memories, or even fragments of them.

Even if I had been the world's worst pilot, why hadn't Ned shoved the rudder to the stop? From his, *Fuck. I can't make it,* he seemed shocked the airplane wasn't doing what he commanded. He wasn't the type of pilot who would have pushed the rudder pedal halfway, then questioned why the airplane wasn't responding when he had additional rudder authority to use.

But I might be too emotionally connected to judge what I heard objectively. Obviously, the NTSB had not viewed our shouts the way I did.

Mrs. Masters and Tippen entered and closed the door behind them.

"You feeling better?" Mrs. Masters asked.

I nodded.

"Are you up to listening again from just before you touched down until you go off the runway?" she asked. "We won't listen to the… after you departed the runway."

"Can I have a sick sac?"

Mrs. Masters pursed her mouth until she saw I was kidding. Her eyes twinkled. "Now that you've heard the recording, this time you might hear something, or notice something, you didn't before."

I'd rather be kicked in my bad leg than listen to our shock and shrieks again. Yet a part of me needed to. My anxiety had been so paralyzing, I probably had missed a lot. Hearing the recording again might be the trigger I needed to remember.

I guzzled more of the soft drink. "Sure. Let's do it." I hope I didn't embarrass myself again.

We donned our headsets and the recording began with the whine of the engines coming through the speakers.

Five hundred, I said.

The engines' whine wasn't constant. It increased then decreased. Ned must've been fighting the gusts to stay on glideslope.

One hundred.

Fifty.

Thirty.

Twenty.

Tippen and Mrs. Masters stared at me, no doubt wondering if I was strong enough to hear this again. I was going to prove I was.

I rested my head in my hands and closed my eyes.

The power decreased. *Ten.*

A couple of seconds later, I said, *Nice.*

The engines went into reverse, then one or both of us gasped. The nose gear slammed to the concrete as the airplane began to veer off the runway.

Whatthefuck? No! No! No! I yelled.

Fuck. I can't make it, Ned shouted.

I raised my hand and the recording stopped.

"Yes?" Eagerness filled Mrs. Masters eyes.

"Can we back up just a couple of seconds and hear that part again?"

"Sure. Why?"

"I thought I heard something." Or, more likely, I wanted to hear something so my mind had fabricated a noise that probably wasn't there.

Mrs. Masters and Tippen exchanged a quick glance.

The recording resumed with me saying, *Nice.* The engines roared in reverse thrust, then one of us gasped. The nose gear touched down with its accompanying chirp.

"There. Did you hear that faint thud?" I spoke loud enough for them to hear me over the recording.

Bosimen stopped the playback.

Mrs. Masters gave Tippen a glance out of the corner of her eye. "Describe what you heard."

"Just as the nose gear hits the runway, there's a very faint thud like—" They're going to think I'm reaching—"a rudder pedal hitting the stop."

The three NTSB investigators did not make eye contact with me or each other.

"Let's listen to it again," Mrs. Masters said. "Tell us the moment you hear what you're referring to."

When the recording resumed, we listened to the engine go into reverse, our gasps, then as the nose gear touched down, "There." I knew I wasn't fabricating it.

Tippen began to carefully fold the wrapper from a piece of gum. Bosimen stared at the computer monitor. His rigidity suggested he didn't want to look away from it. Mrs. Masters swiveled her chair back and forth.

What was up with them? "Can you isolate that noise like they do on CSI?" I asked.

Mrs. Master rolled her eyes. "We already have."

I tried to calm my hope. "And… what was it?"

It was Tippen's turn to glance at her out of the corner of his eye.

"We're not sure." She ran a hand through her short hair.

I frowned. "I thought at times like this you went to an aircraft and recorded possible things that might make that noise. Didn't you test to see if a rudder pedal hitting the stop sounded like the noise on the recording?"

"We did." Tippen looked up. "What we discovered didn't make sense."

When he didn't go on, I asked, "Why not? What did you discover?"

Mrs. Masters twisted in her seat so that she faced Tippen. She wore an expression that conveyed interest in how he would answer.

"The noise... the noise on the recording has an identical signature to a rudder pedal," he sighed, "reaching the end of its travel."

"So why doesn't that make sense?" It seemed crystal clear to me and filled me with relief that Ned and I had tried to keep the aircraft on the runway. This thud and everything we'd yelled as the aircraft departed the runway added up to us fighting in vain to maintain control.

"Because the data from the DFDR does not confirm that fact."

"Then the DFDR is wrong." I couldn't believe they were being so obtuse.

"We doubt it." Tippen's tone was placating.

I shook my head. "I've heard that thud thousands of times before each flight when I check that the rudder pedals move freely and have full travel. That noise on the recording was identical."

"It may seem that way to you." Tippen nodded. "But we can't confirm that fact."

"You heard on the recording the first officer yelled, 'I can't make it.' He was saying the airplane wasn't responding as it was supposed to. He would've only said that after he mashed the pedal to its stop."

Tippen glanced at Mrs. Master.

She stared at him and gave a nod, signaling he could respond.

What was up with these two?

"The data from the DFDR is never wrong. You failed to move the rudder more than forty percent to the right. That leaves us uncertain as to what both your and the first officer's questions meant. We've heard this before. At times of high stress, like you experienced, pilots tend to not be coherent in what they say."

I glared at him. He was trying to downplay what I knew to be fact.

"Did the recording help you remember anything that might clarify this confusion we have?" Mrs. Masters asked.

I bowed my head and shook it, wishing I could say I remembered stomping on the right rudder pedal. If I lied and stated I remembered doing that, would I be proven wrong later?

"Isn't it possible the standby hydraulic pump didn't have sufficient pressure to move the rudder more than forty percent?" My gaze moved back and forth between Mrs. Masters to Tippen.

Mrs. Masters stared at Tippen.

He cleared his throat. "It doesn't matter. The rudder pedals' potentiometers show you didn't move the pedals more than forty percent, which corresponds to rudder travel. And there is no data that the rudder was powered *only* by the standby actuator."

"Yes there is. I sent messages to our dispatcher stating the standby rudder light came on."

This time, Tippen gave Lori the nod to answer this question. "Your company has no record of you sending those messages. Or an MEL procedure being applied to your flight."

"Then you're being deceived. If you haven't seen them, someone has withheld them from you."

"We doubt it." Mrs. Masters said. "We've reviewed the messages you sent and received while waiting for the aircraft, and while in flight. There's no mention of a rudder problem."

"Bullshit. Sphere has kept them from you knowing they screwed up." My outburst didn't seem to affect them.

"How is it you feel your airline," Tippen paused, "screwed up?"

Really? I almost became sarcastic as Natalie had when she explained I couldn't travel. Instead, I worked to keep my tone professional. "They released an aircraft from maintenance that obviously wasn't ready for flight. When we had the standby rudder problem, they ordered us to continue to Dallas instead of returning to San Salvador to have it fixed. Then, when the accident happened, they knew they had to cover up their incompetence. Hence the missing messages."

"Even if those things may be true, that still doesn't explain you not using all the available rudder." Tippen cocked his head as if catching me in a lie.

"Because we couldn't." I enunciated each word. "I don't care what the DFDR says. There's the thud that you've identified as a rudder pedal hitting the stop. We used all the rudder, but the aircraft didn't respond. That, too, we conveyed on the recording."

"I'm sure this is upsetting." Tippen nodded as if to placate me.

"Why would the FO have disconnected the autopilot and said he wanted to see how the aircraft handled if we didn't have a rudder problem?" I tried to keep my tone tempered, but the fact that they couldn't see the obvious angered me.

While staring at the table, Mrs. Masters shook her head.

I thought she had brought me here to reinforce what she suspected.

"The investigation has not concluded," Tippen said. "We'll take your points into consideration as we move forward."

I would not be dismissed.

Leaning forward, I put conviction in my voice. "Find the messages that I sent. They'll prove we had a problem hours before the landing."

"We'll do our best." Tippen wrote MESSAGES in big block letters on the pad in front of him and underlined it three times.

That too was to placate me.

"Do that. Because if you don't, I will." How, I had no idea. "When I do, they'll be used in my defense in the lawsuit brought against me. I don't think you'll want the public finding out the NTSB missed them."

Chapter Thirty

Lori Masters tried to hold her aggravation in check during a meeting with the NTSB investigators. "The captain heard the same thud everyone on the CVR panel noticed. A noise we've established as having an identical signature as a rudder pedal reaching its stop. He was adamant that he's heard that same thud thousands of time before each flight."

"I wouldn't say he was adamant," Tippen said. "Grasping might be a better term. He hadn't heard anything that dismissed his negligence. He's grasping at this unknown thud, hoping to distract us."

"I disagree," Lori said. "His logical questions about why his right leg was injured more than his left are valid. Now he's heard a noise we've dismissed. He's justified in questioning our findings."

"So we need to go take measurements and run more tests," Hume said in a monotone. "We've heard this argument before, Lori. The FAA, Edwards Aerospace, and Sphere Airlines see no reason to."

"Which I question." Ratliff didn't lift his gaze from the tablet computer on which he was reviewing the data from the flight data recorder.

"The fact that the rudder pedal data doesn't agree with this thud Kurz is hanging his defense on isn't reason enough to waste resources trying to placate him," Hume said.

"But Kurz has another valid point. What if he sent messages that we haven't been shown?" Lori flipped her pen onto the table. She didn't understand Hume and Tippen's reluctance to dig deeper into the cause.

"If he had, why wouldn't Sphere show them to us?" Tippen asked. "If they'd made a mistake, they'd pay the fine the FAA would impose and move on. Hiding data from us would be criminal. There's no smoking gun here, Lori."

Lori's heart pounded; she didn't like being ganged up on. Was Ratliff going to join this discussion or be a useless oaf? "Then how do you explain the difference in Kurz's leg injuries, and the rudder pedal noise? Those points haven't been addressed."

"Lori's got a good point." Ratliff turned his attention to those around the conference table. "We've got data that might be corrupt, an unknown noise, and differences in a crewmember's injuries. On top of that, we have three organizations resistant to further investigation. Do they feel these issues are not valid? Or are they worried we might uncover something more complex that'll be costly to correct?"

Finally. Lori took a silent breath.

Hume leaned forward. "They must realize—"

"You've got a good point too, Jeff," Ratliff said. "We may be wasting resources to learn there's nothing to these issues."

It took considerable effort for Lori to not swivel back and forth in her chair.

"Since there is reluctance to conduct further tests, including from some in this office," Ratliff rested his gaze on Hume, "it makes me curious what we'll uncover if we do."

Lori hung onto the silence that followed.

Ratliff tapped a finger on the table for a couple of beats, then said, "Lori will take a team to Dallas and test the rudder pedal potentiometer to see if it measures rudder pedal displacement accurately."

Hume lifted his face to the ceiling.

Lori tried not to, but smiled despite herself.

"Don't think you're being rewarded by forcing me to meet the pilot." Ratliff bore his gaze into Lori. "I don't appreciate you going around Jeff and conducting your own investigation. If you can't follow Jeff's direction, find another job."

Her face warmed. Although admonished, Lori knew this reprimand was to warn the other investigators to toe the line with such a high-profile investigation.

"Yes, sir." She bowed her head.

"You're to *only* do that one test. If the potentiometer does not measure rudder pedal movement correctly, then we'll have a fight on our hands to do further testing. We'll evaluate then how to appease the FAA, Sphere, and Edwards Aerospace as to why we have to test the standby hydraulic system and take measurements." Ratliff glanced from Lori to Hume.

"Understood," Lori said.

Hume slumped but nodded.

To Lori, Ratliff said, "Arrange a time when Edwards Aerospace, Sphere, and the FAA can be present to validate your test. If any party tries to stall when it is accomplished, they'll have to live with the results without their input."

When Lori returned to her desk, there was an email from Bill Kurz that read:

May I please have the name of the dispatcher who worked my flight?

Chapter Thirty-One

After I completed physical therapy, I eased into the backseat of an Uber car and gave the driver Sphere Airlines' corporate address near the airport. Fortunately, the driver didn't engage me in conversation so I could silently rehearse the role I would play at our dispatch center.

At headquarters, I hobbled inside on my crutches with my airline ID hanging from its lanyard, dressed in khakis and a button-up shirt like many who frequented this building.

Having been here several times made it easy to cross the lobby and board the elevator to the fifth floor like I belonged. Regardless, my heart thudded as if I were trespassing.

No doubt this was self-induced. It shouldn't be suspicious for a pilot to seek information on one of his flights. But since learning Sphere had withheld data from the NTSB, an overriding feeling of suspicion consumed me.

The door to our dispatch center required a swipe of an ID and a code punched in. I had no idea what the code was. The last time I had been here, I had been let in by the instructor giving us the tour.

Leaning on my crutches, I pretended to read from my phone.

From inside the room, someone opened the door to exit.

"Can you hold that please?" I hobbled forward.

My crutches had the desired effect and the heavy-set woman stepped back, holding the door for me.

"Thanks," I threw over my shoulder once inside. I hobbled along as if I belonged there. The door closed behind me with a click. The few who turned their attention to me looked away after a moment.

Off to one side were the waist-high cubicles where fifty crew schedulers worked.

Elevated at the back center of the room were the supervisors of crew scheduling, dispatch, and maintenance.

In front of this platform, thirty-five dispatchers sat behind dual monitors they used to prepare flight plans, track flights in the air, monitor airports for departure and arrival delays, and watch the weather across the globe. Taking up the entire wall in front of them were numerous giant, flat screen monitors that showed maps of different parts of the world with numerical blocks signifying a flight's location.

The maintenance technicians occupied the other side of the room. They worked with the dispatchers to get airplanes with mechanical issues corrected.

This time, as when visiting previously, a sense of awe filled me with the complexity of Sphere Airlines' worldwide operations. It was one aspect of working for a major airline I had been proud to be a part of. In my heart, I was just a pilot who loved to fly and would have enjoyed working for an operator of a single airplane. But being part of an organization that employed seventy-five thousand and flew millions around the world on seven hundred airplanes gave me satisfaction that I was part of something bigger than just little ol' me.

Yesterday I looked up on the airline network the name of the dispatcher Mrs. Masters had supplied me with, and pulled up the picture of Kevin Darby. A call confirmed he would be working today. None of the dispatchers nearest me looked like that picture. Toward the center of the group, the dark-haired guy with frameless glasses resembled the thirty-something dispatcher. I hobbled over to get a better look.

When I approached his desk, he glanced up and ran his gaze up and down me.

"Hi. Kevin Darby?"

He nodded, continuing to look at me as he might any stranger who'd approached his desk.

"I'm a 220 pilot. While I'm laid up, they have me working on a pilot newsletter." I berated myself for talking faster than normal.

His eyebrows twitched up.

"I was hoping I could get some information on how our A-CARS messaging system works. If now is not a good time, I can come back later." I knew it was presumptuous of me to expect him to drop what he was doing and answer my questions about the

Aircraft Communication and Reporting System. He might have several flights he needed to get dispatched.

He sighed. "Why me? I know no more about it than any other dispatcher."

"Bryce Marling, the 220 fleet manager, recommended you. I assumed he considered you the expert. Can you suggest who I should talk to?" Another dispatcher could educate me. But I hoped to work with Darby so I could gauge if he was involved in erasing the messages I had sent to him.

"Marling, you said?" Darby frowned. "Doesn't ring any bells."

Relief settled over me. I didn't want him asking Marling later if the info Darby gave me helped with my newsletter.

Darby glanced at his monitors. "I've got to get a flight plan put together. After that, I'll have a few minutes before I get busy again, if you can wait."

"Sure." I didn't want to leave the room and have to admit I couldn't get back in. "Ummm… I'll wait over there until you're ready." I gestured with my chin to what appeared an unoccupied cube.

When I had eased myself into the empty chair, I took a deep breath. So far so good.

For the next fifteen minutes, Darby worked at his computer, answered a few calls, and made a few others. His slouch and attention focused on his monitors gave me the impression he was doing his job and not calling a supervisor to report my presence.

Eventually he stood and stretched, then gestured for me to come over. "I didn't catch your name earlier."

I tried not to stiffen. "Bill."

His eyes didn't narrow, nor did he glance at others he might alert. Instead, he wheeled a chair up next to his desk. "You don't look like you can stand for long." He let out a little laugh.

I chuckled with him. "You got that right."

"What happened to you?" He pointed to the crutches.

"I was in an accident. Nearly lost my right leg."

His face scrunched up. "You alright now?"

"A few more months of therapy and I should be good as new." I wished it would be that quick and easy.

"Good to hear. So, what do you want to know about A-CARS messaging?"

From my backpack, I dug out a pen and notepad. "When a pilot sends you a message, how do you receive it?"

"Oh, it just pops up on the side of my screen." He gestured to one of the monitors. "If one comes up while we're talking, I'll show you."

"Okay. But what I need to explain in the newsletter is how does the message actually get to you? Is it radioed to a ground station where it travels across the internet to reach your computer?"

An enlightened look came to his face. "Oh, I see what you're getting at. Yeah. We use the company, Arinc, who has numerous towers at all the major airports and points in between. When we send a message to an aircraft, or the pilots send one to us, it is transmitted over Arinc's network to reach the dispatcher working the flight, and vice versa. It works kind of like email."

For effect, I made notes, even though I would remember what he said. "How does the network know to send a pilot's message to you and not another dispatcher who might not be working the flight?"

"When I load a flight plan into the system, I include the aircraft that is supposed to receive this information. Each airplane has its own unique code. The flight plan goes to Arinc's network and sits there until that aircraft logs in. Then my computer and the computers on the aircraft are linked. Any information we send to each other follows that now-established path."

I now understood the initialization process the first officer or I did before each flight. "So when a pilot sends you a message, is it stored anywhere?"

Darby lifted his face and considered my question. "Hmmm... I guess it'd be stored on one of our mainframes somewhere. I know they're continuously backed up in case there's a power failure. Once power is restored, we can retrieve the information on flights already airborne. Why?"

I concentrated on making a note so I didn't appear concerned by his question. "Oh... you know," I shrugged, "how paranoid we pilots are. Like what if we'd asked what the latest game scores were, then we had an incident. Could the FAA pull up those messages and feel we hadn't been paying enough attention to the flight?"

He gave a vigorous nod. "Or the dispatcher wasn't monitoring his flights adequately. The FAA criticized me on that during the investigation of our Dallas accident a few months ago." He frowned as he glanced at my crutches, then continued. "Just before that accident, a pilot on another flight sent a message asking if the mechanics had agreed on a new contract. I replied they had. During the accident investigation, the FAA saw that message and asked if I might have prevented the accident if I had been paying more attention to the flight that crashed."

I wondered if that was why it had taken him so long to respond to the message I sent asking about delays at DFW.

I scowled. "Friggin FAA."

"Like they don't have more important things to do."

"Yeah, really." I paused. "Well… what about for disciplinary actions? Say we had a pilot that's a pain in the ass. Could a chief pilot pull up those messages to use against a pilot?"

"I don't know if a chief pilot would have the privileges to pull them up." He waved a hand as if swatting away that answer. "But all they'd have to do is have the director of dispatch do it and email them a copy."

"I wonder how many pilots have sent messages that could have come back to haunt them later? Anyway," I turned serious, "let's say our servers are corrupted, or for some reason the messages a dispatcher or pilot sent back and forth are not backed up, would there be a copy of them on Arinc's servers?"

Darby scrunched up his face. "Hmmm… I don't know how they'd escape being backed up by us, but I suppose there might be a copy on Arinc's computers. You'd have to ask them."

"How long are the backups stored on our computers?"

A shrug. "Beats me."

"Would it be more than two or three months?"

"I really don't know," Darby said. "I assume so."

I tried to appear nonchalant, but my heart thumped hard. "Could we pull up one of my flights to see if the messages are still there?"

"Sure." He turned to his computer. "Give me a date and flight number."

I took a deep breath. "May twenty-first."

He frowned as he selected this date from a pull down menu.

"Ah… let's see… how about flight… 9100?"

He faced me with wide eyes. "Shit!" He shot to his feet. The chair he'd vacated hit the cubicle behind his with a clatter. "You're that captain. You're going to have to leave."

With my hands resting in my lap, I cocked my head. Inside, I didn't feel as calm as I appeared. "Why?"

"I can't talk about that accident." His raised voice attracted the attention of the dispatchers nearby.

"Why not?"

He held his hands up palms out. "You've got to leave." He glanced at the elevated platform at the back of the room.

The supervisors there watched us. One of them stood and made his way down the steps.

"Look, I'm sorry about what happened to you. But I—"

The supervisor came our way.

Darby spun and walked away.

Chapter Thirty-Two

The supervisor who had stepped down from the platform stopped in front of my seated position. His narrowed eyes expressed curiosity. "Can I see some ID?"

I lifted my airline ID so he could read it. Although I kept my face slack and my body language relaxed, I was pissed. Darby's reaction had told me a lot.

After reading my ID, the supervisor glanced at Darby, who paced at the side of the room, shooting glances our way. "Your name seems familiar, Bill. What do you do for Sphere Airlines?"

"I'm a 220 captain writing a newsletter." I'd let him make the connection as to why I might be familiar.

"Wait here." He went to Darby and had a discussion with him. They both looked at me before the supervisor stepped up onto the platform and made a call.

I thought about getting the hell out of there. If Sphere would hide information from the NTSB, and consequently the FAA, how far might they go to keep that information hidden?

But I was dealing with an airline, not the CIA. Besides, how fast could I run on crutches? I decided to let play out whatever was going on to see why Darby couldn't discuss my flight.

Several minutes later, a portly man in dress slacks and a button-up shirt hurried into the room. Dressed in a more distinguished manner than anyone else in the room, it was apparent he was higher up on the pecking order than the supervisor. Following him were two men wearing white shirts with patches sewn onto their breasts that identified them as security.

My stomach knotted as they approached. Yet my pent-up anger welcomed whoever this was.

"You'll have to leave." Portly pointed to the door.

I remained planted. "Who are you, and may I ask why?"

"I'm the senior director of dispatch." He stated that like I should be impressed. "You're in a secure area and don't have authorization to be here." Crimson crept into the man's complexion. "Out. Now!"

Everyone in the room stared at us.

"I've been in this room before. Why can't a captain for our airline be here now?"

"Because. You're. Not. Authorized." Portly might have a heart attack, his face was so red.

"Let's go, sir." One of the security guys grabbed my arm.

Getting to my feet, I said to Portly, "Once outside this room, I need to ask you a few questions."

"No. You're trespassing. Either leave or I'll call the police."

I debated if he would. Since he had made such a scene, he wouldn't want to lose face. The rumor of my arrest would fly through the rumor-hungry airline. My arrest would warn those involved in keeping data from the NTSB that Sphere would jail them if they didn't do as ordered.

Natalie and I couldn't afford to have Tori Killinger bail me out. Being manhandled would set my recovery back.

Outside the dispatcher center, Portly shook a finger in my face. "You are not authorized to be here. Don't ever come back or you'll be arrested."

By nature, I'm not a confrontational person. The few times I had to persuade a passenger to abide by the airline's rules or be pulled from the flight, my authority as a captain gave me the backbone to be challenging. But now, their unscrupulous behavior affected the well-being of Natalie and myself. I unharnessed the aggression I had been restraining.

"Where are the messages I sent regarding the rudder problem?"

Narrowed eyes glared at me. "Get him out of here."

✈✈✈

Outside, I worked my way to a bench to sit and let my pounding heart ease. From inside, the security guards looked out at me.

Replaying Darby's reaction when he realized who I was gave me an idea.

Down the street was Happy Landings, a bar/grill that would be a painful, tiring, walk on crutches, but doable.

There, I ordered coffee, then sent a text to Natalie. *Call me when you have a sec. Something I want to discuss.*

A few minutes later, she did. She must've been between patients. "How'd therapy go?"

"Nancy worked me hard today. I can lift my leg a little higher now."

"Good."

I knew Natalie would be pressed for time, so got to the point. "I went to Sphere's dispatch center after therapy."

"Oh?" She would've expected me to return home to rest.

"They're definitely hiding something."

"Why?"

"I just got kicked out of there. Security guards escorted me to the front door."

"What? Why?"

I explained Darby and Portly's reactions. "If they had nothing to hide, why wouldn't they have shown me there was no record of any messages stored? Why didn't they play along like I must be mistaken?"

Her response was immediate. "Because they know you sent them and it would be damaging to them if they revealed that fact."

"Exactly. They've tipped their hand. You up for a little adventure when you're done work?"

Chapter Thirty-Three

Lori Masters, along with Tippen, had removed the floorboards in the cockpit of the accident aircraft.

She checked the connection of the cable that ran from a laptop to the rudder pedal potentiometer, then fought the urge to run the test before the other interested parties had assembled. In her gut, she knew there was more to the cause of this accident than the crew not using all the available rudder. This test would prove they needed to dig deeper.

Since no one wanted to consider her hypothesis—that the rudder pedal potentiometer was defective—she waited, leaning against the cabin's door, tapping a foot. The representatives from the FAA, Sphere Airlines, and Edwards Aerospace meandered around the hangar, talking on or reading from their phones.

After it seemed they couldn't stall the test any longer, they gathered around the laptop set on a counter in the forward galley.

"Go ahead, Lori." FAA Investigator Bob Cramp glanced at his watch. "Show us we're not wasting our time."

In a moment, he would owe her an apology.

"Go ahead," she said to Tippen.

Crouching where the captain's seat would be, he pushed the right rudder pedal.

Lori and the others watched the indicator on the laptop's screen show the rudder pedal moving from zero, to ten, twenty, then thirty percent. As it approached forty, Lori waited for the needle to stop.

But it didn't.

It continued to move, indicating fifty, then seventy, eighty-five, and stopped at one hundred.

"I'm at the stop," Tippen said.

Beside her, Cramp sighed.

Lori blinked. And blinked again. The indicator continued to show the pedals had moved full travel.

"I'm guessing by everyone but Lori's expression the potentiometer is working correctly." Tippen wore a smug grin.

"Push on the left pedal," Lori said.

On the computer screen, the needle went back to zero, then moved in the opposite direction until it indicated one hundred percent.

She ran a hand through her hair. "Move the right pedal again."

"Really, Lori," Cramp said.

Again, the indicator showed one hundred percent.

"Center the pedals., she said to Tippen, "then move the right one slowly to about halfway, then push it the rest of the way as fast as you can."

She wanted to rule out the chance that the pilots had held the pedal halfway, correcting for the crosswind while they flared to land, then stomped on it to correct for the gust that forced them off the runway. The potentiometer might not capture the rapid movement.

The indicator went to forty-five degrees, paused, then shot to one hundred.

"Well," Cramp said, "it was good to get out of the office for the day."

Beside him, the Edwards Aerospace representative sighed. "I knew this was a waste of time."

Lori paced down the cabin several steps, turned, and returned to the laptop. *What the hell?* "Was there any binding when you moved the pedals?"

"Just the normal resistance from the mechanical linkage." Tippen's tone was matter-of-fact.

With a *come here* gesture, Lori said, "Let me see."

"If there's nothing further, Lori, we'll go catch flights home." Cramp's tone dripped with sarcasm.

Lori didn't bother answering. She didn't care that they thought she had wasted their time. They had ruled out a possibility that hadn't been considered.

What had her clenching her jaw was two well-trained pilots had sat idly by, letting their aircraft go off the runway when it appeared their controls weren't compromised.

Prior to this moment, from the short time she had spent with Bill Kurz, she wouldn't have thought him so incompetent.

After Tippen had moved out of the cockpit, she crouched down where he had been and pushed on the right rudder pedal. She too only felt the normal resistance of the mechanical linkage. Centering the pedals, she moved the right one slowly to the middle of its travel, then shoved it as fast as she could. The force to move it didn't change.

Tippen stood at the laptop. "Still showing full travel."

There was no need to test the first officer's pedals. The two pilots' controls were mechanically linked to each other. If the captain pushed his right pedal, the first officer's moved accordingly.

In her mind, she reviewed the rudder system schematic. She had studied it so much, she could draw it from memory. "We can't rule out that something prevented the pedals from moving beyond forty percent and was dislodged when the aircraft tumbled."

"We've been over that." Tippen shook his head. "Because of the damage to the aft end of the fuselage, we'll never know if that was a possibility."

"We need to inspect the airframe again. We've missed something."

Behind her, Tippen growled. "Lori, we're to only accomplish this one test. It proved the pilots didn't use all the available rudder. We're done here."

With a flashlight, she shone a beam on the area around the base of the rudder pedals. There were no stray items laying on the fuselage skin that could've been stuck in the pedal mechanism and had come free. She didn't see any markings on the olive-green primer from something trapped in the rudder pedal arms that scratched it when the pedals moved.

"Damn!" She'd been so confident.

In the galley came the sound of the cable from the laptop hitting the floor and a thud from the screen being closed.

Her flashlight beam traced the control rods from the captain's pedals to the bell-crank that linked the two pilots' controls together with no indications anything had obstructed its movement.

She stepped across the center console and crouched down to inspect the first officer's side. That side too showed no evidence of control movement infringement.

Shining her light over the potentiometer, she frowned. The screws that fastened it in place appeared new. There was no grime or discoloring that the unit would have in the several years it had been installed since it was new. The wires that ran from the potentiometer had a thin coating of dust on them.

Why would the potentiometer seem new when everything around it didn't?

When she reached to remove the plug from the laptop's cable, the beam from her light dipped and shone on the inside skin of the aircraft's belly. A white plastic tie-wrap that had been cut from a wire bundle laid there.

It wasn't uncommon to find loose nuts or screws when inspecting an aircraft that had been flying for some time. Mechanics often dropped items while working in tight places. It was easier to leave it than try to fish it out of a tiny crevice.

She was about to dismiss its presence when she noticed an area around the wires that ran from the potentiometer had a band the width of a tie-wrap that was dust free.

On her belly, she stretched out to retrieve the tie-wrap, but her short arms put it out of reach. "Aaron, you still back there?"

No response.

With a heave, she got to her feet and moved to the aircraft's door. At the base of the stairs, Tippen and the two Sphere investigators were gathered together.

One of them, Pringer, the operations inspector, stood hunched over like he held something to his stomach. "Then he's running and jiving." Pringer weaved back and forth.

Tippen and Liske, the Sphere maintenance investigator, smiled.

"Good. I'm glad you guys are still here," she said. "Aaron, bring a set of mechanical fingers. I need you to look at something."

He blew out his lips.

Lori got her camera and took pictures of the tie-wrap laying on the fuselage, and the wires with the clean spot.

"What is it?" Tippen sounded annoyed.

After moving out of the cockpit, she explained what she had found and told him where to look.

"Yeah, so what?" he said after he had peered at the aircraft's belly.

The two guys from Sphere stood behind her. To Tippen she said, "Did you have to cut that tie-wrap to attach the laptop's cable?"

"No."

"Look just aft of the potentiometer at the wire bundle. Do you see that area that's cleaner than the remainder of the wire? It looks like that tie-wrap might've secured the wires to the fuselage."

"Yeah. So?"

"Don't you think it's suspicious a tie-wrap happens to be directly under an area where one was attached? Especially since the aircraft rolled violently five revolutions nose to tail. How would the lone tie-wrap remain right below where it was cut off?"

"This aircraft just came out of heavy maintenance," Liske said. "There's probably many stray ones floating around."

"True. But that one appears to be the correct size to wrap around the wires running from the potentiometer."

"Like I said," Liske articulated each word, "there are probably hundreds floating around. They replaced the potentiometer during its inspection and must've forgotten to install a new tie-wrap. During the accident, that one from another wire bundle landed there."

Lori lifted her brow. "What?"

Liske squeezed his eyes shut, then wouldn't meet her eyes. "I said its probably from another bundle."

"The potentiometer was replaced during the inspection?" She couldn't believe they were just now finding that out.

Liske looked anywhere but at her. "I think so. I don't know for sure."

"No." Lori shook her head. "You said it *was* replaced."

Liske's Adam's apple bobbed.

"Which is it?" She tried to engage his eyes.

"What's it matter?" Liske shrugged. "The test you insisted on running proves it worked. Who cares whether it was replaced during the inspection, or a year ago?"

"It matters," she paused to rein in her anger, "because we might not have had to conduct this test if we knew the potentiometer was brand new. Why wasn't this mentioned when you tried to discourage this test from being conducted?"

"I... ah... didn't remember that then." Liske's eye contact was brief.

With a glance at Pringer, the Sphere operations investigator, she asked, "Did you know it had been replaced?"

He met her eyes. "No. First I've heard about it."

She believed him. Turning back to Liske, she asked, "Of the hundreds of parts that were replaced on this aircraft during its inspection, you happen to know that one was replaced? But didn't think to mention this today when we gathered to do this test?" Lori thought about poking a finger in his chest to get him to look at her.

Liske threw out his hands. "Look, I'm not sure if it's new or not. I'll have to check."

"I don't believe you," Lori said.

Red blossomed up Liske's neck.

"If you're unsure, why did you say it was replaced?"

With his hands shoved in his pockets, Liske began to jingle coins. "Look, I might've overheard someone say it was replaced during the inspection. I can't remember for sure. I'll have to look it up."

"Do that. I want a copy of the parts replaced during that inspection."

"That'll take forever." Disbelief filled his voice.

"Too bad."

Liske still wouldn't look at her. "Look, I'm sorry. I just forgot to mention it."

"So you knew it was replaced."

"I just told you, I don't remember. I was just saying I forgot to mention that I heard it might've been replaced."

Lori stared at him.

"Look, I'll get you that list ASAP. I don't know what else I can do."

"You can begin to tell the truth from now on."

"What'll you want to do, Lor?" Tippen asked.

Remembering Ratliff's reprimand about following Hume's direction, she said, "We've gotta call Jeff and discuss this with him."

Chapter Thirty-Four

I stood in front of Happy Landings, constantly glancing at my watch. Natalie was cutting it close. But traffic probably had been bad, or her patients talkative, detaining her from leaving on time. Moments later, her red Venza turned onto the street.

When we drove off, I asked, "How was work?"

The amused frown of hers that I loved filled her face. "The usual. But shouldn't you fill me in on how we're going to get this dispatcher to talk to us?"

"When we get there. Keep going to the stop sign and take a right." I stared at her, waiting for her to tell me about her day.

With a sigh, she told me about the day's frustrations, venting about the office manager's continuous attempts to dictate when and how Natalie and the other nurse practitioners saw patients.

"I might be willing to take Marissa's advice if the support staff, the very people she's in charge of," she shook a finger to emphasis her point, "weren't in constant chaos. What I don't get is why the doctors in our group can't see how she sucks up to them but looks down on everyone else in the practice."

Prior to the accident, I listened so she could vent. I compared Natalie's woes to what pilots griped about with our management. Procedures were implemented that didn't seem to make flying safer or more efficient. Some, it seemed, were changed only because the person in charge wanted things done their way.

But unlike Natalie, I seldom interacted with management unless I screwed up, pissed off a first officer, gate agent, dispatcher, or a flight attendant. To prevent that, I read the bulletins and manual revisions to fly my flights as they dictated. Every nine months a Sphere pilot approved by the FAA to be an instructor administered training in the simulator verifying I was safe, competent, and flew the procedures as spelled out in our manuals. And, once every two years an instructor or FAA official sat on the jump seat and observed one of my flights.

Otherwise, I didn't go to work every day frustrated by how a supervisor might attempt to make my life hell. If I ended up with an office job, would I be micromanaged like my wife?

I listened while guiding her to the parking lot behind Sphere's headquarters so we could watch employees exit and walk to their cars.

"Fill me in again. Why are we following him?"

"When he realized who I was, he said, 'I can't talk about the accident.' Not, 'I don't want to talk about it,' like it's too traumatic for him. It was said defensively. I got the impression if we could get him away from work and alone, he might give us an idea who erased the messages."

"What if he won't talk to us?"

"I'll have to try to convince him otherwise." Although I had never interrogated anyone, our livelihoods were at stake.

"Okay, then." I had heard that *This is a waste of time but I'm going along with you* tone numerous times before.

Several minutes later, numerous people who I recognized as being in the dispatch center departed the building. Kevin Darby wasn't part of this group. Had we missed him?

"What'll we do if he doesn't come out soon?" Natalie tapped her thumbs on the steering wheel in time with the Paul McCartney song playing on the radio.

"Make out until he does?"

She looked over the top of her sunglasses at me while trying not to smile.

"The dispatchers' shift has ended. Unless he had to stay until a flight landed, he should be out soon."

Like me, I knew she was thinking Casey needed to be let out. It had been eight hours since I'd left home.

For several minutes, no one else left or entered the building. We silently watched the door.

Natalie sent several texts and read some email. Forty-five minutes passed. "How will we know if we missed him?"

"Let's give it fifteen more minutes."

Moments later, Darby exited and made a beeline to his car.

When his 3-series BMW coupe sped to the parking lot exit, Natalie followed.

"Ever follow anyone before?" I kept my tone inquisitive but being a captain, the ingrained habit of giving advice to a first officer itched to say something.

"Yeah, just the other day." She said this in a mock matter-of-fact tone.

I said nothing, thinking she was too close to Darby.

We were silent while Darby took us south on Tower Road, then west to Peña Boulevard, then south on Interstate 225.

"Where's he taking us? Aurora?" she asked.

"Let's hope so, and not someplace further south." We were heading in the opposite direction of our home. Every mile doubled the distance we would have to travel before we could let our dog out. "Why don't I call John and Lyn to see if they'll let Casey out?"

"I hate to impose on them. Again." A pause. "Okay."

After I disconnected the call, I said, "John said he didn't mind at all."

"He's a nice guy. We're lucky to have them as neighbors." Her shoulders slumped.

I too worried they might not be our neighbors for long.

My concern we might be on a long journey eased fifteen minutes later when Darby exited 225 and made a right onto E Lliff Avenue then pulled into a sports bar. He went inside without a glance at us as we parked several spots from his.

"Now what?" She put her car in park.

The vehicles in the lot were modern and in good shape. The bar and the businesses surrounding it did not have bars over the windows or graffiti painted on the walls. The patrons inside should be sports fans enjoying a drink after work and not troublemakers who might come to a fellow drinker's aid.

"We go in for a drink and see if he'll talk to us."

Natalie hesitated before killing the engine.

Inside, the noise of several sporting events was being broadcast on numerous large screens. No one paid any attention to us as we entered.

Darby sat alone at the bar, staring into a glass of honey-colored liquid, an empty shot glass in front of him.

I lifted my chin, pointing him out to Natalie. As we approached, his face snapped in my direction. His eyes widened as he glanced at the door, then around the room. "Fuck! What are you doing here?"

I mocked looking surprised. "What a coincidence. I didn't know you'd be here."

From Darby's continuous survey of the room, I suspected he didn't believe me.

"This is my wife, Natalie." To her I said, "This is one of our dispatchers."

The corners of her mouth turned up. Her hand lifted, dropped, then she held it so he could shake it.

A grimace crossed Darby's face before shaking her hand. "I can't talk to you."

"Then don't." I rested my butt on the stool beside him. "We're here to have a drink. Natalie's had a stressful day."

She leaned against the bar beside my stool.

"What can I get you?" the busty bartender with the tight referee shirt asked.

A scotch, even a beer, would be great right now, but wouldn't mix well with the Percocet I had taken while waiting for Natalie. "Club soda for me and a…"

"Chardonnay," she said.

Darby took a gulp of his drink, then fumbled in his rear pocket like he was fishing for a wallet.

"Relax." I gave up on the pretense. "No one knows we followed you here."

"How do you know? I didn't know you'd tailed me."

Good point. I had been watching him and not surveying the cars behind us. I shrugged. "Why would anyone want to follow us?"

Darby waved a credit card at the bartender. "After my shift, I had to go talk to the director of dispatch and tell him everything we'd discussed when you ambushed me."

"Why are they interested in that?"

He gave his head a furious shake. "I was reminded I'm not to talk to *anyone* about dispatching your flight without the director of dispatch and the company attorney present. They've hinted, *not too subtly*, that if I ignore that order, my employment with Sphere will be re-evaluated."

"Why? There was nothing wrong with the aircraft. I never sent any messages stating otherwise. Or so the NTSB believes."

The bartender set Natalie's and my drink down. "Want to start a tab?"

"Sure," I said.

"Close me out." Darby held out a credit card.

"His is on me." I hoped to remove the enmity between us.

Darby shook his credit card. "No."

The bartender frowned before walking off with his card.

From my side, Natalie said, "Bill may never walk without a limp. The estates of two people killed in the accident are suing us. We'll lose everything. We need to know why they're hiding those messages."

Her words eased the rigidity in him. "I'll lose everything too if I'm seen talking to you." He gulped down the rest of his beer.

"Thanks for stopping by." The bartender set Darby's credit card and receipt down.

"What are they afraid of?" I asked.

Another vigorous shake of his head while signing his name.

"Did the NTSB interview you?" I considered snatching up his credit card and not giving it back until he talked. But I feared he'd make a scene, something both of us hoped to avoid.

"Of course." He stuffed his card in his wallet in hurried gestures.

"Since they don't know about the messages we exchanged, you lied during a federal investigation." I paused. "I think that's a felony. Are you prepared to go to prison? Lose your dispatch license? Because I intend to prove the accident wasn't my fault."

A glare was pointed my way.

"Natalie's not lying. We *are* being sued. I'll have you called as a witness and you can lie under oath that we didn't discuss something being wrong with the aircraft and face perjury."

His nostrils flared. "They'll fire me for sure. I've got nothing to live on if I lose my job."

I leaned toward him. "You think I want to live with the guilt of thirty-eight dying from something that wasn't my fault? Or lose our house and retirement?"

When Natalie's hand rested on my shoulder, I leaned back but kept staring at him.

His barstool threatened to fall over when he shoved it back. "Look, I'm sorry about your situation. I really am. But *please* leave me out of this. Please."

"If the situation were reversed, would you do the same?"

He dropped his head. His shoulders rose and fell, then he glanced around the room. "I'd see if Arinc has a copy of those messages."

He left without a backward glance.

Chapter Thirty-Five

Since the next day was Saturday, there would be no one at Arinc who could provide me with a copy of the messages I had sent. That left me with no excuse to avoid paying my condolences to Ned's wife, Alicia.

It had been a month since I had gotten out of rehab. Two since the accident. I should've made this trip, or at least called, long before this. Alicia probably thought I was deliberately avoiding her. I would if I'd been in her position. But if the situation had been reversed and Ned had been the survivor, I knew he would not have been so delinquent.

Initially during the two-hour drive, we were silent. What would we say? Alicia had to resent the fact that I survived but Ned didn't. Would she blame me for his death?

Natalie turned the music down. "I've been thinking about the dispatcher's worries of being fired. If you continue to look into why Sphere deleted your messages, could they fire you?"

"I suppose. Since the NTSB put the cause of the accident squarely on me, it'd be easy to justify giving me the heave-ho. And since the union has been sitting on the sidelines, I doubt they'd step up and fight for me."

If that happened, we'd lose my sick leave and probably disability insurance.

She shifted in her seat.

"Spill it. We need to be open about what we're going through or this will tear us apart." I already carried a planeload of guilt from putting us in this position. Instead of being the jovial woman she was, Natalie now was withdrawn, the fine lines around her mouth and face more prominent.

She sighed. "If we sit back and let Tori Killinger fight the lawsuit, regardless of the outcome, we'll lose everything when you did nothing wrong."

I liked hearing her say that last part of her statement and expressed my admiration.

"If we try to prove the accident wasn't your fault, you could be fired before we can sell our house, it will be foreclosed, and our credit ruined. The equity we have in it will be tied up in the foreclosure and our lawyer may not represent us if she feels we won't be able to pay her."

"Well, when you lay it out like that, things seem pretty bleak." Though I tried to lighten the mood, her comment reawakened the gloom I had shoved aside after hearing the cockpit voice recorder.

"Do you think the NTSB will find those messages and exonerate you of blame?"

The discussion I had with Masters and Tippen after hearing the recording troubled me. "I doubt it. They probably think they are nonexistent."

"We can't have the house foreclosed." She glanced my way. "That'll ruin us. We'll have a hard time renting a dump if our credit is crap."

Regardless of whether I agreed with my wife, she had to face reality. "We can't hope the NTSB will be working on our behalf. They seem satisfied with the preliminary cause."

"Didn't you say you thought that woman... what's her name again?"

"Lori Masters."

"Yeah, her. Didn't you feel she thought something in the preliminary report wasn't right?"

"Kinda. It seemed she was working on her own to figure out what happened. I just don't know how much we can depend on her to help us."

"Call her. Tell her the dispatcher lied. That Sphere deleted your messages. Maybe that'll convince her Sphere is hiding something and she'll dig deeper."

I had intended to do that but wanted to get a copy of those messages from Arinc beforehand. When I emailed a copy of them to Mrs. Masters, in the body of the message I planned to type in bold font, *See. I wasn't lying.* But she did need to know Darby had misled them. "Okay. Good idea."

An hour east of the Denver airport, at the town of Genoa, we turned off I-70 and drove north on a two-lane country road. For as far as we could see, hundreds of windmills turned slowly. "Ned told me he hoped to have a couple of those put on his land to generate some income."

"I wonder if his wife will still consider it."

"If I don't recover enough to fly again, it'd be nice if I did something that was useful. Like building those." I gestured out the windshield. "It'd be satisfying knowing what I did helped the environment and reduced our dependence on foreign oil. I'd go crazy if I sat behind a desk nine to five doing something that didn't matter other than bringing home a paycheck."

The warmth Natalie expressed from my declaration had not been evident since that fateful day. Hell, since I decided to build the airplane. We used to share our thoughts and dreams, knowing the other was the one person to whom we could openly express what was on our minds. Why had I allowed us to drift apart?

We came to an area of trees that covered several acres. A gravel track wound through the middle of them. The mailbox at the end of the drive had *Partin* lettered on it.

"This must be it." Natalie turned onto the driveway. "You ready?"

This wasn't the first time I'd visited family or friends who'd lost a loved one. Before each visit, my mind blanked, not knowing how to act. I had to work at being a good listener or someone to depend on. On the other hand, I disliked those who put on false pretenses or avoided humor, as if making the grieving person laugh was insensitive.

Today, those same feelings clamped down on my gut. Accompanying them were the what-ifs that had clogged my thinking since waking in the hospital. If we had rejected the takeoff, returned to San Salvador, or diverted, Ned would be alive.

To Natalie's question, I nodded.

A couple hundred yards down the drive, we came to a fork. A rectangular ranch home with thin, newly seeded grass sat several car lengths down the gravel drive. Two children's bicycles sat on their sides behind a SUV. "Alicia said their house was at the end of the main driveway." I pointed out the windshield.

Further down the driveway, the trees opened to reveal a two-story home across from several farm buildings. The paint on the clapboards of the home was not peeling or cracked. The windows, smaller than what would be installed if it were built today, shined. The grass was mowed.

One farm building, the largest, was as large as an aircraft hangar, with shiny metal siding as if built within the last few years. The others wore weathered cedar shingles. Their walls were straight and plumb.

A field of corn off to the side of the buildings looked full and healthy.

A boulder filled my throat while visualizing Ned, with his wry grin, walking out of one of those buildings. "I bet it's a lot of work keeping a place like this looking this good. I wonder how Ned found the time to fly for Sphere."

"How's she managing this on her own?" Natalie asked.

We were getting out of the car when the door to the house opened. A woman not much older than Lucas, dressed in jeans and a polo shirt, stepped out. She stopped on the porch, crossed her arms at her chest, uncrossed them, and splayed her fingers several times, then moved down the steps.

"You must be Bill?" the woman said.

I put my crutches under my arms and stepped toward her. I cleared my throat. "Ummm… yeah, hi. Bill Kurz. This is my wife, Natalie."

The woman ran her gaze up and down me. Was she looking for evidence of my injuries?

I'd deliberately worn khakis instead of shorts on this warm day so the ugly scar on my leg didn't stand out to announce I had almost lost it. If I could have gotten around without the crutches, I would have left them in the car.

The woman's mouth pursed and she blinked several times before she covered her eyes. She stomped her foot. "Damn it." Her shoulders shook as she turned away.

I'm not sure whether it was my paternal instinct toward this young woman or the natural action to comfort one in pain that overcame me. But without thought, I stepped close, let my crutches fall behind me, and engulfed her. "I'm so very sorry." She shuddered in my embrace. Emotion threatened to erupt from me, but I shoved it down. My eyes burned from the tears, blurring my vision.

The woman wrapped her arms around me. I hadn't expected that and we swayed toward my right leg, which threatened to give out on me. We might have ended up on the ground if Natalie hadn't come up behind me and supported me.

Ned's wife sobbed into my chest. "Why? Why?" she kept asking.

"I don't know."

When she had herself under control, she stepped back, wiping her cheeks. "I'm sorry. I haven't even introduced myself. I'm Alicia Partin."

Natalie handed me my crutches and said, "It's a pleasure to meet you." Her mascara had run.

Casey sat next to me and lifted a paw to Alicia.

"Well hello there." Alicia bent and petted Casey.

When I thought I could speak without the words coming out gibberish, I said, "I want you to know," I took a deep breath, "the accident wasn't Ned's fault."

A fresh wave of tears spilled down Alicia's cheeks.

"There had to be something wrong with the airplane." My voice wavered so much, I hoped she could understand me. "If Ned couldn't have kept the airplane on the runway, no one could've."

She hugged me again, squeezing so hard I winced from the jolt where my ribs had been fractured. Alicia stepped back, her mouth agape. "I'm so sorry." She covered her face and shook it. "I didn't even think about how badly you must've been hurt."

I shrugged, hoping I masked the stab that shot through me. "It doesn't matter. I'll mend."

A sad smile came to her. "Ned always looked forward to flying with you."

A memory from months ago came to mind. Ned got out of his seat to exit the airplane and preflight the exterior of the aircraft. He patted me on the shoulder. "You sit still. I'll get this," he had said. It was a joke, as the first officer almost always did the exterior inspection.

I expelled a deep breath. "I'll cherish the time I got to spend with him."

Natalie broke the awkward silence that followed. "This is a nice place you have."

Alicia glanced around. "I don't know for how much longer I can call it mine."

"Why?" I asked.

"I've made coffee. Would you like to come inside? I'll explain what we're facing."

Chapter Thirty-Six

We sat around Alicia's kitchen table with mugs of coffee. Casey rested on the floor between Natalie and me.

"Shortly after the accident, a group of lawyers approached me to be included in a lawsuit." Alicia's voice dripped with bitterness. "They were suing Sphere Airlines and Edwards Aerospace on behalf of the victims that lived in Colorado."

I attempted to hide my frown by taking a sip of coffee. That didn't add up with what we had learned about the lawsuit filed against us.

"When it became evident I would be suing you too," she turned to me, "I wanted nothing to do with it. Ned would roll over in his grave."

"Thank you." It amazed me that Ned enjoyed, possibly even respected me so much that he would express that to his wife and she would honor his belief. If she'd joined in the lawsuit against Sphere, Edwards, and us, she might've been able to live comfortably for years to come. The most Natalie got out of me was that the first officers didn't talk too much, or did, or were easy to work with. Had I praised Ned the way he had me?

"A week later, I was served papers," Alicia said. "I'm now being sued by the same lawyers that wanted to represent me."

And lawyers wonder why they have such a bad reputation. "Yeah, I saw you listed as a defendant in the papers served to us."

"Will you be able to keep your farm?" Natalie asked.

Fresh tears pooled in Alicia's eyes.

"No." She retrieved a box of tissues from across the kitchen and pulled a couple from it before dropping the box on the table when she sat. "My mother gave us half the farm after my father died a few years back with the stipulation we build her a house. You might've seen it when you drove down the driveway."

We nodded.

Her face became vacant as if reviewing a memory. "She put the entire farm in our name even though she still owned half of it. Each year, we give her twenty-five percent of the harvest proceeds. But in the eyes of the lawyers, we," she blinked a couple of times, "I own all of it."

I knew where the conversation was going and hated it.

"My mother has lived on these five hundred acres since she and my father married thirty-six years ago. This damn lawsuit will make us sell the only place she's lived her adult life. I won't be able to leave the farm to my kids."

Internally, I kicked myself for feeling so sorry for myself. As I had preached to Lindsey and Lucas numerous times, there was always someone who had it worse.

"I'm so sorry." Natalie held Alicia's hand. "Can you borrow from a bank to pay off the lawsuit?"

Alicia dabbed a tissue at her eyes. "No. We're heavily mortgaged to put in this year's crop and have the loan for my mother's house."

"What are you going to do?" Again, my parental instincts craved a way to help this woman. Since she wasn't much older than our children, I hoped that if Lucas or Lindsey were victims of a situation that threatened their well-being, someone would step up and lessen their burden.

Alicia stood and leaned against the sink, staring out the window. After a moment, she said, "I have no choice but to sell the farm. Several years ago, a large corporation that owns thousands of acres in the area approached us to buy it. Ned and I had hoped to hold out and keep it a family-run farm. I'll have to see if they're still interested."

She turned back to us. "All I know is farming. I don't know how I'll support my children. My mother's retirement was the proceeds from each year's harvest. I just wish so much," she swallowed and choked out, "Ned was here to talk about this mess I'm in."

Natalie and I exchanged a glance. As difficult as our situation was, we had each other.

"I'm sorry. I didn't mean to dump all this on you." Alicia rejoined us at the table. "I'm sure your situation is just as bad."

"Where are your children now?" Natalie asked.

"They're with my mother. I thought it'd be easier."

"Ned loved you all so much. Each time we flew together, he told me about your children's accomplishments and how hard you worked while he was away."

Alicia grasped my hand and gave it a squeeze. For a long moment, she stared at the table before lifting her gaze to me. "What happened on that landing?" She searched my face before turning away. "I'm sorry. You probably have tried to forget the accident."

In the same way I'd try to forget a nightmare. Except this one I didn't wake from.

"We ahh…we got an indication of a problem with the rudder on the takeoff from San Salvador." I summarized what I knew and heard on the cockpit voice recorder, telling her about my missing memory.

Her attention remained focused on me the entire time, with occasional glances at Natalie.

"From what I've pieced together from the video that was on the news and heard on the CVR ah… the cockpit voice recorder, Ned did everything possible to prevent that accident."

She pursed her mouth, blinking several times before another batch of tears dribbled out of her eyes.

"I'm not just saying that to make you feel better." I told her about the thud of the rudder pedal hitting the stop. "The investigation is not over. I'm sure the NTSB will realize we did everything we could."

I decided not to drag her into my belief Sphere was hiding evidence from the NTSB, or that they were reluctant to believe we'd stomped on the rudder. Today was to reassure her that her husband died being the competent pilot I knew him to be.

Her gaze roamed around the kitchen before resting on my face. "Did… did he…" she swallowed, "suffer?"

Our yells and cries amongst the other noises that were captured on the cockpit voice recorder flashed through my head. It seemed we both were shrieking as the aircraft tumbled. But with all the other noises of the airplane being mangled, and my emotional attachment, I could not definitively say Ned died instantly and those were my cries of anguish.

Had the NTSB isolated our screams by doing a voice print to determine if that was the case?

"No. He ah... he must've died instantly." I regretted that my answer was passive.

Regardless, she squeezed her eyes shut and expelled a deep breath before lifting the corners of her pursed mouth. "Thank you."

Natalie and I left some time later, promising to stay in touch.

When we drove past the driveway to Alicia's mother's house, we both looked down it. A boy chased a girl around in the yard. It could have been Lucas and Lindsey years ago. At the same time, we expelled sighs.

Natalie said nothing until we had turned onto the two-lane road. "What can we do to help her?"

"The same thing that would help us. Prove Ned and I weren't the cause."

"I don't care what you have to do. Do that. Find out what was wrong with that airplane. Our lawyer said the way to win the lawsuit was to show the accident wasn't your fault. Prove that so this family's lives aren't ruined."

Although freed to exact some revenge while damning the consequences of being fired, the significance of her decision weighed on me. "You're putting a lot on me. What if I can't prove something was wrong with the airplane?"

A glance that came my way wore a frown. "This from the guy who *had* to build his own airplane."

"What's that supposed to mean?"

"You had to prove to yourself you could build as good an airplane, if not better than anyone else." When I began to defend myself, she held up a hand. "Yes, you like building things and would enjoy flying it more than if you had bought one. But there's that part of you that wants to do something a little better than someone else. It's not a dominant characteristic, but you have this need to prove to yourself you're worthy of any challenge."

Did I?

"Not only do I see it in how you took on building the airplane, you do it skiing. When we ride up the lift, you're watching someone skiing effortlessly down a difficult trail. On the next run, you ski the same trail, mirroring the previous skier. It's like you have to prove you're as good a skier as the one you watched."

I had thought I had been challenging myself to do better; whether it was flying, skiing, or building. Was she right? Could I be so insecure I had to prove I was as good, or better, than someone else? She hadn't mentioned I applied this characteristic to how I treated others, or worked that principal in our marriage.

"I know part of the reason you went to D.C. and to your dispatch center was *you wanted* to prove the NTSB was wrong. Morally, you feel the real cause needs to be known. But you feel challenged. I know you're trying to prevent us from being financially ruined, but your ability as a pilot has been tarnished and you need to prove no other pilot could have prevented that accident."

"Well, yeah." I was about to point out that if one of her patients had died while in her care and she was accused of negligence, she would do the same thing. But her next statement prevented me from getting defensive.

"So, don't act like you doubt you can uncover the truth. I *know* when you're faced with a challenge what the outcome will be."

Chapter Thirty-Seven

How would I prove the accident wasn't my fault or Ned's when the NTSB with their vast experience and resources had not? They had subpoena power to get people to talk to them that I did not. If employees of Sphere were willing to withhold evidence and lie about it to federal authorities, how did little ol' me prove this?

As much as I resisted including them, I had to make the NTSB a part of *my* investigation.

I called Mrs. Masters Monday morning.

"I'm glad you called, Bill. After we met, a group of investigators went to Dallas to test the rudder pedal potentiometer to see if it measured rudder pedal movement correctly."

"What'd you find out?" I sat rigid in my seat, hoping the results would make my crusade needless.

"The test confirmed neither you nor the first officer depressed the rudder pedals more than forty percent of their travel."

Damn. "Why were you testing the potentiometer?" Had they done the test incorrectly? I know I heard a rudder pedal hit a stop. Maybe my determination had pushed them to look further.

"We wanted to confirm the unidentified noise on the CVR wasn't a rudder pedal reaching the end of its travel."

Was that thud the pedals hitting something that blocked them from reaching their limit? "Something blocked the rudder pedals then."

"That's what I suspected too." Masters' tone was as if discussing a problem with a coworker, not someone trying to prove her organization was wrong. "But we cannot find any evidence that the rudder pedals or its linkage were restricted."

Meaning: They still thought Ned and I caused the accident.

"Here's something that can shed some light on this situation," I said. "The dispatcher for the flight lied to you. He remembers we exchanged messages shortly after takeoff that the standby rudder light came on."

"That's not what he reported to us when we interviewed him." Masters' voice was challenging.

"Sphere has threatened to fire him if he discusses the flight without the director of dispatch and the company lawyer present. They've coerced him to lie to you."

A pause. "How did you get this information?"

I explained my visit to the dispatch center, getting kicked out, and following Darby to the bar.

Another pause. "What you're implying is your airline is withholding evidence from the investigation."

"I'm not implying, I know they are. I sent messages that something was wrong with the aircraft. Since you're unware of them, they realize those messages indicate the rudder issue I reported caused the accident."

"Why would they go to such extremes?" Masters' voice was skeptical. "I've worked with some airlines that have taken drastic measures to disguise their negligence. But in this case, if maintenance's work had prevented the rudder from operating correctly, they'd be better off accepting the fine the FAA would impose and implementing the corrective measures the NTSB would recommend and the FAA would demand. If they're deliberately misleading a federal investigation, the FAA will likely shut the airline down. Someone will go to prison."

I had not considered these issues. "Maybe they're worried about the lawsuit filed against them, Edwards Aerospace, the first officer's family, and mine. If they can blame me and the first officer, they won't have to pay up."

"Sphere will have insurance to cover a lawsuit. Why would they risk being shut down to avoid one?"

"I don't know. Maybe they thought if the blame for the accident was put on me, I couldn't sue them." I knew I was grasping. What she said was relevant. "Get a copy of the messages I sent and you'll realize they're up to something. Sphere's datalink provider, Arinc, should have a copy of them."

When another pause dragged on, I wondered if she was a deep thinker or distracted by something else.

"Here's the problem I'll have," she eventually said. "There are many in the investigation that feel the trip to Dallas was a waste of time. All it proved was what had already been established. You and the first officer did not maintain directional control on landing."

I fought the urge to yell into the phone, *because we couldn't.* Since I couldn't remember that, I knew I'd come across as defensive.

"So, convincing my superiors to get a subpoena won't happen."

"Convince them. You'll discover *there are* messages that were withheld from you that prove something was wrong with the rudder system on that approach. If Sphere would hide that evidence from you, what else might they withhold?"

When Masters didn't say anything, I lost all semblance of being cordial. "My wife and I visited the widow of the first officer this weekend. Because something was wrong with the airplane and you and your organization seemed *unable* or *unwilling* to find the real cause, this young woman will lose the farm that has been in her family for two generations. She and her two young children will have no means of income."

I hoped my words were hitting home since the photo on Mrs. Masters' computer suggested she was a mother.

"I've already discovered information you were unaware of and now are dismissing as irrelevant. This will be used to defend us in the lawsuit brought against us and Mrs. Partin. I'll be sure the media gets a copy of it too.

"I. Was. Not. The. Cause. Of. The. Accident."

Chapter Thirty-Eight

After hanging up on Mrs. Masters, I sat at Natalie's computer—could we afford to replace the laptop I lost in the accident?—and looked up a number for Arinc, the company that transferred data to and from Sphere's aircraft.

After being passed off to several people, I reached someone who answered, "Campanella."

I identified myself. "I was the captain on the Sphere flight 9100 that had the accident in DFW a couple of months ago."

"Oh. Okay, uh… sorry to hear about your misfortune. You're obviously okay then."

That was open for debate, but I'd save the sympathy card for later if I needed it. "Thank you for your concern. The reason I'm calling is, somehow, all the messages I sent through ACARS during that flight weren't turned over to the NTSB. Since the copy they have came from Sphere, I suspect Sphere's copy must be corrupt." Not alluding to fraudulent behavior would get what I needed quicker. Otherwise, Campanella might have to consult with his management, possibly even their legal department. "I'd like to get a copy of those messages so that the NTSB will have all the data they need to fully investigate the accident."

"Why doesn't the NTSB subpoena us for them?"

I was afraid he'd ask that. "They're reluctant to believe the data provided by Sphere is inaccurate."

"Well, then, I'm afraid I can't help you."

My hands began to tremble. "I'm being blamed for the accident. Those messages will reveal there was something wrong with the aircraft. Don't I have a right to have them so I can prove I wasn't at fault?"

"Hey, I hear you and understand what you're saying. But unfortunately, you're not our customer. Your employer, Sphere

Airlines, is. Therefore, unless the Director of Dispatch or his superior submits a written request for a copy to be turned over to you, I can't provide you with one."

I massaged my forehead. "Here's the reason I need it. Since the NTSB has put the majority of the accident's blame on me, the estates of two of the people killed in the accident are suing me. To defend myself in the lawsuit, I'll need a copy of those messages."

"Then have your lawyer get a subpoena."

"I was trying to do as much of the leg work as I could, as the legal fees are going to break us. We'll have to sell our home and raid our retirement. On top of that, I might not be able to work again."

"Look, I feel bad for you. Hell, from what I saw on the news, I'm surprised you're alive. I'd like to help if I could. But we have a strict policy of not releasing data unless authorized by our client or issued a subpoena." A pause. "Can't you get the Director of Dispatch to request this data? If their copy is corrupted, I'm sure they'd want to help the NTSB as much as they could."

I debated if I wanted to forewarn him that Sphere didn't want Arinc's copy of my messages revealed. Instead, I said, "Would you please make sure a copy of those messages is backed up and stored in a secure location? My lawyer will be getting a subpoena for them."

But my warning was lost on him. "No problem. When we get the subpoena, we'll send them along to your lawyer."

"I'm very serious here. I need a copy of those messages stored where a hacker can't break into your system and delete them. At this point, I wouldn't be surprised if that happened."

"You've got nothing to worry about. We've never lost any of our clients' data."

I hoped it stayed that way.

My next call was to Tori Killinger to explain the need for a subpoena. She took down the information Campanella gave me.

"When we get that far into the case, I'll request one from a judge."

"Why can't you get one immediately? Those messages will prove there was something wrong with the aircraft hours prior to the accident. They just might get the lawsuit dismissed." I knew I sounded exasperated but didn't care.

"It's up to the plaintiffs to identify why they feel you're guilty of negligence. Until I discover how they intend to prove that, I don't want to tip their hand and begin issuing subpoenas for information that'll help prove your innocence. It might reveal aspects of the case they were unaware of."

What she said sounded reasonable. Or, was she trying to keep this case alive for the billable hours? "Okay. I'm just worried Sphere will somehow make those messages disappear."

"If that were to happen, and we can prove that, they'll have sealed their fate in court."

I wanted to remind her that evidence gets lost all the time. But she knew more about that than I.

On the company's internet, which I luckily still had access to, I got the name of the Director of Maintenance for Sphere's hangar here in Denver.

After calling and arranging a meeting, I found Natalie in the garage, stirring a can of deck stain.

"Will you please drive me to Sphere's hangar?"

"Why?"

Her question dripped with innuendo. She had listened to my side of the previous conversations and heard my disappointment. Was she feeling this too was a waste of time? Or, now that she was motivated to begin the chore she wanted my help with last year, was she resistant to me pulling her from it again? Or, did she simply want to know why I wanted to go there?

"I want to know what the director of maintenance there thinks of San Salvador's work. I could call him, but in person I can judge whether he's telling the truth."

"Won't he be as reluctant to talk to you as the dispatcher was?"

"I'm using the same pretense I used before. That I'm writing a newsletter about maintenance inspections while laid up."

She smirked. "Don't you think they'll catch on to that?"

"Sphere Airlines has over seventy thousand employees spread across the globe. They're so big and departmental, one group of people has no idea what another is doing. I doubt a company-wide email has been sent out warning *everyone* not to talk to me. If I can't remember a first officer I flew with a month ago, it is unlikely a maintenance supervisor will remember I was in the accident two months ago."

"Let's hope not."

"Why would he have agreed to meet me if he's not going to talk to me?"

"I don't know." She hammered the lid closed on the stain. "Maybe to see what you're trying to find out?"

She had a point. How many people could I talk to before I was terminated and prevented from getting the information I needed to exonerate Ned and me?

At the hangar, a man dressed in the mechanic's uniform of navy-blue pants and gray shirt pointed out the director's office: up four flights of stairs. Luckily there was an elevator.

At that office, a balding man typed at a computer. "Mr. Harting?"

He glanced at me over the top of his glasses. "Yes?"

"I'm—"

"Bill Kurz." The man expression was flat, filled with apathy as if suspicious of my intentions.

Natalie stiffened. I'd be hearing about this later.

During our brief conversation on the phone, I had found Harting affable. Obviously, I was wrong.

"You told me you were laid up. Apparently, you are." Harting's face softened while his gaze traveled up and down me. "It must be a bitch getting around on those things."

My tension eased that my name hadn't registered with him. "That's an understatement. This is my wife and chauffer, Natalie."

He stood and shook our hands.

"How is it a pilot can marry such a lovely woman? Didn't anyone warn you about becoming attached to a pilot?"

Natalie's pursed lips turned up. "No, but I wish they had. It would've saved me a lot of grief over the years."

If I wasn't nervous, I might've joked that she only married me for the flight benefits.

"Have a seat." Harting sat. "So, what can I tell you about maintenance inspections?"

Digging out my pen and notepad, I asked about the different types of inspections, how often each happened, and what was inspected during each. I took copious notes as if I were writing a newsletter.

Natalie sat with her hands in her lap, seeming to follow along in the conversation. Then her face went slack and her eyes glazed over. I'd be just as bored if listening in to her and a colleague discussing health care.

After thirty minutes of questions that were occasionally interrupted by Harting getting phone calls, I approached the subject I had come to really ask about. "Are all these inspections completed at Sphere Airlines hangars?"

He scowled. "Yes, except the C-checks. The one where they strip the aircraft of its interior and examine the entire airframe. They're becoming farmed out to other facilities."

I feigned surprise. "Oh. Where are they done?"

"The B777s, B757s, and EA330s are done in Hong Kong."

"Hong Kong?" This time it was easy to act surprised.

"Yeah, like everything else in this country, the Chinese are doing what Americans used to."

I nodded. "What about the 220s? Where are they done?"

A heavy sigh. "Until recently, they were done in house. We're now using a place in El Salvador."

Natalie shifted in her seat.

"Really? You mean... we can fly an aircraft down there and back empty and it's still cheaper than doing it at our own facilities?" After the standby rudder light illuminated, Ned and I had questioned if cheap labor in the Central American country might not be worth the price.

"From what we're told, it's significantly cheaper. I don't know the exact number, but it must be significant." A sigh escaped him. "You heard the mechanics got a new contract?"

The change of subject jarred me, until I realized where Harting was taking it. I nodded.

Ned and I had discussed this on the flight to DFW. It was of interest to us since the pilots' contract was being negotiated at the same time. If the mechanics got a raise, it looked good for the pilots to get one too.

"They got a substantial raise and more benefits," Harting said. "It will cost Sphere an additional two hundred and fifty million dollars over the four years of the contract's term."

It still baffled me that the one hundred seventy passengers I flew on my flights generated enough revenue to cover these staggering numbers. But Sphere flew three thousand flights a day and some had twice the number of passengers than my flights carried, and to the lucrative international destinations.

"You know how those bean counters in the ivory tower think." Harting folded his hands over his ample belly. "They aren't going to give the mechanics a quarter of a billion dollar raise if they don't make cuts somewhere."

"So, if the mechanics want a raise, they have to allow outsourcing to cheaper facilities," I said.

Harting nodded.

"Won't some of them lose their jobs?" Natalie asked.

The maintenance director lifted his round shoulders and let them fall. "Probably. But every mechanic except the most junior ones hopes a furlough won't affect them. Even if it did, until they're on the street, they'd rather bring home a bigger paycheck than stand on principles."

"That's the reality of the American worker today." I shook my head. "Will having all the major inspections completed outside the company lower maintenance standards?"

For a moment, Harting rubbed his jaw. "I hate to say this, but not really."

"Why do you hate to say that?" I asked.

"I wish the aircraft would return to service with problems our guys had to correct. The additional time the aircraft was out of service and the cost to correct those issues would make the company realize they weren't saving any money and return the work in house. Or, the FAA would realize aircraft were not being inspected as spelled out in the maintenance manuals and prevent us from using the vendors."

"But that's not the case."

"The Chinese have their act together. The aircraft coming from their shops are as good as our guys would do. I don't know about El Salvador. We've only been using them three months and the aircraft returning from there fly into DFW before going back to the line."

"Oh?" I hoped my disappointment didn't show.

Natalie squirmed.

"I have to wonder though," Harting frowned. "Even though the crew got blamed for the accident in DFW, there must've been something wrong with the aircraft. Something that prevented them from landing safely."

I avoided glancing at my wife, knowing it'd be hard to mask the glee that someone didn't feel I was incompetent. "Wh... why do you say that?"

"I've ridden in the cockpit of our flights hundreds of times. Our pilots are as good as any other airlines'. If the accident happened on a routine flight, I'd think they experienced a gust that exceeded the capabilities of the aircraft. But since the aircraft landing before ours had no problem and this was the aircraft's first flight after a major maintenance inspection? Come on. That accident wasn't the crew's fault. I hope the NTSB finally figures that out and exonerates them."

A frown came to him as he glanced at my crutches leaning against the desk. "Were you the captain on that flight?"

Chapter Thirty-Nine

I tried to slow the hammering of my heart. Harting's question seemed harmless, but if I confirmed I was the accident captain, would an avenue of figuring out what had been wrong with the aircraft be closed? Would whoever was withholding information from the NTSB hear about another one of my visits and have me fired?

Instinct told me Harting had simply put together my injuries and questions and was curious. Everyone at the airline who had contact with our pilots had probably racked their brain, wondering if they knew the crew of the accident. Those who might've put a face to our names would've questioned if we were so incompetent we would allow our aircraft to crash.

I turned to Natalie and lifted my brow.

She nodded.

"Yeah, I... I flew that flight." The tension that made me rigid in the last few moments slackened but didn't relax its grip on me.

"Shit! You're lucky to be alive."

I blinked away the memory of Ned's bulging, lifeless eye.

"Why didn't you tell me?" There wasn't any anger in his voice at being played.

I wiped the sweat from my forehead. "Ah... like you said," I decided to take the plunge and trust him, "we too feel there was something wrong with the aircraft. But it seems the company is trying to prevent that from being known."

His eyes narrowed. "Really? How?"

If he was an actor trying to extract information from us by playing dumb, he was a damned good one. After a calming breath, I told him about the standby rudder light coming on, communicating with the dispatcher, and those messages going missing.

Harting leaned back in his chair, his face still lined with suspicion. "Does the NTSB or FAA know that?"

"Yes."

"And they're not doing anything about it?" Disbelief filled his voice.

I explained the NTSB was relying on the rudder position data. "They've been reluctant to believe me since I can't remember the accident."

"You can't remember the accident?"

"It's a common occurrence for victims of trauma to not remember the event," Natalie said in the same clinical tone she would use if explaining high blood pressure.

He rocked his chair back and forth with a thoughtful expression.

I hadn't come here expecting to ask this question, but decided to pounce on what seemed like an opportunity we shouldn't pass up. "Can you see what was worked on during my aircraft's inspection?"

He glanced at his watch and turned to his computer. "Like was the rudder or its systems overhauled?"

"Yeah." I smiled at Natalie, conveying that we hadn't wasted our time coming here.

I doubted Harting would find anything incriminating. The NTSB would've looked at the same records. But it seemed the right placed to start.

Natalie's shoulders had relaxed from their hunched position a few minutes ago. She turned her gleaming eyes to me with that excited expression of hers I loved.

"Do you remember the tail number of that aircraft?" Harting stared at his monitor.

It would be a number I'd never forget.

He typed the digits I gave him, then frowned. "Access denied. What was that number again?" The computer keys clicked. "It's not letting me look at it. I can look at any of our seven hundred aircraft. Even the ones removed from service and sitting in the desert waiting to be sold. If I were doing this from home, I could understand it. But here on the company network? Let me call someone in records." He lifted his phone.

"Before you do, you should know the dispatcher of that flight has been threatened to be terminated if he talks to anyone about the flight without the director of dispatch and the company lawyer present."

The phone clunked back in the cradle. "So, you're telling me if I ask around about this, whoever is hiding information from the feds could make trouble for me?"

"Yeah."

"So this whole writing a newsletter thing was just a way to get information without the higher-ups knowing?"

I expressed my regret. "Sorry."

To Natalie he said, "This is why you shouldn't have married a pilot. You can't trust them." His smile eliminated any mistrust his statement had created.

He rocked his chair more. "So, you're digging into this because you worry the company will prevent the NTSB from finding the truth? Are you that insecure you need to prove that you're not a bad pilot?"

I smiled, knowing he was joking.

Natalie had slid to the edge of her seat. After she detailed the lawsuit we and Alicia faced, Harting shook his head. "Christ."

"What do you know about the rudder system of the 220?" I asked.

"Not much. When I was turning wrenches, we didn't have them. Why? What's your question?"

"The only reason I know for the standby rudder light to come on is because the A and B rudder actuators have been disabled because of the force/fight protection. Does that imply something jammed those two actuators, preventing them from moving the rudder?"

"Probably." Another glance at his watch. "Like I said, I'm not the expert." He flashed a smile. "But I have a bunch of guys under me who are." He held up his hands when I straightened to speak. "Don't worry. I can ask questions without raising any suspicions."

I eased back into my seat, grateful we finally had an ally.

"I'm sorry to cut this short, but I have to be on a conference call in a few minutes. Let me ask around, *discretely*, and I'll give you a call."

We stood. While I got my crutches under me, Natalie said, "Thank you. You don't know what a relief it is to have someone helping us."

"It's the least I can do." When he walked around his desk to say goodbye, Natalie stepped up and kissed him on the cheek, making him blush.

When we stepped out of the elevator on the hangar floor, I stopped to admire a 757. Russell had been flying this model when he retired. It was an aircraft I too had hoped to fly. Through the open doors of the hangar, the familiar whine that was deeper in pitch than other jets announced the arrival of a 220. It turned from a taxiway onto the hangar's ramp, then shut down. I sighed. Would I fly another one?

Natalie must have sensed my need to soak up the environment that had fulfilled me. She stood by my side without saying a word.

Stairs were pushed up to the cabin door, which opened a moment later. One of the pilots exited and looked into the hangar. He was a lanky man.

"Shit! Let's go." I turned and hurried off as fast as I could make my crutches move.

"What is it?" Natalie caught up to me.

"That's Marling."

She hurried on ahead and held the door to the parking lot for me.

Before stepping out, I glanced back through the hangar.

With a hurried pace, Marling was halfway between the 220 and the hangar.

We scrambled into the car and backed out of the parking space. The hangar door opened and Marling stared at us as we drove off.

Chapter Forty

Marling had to know why Natalie and I had been at the hangar. Since it was unlikely I had gone there to walk around an EA-220, or sit in one and reminisce, there had to be only one reason for us to be there. Our hasty retreat would only add to his suspicion.

If the airline was intent on hiding damaging details from the NTSB, they wouldn't like me attempting to dig it up. The easiest way to prevent me without drawing any attention to their actions would be to fire me. Without my airline ID, I couldn't enter the dispatch center or hangar. Revoking my access to the company's computer network would also hinder me.

"What do we do now?" Natalie drove fast, glancing in the mirrors often.

She must've had visions of Marling ordering armed men to intercept us and do unthinkable things. Although I thought that unlikely, I couldn't rule it out. The airline had two hundred and fifty million dollars' worth of reasons to silence us. I wished I had calming words to alleviate her concerns, something a husband should have. "Before I become what may seem like a disgruntled ex-employee, I need to tell the NTSB what we just learned."

Mrs. Masters would not like hearing from me twice in one day.

"Masters."

I identified myself and told her she was on speaker with Natalie. "We just talked to the director of maintenance at our Denver hangar." I filled her in on the revelation of the mechanics' new contract allowing outsourcing of maintenance. "Could this cheaper facility's maintenance have caused the accident?"

"We inspected the maintenance facility." Masters' tone hinted at being annoyed. "Everything was in order. The aircraft had been inspected as outlined in the maintenance manuals."

"Even though they documented they did the work correctly, they still might've forgotten a wrench in the rudder mechanism."

Silence came from the phone for several seconds. Had I touched on something not considered?

Then Mrs. Masters spoke in a measured voice. "Bill, this isn't the first accident the NTSB has investigated. We don't just check records to verify they are in order. In addition to checking the control mechanism, we questioned the technicians who'd worked on the aircraft. Those interviews did not suggest they were covering up any negligence."

From my reading of accident reports before I was involved in one, I suspected as much. "Something is fishy, though. The director couldn't pull up the maintenance record for my aircraft. He was locked out. Yet he can pull up any of our other aircraft."

"Maybe it's been restricted so that its records aren't tampered with while the investigation is ongoing."

"Yeah, maybe. Have you reviewed the maintenance records? Did anything stand out as not quite right that was easy to overlook?"

"Me? No. That's not my area of expertise. I'm an operations investigator. But I have reviewed a list of parts that were replaced during... "

I frowned. "If maintenance isn't your expertise, why were you looking at a list of replaced parts?"

"There was..." she paused. "I'm not at liberty to say why."

Natalie and I glanced at each other with furrowed brows.

"Let me get this straight. As an operations investigator, you were looking at a list of replaced parts?" I asked.

Mrs. Masters didn't respond.

"May I ask when you looked at this list?"

"Look, I've a ton of work I need to attend to."

"So now you're blowing me off." I didn't regret expressing my frustration.

"I'm not blowing you off. I don't need to justify my... or anyone else's actions involved in the investigation."

"If I hadn't questioned why one of my legs was injured more than the other, would you have asked me to hear the CVR so soon?"

Natalie had pulled her lips into a thin line.

"I can understand your frustration, but since you've never been involved in an aircraft accident investigation, you don't know the protocols that have to be followed."

That came across as a parent lecturing a child, telling them they didn't know as much as they thought. It raised my hackles. After a calming breath, I softened my tone. "I'm sorry for getting short. I'm..." She didn't need to hear again about the lawsuit and my being in constant pain. "Can I get a copy of that parts list?"

"What is it you think you'll discover that the numerous experienced investigators at the NTSB didn't?"

"A fresh set of eyes might find something that was overlooked." I knew I was reaching.

"I can't turn over data from an ongoing investigation. But while I've got you on the phone, I have a question."

"Go ahead."

"Did you do a control check before you began taxiing in San Salvador?"

"Of course," I said.

"Including the rudder pedals? Did you push them to the stop? Or just part way?"

"The most dangerous flight a pilot can make is with an aircraft that just had maintenance performed on it. So yes, I moved both the yoke and rudder pedals to their stops in all directions to make sure they weren't restricted. Something I do on every flight."

"Was there any resistance or binding?"

"No." I wanted to lecture her that wasn't my first flight, but held my tongue.

"Was either or both of yours or the first officer's seat position different than when you did that check?"

She was trying to figure out why we didn't deflect the rudder more than halfway on landing if I could push the rudder to its limit before takeoff. "I can't speak for the first officer, but it seemed he was sitting in the same position during the approach as he was when we did the flight control check. I know I was."

"Okay."

Again, I hated I couldn't remember the accident. The need was strong to tell her I had the rudder jammed against the stop before we went off the runway, but the aircraft didn't respond to that input.

Then a thought clicked into place that had occurred to me while talking to Harting. "Now I have a question for you."

"I can't promise I'll answer it, but go ahead."

"Well, actually, I have two. Did the FAA go with you when you inspected the maintenance facility in San Salvador?"

"Yes, they're part of the investigative team. If we'd discovered irregularities, they're the agency with the authority to impose fines, violations, or halt its operations. Why do you ask?"

"I'm wondering if one of them was that guy who grilled me at my hearing. Knowing the lucrative contract San Salvador has with Sphere might disappear if this aggressive inspector determines they screwed up, they might answer his questions however they thought would keep that contract."

"Inspector Cramp is an operations inspector. I doubt he inspected the maintenance facility."

"Did the FAA guys here in Denver who are responsible for overseeing Sphere's maintenance investigate the facility with your guys?"

"I wasn't a part of that visit since it didn't concern my area of expertise. Therefore, I don't know who went. Why?"

"If my accident was caused by shoddy maintenance, it might derail someone's career in the FAA who is responsible for overseeing our maintenance. Someone from the Denver office might've flown to San Salvador before your investigators arrived to make sure nothing made them look bad."

"I doubt that happened. Besides, our investigators were probably at the facility in San Salvador within a day of your accident. It'd be impossible to hide negligent maintenance standards in a few hours."

"Inspector Cramp seemed like he had an agenda." The memory of him shaking his head as I answered questions still made me grit my teeth. "Is he always that way? He gave me the impression he *needed* to blame me." I sounded insecure.

"Inspector Cramp... I think it would be best if I don't comment." Her voice was halting.

"Why? Did you feel he had an agenda?"

"Were there any more questions?"

I barred my teeth and pretended to choke the phone. That elicited a smile from Natalie.

"No. What... what if..." I had gotten so sidetracked letting Masters know I was pissed at Cramp, I had forgotten the train of thought I had. Then it returned. "What if the FAA's oversight of the maintenance facility was lacking. What might happen if my accident reveals that?"

"Do you have any proof of this?"

No, other than it would be harder for the FAA to monitor the maintenance practices of a foreign contractor than one in the states. "I'm just wondering what will happen if that was the case."

There was a pause. When she spoke, she did so as if weighing her words. "If the FAA was negligent in their duties, there might be a Congressional hearing at which individuals from the FAA would have to testify. From that hearing, changes would be handed down that the FAA would have to implement. Most likely, key individuals at the FAA would lose their jobs."

I hadn't thought of that. If—and this was a huge *if* since it was merely a conjecture—the FAA or individuals there were negligent in their duties and working with Sphere to hide data from the NTSB, they would probably be very aggressive in assuring that information stayed buried.

I thanked Mrs. Masters and said goodbye.

Natalie stared at the road with that wide-eyed look she had when Tori Killinger spelled out all we could lose in the lawsuit.

How did we prove something was wrong with the aircraft with such powerful, resourceful people working against us?

Chapter Forty-One

The next morning, the principal investigators from the NTSB, FAA, Sphere Airlines, and Edwards Aerospace sat at a conference table at the NTSB headquarters in D.C.

Jeff Hume, the NTSB investigator in charge, went around the room and asked each representative to update the others on open items in the investigation.

Lori Masters had deliberately placed herself next to Hume knowing he liked to go around the table clockwise. She would be the last to speak.

Though the details being discussed were relevant and informative, she knew her questions would shake up the investigation. She circled her foot round and round.

"Our records indicate," Sphere Airlines operations investigator Josh Pringer said, "both Captain Kurz and First Officer Partin were trained in gusty crosswind landings. That should have prepared them for the crosswind they experienced. We're just as confused as everyone why these two competent pilots used less than half the available rudder."

"There is that report of the first officer having to take the controls from Kurz." Bob Cramp looked over the top of his glasses at Pringer. "You might have a training problem?"

"At this time, we cannot determine that. The environment data from the time of the accident will be programed into our simulators. Every crew going through recurrent training will experience the same scenario that Kurz and Partin experienced. If we discover we have a problem, we'll administer additional training." He studied the tablet computer in front of him. "That's it for me."

"Alright." Hume typed a note on his own tablet. "Lori?"

"Sean," Lori looked across the table to the Edwards Aerospace maintenance specialist, "what parameters would require a rudder pedal potentiometer to be changed?"

Around the table, there were several sighs, a groan, and an exaggerated eye roll.

Before Sean Hayden could speak, Cramp turned his attention to Lori. "This was addressed when you wasted our time going to DFW. Why are you rehashing this again?"

Before Lori could respond, Hume did. "Because the NTSB would like to know what would require a potentiometer to be changed. That wasn't addressed at DFW."

She steadied her foot.

After Lori informed Hume about the stray tie-wrap she'd discovered and Liske blurting out that the potentiometer had been replaced during the inspection, Lori wasn't sure Hume bought into her suspicion that the potentiometer had been changed after the accident.

"It shouldn't matter when one is required to be changed," Corey Liske said. "It was established the one on the accident aircraft recorded full pedal movement. Why are we looking at something that has no bearing on the accident's cause?"

"Sean?" Lori avoided looking Liske's way, knowing she wouldn't be able to control her glare.

The Edwards Aerospace maintenance specialist glanced from Cramp to Liske before responding. "A faulty one would send a signal to the FRU, the fault recoding unit, located in the electronics compartment. The code would tell the maintenance tech the unit was malfunctioning."

"Is the potentiometer routinely replaced?" Lori asked.

"As I mentioned in Dallas," Liske took in the others at the table with raised eyebrows as if seeking assistance in moving off this subject, "the one on the accident aircraft had been replaced during its C check in San Salvador."

Cramp picked up his phone and began typing with one finger.

"Since it was replaced," Liske continued, "what is the point of learning how often one is replaced?"

Cramp set his phone down while looking at the closed glass door of the conference room.

"Yes, you did mention that," Lori said to Liske. "Regardless, I want to know how often they are changed."

"I agree with Corey," Cramp said. "Why are we wasting everyone's time for you to learn something that is not relevant?"

Folding his hands on the table, Pringer said, "She's not wasting mine. I'd like to know."

Hayden paused, as if waiting for someone else to voice his disapproval. "There is no specified replacement interval. They're replaced as needed."

"So, the only time an operator would replace one is when it sends a signal to the FRU that it was faulty?" Lori asked.

"That's correct."

"Who would have access to the fault recording unit?" Lori asked. "Would a pilot?"

"Normally, only a maintenance technician," Hayden said.

The door to the conference room opened and Ratliff stepped into the room.

Lori began circling her foot again.

"I'm glad you're here." Cramp nodded at Lori. "One of your investigators is, yet again, wasting everyone's time on the rudder pedal issue that's already been dismissed."

"She's not wasting mine." Pringer stared at Cramp as if challenging him.

Ratliff's gaze took in everyone's body language. Lori worried he'd side with Cramp and shut her down. Hume had briefed Ratliff about the potentiometer passing its test. Since then, it seemed he'd been keeping his distance from her.

"I'm sure Lori has a valid reason for asking her questions." He took a seat behind her against a wall.

She expelled a silent breath. "How often would a maintenance tech check the FRU?" She directed her question to Hayden.

Liske kept his face pointed at the table, the muscles in his jaw working.

"During the daily inspection when fluid levels and a walk-around inspection is completed," Hayden said.

"So an operator wouldn't replace a potentiometer routinely?" Lori asked.

"Aaron, really." Cramp faced Ratliff. "This has been established."

From behind her, Ratliff said, "Continue, Lori."

"That's correct," Hayden nodded. "In today's cost-cutting environment, an airline most likely wouldn't replace one on a routine basis."

"How expensive is each potentiometer?" Lori asked.

"I'm not sure." Hayden scratched his head. "As a guess, I'd say a thousand dollars a unit."

Lori turned to Liske. "Corey, does Sphere have that kind of profit to replace a thousand-dollar part when the one installed is working correctly?"

Liske squirmed. "I'm... I'm not sure I get what you're asking."

"You told me the potentiometer was replaced during the accident aircraft's C-check. There is no record in the maintenance records that the one on the aircraft was defective. So, does Sphere routinely change components that are working correctly that don't have a time limit?"

The pen Liske held clicked several times. "I'd have to check on that. The requirements on the different fleet types vary."

"Yes, please check later. But off the top of your head, would you say it's Sphere practice to do that?"

"I... ah..." Liske cleared his throat. "I hate to commit to an answer in case I'm wrong. You know, I don't want to be giving less than factual information."

Lori knew that was a dig at her for reprimanding him in Dallas to tell the truth. "I won't hold you to your answer if you find out later you were wrong. But as Sphere maintenance specialist, you must have an idea if that is done routinely."

"Routinely, no, I can't say that we do. We must've... ah... thought in this particular case it would probably be a good idea to replace it while we had the aircraft torn apart." Click click. "They're pretty hard to get at."

"Yeah, I can verify that fact." Lori worked her shoulders, remembering lying on her belly and stretching to attach the cable from the laptop to the one they tested.

Around the table, several smiled.

"So, if we check other aircraft that have recently had C-checks, we'll discover the potentiometer on those aircraft had also been replaced?"

Liske swallowed. "Well... one might've been malfunctioning at some point and replaced prior to its C-check, so we probably wouldn't replace it then. They do go bad occasionally."

"How often would they fail?" Lori asked, diverting her attention to Liske to Hayden.

Both paused as if waiting for the other to answer.

"Bob?" Lori asked.

"Initially, we had a batch that failed after the aircraft had flown approximately two thousand hours. We clamped down on the vendor and their quality control improved. Now a failure of one is almost nonexistent."

"Was the one installed on the accident aircraft from this initial batch?" Lori tried to quell her excitement. This might be the information she needed.

"Heck if I know," Liske said. "We get so many service bulletins for all the different aircraft, no one can keep track of what parts need to be replaced."

Lori leaned forward against the edge of the table but folded her arms, hoping it masked her anger that he thought she could easily be fooled. If Sphere could not implement the service bulletins the aircraft manufacturers issued because, "no one could keep up with them," the FAA would shut the airline down.

Cramp stared at the table in front of him, his body rigid. Why wasn't he intrigued Sphere admitted they couldn't track maintenance as required by regulation?

"I bet your parts tracking software can pull that information up," Lori said. "Why don't you look into this and get back to us?"

Liske blew out a breath. "That'll... that'll be pretty time-consuming. If the part number is the same for the newer potentiometer, it'll be difficult to figure out if the one on the accident aircraft was part of the defective batch or a newer one."

Liske straightened. "If the accident aircraft had a faulty unit installed, it was probably why it was replaced during its inspection."

Hayden shifted in his seat.

"Bob," Lori said and directed her attention to him. "Would the part number be the same?"

Hayden's chest rose and fell. "No."

"Correct me if I'm wrong, Corey," Lori said. "Since the part numbers are different, in a few keystrokes, you can look up if an aircraft had one part removed and another replaced with a newer part."

Looking anywhere but at Lori, Liske replied, "It's a bit more complicated than that. But I'll see what I can find out."

"Do that. From you, Bob, I'd like the dates and quantities of potentiometers you've shipped to Sphere, and where they were shipped to."

Cramp shook his head.

"Can we have this information when we meet again?" Hume asked.

Liske grimaced. "Ah…I'll try."

"Do more than try." Hume typed into this tablet.

Cramp dropped his glasses onto the table with a clatter. "Can I ask what this accomplished? What does it matter that Sphere replaces parts more often than required? If anything, they're more safety conscious than the regulations dictate."

Ratliff stood. "It showed the investigation is not concluded and the NTSB will not be misled." He looked at each person before leaving the room.

Lori relaxed her shoulders. The support he had given her was like a refreshing drink.

The silence in the room lasted a moment before Hume asked Lori, "Do you have anything else?"

She wanted to ask who from the FAA had inspected the San Salvador maintenance facility after the accident and when they arrived, but withheld those questions. She hadn't done the research to know if she was being bullshitted. "That's it for now."

"See everyone soon then," Hume said.

✈ ✈ ✈

After the meeting, Lori typed up her notes then went to Hume's office to discuss the meeting. As she approached his door, Ratliff walked out and met her stare without any emotion as he continued down the hall.

Through his glass wall, Hume flagged her in. "What's up?"

Stopping in front of Hume's desk, Lori questioned if Ratliff's support was out of obligation to support a fellow NTSB investigator. Or was he displeased the other investigative parties hadn't considered the issues she brought up? Not being a pat-on-the-back kind of leader, was he incapable of expressing his respect for her diligence and dwelling on the incompetence of others?

"Lori?" Hume frowned at her.

She sat to prevent herself from pacing. "Have you worked with Bob Cramp before?"

"Yeah, but this is the first time he's been the lead FAA accident prevention specialist. Why?"

"Was he always so antagonistic?"

Hume swayed his head left and right in a maybe gesture. "Not really. He's always been a little too eager to voice his opinion, but he seems more inclined this time."

"That's what I thought, too. Has he always been prone to blame the pilots rather than consider other aspects that contributed to an accident's cause?"

An exhale vibrated Hume's lips. "I guess. As you know, human error is the majority of causes. Why are you asking about him?"

"It strikes me as odd that since his background is operations, he challenges us when we bring up maintenance issues." This thought had manifested in her before, but her conversation with Bill yesterday, and Cramp's attitude today, refreshed it.

"He's probably just trying to keep the investigation moving along. I hear the FAA Administrator is demanding daily updates from him. He might've told the administrator the investigation was almost wrapped up and it was pilot error. Now when we're looking at other contributing factors, he might be worried he'll look clueless."

Are we *looking at other factors?* To her, it seemed she was the only one considering other aspects. Hume and Ratliff's support might've only been an appearance of solidarity. If she didn't prove something else prevented the crew from staying on the runway, would they let her dangle on her own? "Let's hope it's only that."

"You do realize your questions probably won't make anyone come forward and admit they changed the potentiometer after the accident, and why they did," Hume said. "You didn't reveal a smoking gun."

"No. But it puts everyone on notice, we're—" *I am*— "suspicious something else was going on. That we're still looking at everything. We need to go back to Dallas and test the fault recording unit."

Hume slouched. "For the sake of appeasing you—"

"Appeasing me? Aren't you—" The raised palm facing her shut her up.

"Let's hypothesize the potentiometer had been changed after the accident."

Inwardly, she bristled at the use of *hypothesize*.

"If we test the FRU and it tells us the one installed when the aircraft left San Salvador recorded a fault from the rudder pedal potentiometer, it doesn't exonerate the crew. The rudder only deflected forty-five percent. Even if the potentiometer was defective and unable to record a pedal deflection correctly, the rudder data indicated the crew didn't use all the available authority. The odds of the rudder pedal and rudder potentiometers both being defective is off the charts."

With conscious effort, Lori kept from standing so she could pace. "Regardless, we need to test the fault recording unit. If it shows the pedal potentiometer was not defective, why was it changed after the accident?"

"We don't know that it was." Hume's voice was sharp.

All sense of being cordial left her. "The tie-wrap I found under the potentiometer was the correct size for the one missing on the wire bundle. The wires where it would've been attached were cleaner than on either side of it. When confronted, the Sphere maintenance rep just happens to know it had been changed. His attitude," she pointed toward the conference room, "showed he's worried we'll discover that. The potentiometer was changed." She stated the last sentence through gritted teeth.

"Or he gets nervous being confronted." Hume returned her glare.

"Someone is worried we'll link the difference in the captain's injuries to something bigger. If the captain had done nothing, like everyone wants to claim, why is his right leg injured more than his left?"

Hume sighed. "Obviously, the way the aircraft tumbled caused the right side of his instrument panel to crush it."

"That's a conjecture you should've let me prove when I was in Dallas. Kurz isn't stupid. He'll have his lawyer hire investigators to measure the damaged aircraft against an undamaged one. If those measurements prove his theory is correct, how will we explain why we did not?"

Hume straightened. "Did you share your theory with him on his leg injuries?"

She scowled. "Of course not. He pointed out that discrepancy to me. He's not sitting around hoping to put this all behind him. He's attempting to prove thirty-eight deaths weren't his fault. If we don't take those measurements and test the FRU, and learn why the rudder moved more than the pedals, it'll come back to bite us in the ass."

Chapter Forty-Two

The day after Natalie and I went to the hangar, I was face down on the floor, grunting through extensions and flexions. I'd lift my leg as high as I could, holding it there while it felt like it was being torn off, before lowering it to rest on the floor. Then I would lift my lower leg toward my butt, bending my knee as much as I could, before returning my foot to the floor. It was debatable which of the two exercises was the most torturous.

My cell phone rang with the Imperial March. My body hummed while I debated answering it or letting it go to voicemail so I could prepare for the conversation that would be crushing. If it wasn't Marling requesting my presence with my company ID, it would be someone from human resources making that request so they could terminate my employment.

But, it might be Harting calling with maintenance information.

"Bill, this isn't a bad time, is it?" the maintenance director asked.

Had he picked up on my rapid breathing from my exertions? I rolled to my back. An old man could have done that with less effort. "No. It's a welcome break."

"Hey, I was having a conversation with a supervisor I've known for years who, like me, doesn't like management having our airplanes inspected outside the country."

"Yeah?"

"I told him I'd been wondering about our accident a couple of months ago and downloaded the preliminary report. I actually did that, by the way."

"Yet you're still willing to talk to the airline's worst pilot."

"After meeting you and reading that report, yeah. I'm convinced something is being covered up."

The feeling of gratitude for him grew. "That's good to know."

"So I told my buddy I couldn't believe one of our crews would be so incompetent, you know, to get a feel for how he'd react."

Since the accident, I hadn't talked to anyone from Sphere other than Marling. Unlike other occupations where coworkers saw each other daily, a major airline's pilot population was so large and spread out, I seldom flew with the same first officer more than twice a year, if ever again. Occasionally we might see each other in the flight planning areas or pass in the terminal. The same was true with the flight attendants and gate agents. That environment made it difficult to develop friendships with coworkers.

Still, it troubled me that no one came forward to rebut what asshole Obermiller claimed about my abilities. There were a handful of first officers and captains I had flown with enough to know I was competent. And knowing how charismatic Ned was, it surprised me that no captain spoke up for him.

"What'd he say?" I held my breath.

"He said he'd encountered a few assholes but doubted any would use only half the available rudder and let the aircraft go off the runway."

"I feel his characterization is accurate."

"I'm sure you guys have a few mechanics you don't think too highly of."

"There's a couple who are less personable than others."

Harting chuckled. "I like that. Less personable. Anyway, I told my buddy, as if I'd learned this from the accident report, that there was some suspicion about the standby rudder actuator powering the rudder at the time of the accident. I also informed him that maintenance control had MELed the light being on while the aircraft was in flight."

"What'd he say?" I worried he might say, *No way would the standby rudder actuator be powering the rudder. It's never happened before on an EA-220.* But I was surprised.

"Well, his comment went something like, 'What? Maintenance control MELed it without performing the maintenance functions first?' I wish I'd thought of this while you were here yesterday," Harting said. "If you look at the MEL procedures for that malfunction, maintenance is to perform tasks before they certify the flight can operate with that light inoperative. They have to do those procedures before each flight."

Ned and I had discussed this too.

"So MELing the light while the aircraft was in flight was illegal," I said.

"Oh, yeah. So my buddy was going to call someone he knew working in maintenance control," I sat up, "but I persuaded him that wasn't necessary. That I was sure the NTSB and FAA would figure that all out."

"Did you convince him?" Normally I would be glad our maintenance guys would review mistakes that had been made so they wouldn't happen again. But if Harting's buddy questioned maintenance control, whoever at Sphere was keeping data from the NTSB would be alerted.

"Yeah, I'm pretty sure he's placated. Together we looked up who had been manning the desk that day so that we could *potentially* bring it up in case the NTSB misses this mistake."

That eased the tightness in my shoulders, but not entirely.

"But between you and me, the NTSB will never learn of this blunder," Harting said. "Like your missing messages, the company has buried this mistake."

"I don't doubt that you're right."

"Oh, I know I'm right. We keep a history of every MEL we've applied so we can track how quickly we repaired the malfunction. And guess what?"

"There's no record of the accident airplane having the standby rudder on light MELed."

"Bingo. Either they didn't enter the procedure in the computer or went back in after the accident and deleted it."

The latter is what I suspected.

"If the FAA learns that, they'll shit their pants," Harting said. "Either one of those is a violation. Do you suppose that's why the company seems content to let you take the blame? That'd be a two-hundred-twenty-thousand-dollar fine."

I thought about that a moment before responding. "Possibly, but I doubt it. Two hundred twenty thousand dollars is a huge amount of money to you or me. But to our airline that generates several billion dollars a year in revenue, it's not as significant."

"It wouldn't surprise me, the way they're trying to cut costs wherever they can."

Was it that simple? "Yeah, but aren't we fined at least a couple of times a year on maintenance issues? If so, what's another one?"

A sigh came from the phone. "Yeah, you're probably right. So we're back to suspecting the company is covering up the faulty maintenance performed in San Salvador?"

"It's as you put it," I said. "The airline has a quarter of a billion dollars' worth of reasons to continue using that facility. If the accident sheds light on the fact maintenance isn't being performed correctly, they'll lose the use of that hangar."

"Any ideas how I—" I almost said *we* since he seemed engaged in the matter—"can prove this?"

"Well, I have one. Why don't you confront the guy working maintenance control that day?"

"That's not going to work." I told him about my visit to the dispatch center where maintenance control was located.

"Hang on." Harting's voice was muffled like he held the phone between his shoulder and cheek. The faint clicking of computer keys sounded. "Want the guy's home address? My buddy feels the guy on duty that day is a good guy, but pliable. He might've been pressured into applying the MEL the day of your accident, then forced to delete it. If you show up at his home on your crutches with that lovely wife of yours, and explain what you're going through, you might get the truth out of him."

Or it might alert the airline that I continued to nose around and get me fired sooner.

Chapter Forty-Three

That evening, Natalie and I drove to the town of Brighton, a suburb located twenty minutes to the northwest of the Denver Airport.

The two-story home we parked in front of was sided in clapboards with stone quoins. The other homes in this well-kept, middle-income neighborhood were similar in appearance. The minivan and pickup parked in the driveway appeared to be a couple of years old. The two-car garage door was open and several bicycles of various sizes leaned against the wall or on their kickstands.

"Nice looking place," Natalie observed.

"Yes." From the lack of moving boxes and haphazardness of the garage, it appeared the maintenance controller who lived here had not been paid hush money that he splurged on this home or new cars. But maybe the children's college funds had gotten a boost.

Flowers lined the sidewalk to the door and mulch that appeared to have been spread this spring surrounded the base of the several year-old trees in the front lawn.

At the front door, I pushed the doorbell and heard it ring inside. A moment later, a woman I guessed to be in her forties who had succumbed to middle-aged weight gain answered. "May I help you?"

Natalie stood at my side dressed in jeans and a short-sleeved blouse.

I'd deliberately worn shorts so the ugly red scar running down my leg was visible. I exaggerated leaning on my crutches. "Is Tucker Cunningham here?"

The woman ran her eyes up and down both of us. "And you are?"

"Captain Bill Kurz and his wife, Natalie."

Wrinkles spread across the woman's forehead. "Just a moment." She closed the door.

Since she didn't say he wasn't there, I was relieved he wasn't working an evening shift. If he had been, not only would it have been a wasted trip, he'd be alerted to our visit and could prepare for our return.

A minute later, a middle-aged man with the beginnings of a protruding belly opened the door. He gave us the same once over his wife had and asked the same question.

"I was the captain on flight 9100 that crashed in Dallas."

Cunningham recoiled.

Although I wanted to grab his shirt collar and ask why he'd lied to the NTSB and FAA, I decided to come across as a fellow concerned employee. "Were you working as the maintenance controller on the day of the accident?" I knew he had been. But I had learned that if I already knew an answer before asking the question, I could tell a lot about a person.

"Why do you ask?"

"We have some questions about the MEL that was issued after I took off from San Salvador. It isn't mentioned in the NTSB's preliminary report."

The whites of Cunningham's eyes became prominent. He glanced around us into the street. "I don't know what you're talking about."

Yeah, like hell. "Well, during takeoff, the standby rudder light came on, and I sent a message to the dispatcher asking if we should return to San Salvador to have it fixed. Instead, an MEL was sent to us."

Cunningham stuffed his hands in his pockets.

"Do remember issuing that MEL?"

He glanced over his shoulder and discovered that Mrs. Cunningham stood within earshot and was watching us. Mister stepped out onto the porch and pulled the door closed but didn't latch it. "I'm sorry. I don't know what you're talking about." His voice trembled. "So I'll have to ask you to leave."

"This is a nice home," Natalie said as she might to an acquaintance, but with her voice louder than conversational. She must've wanted the wife to hear her. "We're going to lose ours because we're being sued for something that wasn't Bill's fault."

Like me, Natalie must've suspected the wife knew nothing of her husband's involvement in the accident.

You go, Honey. I wanted to give her a hug but kept my concerned expression glued on my face.

Cunningham focused on Natalie with a frown.

"Since the NTSB doesn't know something was wrong with the airplane," I said, "I'm getting blamed for the accident. The attorneys for the people who died in the crash are suing us."

"We're going to lose our home, savings, and retirement. Bill may never fly again and will limp the rest of his life." Natalie expelled an overly dramatic sigh. "The first officer's wife and two young children will lose their family farm and become homeless."

That served the intended purpose, as Cunningham gave me another once over, staring at my leg.

"Look... ummm... I don't know what this has to ummm... do with me. So, I'd like you to—"

"If you think the airline will back you up when the NTSB discovers there was something wrong with the airplane, you're in for a rude awakening. They've hung me out on my own and they'll do the same to you."

"Get off my property." Although he barked this out, the quiver in his voice was prominent.

The door behind him opened enough for the wife to peer out.

"Look, I don't mean to trouble you with this, but the accident wasn't my fault. If you tell the NTSB there was something wrong with the airplane, we have a chance of winning the lawsuit."

His wife stepped out. "What's he talking about?"

"Go inside," Cunningham said. "I'll be in in just a sec."

The wife hesitated before closing the door partially. I suspected she had her ear to the crack.

"If you come forward before the NTSB questions you again, I'm sure they won't consider your first testimony a lie and have you arrested for obstructing a federal investigation."

"Isn't that a felony?" Natalie asked me.

I'd kiss her for that later.

The maintenance controller stared off to the side, his face vacant.

"Can you keep your A and P license if you have a felony on your record?" I referred to his Airframe and Power Plant license that all mechanics had to earn.

The door opened again. "Tuck, what're they talking about?"

"Your husband needs to do the right thing if you want to keep your home," Natalie said.

"Tuck?" The wife's eyes widened.

The gratitude I felt for Natalie bloomed inside me but I did not show it. If she had stayed in the car, this conversation might not have reached his wife the way it had. Without her, I might have come across as a finger-pointing victim.

"You need to leave now." Mr. Cunningham's words had lost their bite.

Like the dispatcher, he probably had been pressured into lying to the NTSB. As time passed without any consequences from that subterfuge affecting him, he probably thought nothing would come of it. Now he knew he faced life-altering matters he couldn't ignore anymore.

"Again, I apologize for involving you in this mess." Being in a similar position, I truly felt sorry for what he was going through. But if he continued to lie and expect Sphere to stand behind him, there wasn't anything I could do for him. "Why the accident happened will come out and the airline will look to blame whoever they can so that they aren't held responsible."

"Tucker?"

"We'll leave now, as you and your wife have some talking to do." Natalie stepped off the porch.

I knew how that conversation would go if someone had shown up at our house with these details and it was the first Natalie had heard about them. Not only had he lied during a federal investigation, probably more problematic was he hadn't told his wife.

"Do the right thing." I pivoted and exaggerated my difficulty in getting down the steps on my crutches. I hoped I didn't look too pathetic.

Chapter Forty-Four

After physical therapy, Russell dropped me off at home, where I took a Percocet and settled onto the couch. Since Natalie was at work, other than Casey's breathing from the floor beside me, the house was quiet, which could lull me to sleep.

While waiting for the narcotic to take the edge off the elevated pain level after PT—Natalie's term, as I would've said it hurt like a bastard—I concentrated on what we had discovered the last couple of days.

A smile touched me while remembering how Natalie and I had worked toward a solution to our problems. Her presence had helped charm Harting, who had become a valuable asset. Then last night, she had been resourceful in getting Cunningham's wife involved in the conversation. Although we didn't learn anything from him, instinct suggested Mrs. Cunningham was now thinking about her husband sitting in prison and she and their children homeless. Hopefully, she'd pressure him to tell the NTSB that he knew about the standby rudder light.

Even if nothing came from talking to Darby, Harting, or Cunningham, the conversations Natalie and I had during the drive to those encounters had been engaging. They reminded me of when we had dated and were first married. Though the subject of where we might live and what I possibly might do if I couldn't fly again weren't topics I cherished discussing, some of the gloom I had wallowed in was not as consuming. Whatever the outcome of the lawsuit against us, I suspected our marriage would be stronger.

✈ ✈ ✈

The airplane drifted to the side of the runway.

This wasn't like any airplane I had ever flown. The windshield resembled the giant screens in the dispatcher center. "Rudder. Rudder," I yelled.

The drift toward the grass increased. "Rudder, dammit."

"Why isn't the aircraft responding?" I asked.

"Unknown," a voice I didn't recognize said.

The side of the runway raced toward us, as rapidly as a video on fast forward.

Then colors. Blue, green, and black the dominant ones. Red flowed in from the edges, drowning out the other colors. Faces bobbed to the surface. One was Ned's. The others I didn't recognize.

Casey's frantic laps of my cheek woke me with a start.

"Ahh," I yelled to bring myself fully out of the nightmare. I shook my head, hoping to shake off the images, and dropped a hand to Casey's head. "I'm okay." I petted her. "Was I crying out?"

Our faithful friend sat, her eyes slitting as she savored my strokes.

Images from the nightmare continued to play in my head. My pain was as bad as it had been after therapy. I suspected I had flexed my leg, trying to stomp on an imaginary rudder pedal. Or was this memory pain from when I woke after the accident?

Another shake of my head didn't dissolve the weird scenes into the netherworld.

I'd slept for thirty minutes and I was far from refreshed. I couldn't take another Percocet for another couple of hours. I would spend that time squirming and rubbing my leg.

I hobbled into the kitchen and put a mug under the Keurig's discharge and waited for a much-needed cup of java to be spit out. When the cup was full, with a series of sliding the mug along the countertop as far as I could reach, then hobbling over and repeating the process, I got as close to the table as the countertops allowed. Gritting my teeth, I took a step with only one crutch, something I wasn't supposed to be doing yet, holding the mug in my other hand, and carried it the additional four feet to the table. My leg threatened to buckle, so I plopped the mug onto the table's surface, sloshing coffee before dropping into a chair.

I cocked my arm to throw the crutch across the room. Then reason took over before I succumbed to my anger. Without it, I'd be stuck at the table unless I lowered to the floor and dragged myself on my butt to the crutch.

Damn, I hated this. When would I be more self-sufficient and able to carry a cup of coffee or a meal to the table? Drive, not depending on others?

To get off the pity-pot, I tried to consider other ways I could prove Sphere was deceiving the NTSB. Memories of that weird nightmare kept surfacing. Was my subconscious trying to tell me something I should know, or realize?

On the drive from physical therapy, Russell had questioned when I would need his help with the airplane. I'd blown him off, as I didn't know. I'd never sold an airplane, let alone a partially completed one. What should I list it for? What did I do to prepare for the sale?

While pondering these unknowns, something from my nightmare hit me. Could the standby rudder light illuminating be a mechanical problem that the airline had never experienced? I had suspected that when talking to Harting on the phone. It wasn't something discussed in recurrent training or that we had to practice in the simulator.

Was that why they had us continue to DFW, because they didn't realize how severe the problem was? Still, why not admit they made a mistake to the NTSB and FAA even though they'd get fined? Covering up that error would be more damaging to them in the end.

In my head, I played over the sequence of events that had happened when I informed Darby, then texted Natalie. *I've thought of something that might get Cunningham to talk to us. Want to drive over there again this evening?*

Her reply came back awhile later. *K What'd you think of?*

It would take too long to type out in a text, and I knew she couldn't take a phone call. *Tell you when you get home tonight.*

Chapter Forty-Five

On the thirty-minute drive to the Cunningham's, I filled Natalie in on how I hoped we could convince the Mister to talk to us. "Remember how I told you after we took off from San Salvador, I sent a message to the dispatcher, telling them about the standby rudder light illuminating?"

"Yes."

"When I asked if they wanted us to return to San Salvador, Darby would've consulted with maintenance before telling us to continue to DFW. So he either walked over to the maintenance controller's side of the dispatch center and talked to Cunningham, or probably called him."

"Okay." She turned out of our neighborhood onto East Baseline Road.

"If it had been a routine line flight with a maintenance issue, the dispatcher and maintenance controller would have talked about the severity of the problem and whether the flight should land immediately at the nearest suitable airport or continue on to its destination."

Her eyebrows rose. "What type of problem would've made them decide to have you land immediately?" Since I had never had to do that in my career, she probably never considered that this could happen.

"Oh, an engine failure or fire, a pressurization problem, a severe hydraulic issue, or as in our case, a flight control problem."

My attempt to gloss over those issues hadn't worked, given the wide-eyed look she gave me. "Okay." She dragged that word out.

"Most of the time, our maintenance problems are the cabin equipment, like a reading light not working, a seatback that won't stay upright, or a clogged sink drain. The ones that aren't cabin issues usually are minor and we can safely continue to the destination without compromising safety."

"But that wasn't the case this time." She stated this like I didn't know that. But after twenty-eight years of marriage, I knew this was her way of acknowledging she was following my thinking.

"Right. Maybe they didn't think about the potential for limited rudder authority. Or they did but thought the thunderstorms would pass to the south of Dallas and not affect us. Or," I paused for dramatic effect, "they were clueless to the severity of our problem and based their decision on needing the aircraft in Dallas to fly a flight."

"Wouldn't they have to fix the airplane before it flew the next flight?"

"Yes. But they had probably never experienced the problem Ned and I had and didn't know how complex an issue it might be to fix."

"Really?"

"Yeah. We were essentially on the backup to the backup system. There are two main actuators that move the rudder. Each is powered by a separate hydraulic system. Alone, either one can move the rudder if the other becomes jammed or its hydraulic system fails for some reason. Only if both main actuators are not functioning—which I've never heard of happening—does the standby rudder actuator move the rudder. So my guess is someone, Cunningham probably, called San Salvador and asked if their work prevented the two main actuators from working. Or, how long it'd take them to fix the problem. Maybe after that discussion, Cunningham thought our guys in Dallas could fix the problem sooner."

She nodded several times like she thought that was possible.

"Since this was an unknown issue they never experienced, maybe they didn't make that call. They might've thought it was just a fault in the logic that made the annunciator light illuminate; an electrical glitch or something that could be fixed quickly when the aircraft returned to DFW. Hence the reason they issued the MEL for the standby rudder light that disappeared after the accident. After we crashed, they realized we had a bigger problem than they suspected."

"I suppose." Natalie wore a frown. "So… what is Cunningham going to tell us that he didn't last night?"

"Well, if you or I took a car in to be serviced and it came out with a problem, we'd have the same shop fix it. So I'm guessing Cunningham had to contact whoever was responsible for sending aircraft to San Salvador to see what they wanted to do. Did they want the guys who created the problem to fix it? Or have our guys in DFW correct San Salvador's mistake? Or, after discussing the problem with San Salvador and finding their knowledge with this malfunction lacking, they determined it would be better for our guys to sort out what caused it. I'm hoping if Cunningham feels by naming whoever made that decision, we'll leave him alone."

"Do you think Cunningham will tell us that? He seemed reluctant to talk about any aspect of the accident."

"If it seems we're not trying to implicate him in any way, maybe." I rested my hand on her thigh. "If his wife is there again, work on her like you cleverly did last night. If she feels they can avoid any legal issues by giving us what we want, I'm hoping she'll pressure him to talk."

✈✈✈

At the Cunninghams' front door, I rang the doorbell. If he refused to help us, it would be hard to not become belligerent.

Natalie grasped my arm a moment while exhaling a deep breath. Her eyes sparkled with mischief, pulling a smile from me. Damn, I was lucky to be married to her.

The door was opened by a teenage boy who stared at us with the bored indifference only a teen could master.

"Hi, is your father home?" I pasted on the smile I gave Lucas and Lindsey's friends.

"Dad, someone wants to talk to you," the teen yelled over his shoulder before walking off and leaving us at the open door.

Natalie and I exchanged frowns. Our children wouldn't have left strangers at the opened door.

Cunningham met the son in the hall without looking at the door. "Who is it?"

The teen shrugged and disappeared around a corner.

When Cunningham saw us, he stood in place, stuffed his hands in his pockets, then walked to us. He withdrew his hands and pointed a finger at us. "Look, I told you to leave me alone last night. Don't ever come back here or I'll call the police."

Before he slammed the door in our faces, I blurted out, "Give us a name and we'll leave you alone."

Cunningham narrowed his eyes. "Name? What name?"

"When you heard about the problem I had after taking off from San Salvador, you must've called somebody above you to decide if we should go back there and have the problem fixed, or continue to Dallas. Who made that decision?"

"If you tell us that, we won't tell anyone how we found out." Natalie gave him the look she must've given her patients numerous times to calm their worries.

Mrs. Cunningham stepped into the hall, then came to her husband's side with a furrowed brow. "What do they want?"

"We're sorry to trouble you again." Natalie's tone was sympathetic. "Don't you just hate those people who show up unannounced? I do."

Mrs. Cunningham's glower softened, no doubt wondering how to respond to Natalie.

"Bill had a question for your husband, then we'll be leaving," Natalie said.

With her frown still in place, Mrs. Cunningham said, "We talked to a lawyer today. He told us to not talk to anyone without him present."

Obviously, bringing her into the conversation last night had brought that about. That might've worked against us.

I sighed. "Yeah, we have an expensive lawyer too who probably would be unhappy we're talking to you without her present."

Natalie nodded, wearing a knowing expression a wife wears when her husband has done something stupid. "Oh, yeah. She'd be livid."

Neither of us knew that. But Natalie's belligerent wife routine had prevented the door from being closed on us. "Our lawyers aren't the ones who will lose everything if the NTSB doesn't uncover the truth. I understand your concern, but if you tell us who decided to have us continue to Dallas, we'll never bother you again."

Mrs. Cunningham nudged her husband.

"If I tell you, what are you going to do?" Mister said.

He must be worried I'd tell the NTSB or FAA where I got my information.

I pasted on my poor-ole'-me expression. "We'll convince him to do the right thing and tell the NTSB why he made that decision." As soon as I said that, I knew how pathetic it was.

Mister snorted. "Really. He talked to the NTSB months ago. They didn't seem concerned by what he had to say. So how are *you* going to pressure him to change what he said to them?"

So, there was somebody above Cunningham who'd made the decision. "Well, then, I'll give him a printout of the messages I sent to the dispatcher after the standby rudder light illuminated. The ones that have been deleted from the copy Sphere provided the NTSB with. I talked to Arinc. They're mailing me a copy of those messages." Even though this was a lie, Cunningham didn't know that.

"Ouch." Natalie scrunched up her face. "The NTSB won't take it lightly that his superior," she gestured to Mister, "lied to them."

I nodded. "Probably not." I watched Cunningham to see if he realized he too would be in trouble since he hadn't mentioned to the NTSB he knew the standby rudder light had illuminated.

The Cunninghams turned to each other with an expression I thought searched from the other what they should do.

"If your supervisor doesn't admit he lied about the standby rudder light, when the NTSB reads the messages that haven't been shown to them, they'll know he withheld information from a federal investigation." I thought I sounded convincing even if I was spewing bullshit.

Misses nudged her husband again.

"You don't realize how high up this guy is, do you?" Mister said. "He's used to arguing with the FAA on a daily basis. The corporate attorney is probably just down the hall from his office. You won't even be allowed to talk to him."

"If he's as high as you say," I lifted my brow, "do you think he's going to allow the real cause of the accident to be put on him? He'll claim he knew nothing about the standby rudder problem. You must not have told him about it."

Natalie made a show of looking around the Cunninghams into the house. "This is a nice home. It'd be too bad to lose it for being loyal."

"If he tells you who made that decision, what assurance do we have we won't be in further trouble?" Misses asked.

Even though I had fabricated innuendos to get details from them, I wouldn't mislead them. "None. Everything I learn, with the exception of where I'll get this name, I'm going to give to the NTSB. When they discover what really happened, they'll probably re-question everybody."

When Mister didn't say anything, I added, "If you were in my position and saw the faces of the thirty-eight that died in your dreams, wouldn't you want someone who could prove the accident wasn't your fault helping you?"

Natalie turned to me. On the ride home, I suspected she'd be asking about that.

With a hung head, Mister expelled a sigh. "For my own protection, I'm not going to give you a name. If I were you, I'd look at who has the most to lose if it's discovered the aircraft returning from San Salvador have discrepancies we have to fix before they can return to service."

I recoiled from this revelation. "There have been more than one aircraft returning with problems?"

Mister squeezed his eyes shut. "I'm not saying any more. Now please, leave us alone."

Misses yanked her husband back and slammed the door.

Chapter Forty-Six

In the car, the realization of what we'd just learned both lifted me and troubled me.

"Your aircraft wasn't the only one that came from San Salvador with something wrong with it?" Natalie's words came fast, the way they did when she was excited. "Does that mean they shouldn't be working on your airplanes?"

"I would say no, they shouldn't. And this explains why it seems Sphere is conspiring to put all the blame on me. If my aircraft had been the only one with a defect, they'd be better off acknowledging that fact and accepting the fine the FAA would impose."

"But more than one aircraft returned with problems." Natalie gestured to accent her point.

"And since it has been a problem for several months, and Sphere hasn't done anything to correct that issue, the fine could be huge. The FAA might prevent them from using San Salvador."

"Would Sphere have to do the inspections at their hangars? Or find another facility?" Natalie asked.

"We might not have the manpower or hangar space. And arranging another facility might take months. Aircraft that need inspections would be parked until they were completed. Flights would have to be cancelled." I slumped in my seat. "How could I have been so short-sighted?"

Natalie took my hand. "You've had a lot on your mind."

Another thought exploded in my head. "No wonder."

"What?" Natalie gave my hand a shake.

"That probably explains why the FAA rode my ass during my hearing. They didn't want it to come out that they hadn't shut down a maintenance facility with sloppy workmanship. You remember the conversation we had with Mrs. Masters. If that was discovered, it would generate national news and convene a congressional hearing. People at the FAA will be fired."

Natalie scrunched up her face the way she did when she asked a question she wasn't sure how to word. "So… what… Sphere and the FAA are covering up the accident's cause together? That doesn't make sense."

No, it didn't.

"Did the FAA have Sphere delete your messages? Or can they do that on their own?"

"I don't think so. Someone at Sphere would have had to erase them." Was it a coincidence the airline and FAA had separately worked to blame me? "Without knowing how the FAA approves a maintenance facility so an airline can use it, and how often they inspect it after that, or what they'd do if aircraft leaving there aren't repaired correctly, I can't answer accurately how involved the FAA might be in the conspiracy."

Dismissing what I didn't know cleared my mind. My thoughts came fast, and I tried to keep up with them. "Maybe there are individuals at both organizations who know their heads will roll if their bosses find out San Salvador should've been shut down. The FAA will question why the inspector responsible for overseeing that facility hasn't done that."

"And at Sphere?" Natalie asked.

"The VPs will question why whoever chose San Salvador hasn't fixed the problem or stopped sending aircraft there. So maybe the inspector and the guy at Sphere approached each other to look for a way to get themselves out of the fix they were in. If it was pilot error, they must've hoped the NTSB wouldn't dig deeper into the airline's maintenance."

I straightened. "Or maybe Sphere wanted to use San Salvador before the FAA could arrange an inspection. So they convinced the FAA to approve it on condition Sphere maintenance inspectors oversaw the mechanics working on the first few aircraft."

"Would the FAA do that?" Natalie asked.

"Maybe, but I doubt it. An airline can't use a new examiner until the FAA observes them conducting a pilot's check-ride. I doubt the FAA would let Sphere use a new maintenance facility until they watched them inspecting an aircraft."

Then an even more troubling thought popped up. "Has Sphere bribed someone at FAA to approve the facility without inspecting it?"

"Bribed? Has that happened before?"

"Not that I know of. Even though it's unheard of, what's to prevent it in the airline industry when it happens in others?"

Though this seemed plausible, I prayed it was unlikely. How many flights were flying at that moment that shouldn't have left the ground because of improper maintenance? And the individuals at the government agency tasked with making sure that didn't happen beefed up their bank balance instead of doing their jobs?

The difficulties of pulling off this conspiracy must've shown on me.

"What?" Natalie asked.

"It seems there'd have to be numerous people at both the FAA and Sphere working to bury this problem. For my messages to go missing, someone in dispatch would have to delete them. Dispatch and maintenance are two different departments. When the accident happened, each entity would pull away from the other to assure they weren't linked as a contributing factor. So for my messages to go missing over a maintenance issue, someone in dispatch had to work with someone in maintenance to make that happen."

My next comment showed how naïve I was, but I could share this stuff with my wife. "I mean... how do you approach someone with a blunder this big and ask them to help you bury it, knowing you both could go to jail?"

"If you have dirt on them, you call in the favor."

"How is it you know that?" I flashed the expression we gave our children when they knew something we wished they didn't.

With a zipping motion across her lips, she worked to hide a smile before it faded. "Maybe someone at the top of your airline knew about the maintenance issues and ordered someone in dispatch to erase your messages. Like you said, the fine could be huuggee."

"If that's true, we now have several people from different departments involved in this conspiracy. If either one felt their well-being was on the line, wouldn't they likely rat out the other?"

"Unless they worried doing that would implicate themselves," Natalie said.

"Good point." I nodded. "So Sphere is sitting on a keg of dynamite, hoping it doesn't explode. At the FAA, whoever oversees Sphere's maintenance, or at least approves the facilities Sphere uses, would have to approach the lead FAA accident investigator and convince him he needs to prove it was pilot error. By doing that, the maintenance inspector exposed he didn't do his job. The accident investigator would then hold the maintenance dude's future in his hand. That'd be a huge risk."

Natalie stared at the mirror before returning her attention to the road. "Unless the FAA maintenance guy went to the investigator and split whatever money Sphere bribed him with."

"You're supposed to be pointing out how unlikely these scenarios are instead of finding ways for them to work." My mock glare didn't smooth out the wrinkles on her forehead.

Then the huge flaw in this line of thinking hit me. "How did they even know they could blame Ned and me? From the beginning, or at least until I began watching the news—" As soon as those words left me, I regretted them.

Natalie scowled.

"—they made it seem Ned and I were careless for continuing an approach with an approaching thunderstorm. It was our judgement they questioned, not our ability to land in a crosswind. It was only after the data from the flight data recorder revealed we hadn't used all the available rudder that they questioned our piloting skills. If the flight data recorder showed we had the rudder pedal crammed to the stop, the NTSB would've been crawling all over the maintenance facility."

"I see what you mean." Natalie's glance lingered on the mirror.

The thud I heard on the cockpit voice recorder replayed in my head. "I refuse to believe either one of us didn't push the pedal to the stop."

"Call Mrs. Masters. Right now." Natalie's tone rang with anger. "Tell her what we just found out."

"Not until I have more proof."

"Why? We were just told that other aircraft returning from San Salvador were not fixed right. Numerous people have lied to the NTSB. They can look into that and realize you've been telling the truth and your aircraft had something wrong it."

Anyone who didn't know us would think our escalated voices signaled an argument.

"What if the NTSB is in on the conspiracy?"

"They're supposed to be an independent agency removed from political influence." Again, she stared at the mirror longer than a glance.

I made air quotes. "'Supposed to be' are the key words. We see it on the news all the time. In this case, the FAA is worried they'll be sitting before a congressional hearing. The FAA administrator calls the senators on the committee responsible for funding the NTSB and asks them to lean on them. A few phone calls later, the data from the DFDR shows Ned and I didn't use all the rudder. Instant pilot error."

She lifted her eyebrows.

"Or, the guy at Sphere who might've bribed the FAA also bribed someone at the NTSB. I'm not saying a word about this to anyone else until I learn more."

When she studied behind us again, I stared out the back glass. "Anyone back there?"

A shake of her head. "I don't think so. But all this talk of people covering up a multimillion dollar mistake has got me nervous."

I rested my hand on her thigh. "Yeah, me too."

Chapter Forty-Seven

The next day, I gave Harting what I thought would be enough time to get to his office at the hangar and read his email and listen to his voice mail before I phoned him.

"Bill, I'm glad you called."

"Yeah." Had he heard through the maintenance grapevine about our visits to the Cunninghams' and wanted to warn me word was out on my activities?

"Do you know a Bryce Marling?"

Worry straightened my spine. "Yes. He's the two-twenty fleet manager." And a crafty son of a bitch.

"He popped into my office the day before yesterday."

"What'd he want?"

"Said he saw you here and wondered if I'd talked to you."

"And?" My heart pounded. Since Marling had seen Natalie and me running from him at the hangar, he had to know we were doing something dubious.

"I couldn't outright lie to him since I didn't know who might've seen us together. So I went with the story you used. That you were writing a newsletter explaining maintenance inspections."

Marling would know that was bogus since he'd be the one to assign that task.

"Maybe you are," Harting said. "You don't seem like a sit around and do-nothing kind of guy. While you're recuperating, maybe you realized you didn't know about aircraft inspections and thought it'd be educational to other pilots. So you're taking it upon yourself to educate them."

I doubted that would work.

"You're probably going to present the report to him when you complete your research." Harting had obviously been thinking of a cover story for me.

I smiled at his resourcefulness, even if it was far-fetched. "Ah... yeah, I was working on that just now." Did I still have the notes I took?

"That's what I thought."

"How'd he know to come to you?"

"Not sure. He said he'd seen one of our pilots here who was out on sick leave and was wondering what he was doing. I guess he asked around until he came to me."

That made sense.

"Seems like a decent guy. If I were to judge how he felt about you writing a newsletter while out sick, I'd say he seemed pleased."

"Pleased?" That's the last thing I'd expect him to be.

"Yeah. Said he was glad you were making good use of your time."

On the legal pad where I planned to write notes, I wrote in big block letters *WTF*.

"I'm no expert at how flight ops works, but isn't your supervisor the chief pilot?" Harting asked.

"Yes. But Marling has been assisting me since the accident."

"Well, that explains why he would know you were out sick. Even though I'm the director of the hangar, I wouldn't know who or how many mechanics were out sick. But I do wonder why someone in training, and a manager no less, is checking up on you. Isn't that normally an assistant chief pilot's job?"

"I've wondered this numerous times. I suspect he's watching me to see if I might reveal anything harmful to the company." But I was beginning to doubt the concern. After finding out I was supposedly writing a newsletter, why didn't he call to ask about it?

"Makes sense. I hope I didn't make things difficult for you."

"Time will tell," I said. "I really appreciate you covering for me. You got time for a few questions?"

"I have a meeting in a bit, but go ahead."

"How difficult would it be to look up how many aircraft return from San Salvador with write-ups?"

A pause before Harting asked, "How many? Are you inferring more than yours had a problem on their return flights?"

"Yes."

"Shit. Where'd you learn this?" His tone of voice was a growl.

"Cunningham let it slip."

"So... he's involved in keeping the NTSB and FAA in the dark about your rudder problem."

"Oh yeah. After Natalie and I put the fear of going to prison and being sued in him, he hired a lawyer."

"What else did he say?"

"Hardly anything. But he confirmed he consulted with somebody above him on whether we should return to San Salvador when we reported the standby rudder ON light illuminating. Somebody he says is used to arguing with the FAA daily."

"That must've been Carl Bladen. He's the VP who chose San Salvador."

I wrote this name down. "What's he the vice president of?"

"International aircraft inspections."

"Is there a VP for domestic inspections?" I asked.

"Yeah."

It seemed Sphere had a vice president for almost everything. "Bladen will probably lose his bonus if the accident was attributed to a facility he's responsible for."

"I hope they fire the asshole. It surprised many of us when he was chosen for that position."

"Oh. Why?"

"He's not the sharpest tool in the box, and an arrogant prick on top of that. He's gotten where he is by kissing ass."

I smiled. "Pilots think the same thing about the management in flight ops."

A chuckle. "Yeah, I bet they do."

"Would Bladen be resourceful enough to mislead the NTSB, FAA, and the rest of the company?" I explained all the people that Natalie and I discussed that had to be involved to delude the investigation.

"Hmmm... I'm inclined to say no. But he's probably in charge of a half a billion-dollar budget. If he figured out a way to siphon cash out of it, he'd have some substantial bribe money."

"Yes, he would." How did I overcome that kind of power? It would be hard for someone at the airline to turn down a vice president's requests. Especially if they were a smooth talker, as most individuals noted for kissing ass were prone to be. Throw in some cash and persuasion that influencing the investigation was for the good of all parties concerned, and most people would do as requested.

"Which gets me back to my original question. How difficult would it be to find out which aircraft were inspected in San Salvador, and did they return from there with write-ups?"

Harting didn't answer. Was he thinking of excuses to avoid the task because of the difficulty Bladen might make for him?

"I'm thinking," Harting finally said. "It'll take me awhile."

"How long is awhile?"

"Well… if I do the work myself, a couple of days."

He must've heard my sigh.

"I've got meetings I can't skip. But if I use the buddy I mentioned earlier, I could probably have something for you this afternoon."

Allowing someone else in on this detail was another person who might leak what I was up to. The proof I needed could then disappear. "Do you trust him?"

"Yeah, I do. I'll still keep him somewhat in the dark about why I'm looking into this. If Bladen has coded things to bury these writeups, my pal is faster at digging out this information."

"I'll have to trust your judgment." I regretted saying that.

"Yeah, I guess you will."

"Hey… I'm sorry. I didn't—"

"Don't worry about it. You've got a lot on your mind."

The man's understanding was comforting. "Next question, if you have the time. How does the FAA approve facilities for Sphere to use?"

"In a nutshell, they inspect the facility to make sure they have the capability to work on our aircraft. They look at mechanic certificates and experience, aircraft maintenance manuals, and if they have the tools to overhaul our aircraft. Then when our first aircraft is inspected, they watch the work being performed. Something like a C check, which takes weeks, they'll randomly inspect the work to confirm the mechanics know what they're doing."

"And after that initial check, do they ever go back and check again?"

"Yes. At least once a year. Unless they have reason to believe the work isn't being accomplished to standards."

"What would happen then?"

"If it were an occasional aircraft, mostly likely they would make us document what we've done to correct that issue. If it is, as you say, several aircraft, they'd stop us from using the facility."

"If you were the PMI for Sphere," I used the acronym for the FAA individual known as the principal maintenance inspector, "and you learned we were using a facility with improper maintenance procedures that probably contributed to an accident with numerous fatalities, what would be going through your mind?"

"I'd be looking for another job. Since we still have the same PMI, I'm wondering why. Is the FAA hoping the NTSB doesn't discover their oversight has been inadequate?"

Or more likely, powerful people were working to keep the FAA from appearing inept. "What would the airline do to Bladen?" I asked.

Harting grunted. "Under a less extreme situation, that asshole would probably get promoted. But knowing the liability the airline would be exposed to, they'd probably retire him with a comfortable severance package. You or I'd be out the door on our own."

He paused. "I'm sorry. I didn't mean to remin—"

"With your help, hopefully, I can prevent that. But in this case, with the lawsuits I'm involved in, Sphere would seem culpable if they retired him with a healthy pay package."

"True. But knowing the asshole, Bladen has already figured out someone he can blame for San Salvador's problem. If I had anything to do with that facility, I'd be watching my back."

Chapter Forty-Eight

Late that afternoon, I completed another circuit of hobbling through the kitchen to the family room, with a pause at the patio door to view the mountains, then back to the kitchen. Luckily, Casey stayed out of my way. Stepping over her on crutches was difficult.

I justified my restlessness while waiting for Harting's buddy to call as exercise. Natalie and the physical therapists would have rolled their eyes at me.

Since it was late afternoon, I worried that word of Harting's digging had reached Bladen, and Harting had been shut down.

How would I get the information I needed without him?

My phone chimed with the Imperial March. Either Harting was calling with the information or someone from Sphere's human resources was requesting my presence. I braced myself and answered.

"Do you like barbecue?" Harting asked without any greeting.

"Yes, but did you—"

"Great. There's a place I know with great ribs in the Larkridge shopping center off Washington Street. You know where it is?"

That was minutes away. "Yeah, but what—"

"Great. When can you be there?"

Obviously, he didn't want to discuss what he had learned over the phone. "Well, Natalie isn't home yet and may not be for two hours."

"Seven work for you, then?"

"Sure." Natalie wasn't fond of barbecue. But if Harting wanted to discuss something that would help us, she'd be eager to eat whatever was available.

"See you then." He hung up.

✈✈✈

Natalie and I spotted Harting sitting near the back of the restaurant, facing the door. He acknowledged us with a lift of his long neck beer.

Hobbling over to him, I realized the little things that I had taken for granted prior to getting around on crutches. Several times I had to turn sideways and shuffle to get between chairs, always on alert for someone who might slide out a chair or a foot into my leg.

After sitting, Harting smiled at Natalie. "I still haven't figured out what you see in him."

Natalie's eyes sparkled. "Lately I'm wondering that myself. He hasn't done a load of laundry since he came home. Nor vacuumed, or had dinner ready." She worked at looking disgusted. "He's always got some flimsy excuse about being disabled. Don't get me started on the yard work."

Although said in jest, her comments touched on my many regrets. I pretended to let her remarks roll off me. "I'm a good listener, though." I batted my eyes.

The humor left the hangar manager's face. "I'm sorry for making you meet me here. I wasn't comfortable sharing—"

"Hi, I'm Cindy. I'll be taking care of you tonight. Can I start you off with anything to drink?" She handed out menus.

Natalie ordered white wine while I stuck to coffee.

When she left, Harting glanced around before leaning in to talk. "What I discovered is troubling."

"How so?" I asked.

From a computer bag, he withdrew several sheets of paper and handed them to me. "Your aircraft was the sixth one sent to San Salvador in the three months we've been using the facility. The first one," he pointed on the paper to a series of digits that represented an aircraft number, "came out of inspection and made its flight back to Dallas without any problems."

He stopped to take a chug from his beer. "As you can see, the remaining aircraft didn't do so well."

"So, the first one, the one the FAA would've been present to observe being inspected, had been maintained correctly."

Harting nodded.

I skimmed the work done on the aircraft and what discrepancies they had on the return flight back to the States.

"Here you go." Cindy set Natalie's wine in front of her.

I pulled the papers to my chest, as if I didn't want them spilled on. It was probably an unnecessary precaution, as I doubted the waitress could understand it and report to someone what we were discussing. I could barely decipher the information on them.

"Are you ready to order?" she asked after setting my coffee down.

"Can you give us a few minutes?" Harting flashed a smile.

"Sure." She moved to the table next to ours without a glance back at us and began stacking the dirty dishes.

I perused the papers while Cindy straightened the chairs, then loaded her arms with the dishes, then walked off.

When she was finally out of earshot, I said, "The returning aircraft had a duct overheat, a cracked windshield, a landing gear down annunciator not working, a hydraulic low level indication..." With a frown, I turned over the last page to see it was blank, then went back and counted the number of maintenance issues. "There should also be a standby rud—" I shook my head.

"What?" Natalie asked.

"The sixth aircraft was mine. Since the cause of the accident is being hidden, the standby rudder problem wouldn't be listed."

"Does this mean Sphere shouldn't be using that shop?" Natalie asked Harting.

"No," Harting said, "we should not."

"I'm surprised we still are." I continued to read the papers. "Repairing the windshield was probably what... a ten thousand dollar repair?"

"Counting the parts, labor, and aircraft downtime, probably triple that," Harting said. "Here's what's interesting about this. See this code?" He pointed to the column with an alpha-numeric symbol. "On every one of those returning aircraft, the maintenance codes indicates the maintenance issue was discovered on the first revenue flight after returning to the States. Not on the maintenance ferry flight back."

With a lifted eyebrow, I stared at him.

"What does that mean?" Natalie asked.

He directed his attention to Natalie. "We code when a discrepancy is reported differently for each phase of flight. Something discovered when the pilots do the preflight is coded differently than if they report it after pushing back from the gate, or in flight, or after they've landed."

She looked from me to Harting. "So why is that significant?"

"Because we track aircraft on reposition flights differently than revenue flights. Someone wanted it kept secret that those discrepancies," he tapped the papers, "are occurring on the return maintenance flights."

Although this agreed with what Cunningham had let slip, I needed to play devil's advocate. "How do you know? They might not have been discovered until after the aircraft returned."

"Because my buddy had to dig to discover this. Someone went into the aircraft's record and changed the code after it was reported." Harting finished his beer.

I didn't know enough about how the maintenance department coded discrepancies to ask for clarification. My befuddlement must've been evident.

"When did you notify us about your standby rudder ON light illuminating?" he asked.

"Shortly after takeoff."

"Did you send a maintenance discrepancy through the aircraft's electronic logbook?"

I scowled. "Of course."

"The maintenance tracking software would've seen you were airborne and coded that writeup as occurring in flight. Those discrepancies," Harting pointed at the papers, "were coded as pilot preflight on the revenue flight after returning to Dallas."

I scoured the pages, looking for a clue that would indicate tampering. "So... how do you know the record was changed?" Harting's buddy must be good, as I saw nothing to indicate a problem.

"My guy noticed the date and time when the discrepancy was recorded was off by hours, and in several cases a day or two, before the code for it would indicate. Those discrepancies were actually reported while the aircraft was in flight on its way to Dallas."

I nodded, understanding what he was saying.

"If the pilots had sent in the write-up while in flight from San Salvador," he said for Natalie's benefit, "the software would have shown the discrepancy happened on a maintenance reposition flight. Not during a preflight before the next flight.

"What I don't get is why this wasn't discovered before now," Harting said. "Weekly, the VPs go over when we had to fix something so they can get on our ass to make the airline more reliable. If, for example, you guys report during your preflight that the engines need oil, and this happens several times, then we get a bulletin reinforcing the need to check oil levels during our preflight inspections."

"You ready to order yet?"

I'd been concentrating on the how and why someone was changing these maintenance codes. I hadn't sensed Cindy's arrival.

Harting flashed the woman another smile. "Sorry, we've been catching up. Can we get another round?"

"Sure. Take your time." She stepped back and studied her notepad before walking off.

When she was gone, I sighed. "Bladen changed them to cover up his incompetence. The facility he chose is costing Sphere money, not saving it like he probably promised." I threw the papers on the table. "Since this hasn't been caught before, the accident scared the shit out of the bastard. Not only will he be fired, he too might be sued."

"Bill." Natalie glanced around to see if my raised voice had drawn any attention.

Harting nodded.

"What if someone above him is involved in this too?" Natalie's voice was just above a whisper.

Harting picked at his beer label. "That would explain why this wasn't discovered before now."

Why would an airline continue to use a facility that would tarnish their safety and on time reputation? Then it came to me. "San Salvador might be giving Bladen and whoever kickbacks for using the facility. After the accident they must've worried, and probably still do, that it would be revealed that the hangar they selected to get rich from had put thousands of lives at risk. If this comes out, the lawsuits could be staggering."

I made two fists. While I worried about keeping my leg, were company officials terrified their get rich scheme might end?

"This is what we needed." Natalie wore the excited expression I usually enjoyed.

It was, and something I'd treasure revealing. Who better than the guy with nothing to lose? Still…

"What?" Natalie asked.

"This doesn't prove my aircraft had something wrong with it."

My wife's shoulders slumped.

"Well…" Harting twisted his mouth left then right, "one might make the case if the previous four aircraft were returned to service with issues, yours might've been too."

He was reaching, but I appreciated his comment. "I doubt that'll convince a jury. They'll still have the rudder pedal data showing we didn't use all of the available travel."

"If nothing else, your accident will close the facility and make our flights safer," he said.

"I'm sure the first officer's widow won't share your gratitude," I said.

Harting sighed. "Yeah, that was a very inconsiderate thing to say."

Stuck with no other alternative, I reconsidered something I had given thought to but rejected. "I need to go to San Salvador and talk to the mechanics who worked on my aircraft." Could I board a flight without becoming a trembling, distraught wreck?

Natalie's eyes widened before the determined refusal I'd seen numerous times filled her face. "What? No. Way."

"It's the only way to find out what might've caused the accident. You've heard Mrs. Masters. The crash destroyed any evidence something was wrong with the aircraft."

"You're not going to San Salvador."

"I need to. Or we're going to be homeless."

Harting sat back and glanced from one of us to the other. His expression said he wished he wasn't there.

"How are you going to get the mechanics to tell you something they wouldn't reveal to the NTSB?"

I didn't want to mention I might have to bribe them with money we couldn't afford to give out. I patted my crutches and pasted on the expression I wore when making light of something. "Sympathy factor."

"This isn't funny, Bill. You've told me it is ranked the number three city in the world with the most murders. When on a layover there, you didn't leave the hotel. Now you're going to waltz around, in your condition, and get people who have lied to the FAA and NTSB to open up to you?"

Although a good point, I couldn't hide that it hurt. A component of the anger that had festered within me for two months was how my wife looked at me as less of a man. It wasn't Natalie's fault she now had to worry about me.

She reached across the table, attempting to get me to take her hand. "You couldn't find out why your flight was delayed because the guys working on your aircraft didn't speak English." Her tone had softened. "How're you going to ask them questions?"

I took her hand. "I don't know."

"We have a liaison down there," Harting said. "He's a Sphere mechanic assigned to San Salvador as a representative of the airline. One of the requirements for his position was he needed to speak Spanish."

I turned to him, the gears in my mind turning.

"I'm not sure if he'd be of any help, as I don't know where his loyalties lie." Harting shrugged. "Five improperly maintained aircraft have left the facility he's supposed to be overseeing. One has drawn significant attention. He's probably nervous his job is on the line. Then there's the fact the NTSB and FAA would've already talked to him and apparently were convinced he had nothing to hide. But should you decide to go there, I can put you in touch with him."

While I thought that over, I noted Natalie's shake of her head.

"Thanks. I'll think about it. Bladen might've already gotten to him and it'd be a wasted trip."

Natalie's pursed mouth softened.

"What's his name?" I took out a pen to write it down.

"Manuel Gervasi."

He was someone I would meet in a very short time.

Chapter Forty-Nine

The next day after Natalie had left for work, I ate a bowl of oatmeal and thought about what I had uncovered, hoping I would figure out an immediate solution to our situation.

The messages I had sent would prove I had been hampered from preventing the accident. They would come to light after our attorney requested a subpoena to have Arinc turn them over—providing Sphere didn't find a way to make them vanish. When Ms. Killinger would request those messages was still up in the air.

Even with them, the lawsuit against us probably wouldn't be dismissed. Although it was more difficult to prove Ned and I were negligent, the most likely scenario, according to our attorney, was that the lawyers for the victims might press on, hoping we'd settle out of court to avoid a prolonged lawsuit that would rack up attorney fees and emotional toil.

Natalie and I would be financially ruined.

And for something that wasn't Ned's fault, Alicia would lose the family farm she grew up on and hoped to pass down to her children.

If a mechanic would come forward stating the aircraft had a problem when it left San Salvador, that too would help drive a nail in the coffin of the lawsuit.

As was pointed out last night, getting one to make that confession would be difficult. If we had the resources, our attorney or her investigator could go to San Salvador with an interpreter and question everyone who'd worked on the aircraft. If someone who'd been brave enough to lie to the NTSB and FAA had a change of heart and admitted there was a problem—a huge *if*—then there'd also be the expense of flying them to the states for the deposition and trial.

Or, if someone at Sphere acknowledged they knew the aircraft left San Salvador with a rudder problem, that would establish Ned and I were as much victims as were those on the regional jet.

If I could get the NTSB to re-interview Darby, he might buckle under pressure and remember the messages. Or he might on the witness stand in our lawsuit. The same might be said of Cunningham. But we would not go to trial for a year or more and would be penniless before then. Would anyone care then that Ned and I had been powerless to prevent the accident because Sphere had valued profit over safety?

How would I feel when a jury ruled we were not complicit? Although no doubt overwhelming, what Alicia, Natalie, and I had to give up in the meantime would take away from the euphoria.

So, the only way I could see to get the lawsuit eliminated was to lean on Bladen.

If he learned his corruption was about to be revealed, he might come forward if he felt he could work out a plea bargain. Especially if he wasn't the only one at Sphere involved in keeping San Salvador in operation. Getting him to rat out an accomplice before they could point a finger at him could work in our favor.

It was wishful thinking. Still, I wasn't going to sit back and let my destiny be determined by others who didn't have a vested interest in it. As Harting accurately characterized, I was not a sit-around-and-do-nothing kind of guy. I had sat around enough the last couple of months. I would need a support group soon.

Approaching Bladen would risk revealing how I learned he had misled the airline, FAA, and NTSB. He would most likely destroy the evidence that could ruin his life.

But I knew a way to convince him doing that was futile.

✈ ✈ ✈

The Uber dropped me off at headquarters. Working my way across the building's lobby to the elevators, I became aware of the same tingling tension I experienced prior to a check-ride for a new airplane. My last visit to this building ended with security guards escorting me from the building. Would they tackle me today?

Telling myself this was an airline corporate office and not NORAD, and the most likely scenario would be they'd ask me to leave, eased some of the tightness in my shoulders.

Several hundred people traipsed through this building daily, and the chances of security remembering me were slim. But my crutches drew people's attention. Would that pique a guard's scrutiny?

Other than a momentary lift of people's gaze from their phones, I boarded an elevator with two others and rode up without being questioned.

I reached inside my sport coat pocket and turned on the recorder function of my phone.

Two floors above the dispatch center, I exited the elevator to face a floor partitioned in offices.

Reaching the one with Bladen's name on it, I barged in the open door without stopping to compose myself.

The empty office was a huge letdown for the vocal battle I was prepared for.

The laptop's screen displayed an email program. It surprised me that someone guilty of fraud would be careless about leaving their computer unlocked. If I knew how long he might be away, I might have perused it for anything incriminating.

But someone walking by might question why I was sitting at his computer.

A trip to the men's room would relieve the anxiety-induced pressure in my bladder and stall my decision to surf his computer or wait for him.

As I backed up to the restroom door, it was opened from inside by a man with a round face, pencil-width mustache, and thinning light hair that matched the photo I'd looked up on the airline directory.

Bladen.

The man responsible for ending Ned's life and changing mine stepped back, holding the door. "After you."

He lifted his brow when I hesitated.

I continued in. "Thanks."

Without a backward glance, he strolled out.

After relieving myself, I steeled my resolve, restarted the recorder that I had shut off, and hobbled back to the asshole's office.

His door was closed. I shoved it open without knocking and hobbled in.

He turned from his computer, wearing a scowl.

"I thought it was time we met." I hated the tremble in my voice.

The stare he gave me was one of recognition. I suspected it was from our meeting at the restroom and not from knowing who I was.

"I'm Bill Kurz, the captain of flight 9100 from a couple of months ago."

Incomprehension wrinkled his forehead before his wide-eyed gaze traveled the length of me. His hands paused on the arms of his chair as if debating whether he should stand to greet me. After he rose, he leaned over his desk with his hand thrust out. "It's good to meet you. How're you doing?"

"I've been better. You are Carl Bladen, aren't you?" I wanted his identity established on the recording.

"Yeah." He searched my face and dropped his hand I hadn't shaken. "What can I do for you?"

Without being offered, I sat in a chair across from his desk, glad to take the weight off my trembling legs. I had rehearsed my conversation, hoping that by laying out the facts in a conversational tone, I'd get his cooperation easier than if I began verbally assaulting him. At that moment, it was hard to rein in my anger.

I took a deep breath. "I'm a little confused. In the NTSB's preliminary report of the accident, there's no mention of the messages I sent after taking off from San Salvador and reporting a problem with the rudder. What happened to them?"

It was brief, but his eyes narrowed before he busied himself straightening papers on his desk. "What you're talking about?"

"When I took off from San Salvador, I sent a message to the dispatcher that the standby rudder ON light had illuminated and did they want us to return and have it fixed or continue to Dallas. Since the aircraft had just come out of a maintenance facility you're in charge of, they would've consulted you."

His gaze darted to the side, paused there, then back to me.

"The NTSB mentions discussing the aircraft's inspection with you," I said. "But not the malfunction we experienced. Or why you decided to have us continue to Dallas. Don't you think it was relevant to the investigation?"

He frowned. "There was something wrong with the aircraft?"

"You know there was."

"Do I?"

I wanted to ask if he had practiced this act before the NTSB questioned him. "Is it easier months later to deny your decision?"

His expression sharpened. "You'd be wise to remember who you're talking to. You may not work in my department, but insulting a vice president could be disastrous for your career."

My aluminum crutches rattled when I patted them. "My flying days may be over." It shocked me at the ease with which I said that. I had not come consciously to that realization.

His gaze dropped.

"Why doesn't the airline, or more accurately you, want the NTSB and FAA to know aircraft return from San Salvador with write-ups our mechanics have to fix? Is the deal so good with that facility you don't want to lose it?"

"Aircraft returned from San Salvador with maintenance issues?"

His confusion seemed legitimate, giving me pause. Then I reminded myself he'd gotten where he was by being a manipulator.

"If they had, the FAA would have prevented us from using that facility." He stated this as a fact with his brow pulled down.

"Not if they didn't know about them."

Then he acted as if enlightened. "And I suppose you think I'm the one hiding this from them." He whistled. "Wow, you've dreamed up quite some conspiracy."

"I know you've changed records to hide the bad decisions you made."

He leaned back, folding his hands over his round stomach. "Where does your inability to land in a crosswind play into this little scenario you've dreamed up?"

My face warmed. I fought the urge to yell *I would've prevented the accident if the rudder had worked as designed.* When I shifted, I grimaced from the spike of pain that shot up my leg.

"So... I'm curious. Why do you think this fantasy you've dreamed up is true? The NTSB with all their experience isn't suspicious of these accusations." He said that like we were friends contemplating some unknown hypothesis.

I put conviction in my voice. "Aren't they?"

"Enlighten me. Because I would think that being as actively involved in the investigation as I am, I would know what they're interested in."

"What they're about to learn is five aircraft have returned from San Salvador that had write-ups occur on the flights back. Records have been changed to show that those discrepancies were reported on the next revenue flights."

His gaze shifted to the side before returning to me. The amused expression he wore planted back in place. "And you know this how?"

"I have my sources."

He smirked. "I'm glad you paid me this visit. If any of this is true," he cocked his head as if doubting it, "you've informed me I might have an enemy in the company."

For the first time since meeting Harting, I questioned his motivation for helping me.

"I'll have to figure out who *might* be trying to make me appear culpable." Bladen stared off to the side.

Was he thinking who he could frame for his incompetence or truly concerned he was being set up?

"Nothing is ever your fault, is it?" I said to mask my doubt and hoping I'd rile him up. I really wanted this smug bastard to be guilty. "Have you risen to the position by blaming others for your failures?"

He glared at me.

A glow of satisfaction warmed me.

"No, you've been talking to someone. Someone who wants to make me look suspect. They planted these fictitious maintenance issues."

Harting's dislike for Bladen was no secret. He also didn't like that aircraft were being inspected outside of the country. Had he framed Bladen to look incompetent to get even with a nemesis and/or punish the company?

"You probably wouldn't enlighten me who my enemy is?" He asked that like we were buds.

I smirked and forced bravado into my voice. "Did you get to this position by being paranoid of those working under you? Maybe if you tried to show admiration and respect instead of suspicion and criticism for others, you wouldn't have this concern."

It was like a switch had been flipped. Crimson creeped up his neck. "You have no idea what it takes to run a department this size with a half a billion-dollar budget. I started out as a line mechanic and worked my ass off to get to this position. I know you pilots sitting in the cockpit in your white shirts watching a computer do your job makes you feel superior to others. You have no idea the decisions I make for the sake of the company. Daily I make choices that keep this company operating and affects whether it makes a profit."

Some of the suspicion I held that Harting was using me diminished with Bladen's arrogance. "You need to come forward and admit your facility should have been shut down."

"Really? Why *should* I?"

"Because the NTSB and FAA are about to get the proof San Salvador should never have been selected. That'll reopen the investigation into the maintenance performed on my aircraft."

The color of his face was still an unhealthy red.

"You've done a good job of misleading everyone until now. Even though you managed to get the mechanics in San Salvador to lie during the investigation, this has gotten too big to hide. You may get some of the mechanics in Dallas to deny that they hadn't repaired write-ups San Salvador should've fixed. But not all of them. You think they'll lie while under oath during the lawsuits against me?" I lifted an eyebrow.

Although Bladen faced me, his face a mask of rage, his gaze was faraway. Was he conspiring how he'd cover this up? Or what he might do to me?

"There'll be a history of parts Dallas used," I said. "The delays those aircraft incurred will be reevaluated. Come forward with this while you can. It'll be better for you."

He focused on me. "Get the fuck out of my office."

At the door, I turned to him, exaggerating my lean on the crutches. "Do you lose sleep that thirty-eight died and ten others were severely injured, their lives forever changed, because you were greedy?"

He turned from me, focusing on the corner of his office, his jaw working.

I deliberately left his door open.

Chapter Fifty

On my way to the lobby, the elevator stopped on the floor below Bladen's where flight operations were located.

Although unlikely, I did not want a pilot I knew to board so that I would have to explain why I was descending from the executive level. The fewer who knew what I was up to, the less likely I'd be thwarted from proving something was wrong with the aircraft.

Two women stepped onto the elevator.

"—thunderstorms in the northeast have already canceled fifty flights," one said.

"I hear it'll be more by the end of the day," the other said.

A silent sigh escaped me with the realization of how much I missed being an integral part of an airline. Before the accident, when on a day off and hearing about weather affecting operations, I smiled, grateful it wasn't impacting my life. Now, I'd love to be number twenty in line at Newark, making my tenth announcement over the PA to tell the passengers I had no update as to when we would take off.

The elevator doors had almost slid closed when a hand shoved into the opening, retracting them. Marling started in, recoiled when he saw me, then continued in wearing a frown.

Shit!

When his gaze lifted as if looking up to the floors I'd come from, he worked at hiding a smile. "Bill. What brings you here?"

My shock at seeing him had to be evident. My heart hammered so hard, I shuddered with each beat.

My suspicion that Bladen was being framed had me considering if Marling could be responsible. Had he and Harting cooked up the details that made Bladen seem incompetent so that Marling didn't take a hit for insufficient crosswind training for

EA-220 crews? That seemed a stretch. If the NTSB ruled that was a contributing factor in the cause, the worst that would happen was the FAA would demand additional training for all crews.

Probably answering Marling's question with *I'm hoping to bring the airline down* was the wrong thing to say. Instead, I went with what he might believe. "I've taken it upon myself to write a newsletter about aircraft inspections."

He smiled as if in on the joke. "That's good. When do I get to see what you've got?"

Shit if I know. "Soon."

"Good."

The elevator stopped at the next floor and the two women got off, leaving Marling and me alone.

When we started down, he gave me a once over. "It's good to see you out and about and making good use of your time."

Weren't those the exact words Harting had used? "Thanks. It's slow going, but getting a little easier."

"That's good to hear." While he stared at the floor indicator, he said, "Any word from the NTSB on how the investigation is going?"

Had I mentioned to him that Mrs. Masters and I occasionally conversed? Or was he simply making small talk? "No, not in a while."

"Must be going as one would expect, then. It'd be nice if they discovered something that'd shed new light on the cause."

Did he lift an eyebrow? "Yeah, wouldn't it?"

"I can't help but think that since the aircraft came out of an inspection, something had been wrong with it." He met my eyes. "Like you stated in your testimony."

I bent my knee, lifting my foot toward my butt, hoping to relieve the ache that had elevated in the last few minutes. "Do you have any suspicions of what that might be?"

"Me?" He lifted his brow. "No."

I bet. "I never asked, but I assume, if the NTSB continues to put the majority of the cause on the first officer and me, it'll affect your chances of promotion."

He sighed. "Yeah, I suppose it could."

The elevator slid to a stop. He blocked the doors open and gestured for me to exit.

As I hobbled past him, he said, "You don't need to worry about that. I feel I'm going to be okay."

With a nod, I continued toward the building's front exit. He walked alongside me instead of going to the rear, where he had probably parked.

At the front door, he stepped out and held it for me. "Is there anything you'd like to share with me?" From his expression, it would be easy to think he was sincere.

"Our health insurance is crappy. It doesn't cover shit."

"I'm sorry to hear that." He gave my shoulder a pat as I hobbled past him. "You keep at what you're doing. I'm sure... I'm sure it'll all work out in the end."

What the hell? I directed my frown to the Uber waiting for me to keep Marling from seeing it.

He went back into the building.

✈ ✈ ✈

Casey greeted me at our door, wagging her tail.

Every time we returned, regardless of how long she'd been home alone, she acted as if it was the best thing in the world.

Her attitude eased me out of the doldrums I'd slipped into on the ride home while I replayed both conversations I'd had at Sphere's headquarters.

After I let her out and gave her a treat, Casey laid beside me on the couch, her head resting on my good leg. The calming effect of our faithful companion made me grateful she had been there for Natalie while I was in the hospital and rehab. Faced with the uncertainties confronting us, it must've been lonely for Natalie without me or the kids here.

After replaying the conversation I had recorded of Bladen, I laid my head on the back of the couch, wishing I hadn't shut the recorder off. It would be nice to go over what Marling had said so I could analyze it in more depth.

I had captured Bladen's arrogance, and as much as I hated to admit it, his suspicion. Either he was a crafty son-of-a-bitch or he was being set up.

Marling's appearance right afterward added to my suspicion of coordinated efforts to mislead the NTSB. Was I being followed and he waited to approach me after I met with Bladen as a warning I was being watched? Or was I being paranoid and his appearance was coincidental?

After running these thoughts over and over in my head, I knew the only thing left to do was follow through on the threat I had made to Bladen.

Mrs. Masters answered my call on the third ring.

"Did you know my aircraft was the sixth that the hangar in San Salvador worked on for Sphere?"

"Bill?"

"Yeah. Did you know that?"

"I don't remember the exact number. But I knew several of your aircraft had."

"Did you know the last five had write-ups on the flight back?" Why hadn't she told me about this stuff?

"No." Suspicion tinged her tone. "What needed to be fixed?"

I read from the list Harting had given me. "I know most of those items could've occurred after maintenance as extensive as a C-check. But every aircraft after the one the FAA observed being inspected to approve the facility had a problem on the next flight. And the one that had the windshield crack had it replaced during the inspection. Come on. That's kind of a big coincidence, don't you think?"

"Where'd you get this information?"

"A source." I didn't want her interviewing Harting since I was unsure of his motivation. "I can send you the list I have." If what Harting had given me was a fabrication, even though I might lose some credibility, the NTSB could discover that easier than I could.

"Alright."

I was sending her crucial information she didn't have, and she acted put upon? "What's interesting about this list is it shows the write-ups were discovered on the first revenue flight *after* the maintenance ferry flight. Someone didn't want it known that aircraft returning from San Salvador were improperly maintained."

"Maybe those items were discovered on the next flight."

"That's a good assumption. But I was led to these issues by someone who let it slip that wasn't the case."

"I'll take a look at what you have." This came out as a sigh.

"I could point out the significance about the code listing when these write-ups were discovered is bogus, but since this isn't your first accident you've investigated, I'm sure you'll figure it out." It was a small dig at her lack of enthusiasm and to get even for something she'd said in an earlier conversation.

"I'll need to know where you got this list so we can verify its accuracy."

If she would just look at the damn list instead of being confrontational, she would learn a lot more. "I suggest you look at who has the most to gain by burying the fact that aircraft return from their C-check with write-ups."

A sigh. "I know you're upset with us for not finding something that'll absolve you of blame. This is still an ongoing investigation. Any information that will help us understand why your aircraft departed the runway will be considered. So please, quit being vague with your suggestions. Tell me what you've learned and how you became aware of it and I'll look into it."

I had to believe her. I couldn't do this without her. "I just met with Carl Bladen, the vice president of international aircraft inspections. He's responsible for selecting San Salvador."

"I remember the name. We interviewed him."

"You should do that again." For all the good that'd do if they couldn't determine people lied to them.

"Why?" She was skeptical again.

"When I informed him I knew about the aircraft returning with write-ups, he went ballistic. He realized it's being uncovered that the facility he chose, and continues to use, isn't maintaining our aircraft correctly. My guess, he's getting kickbacks for sending aircraft there."

"Let's deal with the facts and not speculate."

"Here's one. He pretended to not remember that he was consulted on whether we should return to San Salvador after I sent the message asking that." I realized *pretend* was another speculation.

"Did you ask him specifically if he was consulted?" Masters asked.

Like an idiot, no. But I remember his answer. "I recorded our conversation. I can send you a copy of it. When you listen to it, you'll hear he evaded answering my questions."

"Did he know you were recording the conversation?"

"No." Like he would've said what he did if he knew that.

"Then I can't use it."

I pointed my face at the ceiling and sighed. "Regardless, you should listen to it. Even though he didn't admit he was misleading the investigation, he didn't deny it either. He's covering something up."

"How again did you come to suspect him?"

"Someone suggested I consider who had the most to lose if it was discovered aircraft return from San Salvador with write-ups. The vice president of international aircraft inspections seemed the most likely person."

"Who is this someone?"

Just look into what I've told you. "I won't disclose that. I promised I wouldn't reveal where I got this information." Although I really wanted to give her Cunningham's name so that he would be questioned again.

"You need to understand the trouble you could be in if you're hindering a federal investigation." There was an edge to her voice. "You can be re-interviewed with the FAA present at any time. If it is proven you lied to us, or withheld information, they could take certificate action against you which could also include a fine. If it is determined you are criminally hindering the investigation, the FBI could arrest you."

Telling Cunningham he could go to prison had not been a lie. I could too if I wasn't careful. Yet, it infuriated me she was hinting I was the one misleading the NTSB.

I tempered that anger. "I'm sorry. I didn't mean to come across so condescending. It's just... it's just hard when I know I would've prevented this accident if I could have and can't remember trying. And everyone I talk to is evasive. Or won't admit they knew we had a rudder problem."

Mrs. Master's silence ran on so long, I considered apologizing more. As infuriating as our relationship was, I couldn't make Sphere accountable without the NTSB.

Eventually, I heard her sigh. The bite in her voice had vanished. "The accident I told you I was in, my husband and I were initially suspected of causing it and were arrested for some serious crimes. So, I do understand what you're going through. I really do. That being said, I still have a job to do."

What had she and her husband been involved in? I wish I knew where and when the accident occurred so I could look it up on the NTSB database.

Sharing her history made me look at her in a new light. I felt I could trust her. "Again, I'm sorry. It's been so frustrating and I've taken my anger out on you when it wasn't justified."

"I feel..." Her voice lowered to just above a whisper. "What I'm about to tell you could get me fired. But you deserve to know."

I straightened.

"I feel the rudder pedal potentiometer on your aircraft was defective during the accident flight. I think it was changed before we tested it."

It took me a moment to figure out what she was saying. When I did, the weight burdening my soul since the accident was gone.

What she admitted didn't prove I had tried to keep us on the runway, but it showed someone suspected I might've tried to.

I mouthed a silent *yes* while pumping my fist.

The thud on the cockpit voice recorder wasn't a noise I emotionally created. This tidbit she had been unable to share reinforced my conviction that Ned and I had tried to keep the airplane on the runway, but had been unable.

Why could she not inform me of this? "Are you on speaker?"

"No."

"For someone who wants to deal in only the facts, why do you say you *feel* it was defective, and *think* it was changed?"

"Ahh... I need a cup of coffee. I'll have to call you back." She disconnected.

I frowned at the phone. Had someone approached her desk?

Several minutes later, she called me back. Traffic noise filled the background. She explained how my mentioning the differences in my leg injuries had made her study the data from the flight data recorder in more depth. From this, she had learned the rudder pedal movement corresponded to the amount the rudder deflected, until just before we departed the runway. Then, the pedals didn't move more than forty percent, but the rudder went to forty-five.

She also revealed the NTSB had no explanation for the sound on the cockpit voice recorder other than a rudder pedal hitting the stop. But since the rudder pedal data showed we didn't use more than forty percent, they felt it was an unknown nosie they hadn't identified.

These details helped her convince her superiors they needed to test the potentiometer. During that test, she discovered a loose tie-wrap the exact size as one missing on the wire bundle running from the potentiometer. That made her suspicious and she examined the potentiometer closer. Unlike the wires and framework near it, the potentiometer was grime and dust free.

"Something else that is suspicious is the maintenance investigator for your airline happened to mention after our test that the potentiometer had been replaced during the C-check. If he knew it had been replaced, why didn't he mention that beforehand? He must've been attempting to hide that Sphere changed it before we tested it."

Although I felt vindicated, anger festered and made me want to fidget. I fought to stay still to prevent aggravating my injuries. "Why am I just learning of this now?"

"That's why I'm walking the streets. There are parties in the investigation who don't buy into my theory—"

"Theory?" It was *the evidence* I'd been looking for.

"It's a theory because I can't prove *at this time* that the potentiometer was changed. To others, it appears to have been working correctly at the time of the accident."

"Who doesn't want to believe this?" The urge to pace had me shuffling to the edge of the couch until I realized I couldn't hold the phone and walk on my crutches.

"The... At this point, I think it is best if I refrain from mentioning that. I've told you this as I'm on your side, Bill. I truly believe you wouldn't have let your aircraft go off the runway. There had to be something wrong with the rudder, as you've said all along."

Finally! "You..." I choked down the sudden eruption of emotion. "You don't know how good it is to finally hear someone say that." I blew out a breath and blinked several times. That didn't work. Tears trickled down my cheeks. It must be the damn narcotics.

I ran a hand under each eye. "Thank you for telling me that."

"Now that you know I'm on your side, will you tell me who this source of yours is?"

I wanted to spill my guts. But I had given my word. "Before I answer your question, I must ask what'll happen to this individual if you've already talked to him and you now learn he lied to you?"

"We've already talked to him?"

I didn't feel a need to answer that.

"Shit. If we discover this individual misled us, he, or she, could face the charges I mentioned earlier. Why would they have falsified information?" She truly seemed surprised.

"They were threatened to be fired."

"Wait a minute. You told me earlier the dispatcher had not been truthful when we interviewed him. Now you're saying, they. There's more than one?"

"Yes."

"Damn." A pause. "Damn! These individuals would risk being arrested just to keep their job?"

"I doubt they realized the trouble they could be in. Or were misled by their superiors. They might've been told there was not enough data to prove otherwise. By falsely testifying to you, you wouldn't learn it was a lie. I realize this is just my opinion. But from having met them, I truly feel they didn't understand the severity of their actions."

"Besides the dispatcher, who else have you talked to?"

I ran a hand down Casey's side before answering. I wouldn't risk being arrested and fined to protect Cunningham. I wasn't the one who'd lied to the NTSB. "Can you give me a day before I tell you?"

"Why?"

"I gave my word no one would learn where I got the information I used to accuse Bladen of covering up maintenance's role in the accident. I need to warn this person I can't fulfill that promise."

"I'll give you two hours."

"Okay." I hoped I could reach Cunningham in that time. "Do you want a copy of my conversation with Bladen?"

"Ummm… if he didn't confirm or deny there was anything wrong with the aircraft, I don't see the point since we can't use it."

"Are you going to re-interview him?" I crossed my fingers.

"That'll depend on what the two people you've been talking to tell us. Have you talked to anyone else we've already interviewed?"

"Not at this time." That was not a lie since they had not talked to Harting.

I could have told her about him, but decided to talk to him first and get a feel for his role in this conspiracy.

Chapter Fifty-One

Out the aircraft's windshield, the runway slewed to the right.
Casey barked. And barked again.
She reinforced my need to do something about the impending
exit from the runway. But I was powerless to do anything.

I bolted awake. Casey wasn't a part of the familiar nightmare.
Someone or something was intruding on her domain.

She wasn't at the patio door where she warned squirrels they
were trespassing on her deck. Her barks came from the front of the
house.

A crash and clinging of glass shot me to my feet faster than I
had in months.

Casey's bark deepened with more menace. Glass crunched
followed by a whimper. She resumed warning the intruder this
house was off-limits.

I hustled to the dining room as fast as I could on my crutches.
Shards of glass littered the floor with triangular pieces still stuck in
the broken window frame.

Casey had her front paws on the sill. Spittle flew from her
mouth with each bark that ended with a growl in her throat.

This was a different dog than we had lived with the last eight
years. We had always joked that if anyone broke in, Casey would
drop a ball at their feet and wag her tail at them.

In the street, a silver two-door hatchback, a Kia or Hyundai,
sped away. Its exhaust had been modified, making it louder and
sounding like a long, continuous fart.

Why would a vandal modify their car to make it noticeable?

Then the blood running down the wall stole my attention.
Tracks of it marked the floor.

"Casey, come." I hobbled back into the family room, hoping
she'd follow.

My faithful friend was having nothing of it. She continued to warn the vandal not to enter this house or they'd deal with her.

I swept pieces of the window away with my sneakered foot to make a path. "It's okay, girl. They're gone." I hoped. I inspected the driveway and didn't see anyone. I gave her a pet. "Good girl. Let's go." I gave her a shove. The glimmer of small pieces of glass still littered the path.

"Casey. Go." I used the tone of voice that told her there was no budging from this command. I reinforced with a push.

A questioning look was thrown my way before her front paws dropped to the floor. After taking a step, she whimpered and lifted a paw and stared up at me.

My anger at what I hoped was only a vandal escalated.

It also enraged me I couldn't kneel and examine her foot and hopefully remove the glass that was probably imbedded in it. I dragged a chair from the table into the foyer and lowered into it. I clapped. "Casey, come. Come on girl."

She took a step favoring her right front paw and left rear, then laid on the floor several feet from me, licking her front paw.

With a grimace, I eased onto the floor and slid toward her. "Come girl." I snagged her collar and pulled her head into my lap.

Out of habit, I patted my shirt to get my glasses. They lay on the coffee table where I'd been reading Harting's document before I fell asleep. I squinted to inspect the bloody front paw. My thumb stung when I ran it over the cut in her center pad.

In the time it would take me to stand and get my glasses, trek across the driveway to retrieve a pair of needle-nose pliers from the hangar, or find a pair of tweezers in the bathroom, Casey would have her tongue sliced open from licking the splinter of glass.

Blood continued to ooze out the cut.

Rolling her onto her back, I inspected the rear paw that was leaving bloody prints. If there was glass in it, I couldn't see it or feel it. If Natalie was home, she would know if Casey needed stitches.

The phone in my pocket chimed. It was an unknown caller. "What?"

"Quit looking into the accident," a male voice said. "If you don't, you'll experience more than a broken window."

My grip on the phone tightened. "Who is this?"

The caller disconnected.

I almost yelled *bastard*, but held back. It would rile Casey up.

She kept trying to lick her bloody paws.

I smacked the floor, frustrated at being unable to carry her to the car and drive her to the vet.

Was that Bladen who'd called?

No, the caller's voice was deeper. If he had climbed through the window right then, after what he had put me through and after injuring our dog, he would see how months of pent-up anger could make a cripple a raging menace.

When Casey attempted to lick again, I swallowed my pride and called Russell.

He agreed to rush over and take Casey and me to the vet. The broken window and a call to the police would have to wait.

➤➤➤

When Natalie arrived home that night, she hurried to the couch, where Casey and I were trying to relax. After the morning I had, trying was the keyword. Who was threatening me?

"Hi. How was your day?" I was interested but knew discussing her day was the last thing on her mind. It would also be difficult to listen actively with the turmoil running through my head.

From the fury that lined her face, I pitied the drivers she had faced on the way here. Maybe I shouldn't have sent the numerous texts explaining what had happened.

Natalie knelt and ran a hand along Casey's flank, then examined the bandages on her paws. "You okay, girl?"

"She'll be all right. She walks gingerly, but that's not holding her back." I braced for the eruption I thought was imminent from Natalie, but she stood to inspect the damage to the dining room window. With her hands on her hips she looked at the piece of plywood Russell had fastened over the broken window.

"What's that going to cost us?" She passed through the family room to our bedroom without stopping to hear my answer.

I could play the cripple and remain on the couch. Or use the excuse that if I followed her, Casey would too, which would cause her pain. But we needed to discuss what had happened.

In the bedroom, I found Natalie standing in the closet, changing out of her work clothes in hurried motions.

I sat on the edge of the bed. "Should we pay for the window ourselves or file an insurance claim?"

Casey limped in and lay at my feet.

"Since we won't own this place much longer, what do we care if the rates go up." She kicked the pants off and pulled jeans from a hanger.

I admired her near-nakedness and thought about complimenting her figure. I'd done that before at a time like this, though, and it had been the wrong thing to say.

"Yeah, you're right." If I hadn't seen Bladen, Casey wouldn't have been injured. This was more mayhem that I'd brought into our life. But dammit, I was not going to sit back and lose everything because someone was corrupt.

Squirming, she pulled up the jeans and fastened them, then unhooked her bra, dropping it on the slacks.

I would never tire of seeing my wife undressed.

She faced me, her shoulders lifted and fell, then she pulled on a t-shirt.

That pause of standing before me topless was for my benefit. She wasn't blaming me for Casey's injuries. If she had turned away from me, I wouldn't have been so sure.

When she sat beside me, she rested a hand on my leg while petting Casey with her foot. "I'd like to kill whoever did this to her."

"Me too."

"It's bad enough they did something that crippled you and killed Ned and will make us lose our homes. But on top of that, they've hurt our dog." She turned her attention to me. "What can I do to help you? I want whoever is responsible to lose their job and be put in prison."

"I wish I could give you a list of tasks that need completing, but I'm going on instinct."

"What're you going to do next?"

I blew out a sigh. "Tomorrow morning I'm doing something that'll end my career if I'm ever able to fly again."

"And that is?"

"Break an unwritten rule. I'm going to the FAA with the list Harting gave us."

She sat on the floor next to Casey and continued to pet her. "Why is that an unwritten rule?"

"Because an airline would prefer a pilot came to them with any safety-related issues so they could fix them on their own. Getting the FAA involved first puts them under a microscope. There might be fines levied and procedural changes implemented that the airline has no say in developing."

She nodded.

"If I'm able to fly again and Sphere hasn't already fired me, my every action will be scrutinized. I'll probably have to pass the check-ride from hell. Then will be called into the chief pilot's office every time I fly through turbulence that wasn't forecasted, or my flight arrives at the gate a minute late."

"Do you want to return to the airline that blamed you for something that was their fault?"

Did I? If Sphere had initially admitted their maintenance vendor was the cause and had stood behind Ned and me, I'd probably return to work when I could. But now, if I was successful at proving they tried to cover up that fact, would I want to?

"No. I guess I don't." It was hard to say those words. Holding onto the dream of returning to what I knew and loved had been therapeutic.

But admitting that removed the few restraints holding me back from getting even for the hell our lives were now. When I met with the FAA the next day, they would see a force to be reckoned with.

Chapter Fifty-Two

At the FAA Flight Standards District office on the south side of the Denver airport, I introduced myself to the receptionist.

She made a call. "They'll be with you in a moment," she said to me.

They? I expected to be meeting only the PMI, the inspector responsible for overseeing Sphere's maintenance. Was another maintenance inspector joining us as a show of force?

Forty minutes later, a overweight man my age stepped into the reception area. "Captain Kurz?"

"Yes." After a glance at my watch, I got to my feet.

"Harvey Straub. I'm the assistant PMI for Sphere."

I extended my hand. "Hi. Thank you for meeting with me." Was that wait deliberate?

"This way." Without shaking my hand, he turned and strolled down a hall.

Alrighty. I'd experienced FAA inspectors that were inimical, but Straub took it to the extreme.

Or was he in on the conspiracy against me?

Straub waltzed into a glass walled conference room and waited for me to enter.

I paused at the door's threshold. Inside sat Cramp. He watched me with narrowed eyes.

"This is Jay Kearse, the PMI." Straub gestured to the other man. "And Bob Cramp from D.C., who works in the office of investigation and prevention. Bill Kurtz." Both Cramp and Kearse's expressions were frosty as they looked me over. They eased out of their chairs and extended their hands.

I was meeting with them to report potential safety violations they did not know about and they treated me like I'd turned them in to the FAA Administrator.

The two from Denver seemed jovial compared to Cramp. While squeezing the shit out of my hand, he addressed me as *Captain* in a tone that made the title derogatory.

"Have a seat," Kearse said. The three sat across the table from me with Kearse in the middle, Straub to his right. "So, I understand you have some maintenance issues *you* feel we need to know about."

"Yes." I considered asking for drink of water to wet my parched mouth, but pressed on to get the meeting over with. From my backpack, I withdrew the folder with copies of the information Harting had given me and slid the sheets across the table.

The three huddled together to read. After they had scanned the pages, Straub opened a folder in front of him and pulled out a packet of paper stapled together. He held it up so I couldn't read it. In whispered voices, they pointed to my sheet and the paper Straub held.

Kearse looked over the top of his glasses at me. "What is it you are trying to do?"

"Bring to your attention write-ups that occur on flights after a C-check that a maintenance contractor working for Sphere Airlines is responsible for."

"Says who?"

I frowned. "Says who... what?"

Cramp rolled his eyes.

"Who says this contractor is responsible for the write-ups?" Kearse articulated each word as if I was hard of hearing.

I thought about cupping my hands behind my ears and saying, *What*? but refrained, not wanting to escalate the tension.

I knew they wanted to know who I had gotten this information from. I'd tried to call Harting yesterday and again this morning and left messages for him to call. Still unclear about his involvement, I decided to refrain from giving them his name. "I'm not sure what you're asking?"

Cramp expelled a loud sigh.

Kearse took off his glasses and leaned toward me. "You're a pilot for Sphere Airlines, correct?"

I nodded.

"I'm wondering why a pilot would have access to maintenance records and what he hopes to gain by bringing them to the FAA."

Since he didn't ask a question, I simply said, "Okay."

When they realized I wasn't going to continue, Cramp said, "Told you he wasn't very forthcoming."

My face warmed. "If you have a question, ask it."

Straub shook his head.

"How did you get this information?" Kearse waved my sheets of paper.

I held back from saying *now that wasn't so bad, was it?* "At this time, that information will remain confidential. Why is that important?"

"Because we must gauge why you're bringing this information to us," Kearse said.

It was decision time. Continue being mister nice guy or make them realize I would not be shut up.

"I'm delivering information about an airline's unsafe maintenance practices to the agency that should have already discovered it on their own." I met the eyes of all three.

They glared back at me.

"How do you know we haven't?" Kearse asked.

"Since Inspector Cramp is here, you're obviously aware I was involved in an accident. If you knew Sphere's aircraft return from being inspected by a foreign vendor with write-ups and you haven't done anything about it, the estates of the thirty-eight that died and the ten severely injured in my accident will find that interesting."

The silence that followed was gratifying.

Staub leaned forward. "So that's your intention. To try to make the FAA look bad?"

I took a deliberate deep breath. "No. I thought this was information you were unaware of and would be interested in knowing about. Apparently, I was wrong and I'm wasting my time."

I stuffed my folder and notepad in my backpack.

Kearse cleared his throat. When he spoke, his tone was not as challenging. "We... we just find it curious why a pilot is bringing us this information. It's very irregular."

Again, since he didn't ask a question, I didn't elaborate.

"Are you worried Sphere didn't correct these write-ups before the aircraft flew revenue service?" Straub's tone was less confrontational too.

"No. I'm concerned the facility Sphere contracted with can't return aircraft to service in an airworthy condition."

"And you know this how?" Straub asked.

I gestured at my papers still in front of Kearse. "That record speaks for itself. Five aircraft in a row returned from San Salvador with something failing on the flight back."

Kearse gave a small nod. "These flights might've been maintenance test flights. The purpose of a test flight is to verify the aircraft was repaired correctly."

I had considered this and was ready. "I doubt you would have approved test flights that fly over mountainous terrain and the Gulf of Mexico on three-hour flights. That doesn't sound safe to me."

The three lowered their faces to study the papers in front of them.

"Since these weren't test flights," I continued, "it's common knowledge an aircraft isn't supposed to be released from maintenance unless it has been maintained in accordance with the approved maintenance procedures. In light of the fact these aircraft returned to service with something improperly repaired, I found it interesting the FAA hasn't stopped Sphere from using the vendor doing the work."

Their eyes narrowed.

"But then I thought, maybe you were unaware of this problem. Maybe Sphere hadn't reported these write-ups to you. So... here I am."

Kearse shifted. "Why don't you think we know about these?" He shook the papers I'd given him.

"If only one or two aircraft had problems, it'd be easy to think you were involved and had Sphere implement better oversight of the contractor they're using." I hoped my flattery would ease the tension. "But every aircraft that came from this hangar after you approved it resumed flying with something wrong? That seems like Sphere is keeping secrets from you."

"Why is it *you* dug into maintenances practices?" Straub asked.

"Because there was something wrong with my aircraft that prevented us from keeping it on the runway."

"And there's the real reason he's here." Cramp wore a smug grin.

"What reason is that?" I asked.

"You're looking to mislead the investigation away from the fact you can't land in a crosswind."

I counted to five before answering. "The late first officer or I could land in a crosswind providing the rudder works as designed. From my perspective, I'm not the one misleading the investigation." I lifted an eyebrow. "But there are those involved in the investigation who are refusing to consider other causes that played a role in the accident."

Cramp smirked. "Don't you think we've looked into the fact this aircraft came out of maintenance?"

"Yes."

"Yet, you feel, a pilot with no maintenance history," Cramp looked over the top of his glasses as if looking down at me, "and without a background in aircraft accident investigation, can uncover something the FAA and NTSB with all of their vast experience and resources could not?"

"I find it peculiar that an inspector with no maintenance experience is sitting in on a meeting about maintenance instead of his counterpart."

His face reddened.

Although my heart pounded, it felt great to be trading barbs with him.

"If my aircraft was the only one that returned from San Salvador with a problem, then I wouldn't be wasting your time. But since five in a row did, the FAA has a problem."

"So you're implying these gentlemen aren't doing their jobs." Cramp gestured to the two men in charge of overseeing Sphere's maintenance. "That they're unware of these problems."

"Nope. Not implying that at all."

"Then you're misinformed." Kearse cocked his head. "Sphere Airlines has already self-disclosed these maintenance irregularities."

Even though I attempted to appear stoic, I wondered if the deflation of my assuredness was noticeable. Had Bladen realized I would go the FAA and informed them of what I accused him of hiding? "When did they report them?"

"The FAA does not disclose irrelevant information to parties without a need to know." Kearse said.

"Well, I'll need to know. I'm being sued by the victims in my accident. The fact that aircraft return from an FAA-approved inspection facility improperly maintained will be used in my defense."

The icy stares the three pointed my way increased the already intense atmosphere.

"Until we get a subpoena demanding that information, it will be withheld while we decide how to handle this situation." Kearse's voice wavered.

The speculation that Natalie and I indulged in was no longer innuendo. The FAA was concerned about being held liable. If Sphere had reported these discrepancies as they occurred and the FAA had done nothing about them, they would appear to be inept to the public.

"You're worried it's going to be revealed the FAA didn't oversee a foreign maintenance facility adequately." My self-confidence had returned. "That's why Mr. Cramp is working so hard to put all the blame for the accident on me."

He grunted like what I said was absurd.

"You've delivered the information you thought we needed. That's all for now," Kearse said.

"That explains why you're here." I turned my attention to Cramp. "You flew from D.C. after I called Mr. Kearse yesterday afternoon to make this appointment. Until now, it baffled me why you would attend this meeting since I didn't mention this appointment had anything to do with my accident."

Cramp's withering expression drained from his face.

"You needed to know what I had so you could figure out a way to bury it."

A wry grin worked its way into his expression. "I see you're still unwilling to accept the fact you screwed up."

"If you feel this information is relevant to the accident investigation, why isn't a representative of the NTSB here?"

Cramp shifted his eyes right, then left. "I don't work for the NTSB, so have no control over what they do. Regardless, I'll be informing them of what was discussed."

"No need. They already know."

The frosty glares had returned.

I took my time standing and getting my crutches under me. "See you in court."

✈ ✈ ✈

When I got home, Casey met me as usual.

When I let her out, she limped over to the corner of our yard, squatted, then limped back to me on the deck. We had tried to keep bandages on her feet so nothing in the yard would cause her an infection, but she chewed them off. We knew from a previous experience that a cone on her head would have been pawed off too. Other than letting her out to use the bathroom, we kept her inside.

Until the meeting with the FAA, Natalie and I thought someone at Sphere had injured our dog. Now I was wondering if it might've been someone at the FAA. The vandalism to our home had happened three days after I had met with Bladen. That gave him ample time to self-disclose the maintenance issues. Was the FAA inspector responsible for monitoring San Salvador now being questioned about why he hadn't shut the facility down? Was he the one who had thrown the brick through our window?

Inside, I called Mrs. Masters and told her about the meeting.

"Do you know when Sphere self-disclosed these discrepancies?" There was background noise as if she were talking on a Bluetooth headset.

"No, I don't. I asked that but they wouldn't tell me."

"Maybe Sphere has been disclosing that information as each aircraft returned with a write-up."

"Possibly," I said. "But I doubt it. The FAA tried hard to get me to reveal how I got that information and what I intend to do with it. They must be upset someone at Sphere knew about these discrepancies but didn't tell the FAA."

"Could be. When I get a chance, I'll find out."

"You might be interested to know that Inspector Cramp was at this meeting."

"Bob Cramp?"

"Yep."

"Did he give a reason why he was there?"

"No," I said. "I thought it suspicious not only from how he's treated me, but how coincidental it was. Isn't he based in D.C.?"

"Yes. Hume and Ratliff are going to be pissed. Not at you," she quickly added. "But the FAA."

I smiled. Had the NTSB been playing nice with the FAA but the hammer was now coming down?

"This puts more urgency on the interviews we're going to do."

"Really? You're going to re-interview the dispatcher and maintenance controller?"

"And Bladen and others. I'm on my way to the airport now. Several of us are flying to Denver tonight to conduct them tomorrow morning."

"Cool." Unless they were able to lie convincingly again, things were looking our way.

"I'll call you afterward to let you know how they went."

I couldn't wait to get that call.

Chapter Fifty-Three

It was time to quit procrastinating and prepare to live in the downsized life forced upon us. Together, Natalie and I could stain the deck, paint Lindsey's bedroom, thin out the closets, and the thousand other things needed to make the home presentable.

Although Natalie would help me with the airplane, Russell had hinted several times he was available when I needed him. Sparing her from that burden was something I needed to do for her.

Staying busy would prevent me from wearing a path in the floor while waiting for Mrs. Masters to call and tell me how re-interviewing Sphere employees had gone.

After I called Russell, he pointed out it was a cloudless day with hardly a breeze. He would love the excuse to come over and help me so he could fly his airplane. It was a fifteen-minute flight from his home at Platte Valley, the airport community where he lived just to the north of Denver airport to Erie, the airport where we lived. He had something to take care of first, then would be on his way.

When I lifted my keys from the hook by the back door, Casey stood beside me, looking up at me with her tail wagging. If she knew I was going to the hangar, she wouldn't be so eager to go with me. The hiss from the air compressor, the rattle of the rivet gun, and piercing growl of the grinder had her pawing at the door to get out. Even though I wouldn't be making those noises, I didn't want her stepping in anything that could infect her healing paws.

I gave her a pat. "You stay here, girl. I'll be back in a bit." She sat and lifted a paw, adding to my guilt.

After opening the garage-sized door off the driveway, I hobbled around the airplane to the other side and opened the hangar door. It creaked up, flooding the space with light and revealing the taxiway that led to Erie's single runway.

The view of the Front Range with a few of the peaks covered in snow was spectacular. Gazing across the airport to the southwest, I watched a pilot practice hovering an Enstrom helicopter. To my right, a Cessna 172 flew final to runway one-five and touched down in front of me with a bit of a plop and an accompanying chirp from the main tires.

After glancing back at my partially completed airplane, I let out a long sigh. Would it have been worse to have completed the airplane and started flying it, only then to be crippled? Or, as I faced now, never getting to fly my creation?

Both prospects sucked.

My fists clenched on my crutches. Through no fault of my own, we had to give this all up. "Bastards."

I gazed upon our airplane with the same gratitude and admiration I did our children as they prepared to leave home for college. Then, I had questioned how they had grown so quickly. I was proud of the adults they were becoming, but worried how empty our lives would be without their daily presence.

Today, I marveled that I had created such a beautiful airplane, but worried what I'd do with myself months from now when my injuries were healed and I could continue working on it, but it was no longer ours.

I hobbled over and ran my hand along the leading edge of the wing, appreciating the effort I had taken to drive rivets in a straight line and dimple free. Studying the thousands of other details I had pondered before figuring out now seemed insignificant. I had loved every minute of building this beauty.

At the workbench, I dusted off the opened builder's manual.

Assemble brake lines that will run from wheel cylinders to rudder pedal master cylinders. The specifications of the parts and instructions on how to assemble the tubes that hydraulic fluid passed through to apply the brakes followed that line.

That would have been the next task I completed after Ned and I returned from San Salvador. To the side of the manual was the steel tubing and fittings I would need.

It was tempting to build one line before I catalogued the parts that would go with the airplane. From experience, I knew that was pointless in my condition. The drop to the floor would now be painful and slow. As soon as I got under the wing, I would realize I needed a tool located on the workbench or in my rolling toolbox.

Before that fateful day, sitting and standing several times in quick succession was a routine I took for granted. Now, it would only add to feeling sorry for myself.

A vehicle idling down our driveway brought me out of my funk. The engine stopped and two doors were shut.

I hobbled around the airplane to the door. Two men stood next to a Toyota Sequoia. The driver had thinning hair that was mostly gray and a physique I associated with sitting behind a desk and never exercising. The other had thick dark hair and a round belly. Both wore jackets that seemed unnecessary on this mild day.

Now that reporters, assholes serving us court papers, and vandals had bothered us, I studied the two men with narrowed eyes. "Can I help you?"

"Are you William Kurz?" The driver asked.

"Who's asking?"

Both walked to me, hands dangling at their sides.

Inside the house, Casey barked.

The driver removed his sunglasses and stuck out his hand. "Roger Obeler. I'm Sphere's Director of International Inspections. This is Manuel Gervasi. He's our representative for the San Salvador's maintenance facility."

The mechanic Harting told me about also removed his sunglasses and offered his hand.

Both men's handshakes were firm as they looked me over with pursed mouths.

"Bill Kurz. What can I do for you?"

Although I was concerned why they were here, both men stuffed their hands in their jacket pockets and glanced around as if appreciating our home.

"We understand you visited Carl Bladen last week." Obeler's tone was conversational like two coworkers would use. "We wanted to talk about that meeting."

Both glanced around me into the hangar. "Is that a homebuilt?" Gervasi's voice was Spanish-accented.

"Yeah."

"Which one?" Obeler stared at the airplane.

"An RV-7."

"Can we look at it?" Gervasi asked.

Keeping them in the driveway where a neighbor driving by could see us was the more prudent thing to do. Still, like every builder I'd ever met, I loved showing off my airplane.

I stepped back to let them pass. "Sure."

Casey must not have sensed any distress as she had stopped barking, but she stared at us through the undamaged dining room window.

Both men walked around the airplane, peering at it as only an aficionado would, then moved in to inspect it more closely.

Gervasi sighted down a line of flush rivets that fastened the wing skin to the spar, then ran a finger over them. "Wow. What workmanship."

Obeler stood where the wing met the fuselage and peered inside the cockpit. He studied the fuel lines from both wing tanks that connected to the fuel selector value and the linkage from the two control sticks that ran to the ailerons and elevator. Something heavy in his jacket pocket banged against the fuselage.

If the airplane had been painted, I would have been upset. That object might have damaged the paint.

"Yeah, I'll say," Obeler said. "Are you an A and P?"

"No." I worked to hide my smile that they thought my work as good as a licensed airframe and powerplant mechanic would do.

"How long have you been building it?" Obeler had moved to the front of the airplane and bent to examine where the engine mount was fastened to the firewall.

"About a year and a half. I might be close to flying it if it weren't for these." I patted the crutches.

That gave the men pause, then they turned their attention out the hangar door and made their way there to take in the view.

"This is quite some place you have here." Obeler glanced across the airport. "I can picture you coming home after a stressful day, hopping in that beautiful airplane, and blasting around, working off the day's frustrations."

Most of my days hadn't been frustrating. Regardless, I had planned to do as he said. "The house and airplane are for sale if you're interested."

"Oh?" Obeler lifted his brow. "How come?"

I explained the lawsuit.

Both men shook their heads.

Obeler said, "Ah, man, that sucks. Any way you can beat it?"

"If I can prove the accident wasn't my fault, there's a chance."

The expression they exchanged with each other was unreadable.

"I hope you can." Obeler strolled back into the hangar and leaned against the leading edge of the wing with his arms folded across his chest. "Is there anybody home or someone who might stop by? The conversation we want to have is confidential. We'd be more comfortable knowing no one will walk in on it."

An uneasiness straightened my stance on the crutches. "For the moment."

"After your visit to Bladen a couple of days ago, he's gone on the warpath," Obeler said.

"Oh?" I eased onto a rolling stool. "What's he doing?"

"He's claiming to just now be finding out about the problems that have existed at San Salvador all along," Obeler said. "He's trying to blame someone for the shitty facility he selected."

Gervasi muttered something that sounded like *fucker*.

"How could he have not known about them?" I asked.

"Because the guy's an idiot." Gervasi leaned against my toolbox.

"That's for sure," Obeler said. "Since I'm the next in line below him, you can imagine who he's aiming to hold responsible. And since Manuel oversees San Salvador, he too will be pulled into the tornado Bladen is creating."

Either Bladen was being framed as I had questioned or looking to blame someone else, which I also suspected he might do. I was still leery of why these two had come to me. "I feel for ya, but that doesn't answer why he wouldn't have known about San Salvador's issues. Didn't he get the reports that show every aircraft coming from there had a problem?"

"Yeah, he gets them. Reading and understanding them is another matter." Obeler blew out a sigh. "I'm sorry. I'm venting and didn't mean to trouble you with all this."

"How did he manage to become a VP?" I asked. "What you're saying about him agrees with what I've heard."

"That is a good fucking question." Obeler nodded. "What'd you hear about him?"

"That he's a kiss-ass and not the sharpest tool in the box."

Both men smiled.

"That's a good description," Obeler said. "Where'd you hear that?"

I shrugged. "Someone I've been talking to."

"Somebody on the line, or in management?" Gervasi asked.

"What does it matter?" It worried me Harting still had not returned my calls. He had been so approachable prior to visiting Bladen.

To divert their attention away from who I had been talking to, I asked Gervasi, "Was San Salvador pressured to inspect aircraft without adequate time to be thorough?"

Obeler answered. "Sphere is good at coming up with schedules that work on paper, but impossible to meet out in the field. I'm sure you've seen that on the line."

"Oh, yeah." Numerous times, crews were told an airplane with a mechanical problem would be fixed in time for them to fly their flight. After sitting around the airport for hours, they would eventually run out of duty time, making it evident maintenance's earlier estimate was a fantasy.

"The pressure exerted from above to get the aircraft into and out of inspection has been tremendous." Obeler shook his head. "They don't want to hear we need another day or two for each inspection. If they allowed that, they wouldn't be able to fly as many flights as they had planned."

"Plus another day or so of downtime would drive up the cost of the inspections," Gervasi said. "Something that wasn't budgeted for. So yeah, we're pressured to push aircraft through."

Although the ache in my leg proved Sphere valued their schedule and budget over the safety of their crews and passengers, it was still disheartening to hear.

To prop up my previous belief that the aircraft I had flown were safe because Sphere's mechanics were conscientious, I asked Gervasi the question pilot instructors ask themselves when signing off a student as safe. "Would you have put your family on one of the aircraft leaving San Salvador?"

Gervasi studied the floor. "Yeah." He nodded as if emphasizing that point. "When aircraft left there, I truly thought they were airworthy."

"Including the aircraft I had my accident in?"

The whoop whoop of the helicopter that I had watched earlier filled the hangar as it came to a hover at the end of the runway. The pilot must have been practicing flying a traffic pattern.

After the helicopter was climbing away and the noise had subsided, Gervasi continued to watch it. "Yeah, I would've flown in it."

"Was the rudder control mechanism on my aircraft worked on?"

"As I testified to the NTSB after the accident," Gervasi's tone ringed with impatience, "as per the maintenance manual, it was inspected for wear. The hydraulic components were inspected. Everything looked like it must've when it left the factory. It was reassembled and checked by a mechanic with inspection authorization."

Even though he probably had to say versions of that several times during the investigation, his lack of earnestness was disquieting.

"Was that one of our guys? Or one employed by the hangar in San Salvador?"

"Look, we feel bad, real bad, for what happened to you," Obeler said. "But these are all questions the NTSB asked that we've already answered numerous times months ago."

"On your aircraft, to back up San Salvador's mechanics," Gervasi still stared at the departing helicopter, "before they closed the access panels in the vertical stabilizer, I inspected their work." He glanced at my airplane and tilted his head as if noticing something.

"Well, something happened to it on the takeoff roll. Somebody missed something."

"I can understand why you would need to feel that way." Obeler's tone was sympathetic. "Hell, if it were me, it'd be important to prove it wasn't my fault too. Since you've been so thorough in that attempt, we're wondering where you're getting your information."

Why were they so curious about that?

"The reason we're wondering is, after your visit to the FAA yesterday, they want to inspect the facility in San Salvador again."

I had the urge to pump my fist. Instead, I worked at keeping my expression neutral.

"Instead of questioning each mechanic as they did after your accident, they'll look over their shoulders for several days, questioning their every move," Obeler said. "You must know what that'll be like from having an inspector watching you fly. The mechanics are going to be meticulous and make sure they follow each step in the maintenance manual with exacting detail. Progress will be glacial."

Oh, too bad.

"The C-checks will take longer, which will put them back on the line later than they're scheduled," Obeler said. "That will delay aircraft slated to go in for inspection and they'll have to be parked. Since there won't be enough aircraft to fly all the flights scheduled, we'll have to cancel many. Management will go ballistic. San Salvador was supposed to save us money, not cost us. Heads are going to roll."

Until now, I hadn't realized Sphere pressured the mechanics to work with limited time. If any business should have the philosophy that more time or assets would be allocated when it was determined it was needed, it should be an airline. Otherwise safety, which every airline claimed was their priority, would be compromised.

Obeler cleared his throat. "So, we're wondering how you came to suspect San Salvador's maintenance procedures. The NTSB— and the FAA, I'll add—inspected the facility after the accident and seemed happy."

I frowned. "Don't you think the number of aircraft returning from San Salvador with write-ups is enough to be suspicious of them?"

The shift in the conversation set me on edge. Earlier San Salvador had been considered a shitty facility. Now, it they were justifying the need to continue using it.

"Anyone knows after an aircraft comes out of maintenance, there's a chance something won't work correctly." Gervasi's accent had become pronounced.

"It's one of the reasons aircraft are ferried to Dallas instead of flying a revenue flight," Obeler said. "Any issues can be fixed before we fly passengers. But we're getting off track. Since the NTSB and FAA seemed happy with their post-accident inspection, what made you come to suspect Bladen wasn't doing his job?"

That should be obvious, but I clarified it for them. "Since we had a rudder problem, and knowing the aircraft came out of an inspection, I suspected something hadn't been reassembled correctly. Since San Salvador was Bladen's way to save maintenance mega-millions, I looked into its history. It was then I discovered the write-ups on the returning aircraft."

Tools in my tool chest rattled when Gervasi pushed off it and propped both hands on his hips. "You wouldn't have access to maintenance records. So how did you get that information?"

His aggression startled me.

"Manuel." Obeler shot a frown his way before facing me. "We're asking because it's unfortunate San Salvador's reputation is tarnished by your accident. Because of it, and the focus you've put on the other aircraft returning with minor write-ups, we're wondering if someone is out to promote themselves by making San Salvador look bad."

While I considered, again, the validity of the information Harting had given me, Obeler added, "Rumor has it you may never fly again. Knowing you'll be out of work, I think you can appreciate the fear Manuel and I are feeling. So, we'd appreciate anything you can tell us that would help us eliminate someone thinking only of themselves and not the hundreds of others involved in the San Salvador operation."

The use of one of the words he spoke was ominous. "Eliminate?"

Gervasi took a couple of steps toward me, stopping an arm's length away. "Enough of this bullshit. Tell us where you're getting your information."

His sudden escalation of anger brought me to my feet. A trembling took hold of me, aggravating the ache in my leg and ribs. "It's time for you guys to leave."

Gervasi returned to my tool chest and lifted a hammer from it. "We aren't leaving until you tell us where the fuck you got your information."

I took inventory of the tools nearby I might grab to defend myself. A two foot long pry bar and a couple of screwdrivers on the work bench were my best options.

Obeler blocked my path while removing an automatic pistol from his jacket pocket.

Gervasi walked over and stood beside the windshield of my airplane and lifted the hammer. "Tell us. Or your airplane will become a piece of shit."

Chapter Fifty-Four

Lori Masters and Jeff Hume walked into Bladen's office at the scheduled time.

Lori never knew how re-interviewing someone would go, especially after she'd learned information that conflicted with what the interviewee had previously reported. It said a lot when Bladen didn't have a lawyer waiting with him.

"Mr. Bladen," Hume said, "we're ready for you. If you'd accompany us to the conference room down the hall."

Bladen stared at them before studying his desk. "It'll be beneficial to everyone if my next in line attended this meeting too."

"Who's that?" Hume asked.

"Roger Obeler. He's the Director of International Inspections. He should be in the building."

"Give him a call," Hume said.

Bladen punched in a number. Over the phone's speaker, they heard Obeler's ring several times, then a man's voice told him to leave a message.

After hanging up, Bladen punched in another number. The same voice stated a version of the same message. "Roger. Whatever you're doing, drop it and call me. Now!" He followed that up with a text. "He should call back anytime now." Putting his laptop under an arm, he followed Lori to the conference room.

There, FAA Inspectors Kearse and Straub, who oversaw Sphere's maintenance, watched Bladen enter. Their expressions were those of a parent when a child had done something troubling.

"Jay. Harvey." Bladen nodded at them.

Hume introduced Bob Cramp, and the two shook hands.

"Have a seat." Hume gestured to one in the middle along the side of the conference table. "New information about Sphere's maintenance in San Salvador has come to light and we'd like an explanation of what we've uncovered."

Everyone faced Bladen across the conference table. If Lori had her way, she would have made it less intimidating and had someone sit on Bladen's side. But she wasn't in charge.

"Lori is more familiar with the information," Hume said. "I'll have her do the questioning."

Bladen nodded.

"Information from a concerned party was forwarded to us that revealed every one of Sphere's aircraft, on the flight from San Salvador, with the exception of the first one, encountered mechanical irregularities," Lori said. "Is that information correct?"

A trace of a smile crossed Bladen's face. "Kurtz," he mumbled. "Yes."

"Why wasn't this mentioned when we questioned you after the accident?"

Bladen cleared his throat. "I wasn't aware of it at that time."

Unlike the relaxed posture and the appearance of wanting to be helpful that he exhibited when the NTSB had questioned him previously, he now sat rigid.

She lifted her brow. "You're the Vice President of International Aircraft Inspections. Why wouldn't you know that aircraft returning from one of your inspection facilities experienced problems?"

"It seems that information was being kept from me."

That could be an interesting detail. Or a lie. "Seems? By whom?" she asked.

"By my next in line, the Director of International Inspections, Roger Obeler."

"Why would he keep that information from you?" Lori wished Obeler was sitting here so she could watch his body language.

Bladen said nothing, staring at a spot on the table before letting out a long sigh. "The captain involved in the accident visited me last week. I've done a lot of soul searching since then and researched what he accused me of."

That didn't answer her question, but Lori could tell he was leading to an explanation.

He lifted his head. "I believe Roger wanted the facility in San Salvador to become so prohibitively expensive that we'd quit using it."

That wasn't the answer Lori expected. "Why?"

"When we were selecting outside vendors to conduct inspections on our 220s, the two top contenders were the one in San Salvador and one at Panama City. Roger favored Panama City, but led me to think either one would be suitable. Replaying the conversations we had during that time, I realize I should have paid more attention to the subtle things he said and the actions of the facility managers we met."

"Like what?" Lori asked.

"The managers at Panama City were more cordial to him than the ones at San Salvador. It was more than a business relationship; friendlier, with slaps on the backs and shared jokes. Roger knew the capabilities of the shop and details of the proposed contract with Panama better than he did the one in San Salvador. When we visited each, he pointed out the fifteen-minute drive from Panama City Airport to downtown, with its more European-like culture. How representatives from the airline and FAA would prefer it over the forty-five-minute drive to downtown San Salvador with its Third World atmosphere and high crime rate."

Having visited both countries, Lori agreed. She would rather visit Panama on a regular basis. "Why was San Salvador selected, then?"

"Panama had good points, but San Salvador promised quicker turnarounds and ultimately was cheaper."

"You were the one that decided on San Salvador then?" Lori asked.

A nod. "Yes."

"How did Mr. Obeler take that news?" Hume asked.

"After he reiterated Panama's benefits versus San Salvador's faults," Bladen said, "I informed him I'd made my decision. At the time, I thought he was on board with it."

"You say 'at the time.' You don't now?" Lori asked.

"There's something else you need to know. When my position became available, Roger and I were both considered for it. Obviously, I was awarded it, which surprised me. Roger and Floyd Yagel, the Vice President of Maintenance, are hunting buddies. Other than work, I don't really know Floyd that well. We've also had a few disagreements in the past."

"Why were you were selected over Mr. Obeler?" Lori asked.

"You'll have to ask Floyd. Any reason I could give would be conjecture."

Lori appreciated his honesty without touting he was the preferred choice. "So, you think Mr. Obeler was upset you were appointed the position he wanted, and you didn't select the inspection facility he thought the better choice."

"That's correct."

"So he... what? Kept information from you so your work would come under scrutiny?" Lori considered this might be a fabrication based on fact to take the burden off Bladen's lack of oversight.

"That's exactly what he did. If you'll give me a moment, I'll show you." Bladen opened his laptop and hooked a cable up to the HDMI port. The large screen on the wall lit up, displaying a duplicate to the one on his laptop.

Several mouse clicks later, a report opened. It was similar in appearance to the one Bill had sent her.

"What you see here is a report of aircraft that required maintenance's attention after leaving their inspection facility. Harvey and Jay are familiar with this report."

The two FAA inspectors gave a nod.

Unlike the report Bill had provided, this one showed twenty-one of Sphere's aircraft were inspected at facilities other than Sphere's, including the six at San Salvador. In the three months that the report covered, except for the five returning from San Salvador, one of the aircraft maintained at other facilities reported a mechanical problem on their next flight.

"This column gives a code that indicates when these write-ups were reported." On the screen, Bladen ran the computer's pointer up and down. "With the exception of aircraft leaving San Salvador, all but one write-up was reported in flight."

"Which wasn't the case with San Salvador," Lori said.

The two FAA inspectors who oversaw Sphere whispered to each other.

"That's correct. This code, PP, indicates the pilots discovered the problem during their preflight. The flight numbers associated with them are all revenue flights. In other words, while preparing the aircraft to fly a flight with passengers, the pilots discovered the problem and reported it to maintenance."

Other than learning Sphere's other facilities had a better record than San Salvador, this was information Lori already knew. But she let him continue, knowing he was building to something.

"This report is generated automatically. Only a director or higher can manually change it. I, and the FAA, normally only look at this report on a quarterly basis. I have no reason to, as I let Roger handle the day-to-day issues with our inspection facilities. During a weekly meeting, we discuss issues that came up and how they were dealt with."

Lori could see where he was going, and thought it convenient he had an excuse.

"During the three months we've been using San Salvador, Roger never mentioned five aircraft returning from San Salvador had write-ups." Bladen scanned the faces of the others. "After Captain Kurz's visit, I pulled up this report and couldn't believe I hadn't been made aware of this fact. Roger never mentioned this."

Lori bet Obeler would say differently.

"Then I questioned why this wasn't discovered during your investigation." Bladen nodded at Hume. "So I had our IT department look to see if this report has been manually changed. Normally it shouldn't have been, as we wouldn't be able to address the issues that this report reveals to us."

Bladen let that hang a moment. "A few hours after the accident, Roger's login was used to alter this report."

Chapter Fifty-Five

My hands tightened around the grips of my crutches as the hammer Gervasi swung smacked into the windshield of my airplane. A loud *bong* filled the hangar. Cracks in the Plexiglas streaked out in several directions from the impact.

It had taken me forty hours with Russell's help to fabricate and install the windshield that the bastard had just ruined.

Inside the house, Casey began to bark.

"Well?" Gervasi held the hammer over his head, ready to take another swing.

I could give them Harting's name, hoping they'd go away and prevent the airplane from further damage. But I doubted they'd leave me able to report what they'd done.

This violence, and a gun being pointed at me, proved the information Harting gave me was accurate. He wasn't framing Bladen. It was these bastards. The whole charade about someone thinking only of themselves and not all those involved with San Salvador was just an attempt to get me to give up Harting's name.

I wanted to swear at the asshole but worried how far I could push them.

The hammer came down with another crack. A jagged hole the size of a coffee can was left in the windshield.

Something crystallized that had bothered me.

Five aircraft in a row returned from San Salvador with something malfunctioning. Regardless of my low opinion of the FAA, how could a facility they had approved been so incompetent that that number of aircraft were not maintained correctly? The asshole destroying my airplane must've done something to all five EA-220s.

His sabotage had murdered Ned and thirty-seven others. He had made me a cripple.

Rage, like I had never experienced before, consumed me. I needed to choke the shit out of the hammer-wielding fucker.

I wanted him dead.

While hobbling to him as fast as I could, I concentrated on how I'd lift and flip a crutch to swing it like a bat. Hit him in the side of the head with two months of pent-up anger.

My laser beam focus on accomplishing this prevented me from noticing Obeler stepping up.

He kicked a crutch out from under me.

I went down onto my bad knee, then tumbled to the floor. "Ahhh!" Pain, as bad as when I awoke after the accident, shot up my leg.

With my teeth clenched and eyes squeezed tight, I writhed on the concrete. "Fuck. Fuck. Fuck!" I yelled each expletive louder.

"Where'd you get the information you took to the feds?" Obeler's tone was that a parent would use to question their teen caught drinking.

My agony was so overwhelming, I didn't need to act like I could not answer. I breathed in pants.

The hammer hit aluminum. There was now a dent the size of a grapefruit in the curved leading edge of the wing.

"Oh. Damn," Gervasi said in a mocking tone of disbelief. "That'll be a bitch to repair." He brought the hammer down on top of the wing with a *bong*.

"It's in your best interest to tell us what we want," Obeler said.

"Go to hell!" I continued to roll back and forth on the floor.

"Kick the Gringo in the leg." Gervasi said that as if suggesting the use of a different tool.

An expression of *why didn't I think of that?* crossed Obeler's face.

A rifle shot would not have hurt worse than the impact of his shoe just above the fracture in my femur. The pilot in the helicopter that approached the airport again might've heard the shriek that erupted from me.

My two tormentors stared at each other with wide eyes. They glanced out the hangar door, then the door to the driveway.

Through the pounding in my ears, Casey's menacing bark/growl reached me.

"Who've you been talking to?" Obeler's voice was raised over the noise of the approaching helicopter.

I rolled to my side and emptied that morning's breakfast onto the floor.

If I told them, they would not leave me alive. They could not afford for me to report their assault on me and the airplane. Not with the NTSB investigating why an aircraft that left a facility they were responsible had crashed.

I had to buy time until Russell showed up. Cradling my leg, I rocked, screaming obscenities. I hoped a neighbor might hear.

"Fucker's not going to tell us," Gervasi said. "What if a neighbor comes to see why he's yelling? Or calls la policia."

Obeler ran a hand through his hair. "We can't leave him. He'll rat us out."

"Shoot the fucker." The noise from the approaching helicopter made Gervasi yell.

I hoped Obeler would need a moment to think about that. It would show murdering me weighed on him.

But, almost immediately, he nodded. "Okay, here's what we're going to do. He's upset about the people he killed. How he'll be crippled the rest of his life. Won't get to fly the airplane he's building. He took his remorse out on it before killing himself."

At that moment, a small part of me welcomed ending the pain that had me rolling in my own vomit.

"Do it," Gervasi said without any hesitation. "We have to."

Was a neighbor outside hearing their yells over the noise of the helicopter?

Obeler walked in a circle. "We can't shoot him here. A neighbor will hear. They might see my truck driving off right afterwards."

The helicopter came into view, lowering to a hover over the end of the runway.

My tormentors moved to the sides of the hangar, out of view from the runway.

"Over that noise?" Gervasi pointed.

The helicopter climbed away.

Obeler messed up his hair some more and stopped his strokes with his hand on the top of his head.

The *whap whap whap* of the helicopter's rotor faded as it flew down the runway. It would take a couple of minutes to fly another traffic pattern. Providing the pilot was not done flying for the day.

"I have…" I panted "…someone showing up…" another pant "…at any moment." Would they take their chances and shoot me before the helicopter returned? Or wait until Russell taxied up, then shoot us both.

"He's bullshitting," Gervasi said.

"What if he isn't?" Obeler asked. "He said earlier he was alone *for the moment.*"

The noise from the helicopter rotors faded to almost nothing.

"Give me the gun. I'll do him when the helicopter returns." Gervasi stepped up to Obeler with a hand held out.

"What if it doesn't come back?" Obeler walked to the hangar door, keeping his body sheltered behind the side of the opening, and searched the sky. "We can't wait around. Someone might stop by."

Through clenched teeth, I said, "Sounds like you guys…" another wave of agony threatened to make me spew more. I swallowed it down "…haven't thought this through. Just like you didn't think about…" pant "the shit you'd be in when you sabotaged my aircraft."

Gervasi raised the hammer as if he was going to strike me.

I was already curled in a ball holding my leg. I tucked my head in.

"No," Obeler yelled. "If we want the police to think he shot himself, a bruise will rule out suicide."

"He probably has one where you kicked him."

While Gervasi stared at his boss, I consider kicking him in the balls with my good leg but I couldn't move without elevating the pain. A feeble strike would anger him. He might ignore his boss's warning. But how I wanted to make him feel the agony I was feeling.

I hated I'd allowed them to put me in this position. Why had I let them into the hangar?

"Is there a key on him to that Honda?" Obeler gestured to my SUV parked in the driveway.

When Gervasi reached down to pat my pockets I slapped his hand away. "Fuck off."

He tapped my leg with the hammer where Obeler had kicked me.

I almost blacked out. While I concentrated on staying conscious, I vaguely felt my keys sliding from my pocket. Some tough guy I was.

The tail lights on the Honda flashed.

Casey continued to bark.

Obeler went to my work bench and grabbed a couple of large tie-wraps. "Bind his hands behind him. We'll load him in my truck. You'll follow me in his. He's a skier and probably upset he'll never ski again. We'll drive him to Eldora Mountain, where he'll kill himself."

"How far away is that?"

"An hour," Obeler said.

"An hour? Isn't there anyplace closer?"

"No." Obeler shoved my shoulder with his foot to roll me over.

The twisting made my leg feel like it was being torn off. Fearing they would gag me, I stifled the roar that wanted to spring free.

I fought Gervasi's attempt to pull my arm away from my leg. My defiance lasted until he applied pressure with his foot on my fracture. I put my hands behind me.

How did POWs resist interrogation?

A *zzzzt* sound came from behind me as the binding clamped tight around my wrists. The struggle to free myself chafed the skin. Another tie-wrap was fastened around my ankles. That was pointless. Even if not in agony, I couldn't run away.

Obeler went out to the driveway and returned a moment later.

He patted my pockets and dug out my phone. "What's the passcode?"

"Fuck the damn phone. Let's get out of here." Gervasi wiped the handle of the hammer with a rag.

"He needs a suicide note." Obeler prodded my leg with his toe. "Passcode. Now."

I squeezed my eyes tight, hating what would go through Natalie's mind when she read I was killing myself.

When Obeler's toe touched my leg again, I blurted out, "Seven-nine-four-seven." The first four letters of Natalie's nickname.

After a perusal of the phone's screen, Obeler asked, "You don't text your wife?"

She was not stored in the device as Natalie, Mom, Honey, or even the nickname she hated that some husbands gave their wives, Babe. If he didn't find our texts, I hoped he wouldn't send one.

"Swish?" He scrolled the screen. "Funny name for your wife."

"Fuck, send the damn text," Gervasi said. "It doesn't matter who it's to."

Obeler typed, then set the phone on the work bench.

Would Natalie realize the wording wasn't language I would have used? That if I were ending my life, I'd make it more personal? Would that make her suspicious of Obeler's message?

Fear, regret, and hatred fought to be my dominant emotion. Why hadn't I run on my crutches when I first became suspicious of their motives?

Each tormentor grabbed me by an arm and dragged me, face up, out of the hangar.

While crossing the driveway, I considered yelling. Lyn and John, our closest neighbors, were seldom home during the day. One of the Martins or Templetons occasionally were, but they both lived further away. Would they hear me and come to investigate, or call 911 if they hadn't already? Would my two captors put a bullet in my head and race off?

Or kill my innocent neighbors too?

Casey continued to bark in that menacing growl. She stood with her front paws on the windowsill, her teeth bared.

The sun was blocked by an airplane flying overhead. That ingrained pilot reflex to look up took over.

Russell's white airplane with red and blue stripes snapped into a steep left bank, one thousand feet off the ground, and circled around our home.

Chapter Fifty-Six

Relief flooded through me as Russell stared down at me while circling overhead. Knowing my friend was aware of the predicament I was in filled me with strength. And the hope that I would be rescued lifted the doom making me frantic.

Gervasi and Obeler didn't notice the airplane.

For the first time since we moved here, I wished the Erie airport had a control tower. Russell would have had to contact it before entering the traffic pattern that flew over our house. Since he would be in contact with them, a squeeze of the transmit button on his control stick and he'd be telling the air traffic controllers he was witnessing a kidnapping and to call the police.

Not having that option, the next best one was to radio Denver Approach, the guys in the radar room at Denver Airport, and have them make the call. Or he could use his cell phone even though it was prohibited while in flight.

Since he continued to circle overhead, I hoped he would follow us to Eldora Mountain and guide the police there.

But, he might think I had fallen and a neighbor was rushing me to the hospital. I squirmed, hoping he saw me struggling and unable to move my hands.

My fidgeting caused Gervasi and Obeler to almost drop me before they regained their hold on my arms.

"Asshole." Gervasi kneed me in the ribs, luckily on the side without the broken ones. "How about I kick the shit out of your leg?"

Anything would be better than that. I stilled my shoulders, keeping my gaze from my circling salvation.

They threw my upper half in the back of Obeler's Sequoia, then shoved my lower half in so they could close the door. If Russell wasn't circling overhead, I would have been screaming my head off, both from the agony and in an effort to attract someone's attention. The way they manhandled me should've quelled any doubt Russell might have that these two were not aiding me.

Hopefully he would connect the threat I got after the dining room window was shattered to what he witnessed now.

The hatch slammed. Obeler sat behind the wheel and fired up the engine.

With gritted teeth, I squirmed to get into an upright position and stretch my legs out, easing some of my agony. What I'd give for a Percocet or two.

When Gervasi got in my SUV, I hoped the month it sat idle would prevent it from starting. When the backup lights came on, I silently cursed Honda's dependability.

While driving out of our neighborhood, Obeler's phone chimed. He lifted it to read and almost went off the street. After negotiating the turn, he read some more, then smacked the steering wheel. "Fuck. Fuck. Fuck!"

The throbbing in my leg had gone from a six to a three in the pain evaluation level. I felt every little bump in the road, but coherent thought became possible. Since they planned to kill me— something that at the moment seemed as remote as the concern I had for losing my leg after I woke in the hospital—I hoped to make them see how ludicrous that idea was.

"Bad news?" I asked.

"Shut the fuck up."

"Can't be as bad as the news my wife got two and a half months ago, thanks to you and your partner in crime."

Obeler's shoulders rose and fell several times as if breathing deeply.

With my head resting against the passenger side glass, I spotted Russell overhead in a shallow left turn, circling us. He had climbed, I guessed, to be less noticeable.

"Tell me, when you heard I had crashed, did you do a little happy dance that my accident played right into your scheme? Or did you panic and think about leaving the country?"

"Will you shut the fuck up? I'm trying to think here."

"Well, if you ask the FOs I've flown with, they'll tell you when I'm stressed, I get all chatty." That wasn't true, but he'd never know.

Behind us, Gervasi stayed a couple of car lengths away.

We were driving fast on Route 7. Several years ago, I'd been given a warning for speeding by the Boulder police. I hoped they pulled us over.

"Did you know the NTSB is questioning your boss again?" If I was annoying enough, maybe he'd throw me out of the SUV. "If you hurry, you can take care of me, then get your buddy out of the country before they issue an arrest warrant. That way, you can take the blame all on your own. I'm sure Gervasi will appreciate that."

Except to look up and down the streets we crossed, Obeler stared straight ahead, his jaw muscle flexing.

"You're... you're going to kill me, right?" Even though I hoped my tone was matter of fact, that'd been difficult to say.

A shake of his head. "And to think I thought pilots were a bunch of idiots. Wow, you're brilliant."

"Thanks. Anyway, since the dead can't give up secrets, tell me, what did you do to my airplane that caused the accident?"

For a couple of minutes, road noise was my answer.

I visualized the rudder schematic. "The standby rudder ON light illuminated, telling us the two main actuators were no longer powering the rudder. So, what? You loosened the hydraulic lines to the actuators that let all the fluid leak out?"

Nothing came from my captor.

"No, we didn't get any hydraulic warnings, so it wasn't a hydraulic failure. You must've done something mechanical to it."

Obeler shifted. "Shut. Up."

"What'd you do? Leave a tool in the rudder mechanism so that the force-fight-protection disabled the two main actuators?"

More silence.

"If you'd done that, the NTSB might've found the tool in the wreckage and question what it was doing there. Since they didn't..."

What else could they have done to disable the main actuators? I thought about that as I had when assembling the controls of my airplane. What could go wrong if I forgot...

Surely, they wouldn't have. "You guys put the actuator pins in upside down without their locking collars?"

Obeler's wide eyes met mine in the mirror before they turned away.

Triumph lifted some of my concern that my wild-ass guess was right.

It was standard practice in aviation maintenance to install bolts or pins so that gravity held them in place if their fastener came off. By putting the actuator pins in upside down without anything other than friction to hold them in that position, they could jiggle out.

When I moved the rudder during the flight control check, and while Ned used it to track the runway centerline during the takeoff, the pins worked free.

"That's why the airplane wasn't ready when we got to the hangar that day, and there was scaffolding at the tail. Gervasi was tampering with the rudder. You are so fucked. If I figured it out, the NTSB is going to."

The saboteur sat still, as if moving might reveal something he wanted hidden from me.

"I realize you were framing Bladen. Why, I don't know. If you were making each write-up more severe than the previous one, the pins falling out of the actuators would've been brilliant. Except you didn't consider the thunderstorm. I bet you shit your pants when you heard we crashed."

My soon-to-be murderer's shoulders rose and fell. "Shut. The. Fuck. Up."

I slumped against the side of the cargo area. It was hard to understand how delusional someone was if they would tamper with an aircraft's flight controls. How did I reason with someone like that?

If I hadn't been so determined to prove I hadn't caused the accident, would this have been discovered? The NTSB hadn't been suspicious of this fact since the preliminary report had no mention of it.

I certainly wouldn't feel my life was at risk.

Russell continued to circle above us.

As long as he was there, I still had hope help was on the way.

"What'd Gervasi do to prevent us from moving the rudder pedals more than forty percent?"

Obeler stared straight ahead.

My captor's silence brought out two months of anger. If he wouldn't answer my questions, I would make this ride miserable. "Thirty-eight died and ten were severely injured because you sabotaged an aircraft. What a worthless piece of shit you are." If he got mad enough, he might turn in his seat and try to shoot me. If I ducked behind the backseat, he might miss. His inattention might allow us to go off the road—or attract the attention of the cars going in the opposite direction.

"If you hadn't gone snooping into something that you had no business looking into, we wouldn't have a reason to kill you. If I'd been given Bladen's position instead of that kiss-ass, none of this would've happened."

"Really! All those peoples' lives are ruined because you wanted to get promoted? What an arrogant, narcissistic bastard you are. No wonder they chose Bladen over you."

"Shut the fuck up!"

"Or what? You'll kill me?"

His neck and ears blossomed in red.

When I glanced out the side window, I frantically searched the sky until Russell curved into sight from behind. We approached the outskirts of Boulder. "You're going to rot in prison."

He shook his head.

"I've told the NTSB about the aircraft returning from San Salvador with mechanical issues. The FAA knows." I allowed my hatred for him to fill my voice. "They're questioning your boss today. I'm sure he's spilling his guts and blaming you for San Salvador's problems. They *will* figure out you two were sabotaging aircraft. They'll call in the FBI. Unless you go to some shithole country that doesn't have an extradition agreement with the US, they'll find you."

"Shut. Up!"

"How are you going to leave the country? Non-rev on a Sphere flight using your own passport? Yeah, you've thought this through."

The chiming of his phone pulled his attention. After reading from it, he slammed it into the passenger seat.

"Let me guess. They want to talk to you and are wondering where you are. If my hands weren't tied, I'd offer to text for you. Let them know you can't make it because you're leaving the country."

"Shut. The. Fuck. Up!"

"Here's the biggest reason you'll rot in prison. Look up." Russell was passing in front of us. "See that airplane? It belongs to a friend of mine."

Obeler leaned forward and alternated his gaze from watching Russell to the road.

"He's been following us since you dragged me out of my hangar. He's probably contacted Denver approach and told them he's tracking a kidnapper. We'll probably come to a roadblock at any moment."

"Bullshit."

"When we do, don't say I didn't try to warn you."

Obeler stared at his side mirror, moving his head as if searching for Russell. When he did, he stared at the mirror for several seconds.

Out the back window, I watched Russell continue in a shallow turn to the west. "Ah, here he comes again."

We swerved back and forth in our lane when Obeler reached for his phone. He punched the screen and put the phone to his ear.

"Who you calling? The FAA to report an aircraft following you?" I mocked laughing at my own joke.

"You see that airplane circling above us?" I loved that Obeler's voice had a quiver to it. "Kurz claims it's a friend of his who's been following us since we left his place." A pause. "I don't know if he's bullshitting. Keep watching to see if he stays above us. And watch your mirrors for any police lights."

Another pause, then Obeler said, "Shut up so I can think!"

"Gervasi must get chatty like I do when he's nervous." I loved that Russell's presence had these guys on edge.

"If we can find an overpass with no traffic, we'll shoot him and leave his body there." Another pause. "Fuck if I know. I don't know this area very well. Let me think and I'll call you back."

If they stopped under an overpass, Russell wouldn't see them drag me out of the SUV and kill me. He might follow them when they drove off, not knowing my bleeding body wasn't in the vehicle any longer. I suppose the good news would be he'd eventually lead the police to them. Or one of them if they split up.

Where *were* the police? Russell must've called them.

I forced on a jovial expression and tone. "That was smart, alerting him of how fucked you are. I hope he doesn't speed off and leave you to deal with a hostage and the looming police presence alone."

"Shut. The. Fuck. Up. Or I swear—"

"You'll what? That threat of killing me isn't working since you *claim* that's what you're going to do. You might want to rethink that. Your follow through is non-existent."

I watched him, ready to duck behind the seat if he twisted with the gun in his hand.

"Maybe I'll just pull over and shoot your ass. Regardless of whether that plane is following us, you'll still be dead."

Dark eyes that burned with anger stared at me in the mirror. I needed to stay alive long enough for the police to pull us over.

When we neared the outskirts of Boulder, at the last instant, Obeler swung right and sped down North 75th Street. My threat of a roadblock must have him worried the Boulder police would set one up in town.

What would he and Gervasi do if we came upon one? Neither of them could have a criminal record and be employed by an airline. It would have prevented them from accessing the secure areas of an airport. Their biggest offense prior to today probably was a speeding ticket or lying on their taxes. Taking another human's life was not something they'd contemplated before.

But they were desperate and therefore unpredictable. Would they stop at a roadblock and give up? Attempt to run it?

"Look," I used the same thought-provoking tone I used when discussing low ceilings at our destination with first officers, "making it seem I'd committed suicide won't work. I can't work my feet well enough to drive. So there's no way I would've driven myself to Eldora Mountain. I also can't walk without my crutches. They got left in the hangar. Then there's the issue of where I got the gun. The only pistol I own is still at our house. Why would I buy one to kill myself if I already owned one?"

I paused to let all that sink in. "You're already in enough trouble. Why... why add a murder charge to the list?"

My words were sinking in. Obeler shook his head subtly while searching the sky for Russell, who continued to orbit above us. Or, maybe he was wishing I'd shut up.

"I have nightmares," I said. "I see the faces of the passengers that died in the accident. I'm guessing you didn't intend to cause their deaths. You simply wanted to make your boss look bad. If it weren't for the thunderstorm, we would've landed normally. So I'm guessing those thirty-eight deaths bother you too."

He sat still.

"But, if you're as bothered by their deaths as I am, I suspect killing me in cold blood, someone who's as much a victim as those on the regional jet, will weigh more heavily on you than those other deaths."

He shifted in his seat.

On both sides of the road was farmland with an occasional home or farm building. We hadn't passed a car in the couple of minutes we'd been on this two-lane road.

"Just leave me on the side of the road. You still can make a run for it. If my friend sees you dropping me off, he'll circle overhead until someone stops to check on me. I don't have a phone, so by the time someone does, you'll be long gone."

He rubbed the top of his head.

"Think about it. If it's not later today, then tomorrow the FBI will be looking for you regardless of whether you..." I swallowed the lump in my throat, "kill me. Take the opportunity to get away while you can."

An image of Natalie, Lucas, and Lindsey sitting at my gravesite during my funeral filled my mind. I blinked to hold back the tears. "What will killing me accomplish, other than causing my wife and family more pain?"

We slowed, but for several *long* seconds, Obeler didn't do anything. Then with a glance left and right, he braked hard and pulled to the side of the road.

There wasn't a building within several hundred yards, or an oncoming car. I tried not to get my hopes up, but it was hard not to feel I was being spared. Elation eased some of my trembling. Fear of the uncertainty kept it from dissolving completely.

Gervasi slowed down, then sped away. He wore a frown as he passed us.

Obeler got out and tracked Russell's flight as he made his way to the hatchback.

Russell flew past, then curved around with the nose of the aircraft low, losing altitude. He aimed at us and cruised by just above the trees lining the road.

I pressed my face against the back glass. He was close enough that when he flashed by, I could see the concern on his face.

Obeler lifted the hatch.

I didn't know if I should fear my life would end or be excited he was setting me free.

Fresh air enveloped me. I cowered into a corner, trying to read Obeler's blank expression.

His hands didn't hold the pistol when he grabbed my arm and yanked me almost out.

When he jerked me again, I realized he intended to drop me on the ground. I braced for the agony.

Pain exploded up my leg in white hot bolts.

While panting to stay conscious, I heard doors slam and his SUV sped off.

I writhed, wishing my hands were free so I could hold my leg.

When the roar of a propeller approached, I lifted up on an elbow so my friend could see I was conscious. I raised my head when he flashed by just above the power lines that ran along the road.

Russell pointed in the direction from which we had come.

From my vantage point on the ground, all I saw was heat coming off the road. I had no idea what he was pointing at.

The nose of his aircraft rose as he pulled into a climb, then set up an orbit above me.

Willing every muscle in my body to relax, I concentrated on taking deep, slow breaths.

When the pain slackened and the nausea passed, it hit me: I was alive. For the first time since the accident, jubilation filled me.

Although it was speculation why we could not keep the airplane on the runway, in my heart, I now knew Ned and I hadn't caused the accident. The rudder had been tampered with, preventing us from using all of its authority.

At first, I snickered. Then laughed hysterically. "I didn't cause it," I yelled into the air.

I stared into the sky, noticing how blue it was. The leaves on the trees behind me rustled from the light breeze. Russell had a great day to be flying. I owed him a tank of gas.

The wail of a siren lifted me up on my elbows.

From the direction we'd come, several police cars with their red and blue lights flashing sped toward me.

Chapter Fifty-Seven

Five days later, I eased into a town car at our home.

Out in the street, the media shouted questions, their cameras trained on us.

Natalie leaned in to help with the seatbelt, which brought a smile to me.

If we weren't being filmed, I might've rested my hand on her awesome butt. "I'm sore, not an invalid. You saw the x-ray. I have a bad contortion."

She smiled. "Contusion."

"Oh, yeah. I always get those two words mixed up."

Still leaning in the car, she faced me, her face an inch from mine. "You sure you don't want me to go with you? I know the practice will understand."

Part of her concern was the fear someone else might harm me. I rested a hand on her cheek. "Even though Obeler and Gervasi are out on bail, they'd be idiots to try anything again. The NTSB, FAA, and FBI know they're responsible for the accident and my kidnapping."

"I suppose."

I gave her a kiss. When we reunited after Obeler left me on the side of the road, the need to be affectionate to her had blossomed. I had allowed us to drift apart before the accident. Death had almost taken me twice. I intended to be there for her until we withered away from old age.

"And even though it looks like the lawsuit against us will be dropped, we still need your income. You'd better keep your practice happy."

"I just hate you being questioned again without me there."

I would've enjoyed having her silent support. "It's alright. I'll be okay."

On the ride to a hotel close to the Denver airport where the NTSB, FAA, FBI, and other interested parties would question me about the accident flight and events afterward, I was able to enjoy the passing scenery. Knowing I was not to blame, or at least pretty sure, the tension that had prevented me from relaxing and enjoying the subtle things of life slackened.

Like the media pulling up alongside the town car to take pictures. Three days ago, I would've been annoyed by that. Now, I shook my head. Were there really people interested in seeing me ride in the back of a car, trying to get perspective on everything that had happened in the last two and a half months?

Harting finally returned my calls when he saw on national news that I had been abducted. His daughter, who lived in Portland, Oregon, had twins prematurely. He and his wife had flown there to see their first grandchildren.

Hearing the joy in his voice as he talked about holding both of "the little bundles of love," I regretted that I suspected he had mislead me.

Natalie and I promised to get together with him and his wife.

Compared to the bundle of nerves I was before my hearing two months ago, my anxiety level now was what I experienced before a check-ride. Serene was not the right description, but I hoped I appeared that way. I'm sure that would change when facing the numerous people who'd pick apart every detail of my last flight and how and where I got the information that resulted in Obeler and Gervasi visiting me.

Among those details was the decision I regretted and no doubt would be reminded of. If I had used my authority as the captain of the flight and overridden the airline's decision to continue to Dallas and had returned to San Salvador, Ned and the others would still be alive. Those who lived but were severely burned or injured would be leading normal lives. I wouldn't limp the rest of my life.

I doubted I would ever forgive myself.

Marling met the town car and opened the door for me. "Good to see you, Bill."

"Thanks. And thank you for the ride." I gestured at the car. "I appreciate it."

He waved a hand. "Glad we could help. This way."

He led me to a conference room where the hearing would take place.

Inside, thirty people were gathered in small groups, talking. Others stood alone, reading from or talking on their phones.

Tori Killinger, our attorney, was not among them, but I knew she'd arrive shortly. Accompanying her was an attorney she recommended who represented clients who faced enforcement actions by the FAA. Knowing many were now looking to deflect any culpability in the accident's cause, a lawyer experienced in aviation matters who would look out for my interests was welcomed.

Mrs. Masters was talking to the Edwards Aerospace representative who'd sat in on my hearing while in rehab. She acknowledged me and held up a finger.

Marling paused at the door. "Remember, if at any point you need a break, or are tired and want to call it a day, say the word."

Since the kidnapping, he and Sphere had gone out of their way to make sure I was being taken care of. "Thanks. I'll keep that in mind." I got the impression the airline wanted me in their good graces. They must fear I was going to bring a lawsuit against them. It was something we were considering and hoped Alicia did as well.

Among the group looking to make good with me was the pilots' union. They would have several trained representatives in accident investigations and two attorneys at the hearing to represent my interests. If ever there was a time for the union to support one of their own, it was immediately after my accident. Since they had not, I suspected they were worried about solidarity among their members.

Regardless of the politics and why they had left me to weather the investigation on my own, both Natalie and I found it comforting talking to the union's Critical Incidence Response members. They had visited us the day after I was almost murdered. These pilots and spouses trained as peers to lessen the stress we experienced after the accident were helping us work through the issues we faced. I planned to continue unloading on them in the future.

Mrs. Masters broke from her conversation and with concern etched on her face but warmth brightening her eyes, joined me. "You okay?"

We had talked a couple of times since my kidnapping, but this was the first we had seen each other since I went to D.C. to hear the cockpit voice recorder.

"Yeah." I shrugged. "It could've been worse." The memory of Obeler's anger-filled eyes flashed through my head. *Maybe I'll just shoot you now.*

I expressed my appreciation for her question.

A moment of silence lapsed between us. I wanted to hug her, but refrained from doing so. It would be unprofessional in front of all these people. Words would have to do for now. "Thank you... for believing in me."

She met my eyes. "It was easy to believe you would've prevented the accident if you could have."

I lifted an eyebrow, unsure of why she felt that way.

"Your memory for details, like the song you were humming during the flight, and willingness to state facts, and very accurate ones, without fabrication said a lot. But it was your continuing to question data and look for information to explain what happened that convinced me you weren't someone so complacent he'd let an aircraft go off the runway."

Humbled, I studied my sneakers.

"We've learned a lot in the last few days. Since Obeler and Gervasi's arrests, individually, they're trying to bargain with the FBI for a lighter sentence with information that'll implicate the other."

"Gee. What. A. Shock," I deadpanned.

She smiled. "Your suspicion they tampered with the returning aircraft from San Salvador was correct. When Sphere was looking for a vendor to do the inspections on the EA-220s, Obeler had arranged to get kickbacks from a facility in Panama City for every aircraft Sphere sent there. Since Bladen was promoted over Obeler, and selected San Salvador, Obeler attempted to make Bladen's choice look like the incorrect one."

I shook my head.

"This should enlighten you. They've both admitted Gervasi placed the rudder actuator pins in upside down without the locking collars."

On the ride to Eldora Mountain, Obeler's body language had made me suspect my assumption was correct. Hearing it stated as a fact was freeing. I eased onto a nearby chair.

"You okay?" Mrs. Masters looked concerned.

I nodded. "I am now. Thank you for telling me that."

"You'll love this." She worked at not smiling. "They claim they wouldn't have sabotaged your aircraft if they had known it would've caused an accident."

"Seriously?"

She chuckled. "I know. It's hard to believe."

"I wonder if it bothers them that numerous lives were ruined or changed because of their actions."

"Well... besides those on the regional jet, we've learned of one who will never be the same. A Gary Kinnamann, a maintenance supervisor at DFW, has come forward. It seems that several years ago, he had a drinking problem. His supervisor was Obeler. He got Kinnamann into a rehabilitation program without your airline or the FAA's knowledge. Before we tested the rudder pedal potentiometer, Obeler called in that favor and had him replace it."

She sighed. "Now Kinnamann is facing federal charges for tampering with a federal investigation."

"He had to know that was wrong. Why didn't he say no?"

"He was up for promotion as the DFW maintenance director. Obeler threatened to reveal he'd never reported his drinking problem, which might've prevented his promotion."

"Sheez. Is there no end to this guy's corruption?"

"It appears not. The director of dispatch, Irvin Gayton, has provided us with the unedited record of the messages you sent during the flight."

That news brought a smile to me. Although the actuator pins being installed incorrectly was enough to show that Ned and I had a rudder problem, this was another piece of information that would prove I hadn't been lying all along.

"Gayton's hunting buddies with Obeler. One night after a few too many drinks, Gayton revealed he'd diverted money from his dispatch modernization budget into his private account. Obeler threatened to reveal this fact if Gayton didn't alter your messages."

"Shit." This was the stuff of movies.

"Edwards Aerospace is determining if the rudder standby actuator needs to be modified. One of Sphere's simulators will be programmed to test if the modification is necessary."

"It'll be interesting to see the results of those tests."

"It's too bad you aren't healthy enough to be one of the pilots they use to test if the accident was preventable."

I craved to prove Ned, nor I, could have prevented the accident. But I was confident no pilot in the test group would keep the aircraft from going off the runway.

FAA Inspector Cramp came down the hall, pausing when he noticed Mrs. Masters and me. He swallowed before he stepped up to us, holding out his hand to me. "Captain Kurz. I'm glad you're okay."

I continued to hold onto my crutches and worked at keeping my expression blank.

"Well… ah, sorry for the interruption." He walked off.

I frowned at his retreating back.

After glancing around, she leaned in and lowered her voice. "Now that your abduction and how it related to your accident is headline news, the FAA is worried they'll be sitting in Congressional hearings about lack of oversight of foreign maintenance facilities. Since you are a victim who almost lost his life because of their lack of oversight, they'll probably treat you as a hero for bringing the information to their attention."

I chuckled. "Yeah, that'll happen."

She shrugged. "You never know. What are your plans now?"

"The winter Olympics are in a couple of years. I have a good chance of winning gold in the downhill."

She rolled her eyes.

I blew out a sigh. "We still have to sell our house and find someplace to live that we can afford on my wife's salary. And thanks to Gervasi, I have an airplane worth a lot less that I must part with. After that… who knows. A lot will probably depend on how well I can walk."

She handed me a business card. "That's my husband's. Kyle is a subject matter expert for Boeing. He helps us, the FAA, and airlines that fly Boeings find answers to issues that may arise. I've told him about you and he'd like to meet you. When you feel you can work again, give him a call. If there's an opening, he'll assist you in getting on with them."

A lump formed in my throat at her generosity. "Thank you. That means a lot."

Chapter Fifty-Eight

A month later, I was hobbling around the house on one crutch, loving that I could now carry something with my free arm. Like the empty coffee cup I'd left on the bathroom vanity.

"I think it's ready." Natalie slid a plate of freshly baked cookies onto the kitchen island. The house now had a mouth-watering smell. "Let's go or we'll be here when the Realtor shows up with the client."

This was the second time this prospective buyer wanted to look at the house. If they loved it this time, we would be moving from the home we had planned to retire in.

I snatched a warm cookie off the plate.

"Bill!" With pursed lips but eyes conveying amusement, Natalie rearranged the plate so the cookies were symmetrically spaced out.

While ushering Casey out to Natalie's car, my phone chiming with the Imperial March was a distraction I didn't need.

After the NTSB, FAA, and FBI had concluded questioning me, I hadn't talked to anyone from the airline. I let the call go to voicemail.

In the car, I listened to a message from Marling. Natalie kept glancing from the road to me.

When I lowered the phone, she lifted an eyebrow.

"The CEO of Sphere is stepping aside and wants me to take his place."

"That's nice, dear," she said in a deadpan tone.

"The first policy I'll impose will be to have a nurse practitioner assigned to accompany me all the time. For the aggravation of monitoring a demanding CEO who doesn't always follow his health professional's advice, this NP will be paid half a mil and get stock options."

"Hmmm... half a million. Any NP would be hard-pressed to be with you for that meager salary. I hope there will be spa time during the day."

"Oh most definitely." I nodded. "In the private spa only she and the CEO use."

"What was the call really about?"

"The newly promoted VP of Flight Standards and Training wants to discuss my future at Sphere Airlines."

"Are you getting fired?" All the joviality had left her voice.

"I don't think so. Marling's tone was upbeat."

"Could you work for the company that almost killed you?"

Could I? I had mixed feelings about that. "I don't know. If they hadn't subcontracted their maintenance, the accident probably wouldn't have happened. But Sphere isn't the only airline outsourcing."

She squeezed my hand. "We'll figure that out."

We'd had this discussion numerous times now. What would I do if I could no longer fly? "We could certainly use the money."

✈ ✈ ✈

Three days later, I was in another town car. This time, Sphere was taking me to Ted's Montana Steak House just off Peña Boulevard near Sphere's headquarters. I tried to relax in the backseat and not think about the upcoming meeting and what my future with Sphere might entail.

Still, it was hard not to stop my mind from going round and round on pointless thoughts. Also occupying my mind was our realtor had heard the people who had looked at our house were considering an offer close to what we were asking. We could expect it any day. The number of things we'd have to do a month before moving out seemed overwhelming.

Moving and storing the airplane was the biggest of those items. I doubted I could find a buyer for it in its unfinished, demolished state in that time. Even though I could get more done now that I used one crutch, I couldn't repair the damage Gervasi had done as well as pack up the house and look for another place to live.

At the steakhouse, I was escorted to a table where Marling and a gray-haired man sat. Gray-hair wore a blazer, pinpoint dress shirt, and dress slacks. He and Marling stood as I hobbled up.

Gray-hair offered his hand. "Captain Kurz, Neal Reeves. I'm the Vice President of Flight Standards and Training. It's good to meet you."

"Thank you. You too."

Reeves pulled out a chair and I eased onto it. Watching me, the VP pursed his lips.

After the waiter left with drink orders, Reeves cleared his throat. "I want to thank you for all you did to have the real cause of the accident discovered. In the eyes of senior management, the Board of Directors, and stockholders, you helped make the airline less culpable by bringing to light the fact that two rogue individuals were responsible."

I didn't bother explaining I was doing it for my benefit and not Sphere's. "Thank you."

"I'd also like to apologize for not doing more for you than I did."

I knew Marling had arranged the flights and hotels for Natalie, Lucas, and Lindsey. Sphere had paid for the air ambulance and the trip to D.C. to hear the cockpit voice recorder. But Reeves' statement made it seem he personally had done something for me. Unsure what that was, I didn't thank him.

"You were probably unaware of his purpose, but I had Bryce looking in on you so he could to get to know you better."

"It's been a pleasure." Marling nodded with hint of a smile.

"You see," Reeves said, "I couldn't believe one of our crews wouldn't use as much rudder as necessary to prevent the aircraft from going off the runway. It didn't make sense that someone who had never failed a check-ride, whose instructors had nothing but praise for him, would allow that to happen."

Really? He's just now telling me this? It would have been nice to know the second-highest-ranking pilot at the airline believed in my ability. I would not have felt I was out on my own. I bowed my head to mock being humbled so that my disgust didn't show.

"Since the airplane had just come out of heavy maintenance, I suspected there had to be a mechanical reason you couldn't have stayed on the runway."

It was easy to claim that *now*.

"I hoped Bryce getting to know you would help us steer the investigation away from a training problem."

Ah, the ole department rivalries. Reeves probably would've lost his bonus if the accident was ruled pilot error. But if maintenance was blamed, he could still buy a new Beamer and bank a couple of years' worth of our mortgage payments.

Knowing I was probably expected to acknowledge the *effort* he put out, I pasted on an expression of appreciation. "Thank you."

Reeves expelled a heavy sigh. "Unfortunately, I did a shitty job. For that, I'm sorry."

Ah... yeah.

"From the beginning, I should've let you know I believed in you and was willing to help in whatever way I could. My only excuse is I felt pressured from above to stay on the sidelines of the investigation."

Again, it was easy to say these things *now*. His apology could be a lame excuse—or the truth. I let my frown show my suspicion.

"Did you notice how unsupportive the pilot's union was?" he asked.

Seriously? "Union? We have a pilot's union?"

Reeves smiled. "Did you also notice an agreement in principal for the pilots' contract was suddenly settled shortly after the accident?"

I had no idea where he was going, but he had my attention. "I was a little preoccupied, but Bryce mentioned it when he visited me in the hospital."

"Yeah, I suppose that wouldn't have been something on your mind then." Reeves squeezed his eyes closed a moment. "It was peculiar to me that before the accident the negotiations were dragging along with both sides' proposals quite different. Then a day after the accident, a tentative agreement was reached."

"That is interesting," My mind raced to consider what he was suggesting.

"I'm not part of the negotiating team, so I don't know why they were suddenly able to come to an agreement. When I questioned those involved in the negotiations, I'd get blank stares or politely told to stay out of something that wasn't my concern."

Was he suggesting there was more to misleading the accident's cause than Obeler's greed?

"Since everything the airline does is analyzed by how much it'll cost, I'm sure a study was done comparing the cost of continuing to use San Salvador for maintenance and the pilots getting a contract with a pay raise and some other perks. Another was done comparing the cost to have the aircraft inspected by our own mechanics, or another facility, and the negotiations with the pilots' union continued to drag on."

I nodded.

"This is pure speculation here, but I wonder if the executive VPs, and/or board felt that to keep the union from digging into the accident, they were given what they wanted at the negotiating table and told to let you face the accident on your own."

The knuckles of my fists turned white.

"This is probably a pretty accurate guess, as I know those above me weren't happy you went to the FAA with the maintenance issues you discovered."

The reported multi-million-dollar fine the FAA was threatening to hit Sphere with had been all over the news after my kidnapping.

"Regardless, I'm sure our outside maintenance facilities will be under closer scrutiny. New procedures will be developed to prevent that problem from happening again. The airline will save money and be safer at the same time. We'll continue flying three thousand flights a day, generating a ton of money."

I squirmed and arranged the silverware to hide my dislike of his justification.

The waiter returned with our drinks. "Are you ready to order?"

"No, we need a few more minutes," Reeves said.

After the waiter had left, Reeves poured cream in his coffee. "I'm glad that doesn't seem to please you. It doesn't me either. But if I want to continue trying to make the airline safe for our passengers and crew, I'll have to appear to be letting it go."

The pilots on the line always heard these types of justifications and didn't like them. Unfortunately, that happened to be the reality of working in the huge corporation that was a major airline.

"Appear to let it go?" I asked.

"We'll get to that. First, tell me what would you do to prevent another accident like yours from happening." Reeves' expression was receptive.

Since I hadn't anticipated that question, I was dumbfounded. "Ah... I guess... I'd have a test flight flown before the aircraft left the facility that had performed extensive maintenance, like a C-check."

"Good idea." Reeves nodded. "What else?"

I blew out my cheeks. "Ah... I'd have a technician review with the pilots the maintenance performed on the aircraft. The crew could discuss what to expect and/or look out for. I'd also have the maintenance individual who signed off the aircraft go on the test flight."

Reeves nodded.

"I'd have a group of line pilots for each fleet have more involved training than we normally get. This select group would perform the test flights."

"I like that," Reeves said.

"Yeah, me too," Marling said.

"Anything else?" Reeves asked.

I sipped coffee to stall so I could think. "Considering everything that happened, it'd be nice to have someone in a position who could be the airline's overall accident investigator that wouldn't be politically motivated should there be another accident."

A twinkle came to Reeves' eye. "Explain what you mean."

"In my accident, we had operations investigators, maintenance investigators, and probably a bunch of other groups involved. Each looked out for their area of the investigation without looking for how that affected another area. If someone outside of maintenance had considered San Salvador's practices, I wouldn't have been attacked."

A knowing smile came to the VP. "I'd like you for that position."

I recoiled. "Me?"

Reeves nodded.

"I'm not a management type." *Seriously?*

"God forbid we have another accident. Should we, though, you know better than anyone at the airline what it's like for the crew and their family. You've seen how an investigation runs. I want someone who'll be the airline's go-to person who'll oversee investigations into accidents or incidents and won't rest until all avenues of the investigation are considered. From this, I'll expect that person to implement procedures that'll help prevent another one."

"I'm honored you'd consider me. But you should know I'm no kiss ass. What if my accident had been caused by the crew not using all the available rudder? Are you willing to hear we have a training problem?"

"How else could we correct that problem if someone didn't point that out? And your willingness to be direct is exactly why I want you in that position."

After Marling's call a couple of days ago, I thought I'd be offered a position filing and getting Reeves coffee. Not the airline's head accident investigator.

"If you were forced to the sidelines during my accident," I asked, "why wouldn't someone in this position be pressured the way you were?"

A smile came to Reeves. "That's exactly the kind of thinking I want from the Senior Manager of Accident Investigation and Analysis. To answer your question, right now the FAA is looking to see how we'll prevent another situation like San Salvador. By creating this new position, we will have the FAA's blessing to audit all aspects of the airlines operation to assure them nothing is being hidden from them. And that corrective measures are being implemented to correct any problems that arise.

"This position will be created so that senior management cannot influence it. Because of our misdeeds, the FAA would probably shut the airline down if the Senior Manager of Accident Investigation and Analysis was hampered from doing his job."

It appeared this position would be the airline's version of the NTSB. Knowing how they'd been influenced during my accident's investigation, I couldn't help but be skeptical that whoever held this position at Sphere would also be hindered.

"You've told me you don't know if you'll ever be able to fly again." Marling gestured to my crutch. "The majority of your work will be done sitting at a desk, yet still working in an airline environment, which I know is very addicting."

"We'll keep you on the seniority list," Reeves said. "If you can return to flying, you can fly a trip once a month as a perk to the position. If you ever want to go back to the line, I won't stop you. But only after you train your replacement."

That was enticing. "What does this position pay?"

"I can offer you a fifteen percent pay bump over your pilot salary and stock options. If your job performance is satisfactory, which I don't doubt or I wouldn't be offering you this position, promotions will come fast."

I'm sure I looked shocked. We wouldn't have to sell the house or airplane. But, maybe I should sell the airplane and get rid of the thing that had caused the ordeal we had experienced. "For a while, I'll have to go to physical therapy three days a week. I tire out quickly so won't be able to work full days. I also can't drive yet."

"I see no reason why you can't work part-time until your health has recovered," Reeves said. "Expense the Uber rides."

Crap! I doubted I would find a job that allowed us to maintain our lifestyle, challenge me, and keep the option of flying again available.

And, becoming known in the airline industry as a safety advocate would open more doors than would be available to a line pilot, which would come in handy should there be another accident and Sphere attempted to influence the real cause. If pushing back so that the truth was known got me fired, the experience at Sphere would make it easier to find a comparable position at another airline.

"I'll have to talk this over with my wife." Natalie would have hundreds of questions I was too overwhelmed to ask now.

"Please do." A hint of a smile came to Reeves. "If you accept this position, the first thing I'll want you to do is observe the testing the NTSB does with Edwards Aerospace in the simulator, with the rudder powered only by the standby actuator. Since First Officer Adam Obermiller claims to be an expert at landing in crosswind, I thought he should be the first pilot we use in the test."

I couldn't hold back the smile that broke free. "That'd be great."

After eating a filet mignon that I didn't remember chewing, and in the town car on the way home, I texted Natalie: *We need to talk.*

THE END

Author's Notes

Thank you for reading *Blamed*.

The inspiration for this story came to me while writing my last novel, *Calamity*. In that one, as well as my other novels, Lori Masters and her husband Kyle, an airline instructor, investigate why an airliner had an accident. Like this story, they were thwarted from discovering why two pilots did not fly their flight safely.

In *Calamity*, an airliner landed in Denver during a snowstorm without engine power on either engine and went off the runway. Near the end of the story, Kyle located the first officer of the flight, who had been kept from Lori's investigation, and interviewed him.

I enjoyed writing that scene, as it was the first time in one of my novels that the crew of the accident flight told what they experienced. I hope the reader, experiencing the accident through the pilot's memory, instead of Lori and Kyle speculating on it, had a more vested interest in the outcome of the investigation. I wanted the reader to question, "What would I have done in the first officer's situation?"

I know some of my readers are pilots, or people fascinated with flying. I'm often asked what it is like to fly these wonderful machines. It is hard to convey in words the satisfaction each flight gives me, or express the gratitude I feel to be a part of this profession. Unfortunately, my previous novels didn't convey what an airline pilot experiences, until that scene in *Calamity*.

That got me to thinking about telling a story from the perspective of a pilot who had to explain why he didn't prevent his aircraft from crashing. No pilot wants to become headline news through what might be considered his negligence. Therefore, it was easy to put myself in Bill's place and wonder how I'd feel if his situation happened to me.

For those who have read my previous novels and have been waiting for my next one, I thank you for your patience. I did not intend to make you wait three years.

If you enjoyed *Blamed*, I would appreciate you telling *everyone* you know and leaving a review wherever you can. Reviews, besides making me smile and pat myself on the back, tell me my labor of love was appreciated, or why I might have failed you, the reader.

July 2017

Acknowledgments

This book wouldn't have been written without the help from many.

Pat Jarvis, MD, Jill Jarvis, PA-C, Becky Griffin, APRN for medical advice. They're to blame for Bill not up and walking sooner.

Dr. Scott Griffin, PT DPT and Adrienne Griffin, PT MPT for helping me understand Bill's physical therapy. Blame them for Bill suffering during his recovery.

The following writers read all, of or parts of this story and offered invaluable help. Their comments and suggestions made this a much better story. Allison Maruska, Molly Zucknick, Thom Tate, and J. L. Bradley.

Once again, Susan Gottfried edited this novel taking this stone and doing her best to make a jewel out of it. If there any missing commas, it's her fault.

I wouldn't publish a book without David C. Cassidy's awesome creativity with the coverart and eagle-eye in formatting the manuscript.

Lastly, this book wouldn't exist without my wife Becky's incredible patience and support while I spent endless time alone. There were times I know she wanted to curse me for not putting the wet clothes in the dryer, or the many other requests that went unfulfilled because I was lost in my pretend world. Every author should have a spouse who will spend a huge number of hours proof reading the manuscript numerous times and returning the pages marked in red ink.

Thank you all.

Author Bio

Dana Griffin is a Boeing 737 pilot for a U.S. Airline. He lives in Kentucky with his wife and two four legged children some people call dogs. When not flying, he's working on another airline thriller, or chasing after his twin grandchildren.